FLESH AND BLOOD

ALSO BY JAMES NEAL HARVEY

By Reason of Insanity
Painted Ladies

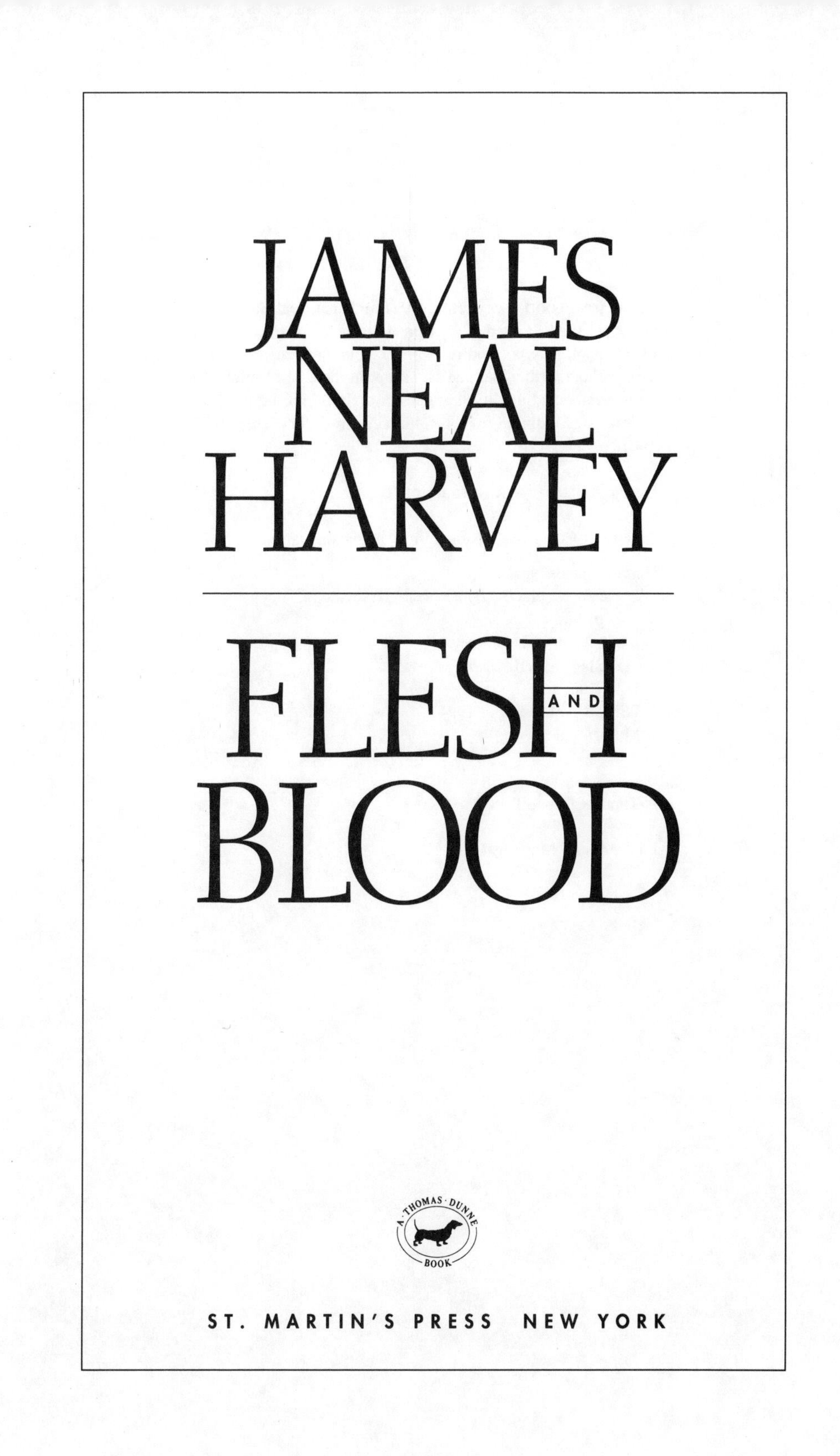

JAMES NEAL HARVEY

FLESH AND BLOOD

A THOMAS DUNNE BOOK

ST. MARTIN'S PRESS NEW YORK

Design by JUDITH A. STAGNITTO

Library of Congress Cataloging-in-Publication Data

Harvey, James Neal.
Flesh and blood / James Neal Harvey.
p. cm.
"A Thomas Dunne book."
ISBN 0-312-10985-7
I. Title.
PS3558.A718F57 1994
813'.54—dc20 94-1033
CIP

A Thomas Dunne Book

First Edition: May 1994

10 9 8 7 6 5 4 3 2 1

THIS BOOK IS FOR DEAN,
MY FAVORITE WRITER.

I wish to thank the following for providing me with expert technical advice as I wrote this book:

Hank Davis, Mgr. Investigations, Barnett Banks; Sidney Arias, Panamanian Investigator, Barnett Banks; Randy Kennedy, Exec. V.P., Executive Airfleet; Harold Shoffiett, Chief Inspector, U.S. Customs, Palm Beach International Airport; Chuck Green, U.S. Customs Inspector (ret.); and my many friends in the New York Police Department, especially former Detective Lieutenant Richard Marcus. Also, my thanks to Robert Garvel, funeral director and master embalmer. Each of you made an important contribution, and I'm extremely grateful.

J. N. H.

FLESH AND BLOOD

1

There were two things Senator Clayton Cunningham III enjoyed having after dinner.

One was a cigar.

The other was a woman.

The cigar had to be Cuban, of course, preferably a Hoyo de Monterrey. It was still impossible to import them directly into the United States, so he had them sent from Montreal. His favorites were the Churchills, eight inches long, thick and dark, with incredibly rich flavor. They cost fifteen dollars apiece, which to him seemed neither expensive nor a bargain. As with most material goods, the price was of little significance. Quality was what mattered.

The quality of the woman was equally important. Like the cigar, she had to be something special: young, with a ripe, firm body. He also preferred her to be reasonably bright, able to display at least a certain amount of what he would define as style. And above all, he wanted her to be enthusiastic.

Tonight he planned to have both the cigar and the woman, and that was a pleasure to contemplate. First, however, there was some disagreeable family business to take care of—which didn't faze him; he believed he could handle anything.

At seventy-two, Cunningham could easily pass for much younger. He was tall and robust, with a flat gut and a full head of black hair that showed only touches of gray in the sideburns. Still a force in New York politics, his career in the U.S. Senate had ended ten years earlier, but after his defeat he'd kept the title. Just as his grandfather had been called the Colonel for the last twenty years of his life, although his military service had amounted to four months in Washington during the war with Spain.

It was the Colonel who had built the original family fortune. A little over a century ago, he'd founded the Cunningham Mining Corporation, which today acted as a holding company for the family's various enterprises. His son, the senator's father, had borne a less flattering nickname. Always in the shadow of the overbearing Colonel, he was called Junior. He died young, along with the senator's mother, in an accident in Europe.

Sitting at the head of the table in the dining room of his mansion on East Seventieth Street in Manhattan, the senator looked at the members of his immediate family. They were all here, joining him for one of the clan's frequent gatherings.

His son, Clayton IV, was seated on the senator's right. Clay ran the family-owned stock brokerage, Cunningham Securities, another enterprise that had been founded by the original Clayton Cunningham, just after World War I. Next to Clay was his chestnut-haired actress wife, Laura Bentley. Laura had retired after her marriage, but she could still be seen occasionally in an old movie on TV.

On the senator's left was his daughter, Ingrid. She headed the other side of the family business, a commercial real estate company with interests in Europe as well as in the United States. An ardent horsewoman, Ingrid owned a stud farm in Connecticut. Beside her was her husband, Kurt Kramer, an aristocratic German adventurer who apparently thought that by marrying into the family he'd struck the mother lode.

At the far end of the table sat Claire Cunningham, the senator's second wife. Claire was sixty years old—attractive, amiable, suitable. And about as exciting as a lukewarm bath.

"When will you be going to Palm Beach, Daddy?" The question came from Ingrid. She was smoothly groomed, her sandy hair pulled back in a French knot.

"Haven't decided yet. In a few weeks, I suppose."

"You'll be there for Christmas, won't you?"

"Oh yes. Wouldn't miss it." In fact, he never had. Each year, the Cunninghams settled in at Casa Mare, their oceanfront villa, for the season. They were all together at Christmas, and then the members would stay for varying periods, some of them through Easter.

It was a tradition begun before the senator was born, and he'd always taken part, although in recent years he'd spent less time there, quickly growing bored with the island's languid pace and itching to get back to the action in New York. This year, he'd leave right after the New Year's celebration. As always, he had much to occupy him here, in politics as well as in business. His wife would stay on in Florida until early spring, which was another reason he'd return to New York early.

Clayton IV turned to the senator. "Did you see we beat Groton, Dad?"

"Certainly did. How'd Skip do—he get into the game?"

"Oh yes. Played most of the first half and all of the second."

"Good for him. He do anything special?"

"Intercepted a pass, made a couple of tackles."

"Excellent."

Skip was Clay's son, Clayton V. As had all the males in the Cunningham family, the boy attended St. George's and was now in the sixth form. He was a strapping youth and the senator was fond of him. He *looked* like a Cunningham—tall, dark, square-jawed.

"Got himself a bloody nose," Clay said proudly. "But it didn't slow him down any. Refused to come out, in fact."

The senator nodded approval. "Glad to hear it."

Football was a form of religion in the family; after St. George's, the men were expected to play at Dartmouth, as had the senator's father, followed by the senator himself and then Clay. Thus Skip would become the fourth Cunningham to wear Dartmouth green.

"He needs to put on some more weight, though," the senator said, "before he can play college ball."

"Oh, I agree," Clay replied. "I've already hired a trainer to work with him right through the summer. I want him to pick up fifteen pounds or so before next season."

"How are his grades?"

Clay shrugged. "Not what they should be, but I'll have him tutored. I'm sure he'll do well when he gets to Dartmouth. Although frankly, I'm disgusted with what's been going on up there."

"So am I," the senator said. "I raised hell at the last meeting of the trustees, and I intend to raise some more at the next one. Women's rights, gay rights, political correctness—Christ, it's hard to recognize the place."

"The admissions policies are what baffle me. Next thing you know, they'll be taking monkeys."

The senator grunted. "They already are."

"What arrogance," Clay went on. "You'd think with all the money we've poured into the place, they'd pay more attention to what we tell them." He looked at his father. "Maybe I ought to be on the board, as well."

The old man scowled. ''Maybe you ought to pay more attention to business before you worry about what the college is doing.''

That brought Clay up short, as the senator had intended. His children were a source of irritation, both of them. In his opinion, they were spoiled and arrogant, seeming to believe good things should come their way automatically, as if having been born Cunninghams was qualification enough.

Moreover, despite their pretended affection for one another, he knew they were in fact intensely jealous, motivated by greed. What these people needed was a good shaking up, and that was exactly what he was going to give them.

The maids were clearing the dessert dishes, and Claire looked down the table at him. ''Shall we have coffee in the library, Clayton?''

''In a few minutes,'' he said. ''But first, there's something I want to say.''

He waited as the conversations trailed off and the others all turned toward him expectantly. For the next few moments, he didn't speak but, instead, raised his gaze to a level above their heads and slowly looked about the room, at the Berchem and Stuart and Hogarth oils in their gilded frames, at the crystal chandelier depending from the high ceiling, at the elaborately carved crown moldings.

It was a technique he'd often used before delivering a political speech and it invariably had the desired effect. Those in the audience were respectful, quiet, sure they were about to hear words of profound importance. Tonight they would, but the message would not make them happy.

The senator lowered his gaze and swept the faces of his family at the same measured pace. He cleared his throat. ''What I want to talk about has to do with your future, Clay. And yours, too, Ingrid. It's the reason I asked you here this evening.''

He paused. ''I want you to know I'm very disturbed by the way our companies are being run. The situation with the brokerage is especially troubling, what with the SEC as well as the district attorney's office nosing around in our activities.''

Clay's face reddened. ''They haven't proved a damn thing.''

''They'd better not,'' the old man snapped. ''Because if they ever did, our interests would be severely damaged. In fact, the entire structure could be put at risk. And what do you think would happen if the media got hold of the story?''

"You're aware of how I've been handling it," Clay said. "It's under control."

"Control isn't good enough. The investigation has been going on much too long. It should be stopped, by whatever means necessary."

Clay returned his father's gaze for a moment, then looked down at his plate.

The senator turned to Ingrid. "What's been happening with Cunningham Ventures is every bit as troubling. The auditors tell me the firm is stretched to the limit financially. If it wasn't for the money coming through the holding company, you'd be in considerable trouble."

She frowned. "It's not my fault that the economy has been in a downturn. When it recovers, so will our business. You know how cyclical real estate is."

"That's only one part of the problem. Even worse is the possibility that the investigation might spread to your operation. If a link could be established, the muckrakers would have a field day. Meantime, you seem more concerned about breeding those horses of yours. You should keep in mind that the Cunninghams have more important goals than winning polo matches."

Ingrid flushed, but at least she didn't avert her eyes. "That's not fair. I'm—"

He raised a hand to cut her off. "Listen to me, both of you. As you are well aware, there is a maxim that this family lives by. A maxim that was created by your great grandfather, the Colonel."

He leaned forward. "Money begets power; power begets money."

The room was silent as he allowed time for the words to sink in. Then he said, "There are times when you seem to forget that. But it's as true now as it was when he was alive. Therefore, I've reached a decision that will show you just how determined I am to correct this erosion of the Cunningham purpose."

He paused again. "Unless I see a marked improvement in your performances, I'm going to make drastic changes in the management of our companies. Moreover, I may also withdraw my support."

They stared at him, stunned.

"You can't say you haven't seen this coming," the senator continued. "I've warned you many times in the past. But apparently you failed to take me seriously. Now, however, you'll have to."

Clay spoke up. ''What if the problems can't be dealt with that easily?''

''Don't weasel with me, young man. There is *nothing* that can't be dealt with, if you're decisive.''

Kurt Kramer cleared his throat as if he was about to say something, but the old man ignored him. He was only a son-in-law, not a blood relative, and therefore didn't count.

''But if we make these, uh, improvements,'' Ingrid said, ''then you'll reconsider? Is that right?''

''Yes, that's correct. But only if I'm completely satisfied.''

The wine they'd had with the main course was outstanding, a '79 Margaux. The senator raised his glass, saying, ''Thank you all for coming,'' and drained it.

No one moved. They continued to eye him as if unable to believe what they'd heard.

He waved a hand. ''Please go on into the library for your coffee and brandy. You'll forgive me for not joining you, but I want to go next door to my office. There are some things I have to do.''

In fact, there were two things, and he was looking forward to enjoying both of them. He got to his feet and left the room.

2

The offices of the Cunningham Foundation were housed in a building adjacent to the senator's home. Like the mansion, it was formally styled and handsome, faced in white limestone. To enter it from his house, it was unnecessary for Clayton Cunningham to go out onto the street; there was a connecting door leading into the building from a rear hallway.

He went through the door, finding the building eerily quiet; the staff had left hours ago. Only the guards and the administrator, Ardis Merritt, would be here now. Ardis lived in an apartment on the top floor.

As Cunningham walked down the corridor, he saw Evan Montrock, chief of security, coming toward him. Balding and solidly built, Montrock was by background and nature ideally suited to his job. A one-time police officer, he was on duty seven days a week, never leaving the building while the senator was present.

"Evening, Senator," Montrock said.

"Good evening, Evan. I'm expecting a visitor. Let me know when she arrives, will you?"

"Yes, sir."

Cunningham walked on down the corridor and went up the back stairway to his suite of offices, flicking on the lights. The suite consisted of an outer sitting area, an office for his secretary, and his own office with connecting bath. He sat at his desk and leafed through the stack of memos and messages, finding nothing that warranted his attention tonight.

This room was his favorite. It was where he not only did much of his work but where he felt most in tune with his heritage. The space was filled with mementos and reminders of the Cunningham family history.

The desk, for example, had been his grandfather's. It was large, built of mahogany, with an inlaid top of red leather and with corners and drawer pulls bound in brass. The chair he was sitting in had also belonged to the first Clayton Cunningham, as had the oversized sofa across the room, both deeply upholstered in the same red leather as on the desk. A pair of matching visitor's chairs were covered in leather as well, but these were forest green, a holdover from the senator's days in Washington.

Across the room was a drop-leaf cherry-wood table, flanked by William and Mary armchairs. He'd bought them years ago in an auction at Sotheby's. Hanging on three of the walls were paintings of the Old West by Frederick Remington, part of his grandfather's collection.

The fourth wall, the one behind his desk, was covered by framed photographs of the senator with famous people, taken at various times in his long and illustrious career. There were photos of him with Governors Dewey, Rockefeller, and Cuomo, with Presidents Johnson, Nixon, Carter, Reagan, and Clinton, with numerous congressmen and mayors and committee heads, and with a sprinkling of show-business personalities.

On the credenza beside his desk was a humidor from Dunhill, made of burled walnut. He opened the box and selected a cigar, holding it to his nose and inhaling its fragrance. Then he cut a slit in the end with a silver pocketknife and placed the cigar on his desk.

There was a knock on the door and Ardis Merritt opened it.

Cunningham looked up. "Hello, Ardis. How are you?"

"Fine, thanks. May I come in?"

"Yes, of course."

She smiled as she entered the room. A plain-featured young woman, she didn't help her appearance by wearing dowdy clothes. Tonight she had on a drab, shapeless skirt and a tan cardigan sweater. Her brown hair was done up in a bun and heavy horn-rimmed glasses covered much of her face. She was carrying a thickly packed manila folder.

He didn't ask her to sit down. "You working late?"

"No, I was watching television. But I do have a few papers for you to sign."

"Uh-huh. Can't they wait till morning?" He wished she'd get out of here. His visitor would arrive at any moment.

"You have a board meeting in the morning, at Fidelity Trust. And this won't take long, I promise."

"Oh, all right." He sat at his desk and she took a chair opposite, opening the folder and placing the stack of papers before him.

He picked up a pen. "What is this stuff?"

"Just the last of this month's bequests. The board has already approved them, but they need your signature."

As he began scribbling his name with the customary whirls and flourishes, he said, "What about the new scanning equipment that's being installed at the hospital? Don't the PR people have something scheduled on that?"

"Not yet. I think they want to be sure they'll have maximum press coverage."

"Fine, but it shouldn't be put off much longer. That's the thing about publicity, you know. If it's to be effective, it has to be a steady barrage. The public's memory is on about the same level as their intelligence."

"I'll speak to the agency first thing, Senator. Incidentally, they said they'd like to have new photos of you. Shall I tell Doris to make an appointment with Bachrach?"

"I suppose so." He went on signing his name. "But what's wrong with the picture they've been using? I like that one."

"So do I. Why don't I just tell them to keep on using it."

He looked up. "Good. We've made a major decision."

Behind the horn-rims, her eyes crinkled. "The wheels of progress are turning."

He signed the last of the papers and shoved the stack back to her.

She gathered the papers and returned them to the folder, then got to her feet. "Thank you, Senator. Is there anything I can do for you?"

"Not just now, thanks. I'm expecting someone."

"Yes, I know. Jessica Silk, for the article she's writing. I checked your appointment calendar. I'll show her in when she arrives."

"You don't have to do that. Montrock knows she's coming."

"It's all right. I like to be helpful, when I can."

He nodded. That was one of the good things about Ardis. As administrator of the Cunningham Foundation, hers was an important position. Yet he never heard any feminist crap from her. She was intensely loyal, always ready to serve him.

"You must have quite a bit of material by now," Ardis said.

He chuckled. "Almost enough for a book, I'd think."

"Have you considered that? Turning it into a book, that is?"

"As a matter of fact, I have. It's something Jessica has been talking about, as well. She wants it to be a biography, but it would also cover my ideas on a lot of different subjects—social issues, politics, and so on."

"I think a book would be wonderful. You've never written one yourself, and yet you've had such a great career. I'll bet it would be a huge hit."

"Oh, I wouldn't go that far. The world is hardly holding its breath waiting for a lot of blather about me." But he was flattered, nevertheless.

The telephone on his desk buzzed softly. He picked it up, listened, said thank you, and hung up.

Ardis stood up. "Is she here?"

"Yes."

"I'll go down for her."

Before he could protest, she turned and left the room.

Alone once more, the senator straightened his tie and brushed his hair back with his hands. He was vain about his appearance; his thick black hair was one of the reasons he managed to keep himself looking so youthful—along with maintaining an interest in activities like the one he'd planned for this evening.

A moment later, a knock again sounded. The door opened and Ardis showed Jessica Silk into the room.

As always when he saw her, Clayton Cunningham felt a surge of pleasure. Silk was stunningly attractive, tall and lissome, with hazel eyes and dark hair that fell to her shoulders in soft waves. Her wide mouth was curved in a smile. She was wearing a navy blue suit with broad shoulders and a short skirt that showed off her legs, which were superb. In her left hand, she carried a black attaché case. He could smell her perfume as she approached his desk.

"Sorry I'm late, Senator."

He took her extended hand in his. "By five minutes? I think I can forgive you."

"Where would you like to work?"

He waved toward the table across the room. "The usual place, I suppose. Gives you room to spread out your notes."

"I made coffee a little while ago," Ardis said. "Let me get you some." She left the office.

Cunningham took the cigar with him to the table. He and Jessica sat down facing each other and she opened her case, taking out a sheaf of papers, along with a pad and a ballpoint.

"How've you been?" she asked. "Have a good week?"

"It would have been a lot better if I'd seen you."

She smiled. "And now you're seeing me."

"Not yet I'm not. I'm just looking at the outer wrapping."

"You make me sound like a present."

He laughed. "Which is exactly how I feel. You're a marvelous present and I can't wait to unwrap you."

"Senator, please. We have work to do."

She was being coy, of course, but that was fine with him. They had plenty of time, and besides, he liked her to resist his approaches a little. Made it more interesting.

The office door opened. Ardis was back, carrying a tray bearing a china coffeepot, cups and saucers, and a small plate of petits fours. She placed the tray in the center of the table and went about setting out its contents.

"Ardis, you're a dear," the senator said.

She smiled as she poured coffee for him and his visitor. "I'll take the tray along. If you need anything else, just buzz me. I'll be up watching TV."

"Thank you."

When she'd left them, Jessica said, "She's quite a help to you, isn't she?"

"Ardis? She's wonderful. And as unassuming as she is, she's

also a crack administrator. Thanks to her, the foundation has never been run more efficiently.''

He picked a book of matches out of an ashtray on the table and lighted the cigar, puffing blue clouds of smoke into the air.

Jennifer leaned forward. ''That's what's so wonderful about you, Senator. With all you have on your mind, you always seem to be aware of somebody doing a good job. And then you're so generous about acknowledging it.''

He puffed on the cigar again, relishing its flavor and aroma. ''It's the way I've lived my life. Choose good people and encourage them to do their best. When they do, reward them.''

''Oh, that's good. I want to use that.'' She made notes on her pad.

''How's it going, by the way?''

''Very well. You've given me so much material.''

He drew on the cigar. ''Glad you're pleased.''

''As you know, I think there's a fine opportunity here for a book.''

''So you've mentioned. Do you really think it would be worth doing?''

''Absolutely. It would be a very good book on the life of a very distinguished man.''

She unbuttoned her jacket, and his gaze went to the blouse she had on under it, her full breasts pushing out the thin white material. She seemed not to notice.

He kept his eyes on her blouse and felt himself stir. ''Well. A book is something I've been giving some thought to, as well . . . ever since you first mentioned the idea. But would many people be interested in reading such a thing?''

Her tone was very earnest. ''I feel certain they would.''

He got up and went to the door, his brow furrowed as if he was deep in thought over her proposal. ''Would it take long to do?''

''That would be up to you. It would depend on how much time you could give it.''

He locked the door, aware that his pulse had picked up for reasons that had nothing to do with the subject they were discussing. ''I see. No deadline, in other words.''

''No.''

''Wouldn't the magazine article take some of the edge off it?''

"Not at all. If anything, the article would help to promote interest in the book."

Returning to the table, he put the cigar into an ashtray and stood beside her. His breathing had quickened, as well. "What do you see as a format? Still think it should be a biography?"

"Yes, but I also think it ought to be much more than that. The book should express your views on how the country should be run, where it should be going."

He took her arm and drew her to her feet. "Sounds like quite a project."

She moved close, her arms encircling his neck. "I think it would be fascinating."

His lips brushed her cheek. "Inspiring?"

"Thrilling."

He pressed his body tightly against hers. His voice grew hoarse. "Thrilling. Yes, I think so, too."

She returned the pressure, tightening her grip on his neck and grinding her pelvis. "I've been looking forward to this for days."

"So have I." He ran his tongue around her mouth and she gasped as his hands slid down her back and gripped her buttocks.

"God, how I want you," she whispered. "You always get me so excited."

He stopped talking then, not wanting anything to intrude on the mood of sensuality. Leading her to the sofa, he fumbled with her clothing, keeping his mouth close to hers, licking, kissing, nipping as they undressed each other.

When they were both naked, he pressed her down onto the squashy leather cushions. He picked up the cigar and puffed on it again, then touched the lighted end against her thigh. She flinched, stifling a cry and inhaling through clenched teeth.

Seeing her reaction was intensely stimulating. He put the cigar back into the ashtray, then lay down on the sofa and took her into his arms.

The sensation of her warm flesh against his was delicious. She was breathing heavily, and he was aware that he'd become as aroused as any man his age could ever hope to get.

He bit her neck and was delighted when she groaned and her body writhed against his. He felt her chest rise and fall with her rapid breathing, felt her lips moving, her tongue licking his ear.

''I have a surprise for you,'' she whispered.

''Wonderful. A new toy?''

''Maybe.''

''What is it?''

''If I told you, it wouldn't be a surprise.''

He kissed her once more and lost himself in a whirl of emotion as they made love. Over the next half hour, his senses seemed to be as gloriously alive as they'd ever been. It was like being young again, he thought. Not pretending, but truly reliving those heady times when he thought his youth and strength would last forever.

When finally he was completely spent, he collapsed and lay sprawled atop her body. He struggled for breath, his pulse still racing, his skin coated with sweat. He was exhausted but happy and deeply contented, waiting for his breathing and heartbeat to return to normal.

A few minutes went by and then she slipped out from under him and got up from the sofa. She was back a moment later, and there was an object in her hand, but he couldn't see what it was.

He raised himself on one elbow. ''What have you got there?''

She smiled. ''Close your eyes and do as I tell you.''

''Is that the new toy?''

''Don't be so nosy. Just close your eyes. You'll love it.''

He did as instructed and she slid back under him and spread her legs. She had to work on him a little, but at last he was able to enter her once more. He was amazed that he could do it, although he realized the prospect of a new experience was reawakening his excitement.

Suddenly, he felt a sensation that was totally different from anything he'd ever known before. He tensed, but she breathed reassurance into his ear, continuing to move in a slow rhythm, and he relaxed and resumed moving with her.

The feeling was fantastic. Whatever she was doing was stirring intense feelings deep inside him. He was infused with lust, rising to a level he wouldn't have thought possible, drawing on reserves he didn't know he had.

At that moment, he felt a violent shock.

The sensation suddenly changed to one of excruciating pain, as if he were in the grip of monstrous pincers that were squeezing the life out of him. He opened his mouth to cry out but was unable to make a sound. Even worse, he couldn't breathe.

The anguish was incredible. He was dimly aware that she was

calling out to him, but the sound of her voice had changed and was much more distant, as if she was shouting across a chasm, yelling to him from a place far away.

The light in the room was changing, as well; it was growing dark. That thought had no sooner registered than he realized he couldn't see.

Which didn't matter anymore; nothing did—except the desire to shut out the awful pain. He wanted desperately to do that, wanted that more than he'd ever wanted anything.

He tried once more to breathe.

And failed.

And then the pain crushed him totally and he felt nothing.

3

In his apartment two blocks from the South Street Seaport, Detective Lieutenant Ben Tolliver got out of bed and stretched. One of the best features of his bedroom was a skylight, and looking up through the slanted bank of windows overhead, he saw that this would be a nice day: cold, probably, but invigorating, with a bright blue sky. And judging from the cloud movement, a fresh breeze was coming out of the north. Scratching his belly reflectively, he went into the bathroom.

He was feeling a little rocky this morning. He'd worked late the night before and then had stopped off at Grady's and put away more bourbon than he should have. But his eyes were clear, their color much the same as the sky he'd been looking at a few moments earlier. The skin under them was smooth and tight and there were no new flecks of gray in his tousled black hair. His mustache could use a trim, however, and his teeth felt as if they were wearing wool socks. He yawned and went to work on the teeth first, scrubbing away the crud with his toothbrush.

Next, he stepped into the shower and stood there for several minutes, letting the hot spray pound his skin. It felt almost as good as a massage. Afterward, he toweled down and took his time shaving.

This was the one time of the day when his thoughts often turned philosophical, probably because he hadn't yet gone to his office at Sixth Precinct headquarters to plunge into the stack of felonies awaiting him there: robberies, burglaries, assaults, rapes, homicides. And today the thoughts were much more agreeable because he didn't plan to go in until later in the morning.

Instead, he'd hit the gym and work out for an hour or so, lose what was left of the hangover. He tried to get there at least once a week and usually failed to make it. Today would be different. He was looking forward to pumping some iron, pounding the speed bag.

He wished he could also drive out into the country, get some fresh air. The trees were bare now, so there was no more color to look at, but at least it would be a change from the crowds and the concrete and the noise and the smoke. Maybe he could do that this weekend.

By and large, Ben Tolliver considered himself a fortunate man. As commander of a detective squad, he was doing the work he wanted to do, and doing it well enough to be in line for a promotion to captain. That was largely the result of having cleared a number of high-profile cases over the past several years, and he was glad they'd come his way. There were plenty of qualified men in the NYPD who hadn't had those breaks, who were sweating it out in the misery precincts of Brownsville and Washington Heights and the South Bronx, with nothing to look forward to but retirement—if they made it that far.

But life was like that, wasn't it? Good was just for openers. After that, you needed luck.

When he'd scraped away the whiskers and trimmed the mustache, he rinsed his jaw and splashed on some after-shave. Then he got dressed in what for him was more or less a standard outfit: gray flannels, white oxford button-down, black loafers, navy blazer.

No ankle holster, however, although wearing one had been a practice he'd followed for years. Recently, he'd switched to new technology, in the form of a custom-made Gaylord that rode in the small of his back and held a .380 Mauser semiautomatic. Unlike his old standby, a Smith & Wesson Detective's Special, the Mauser was compact and flat, carried a nine-shot magazine, and was constructed of alloys that made it much lighter than the Smith. It was also considerably more accurate.

Glancing out the window of his bedroom, the lieutenant thought about how his life had changed in many ways recently—not just in the weapon he was carrying but also in his overall lifestyle. This apartment, for example: It was by far the nicest place he'd ever occupied—it even had a view. From up here, he could see the old sailing ships tied up at their wharves in the Seaport, the Manhattan Bridge spanning the roiling gray waters of the East River, and on the opposite shore, the buildings along the Brooklyn waterfront.

The apartment was another example of what luck could do for you. He'd gotten it because he'd closed an extortion case that had been threatening to put a developer out of business. In gratitude, the developer had offered him the choice space in this building, with a long-term lease at very favorable rates.

Just how ethical that arrangement might be, Tolliver wouldn't worry about. Basically, he was as honest as any cop in the NYPD, and far more than many he knew. If the developer wanted him for a tenant, that was fine with Ben. It was a great place to live.

In the kitchen he got a carton of orange juice out of the fridge and poured himself a glass. As he drank it, he turned on the small Sony radio, which was set on WINS so that he could catch the news whenever he was in here. A sports announcer was estimating the chances of the Giants against Dallas this coming Sunday, draping his comments in black crepe.

Only half-listening, Ben put coffee and water into the Braun on the counter and turned the machine on. Then he dropped two slices of bread into the toaster. The Giants had been crippled by injuries, the announcer was saying, with both their offensive and defensive lines far below strength.

A pitiful story, Tolliver thought, that probably had been put out by the Giants PR office for the Cowboys' benefit.

A rash of commercials followed and mentally he tuned out. So far, he'd bet a total of eighty-two bucks on pro football since the season began, and at this point he was twenty-four in the hole, which went to show what thinking with your emotions instead of your head could do for you.

Another announcer came on. "On a sad note, former U.S. senator Clayton Cunningham died last night, the victim of a heart attack. The senator was in his offices at the Cunningham Foundation, next door to his home on East Seventieth Street, when he was stricken at approximately nine-thirty P.M. At the time, he was being interviewed for a magazine article. The head of one of America's richest and most influential families, Clayton Cunningham served two terms in the Senate and was active in many charities and business affairs, as well as in politics. He was seventy-two years old."

The announcer then went on to outline the high points of the senator's career.

Ben listened closely. Cunningham dead? That was startling news, the senator's age notwithstanding. To say he'd been the head of one of America's richest and most influential families was putting it mildly; the Cunninghams were way up there, almost on the same level as the Rockefellers and the du Ponts and the Kennedys. They'd given millions to charity, had even founded a hospital. And under the senator's direction, their foundation had continued to donate large sums of money to an endless number of good causes.

The man had also been a power in both New York and national politics for as long as Ben could remember. Whether you agreed with his political beliefs or not, most of what he'd engineered and what he stood for was positive. Unlike a good many rich families, the Cunninghams had always displayed strong civic responsibility. The city, and the country as well, would miss him.

But wait a minute.

He died while being interviewed for a magazine article—*at night*? What was that all about?

Or am I just being characteristically suspicious, he asked himself, the result of having spent almost twenty years as a cop in the crime capital of America? It could do that to you, he knew.

The radio continued to babble, but he paid little attention to the remainder of the newscast. He ate the toast smeared with butter and blackberry jam—what the hell, one bunch of doctors said cholesterol would choke your arteries, while another claimed it was good for you—and stopped thinking about the death of the senator. He had other things on his mind—such as his chances for promotion.

The last word he'd had was from his boss, Captain Michael Brennan, zone commander of the Sixth, Ninth, and Tenth Precinct detective squads. Brennan was about to be moved up to the rank of deputy inspector, and it was odds-on Ben would be tapped to take his place. Brennan hadn't come right out and said so, but the implications were clear enough.

It was strange, but as much as Ben wanted the prestige and the respect that went with the job—to say nothing of the extra money—he also felt a certain ambivalence. The further up the chain of command you went, the more you had to deal with politics and administrative work, and those were two aspects of police work he loathed.

Which was another thing about life: Even when it was good, which for most people was unusual, it was never altogether good. There was always a certain amount of shit you had to put up with.

Unless you were somebody like Clayton Cunningham, and how many of those were there?

It would be blustery outside; Ben decided to wear his raincoat. He got it out of the front-hall closet and put it on, then automatically checked to see that he had keys, money clip, wallet, pocketknife, and the case containing his shield and ID. With everything on board, he turned toward the door.

The telephone rang.

For a moment, he was tempted to ignore it and get the hell out of there. Answering telephones early in the morning was dumb.

But then curiosity got to him, as it invariably did. He stepped back into the living room and picked up the instrument. "Tolliver."

"Lieutenant, this is Chief Houlihan."

"Yes, sir."

"Glad I caught you. I called the Sixth and they told me you weren't coming in until later."

The curiosity Ben had felt at hearing the phone ring was nothing compared to what he was experiencing now. Houlihan was in charge of all detectives in the NYPD. For him to contact Tolliver personally was unusual. Normally, he would have gone through either Captain Brennan or Anthony Galupo, chief of detectives in the borough of Manhattan. Was the call in connection with Tolliver's imminent promotion?

Houlihan dispelled that notion with what he said next. "Lieutenant, I have a special assignment for you."

There was a note of annoyance in the chief's tone. "I got a call from the district attorney's office a few minutes ago. They want to borrow an officer who can work on an investigation and be discreet about it. There are certain factors that make the situation sensitive. In other words, the guy has to be able to keep his mouth shut. You understand?"

"Sure, Chief. Can you tell me what it's about?"

"You'll get all that from the DA. Go to his office right away; report directly to him. I'll notify Chief Galupo and Captain Brennan. Brennan will let your squad know you're on a special assignment and that you'll be back in a few days. You got that, Lieutenant?"

"I've got it."

"One other thing. Remember who you work for. No matter what the DA says, I want you to keep us fully informed of what's going on.

Confidentially, of course, through Brennan. As soon as you have this thing sized up, check in.'' He hung up.

When Tolliver put the phone down, he stood there for a moment, again staring out the window. Most of the east wall was glass, to take advantage of the spectacular view. A tugboat was coming down the river, moving fast in the swift current, and streams of vehicles were crawling in both directions across the Manhattan Bridge. Crowds of tourists were already swarming about the Seaport. But Ben only half-saw all that as he turned over the chief's words in his mind.

A special assignment to be undertaken for the DA? One shrouded in secrecy? No wonder the chief had sounded pissed. But then, much of what went on within the DA's office stirred up resentment among the police brass.

For one thing, the DA not only had his own detectives; he had four separate units of them. One consisted of men on loan from the police department who worked on complaints the DA felt warranted independent investigation. Technically, this group was under the command of Houlihan, but that was merely according to a table of organization. In fact, the chief rarely knew what these guys were up to, and as a result, he looked on them with suspicion.

For good reason. Not only did the detectives hide behind a screen erected by the DA's office; they were people with political connections that kept them safely ensconced in their cushy jobs. As investigators, they were very good at typing reports and drinking coffee and calculating their pensions. They were so well insulated that not even Internal Affairs messed with them. The unit was headed by a captain, who had the cushiest job of all.

The second unit was worse. It was comprised of civilian investigators hired by the district attorney and had nothing to do with the NYPD. There were eight or ten of these people, and most cops considered them a bunch of college-trained assholes who were long on theory and short on ability. Some of the time, they investigated complaints against the police that were thought too sensitive for either the review board or IA to handle, which caused cops not merely to hold them in contempt but to hate them.

The third unit was an offshoot of the Rackets Bureau, and the investigators in that one were mostly involved in digging for evidence that could be used in RICO prosecutions. Some of what they did was street work, but mainly it consisted of uncovering paper trails of corruption. This group was headed by a one-time NYPD detective who now had the title of captain, although his command consisted of no more than a dozen men and women.

Lastly, there was the Jade Squad, detectives who dealt with organized crime among Orientals, an area that had burgeoned in New York over the last ten years. The bad guys this unit chased were some of the most difficult to cope with, operating in drugs, extortion, prostitution, and murder according to their own mysterious codes, speaking dozens of different Asian languages and dialects.

So with a mob of his own detectives to choose from, why had the DA asked for a man who had no connection with the office and who wasn't even known to him, except possibly by reputation?

Because, just as Houlihan had said, the assignment was sensitive, requiring an officer who could keep his mouth shut. That meant it would be fraught with political implications, with two or more factions tugging in different directions. The chief was already demanding the police brass be kept informed without the DA knowing it.

In other words, it was the kind of job that offered you a slight chance to help your career and a much larger opportunity to fall on your ass.

He looked at the telephone and wished he hadn't answered it. Then he went into his bedroom and put on a tie, a blue-and-white stripe. After that, he left the apartment, locking and double-locking the door behind him.

4

The Manhattan DA's office was in the Criminal Justice Building, one of the drearier of the many dreary structures housing branches of New York City government. Located at 100 Centre Street, the delapidated pile of stone put Tolliver in mind of a medieval fortress whenever he entered it.

This was where justice was dispensed on an assembly-line basis. Where the courts were in session around the clock, with legions of assistant district attorneys each handling between two hundred and three hundred cases a day, bargaining most of them down to dis cons—charges of disorderly conduct—just to keep things moving. Where in the small hours of the morning, cops slept on the floors of the hallways outside courtrooms, waiting to be called, while inside the rooms harassed judges tried to deal with a flow of cases that grew ever larger, never smaller. It was the Bedlam of criminal law.

As Ben walked in this morning, the south entrance hall was crowded as usual with all types of miscreants—burglars and fare beaters, boosters and prostitutes, muggers and murderers. Moving among them were their lawyers and the vast numbers of clerks and police officers and prison guards and judges and prosecutors who were all part of the system. The granite walls and the gray-green stone floor echoed with the sounds of their chatter and their footsteps.

Tolliver flashed his ID to a court officer and stepped into an elevator. The car was filled with people who looked either nervous or bored—some of them the accused, others their attorneys, still others the accusers. It was impossible to tell who was what. When he got off, he had to show his ID twice more before being admitted to the waiting room outside the DA's private office.

The district attorney of New York County was a famous man from a famous family. Henry Oppenheimer had what probably was the most visible prosecutorial job in the United States. The son of a high-ranking official in the Roosevelt administration, his name was linked with cases that had held the entire nation in thrall, cases the media had exploited endlessly: the Central Park Jogger, the Preppie Murderer, and dozens more. There was never a time when he wasn't at the center of controversy.

It was a job that would have killed many people, but Oppenheimer seemed to relish it. A quiet, soft-spoken man with a kindly face and a wreath of white hair, he looked more like the dean of some remote New England college than what he was: a brilliant legal mind with the tenacity and the killer instinct of a shark. Not since the days of Thomas E. Dewey had the office been occupied by one who understood so well how to use its power.

Tolliver had never met the man, had seen him only a few times, and then at a distance. He told Oppenheimer's secretary who he was and was waved to a bench. Sitting there with his raincoat on his lap, he felt slightly apprehensive, like a kid waiting to be called into the principal's office. Whatever this mysterious assignment turned out to be, he could be sure of one thing: It would have an impact on his career, one way or another. He could only hope it might be for the better.

A steady flow of people were going in and out of the office, all of them stepping briskly, looking important. The secretary and two trial-preparation assistants were screening them, but apparently most of the visitors were staff, bureau chiefs and senior prosecutors. Tolliver imagined he'd have a considerable wait.

Not so. After about ten minutes, one of the TPAs approached the bench he was sitting on and told him to follow her. He did, and a moment later found himself inside a wood-paneled chamber, facing Oppenheimer himself.

For a man his age, the DA appeared to be remarkably fit. Lean and slightly built, he had on a dark gray suit and a red tie that set off the white hair and his ruddy skin. And from his manner, you'd think he had nothing more to do than show interest in a lowly detective squad commander. He shook Ben's hand and smiled warmly. "I've heard a lot about you, Lieutenant. All of it good. In fact, I remember the work you did on a number of difficult cases."

Ben nodded, hoping he seemed modest.

Oppenheimer gestured toward a pair of well-worn brown leather armchairs at the far end of the room. "Let's sit over here, shall we?"

The assistant hung Ben's coat on a clothes tree and bowed out, shutting the door behind her.

Ben sat down and made a quick appraisal of his surroundings. The room contained a scarred desk with stacks of paper covering its surface and a half dozen chairs grouped around a conference table. Behind the desk was an eagle-topped pole with an American flag draped from it. A few framed photographs were hanging on the walls and some old wooden filing cabinets and a pair of bookcases stood against the walls. And that was it. All business, plainly functional, nothing pretentious. Set for action, like the DA himself.

Oppenheimer was watching him, making an appraisal of his own. The smile stayed in place. "Nice morning out there, isn't it?"

"Yes it is," Ben said.

"Fall is my favorite time of year. The summer's over; everybody's back to work. Makes you feel invigorated. But it's over too soon, don't you think? Here we are with Thanksgiving only a few days away. How about a cup of coffee, Lieutenant?"

"If you're having one."

"How do you take it?"

"Black, please."

Oppenheimer picked up a telephone from the small table beside his chair and spoke into it. When he hung up, he said, ''I wonder if you've heard the news about the death of Senator Cunningham.''

In one shot, everything came together. Ben now knew why he was here, why the assignment was one that required the services of a detective who was outside the DA's own forces, why Oppenheimer had requested a man who could be relied upon not to talk about his mission. Apparently, Tolliver wasn't the only one who'd wondered about the way Clayton Cunningham had checked out.

He nodded. ''Yes, sir, I did hear about it—on the radio this morning.''

''A great loss,'' the DA said. ''The senator was a fine man, and a personal friend of mine for many years.''

That was interesting. It was well known that Oppenheimer was on the opposite side of the political spectrum from Cunningham. Apparently when you got to a certain stage, personal feelings transcended politics. Or did they?

''It would be hard to think of anyone who served the people of New York better than he did,'' the DA went on. ''On the national level as well as the state. In fact, the whole family has always been dedicated to public service. They set a great example.''

''I think so, too,'' Ben said.

''But like all public figures,'' Oppenheimer continued, ''they've also received their share of criticism—for political as well as other reasons. No matter how much good one does, you can't expect everyone to love you.'' He smiled. ''One of the hazards of being rich.''

Ben was about to say he wouldn't mind taking the risk, but then he thought better of it.

The door opened and the secretary brought in a tray with coffee and a plate of pastries. She set the tray down on a small table beside the two men.

Oppenheimer looked at the pastries and then at the woman, who was round and gray-haired. ''Helga, what are you trying to do to me? Make me fat?''

''The Danish is for your guest,'' Helga said with a straight face, then left the room.

''That woman has been in charge of me ever since I've had this job,'' the DA said. ''Help yourself, Lieutenant.''

Ben reached for a cup of coffee and then broke off a piece of pastry and ate it.

Oppenheimer took the other cup and sipped the steaming black liquid. "Anyway, I understand there is already a lot of gossip being churned up by the media. Did you get any of that in the newscast you listened to?"

Ben shook his head. "All I heard was a brief announcement that he died."

"I see. Well, it seems they're sniffing around like a pack of hyenas, trying to turn the situation into something sensational."

"I guess that's to be expected."

"Yes, unfortunately. Of course, anything to do with the Cunninghams is news. I'm sure people all over the world are aware of the senator's death by now . . . *and* have heard the rumors."

"What are the media saying?" Ben asked.

"I gather they're trying to suggest something not quite proper was going on. At the time, the senator was being interviewed by a writer who was doing an article on him."

"I did hear that much," Ben said.

The DA was watching him closely. "That's what all the fuss is about. The writer was female. They were in his office, which is in the building next door to his home. The poor man had a heart attack and fell unconscious. By the time help arrived, he was gone."

"Is anyone claiming it wasn't a heart attack?"

"Oh no. Nothing like that. The doctor who examined him has been the family physician for a long time. Name's George Phelps. Heard of him?"

"I don't think so."

"Quite well known in his own right. He's head of cardiology at Manhattan Medical Center, which of course was founded by the Cunninghams. By the senator's grandfather, actually. Dr. Phelps said it was a coronary and that he died almost immediately."

"Will Phelps do the postmortem?"

"There won't be one. The family feels having an autopsy performed would only add fuel to the gossip and conjecture. Dr. Phelps signed the death certificate and that was that—or should have been, anyway."

Ben drank some of his coffee. Something was going on here, but he couldn't put his finger on what it was.

Oppenheimer continued to watch the detective's reactions. "Nevertheless, you can imagine what's coming next. TV and the tabloids will turn out a lot of trash about how there was a relationship between the senator and this writer. A romance, or something like that."

"Who is she?"

"Her name is Jessica Silk. I'm told she's a free-lance journalist who writes for magazines, and that's all I know about her."

Ben wondered whether what the media was stirring up might be true. He tried to put the question diplomatically. "Of course there's nothing to the rumors?"

Oppenheimer sipped his coffee. "I don't think so, although it's possible, of course. There've been stories about the senator and his affairs for years. Many of them well founded, I'm afraid. When his first wife divorced him, a lot of scandalous details were revealed."

"I remember some of that," Ben said.

"On the other hand, he was a very busy man, and the family told the police it wasn't at all unusual for him to work for an hour or two in the evening. After dinner, he'd often go over to his office and catch up on a few things. That was why he scheduled the interview at that time. What's more, he and this woman weren't alone when he suffered the attack."

"Is that so?"

"Yes. You see, the Cunningham Foundation is headquartered in the building. That's the organization that makes grants to various charities and worthwhile educational ventures. The chief administrator of the foundation is a woman who lives there. She was also in the senator's office when he became ill."

"So two women were present."

"Correct. According to the police report, they called for help immediately. The police and an emergency ambulance arrived within minutes. They tried CPR and administered oxygen, but Senator Cunningham was already dead. Dr. Phelps got there not long after, and he said nothing could have saved him."

"Was that the first time the senator had a heart attack?"

"I have no idea. But whether it was or not, this one killed him, almost instantly. And as I say, that should have been the end of the story, except for mourning over the loss of a great man. Unfortunately, it won't be. Which is why I asked for your assistance."

Oppenheimer drained his cup and set it down. "I want you to conduct an investigation, get to the bottom of this. I want to know *exactly* what happened. Not that I expect any surprises, but all these damned rumors should be put to rest."

"You said the police went to the scene? They would have been from the One-nine Precinct."

"Yes, they were." The DA gestured toward his desk. "I had their report faxed to me as soon as I reached my office this morning. The trouble is, a summary by two officers in a patrol car isn't going to do what needs to be done."

"No, I guess not."

"That's why I asked Chief Houlihan to recommend a detective. He suggested you because of your excellent record and your reputation for carrying through on tough assignments."

Oppenheimer paused. "You may be wondering why I didn't put one of our own investigators in charge."

"It did cross my mind," Ben said.

"The reason is that I want this to be treated with total objectivity. And the only way that can happen is for you to be independent. I will ask one of our men to assist you, however. One of the detectives in Captain Brannigan's unit. I've already spoken to Brannigan and cleared it with him."

Sure, Ben thought. I'll be objective and independent, while you're behind the scene, calling the shots.

"You're to get on it immediately," Oppenheimer said. "Chief Houlihan will announce that a special investigator has been assigned."

Ben nodded.

"There is also another situation that has bearing on this. We've been looking into certain irregularities involving Cunningham Securities, a stock brokerage that's one of the family companies. The man who'll be helping you is a detective who's been working on it, along with the ADAs assigned to the case. His name is Jack Mulloy. Do you know him, by any chance?"

"Afraid I don't."

"His work is extremely confidential, of course, but he can provide background information that would be useful to you. I've asked him to give you complete cooperation, and I also sent him a copy of the police report on the senator's death. I told him to expect a visit from you this morning. You'll find him over in the investigators' offices."

"All right, fine."

Oppenheimer paused again. "As I said earlier, Lieutenant, I'm informed that you have an outstanding record."

Ben made no reply.

"And I also happen to know you're being considered for a promotion to captain. You're aware of that, no doubt?"

"I've always hoped it might happen someday," Ben said.

"No reason it shouldn't," the DA continued. "You're bright, and you're politically astute. Both those things were evident to me in the way you handled yourself in our discussion. I'm sure I don't have to point out to you that a job well done here could be very helpful to you."

"I understand," Ben said.

Oppenheimer rose to his feet and went to his desk, returning with an envelope. Ben stood up, as well, and the DA handed him the envelope, saying, "This is a copy of the police report. Get back to me, Lieutenant, as soon as you've looked into the situation and made your initial assessment. I'll tell Helga any call from you is to be put through at once. Incidentally, it's especially important that you exercise caution when you talk to anyone from the media. I'm sure they'll be all over you, but you know how to handle them. You'll be polite and cooperative and what you tell them will amount to nothing. Right?"

"Yes, sir."

The DA held out his hand. "Good luck."

Ben shook the hand and then Oppenheimer returned to his desk, his mind obviously already on another subject.

Tolliver turned and left the office, picking his coat off the rack on the way. While he waited for the elevator, he thought about the situation he was in: caught between the chief of detectives and the district attorney. Wonderful.

But he had to hand it to Oppenheimer. The DA was already protecting his flanks, testing whatever political ramifications might result from Cunningham's death, while he saw to it that the investigation appeared to be the police department's responsibility.

Oppenheimer had implied this was a tough assignment. Why? From everything Ben could see, it was merely a ground ball. A prominent citizen had had a heart attack and died. The media were gossiping, but that was at least half of what their business was about. And even if the rumors were true, was that such a big deal? If the old guy had died in the saddle, what better way to go?

The thing to do was what the DA obviously wanted: wrap this thing up in a tidy bundle with a nice official ribbon tied around it, marked CLOSED.

And then Tolliver could get back to the job of being a cop. He hadn't joined the force to spend his time sweeping up dog shit. But he also knew that if you wanted to make progress in the NYPD, you did what you had to do. The elevator arrived and he stepped into the car.

5

Jack Mulloy was a big man with a square jaw and a balding pate, working in his shirt sleeves at a desk piled high with stacks of paper. A Colt Detective Special was riding on his right hip, but even without it, there was no way you'd make him for anything but a cop. He was on the phone when Tolliver arrived and he waved his visitor to a seat beside his desk.

Ben sat and looked around. There were a dozen similarly laden desks in the area, the men and women working at them busy to the point of seeming harassed. Which was understandable, he thought. If he had to spend his time wading through a paper swamp the way they were doing, he'd go out of his mind.

Mulloy sounded angry. ''Checking confirmations by hand is crazy,'' he said into the phone. ''We should have their computer data to work from. Christ, we'll never get caught up.'' He listened for a moment, then rolled his eyes. ''Request it again, then. Or have Shackley request it. And tell him we need more bodies on this. There's nobody over here that could pitch in, so some of you guys'll have to.''

He listened for another few seconds, growled something unintelligible, and hung up.

Turning, he stuck out a meaty hand. ''You must be Lieutenant Tolliver. Welcome to the fun part of the business. Okay if I call you Ben?''

Tolliver shook the hand. ''Sure. I understand you'll be giving me some help.''

''So I'm told. Too bad about the senator.''

''Yes.''

Mulloy inclined his head toward an office door at one end of the room. ''Captain Brannigan sends regards. He's in a meeting this morning, but he wants you to stop in and say hello when you get a chance.''

''Fine,'' Ben said. ''I'll do that. The DA said you're working on an investigation of Cunningham Securities.''

''That's correct.''

''How's it going?''

''Like everything else around here—slowly. We could use ten times the people we got.''

"You're loaded down, huh?"

"You wouldn't believe it."

"Okay, I understand. I'll try to take as little of your time as possible."

"Hey, don't mind my bitching. I'll be glad to help. At least it'll be more like being back in police work instead of dealing with this shit."

"You been here long?"

"Six years. I was in the job before that, detective third. I retired with a partial disability. That's why I'm on a desk."

"So what's happening with your investigation?"

"It looks like there've been leaks someplace, involving the brokerage's employees. Inside information got out on a couple of acquisition deals. We have some possible suspects but nothing we can prove so far. Even so, two of them were fired, so I guess the company got nervous. The senator's son is the head of it, and he's been stonewalling us."

"What's his name?"

"Clayton the Fourth. He's got a sister named Ingrid who runs another family-owned outfit, a commercial real estate firm."

"How's that one doing?"

"Some problems, from what we can gather, but nothing illegal. At least nothing we know about. Supposedly, they're overextended on a number of very large office-park developments. A lot of the trouble is because Ingrid's a horse nut. She spends more time on her farm than on the business. Her husband is a con artist named Kurt Kramer. He's a German who skipped out of Munich after he got caught running a phony investment scheme."

"He up to something over here?"

"It's possible, but there's no evidence. He calls himself a financial consultant. We're keeping an eye on him, too."

"On the subject of the senator," Ben said.

"Yes?"

"Have you read the police report?"

"Oh yeah." Mulloy flicked a hand at the papers on his desk. "Doesn't look like much, though, huh? The old guy was in his office getting interviewed and his ticker gave out. Another witness was there at the time, which tends to let the air out of the story the media's trying to pump up."

"It should, if the witnesses' statements were accurate."

''Sure, but even if they were lying and the senator was dicking this writer, so what? A guy seventy-two years of age? He should get a fucking medal. So to speak.''

Ben smiled. The thought had occurred to him, as well.

''Here's another possibility,'' Mulloy said. ''Suppose he was getting it on with both of them, had a threesome going. That ought to be worth a parade down Broadway.''

''Except that he wouldn't be around to enjoy it.''

''Okay, so maybe just a twenty-one-gun salute at the funeral. Or the Rockettes could dance or something.''

''Fine, but I think I'd better concentrate on my end of this first. The DA is expecting a report.''

''Fair enough.''

''Off the record,'' Ben said, ''I'm as curious as you are about why he wants the situation investigated at all. Seems to me there'd be less of a public stir about it if the case was just allowed to fade away. After the funeral, it'd be forgotten about.''

''No question. By that time, the media'd be serving up some new scandal.''

''So why not leave it alone? Oppenheimer said he and the senator were personal friends, told me how much he admired him. Wouldn't it have been better to let the old man rest in peace?''

Mulloy chewed his bottom lip as he studied his visitor. ''Tell you what, Ben. Let's you and me have ourselves a cup of coffee, okay? Only not here. There's a deli down the street.''

Tolliver had no need for more coffee, but he understood the signal. ''Sure, let's go.''

Mulloy stood up and retrieved his suit jacket, which had been draped over the back of his chair. He shrugged into it and led the way.

As they stepped toward the elevator, Ben saw that the other man walked with a limp. ''That from the injury you were talking about?''

''Yeah, I was on a drug bust in the Three-four,'' Mulloy said. ''We were in this crapped-out building and I stepped on a piece of rotten flooring. Went right through it, wound up in the basement. I was in and out of hospitals for over a year.''

''Must've been rough.''

Mulloy shrugged. ''At least I get an extra hump on my pension.''

The deli was called Max's, and the pungent aromas inside were a blend of kosher pickles and hot pastrami. They ordered coffee at the counter and then took the plastic containers to one of the small tables.

"You gotta be careful what you say up there," Mulloy said. "Never know who's listening or where it might go."

"Uh-huh."

The detective hunched over his coffee. "You want to know what this is all about, right? Why Oppenheimer is doing this? I'll tell you why. Maybe him and the senator were friends, like he says. Maybe they loved each other dearly—which I doubt, but maybe they did. Whether they did or not, you have to remember the DA is one thing above everything else. And that is, he's a politician."

"I'm sure that's true."

"Good. Because that's the whole key to understanding how he works. See, if the investigation comes up with nothing, so be it. Running it might throw a shadow over Cunningham's memory, but what the hell—that's not the DA's fault, right? The police department did the investigating. All he did was issue a routine order. On the other hand, if there is something to all those rumors, that's not bad, either, from Oppenheimer's point of view. It proves the senator wasn't so high-and-mighty, after all. It'd also make it easier to go forward with the thing I'm working on. Now do you get it?"

"Yeah, I suppose that could make sense."

"Now let me ask you something else. You think Oppenheimer just took it on himself to decide the senator's death ought to be looked into?"

"Why not?"

"Think about it. You got a lot of powerful people who'd have reasons to push him, right?"

"Maybe."

"Maybe is right. There's more undercurrents in that outfit of his than you could count. You take this investigation I'm on. The senior prosecutor is a guy named Fletcher Shackley. He's got a whole raft of ADAs assigned to the case, but where's the progress? We've been on it almost two years now and we're no closer to an indictment than we ever were."

"Why aren't you?"

"I wish I knew. Every time we come up with something that looks solid, it goes up in a puff of smoke."

"Shackley dragging his feet?"

"Maybe. He's got his own agenda, speaking of politics. Far as he's concerned, his current job is just a stepping-stone."

"To what?"

''Who knows? I wouldn't be surprised if he wanted to run for office someplace down the line. Maybe the state legislature, or Congress. Which means he has to be careful not to piss off the wrong people.''

''Interesting.''

Mulloy was thoughtful for a moment. He dumped cream and sugar into his cup. ''You know what, Ben? The job has changed a lot over the past twenty years or so. When I was a uniform, I really believed all that shit about how our duty was to protect the civilians, catch the bad guys.''

Tolliver knew what he was about to hear. It wouldn't be the first time he'd listened to a veteran cop express feelings of disillusionment. And he was sure it wouldn't be the last.

''Nowadays,'' Mulloy went on, ''everything's political—and not just on this level, either. With the DA's office, that's to be expected. But look at the police department. Sure, there was always politics, only now it goes all the way down to the street. A cop who makes a lot of collars is considered a problem. Why? Because arrests are what cause complaints. And yet if the assholes didn't get arrested, they wouldn't have anything to complain about, right? So how do the brass treat that? They tell the cop to cool it, warn him not to make waves. If he gets the message, fine. If he doesn't, he winds up in the tunnel.''

''Yeah, I'm aware,'' Ben said. ''Sometimes the political balance gets tilted in the wrong direction.''

Mulloy's eyebrows lifted. ''Political balance gets tilted? Hey, come on. In this town, there isn't any balance. It's so heavy in favor of the bad guys, cops don't worry about stopping trouble anymore; they worry about staying out of it themselves.''

''That's why it needs to get tilted back again.''

''You think that's ever gonna happen? Look at what's been going on here. Take the thing in Washington Heights. A convicted drug dealer tries to kill a cop. The cop shoots him. So the mayor goes to the dealer's family and offers condolences and then he has the city pay for the bum's funeral. Acts like the cop was the criminal. And that's just one case. You think the city can ever have an effective force again? Please.''

''So what's your point?''

''My point is, the job today is *all* politics. Including this assignment Oppenheimer handed you. It doesn't matter to me—I just have to ride the desk a few more years and then I get another pension on top of the one I got now. But what you've gotta do is be careful. This thing may look simple, but it could be a mine field. I'll give you all the help I can, but watch your step, okay?''

''Sure,'' Ben said. ''Thanks for the advice.''

6

Tolliver decided to talk to Ardis Merritt first, on the grounds that she was the more neutral of the two women. The writer was the one the media were using to churn up their gossip; he'd get to her later. The police report said the foundation was located next door to the senator's home on East Seventieth Street. Ben got into his car and headed for the entrance ramp to the FDR Drive.

The car he was driving was a new Ford that had been prepared by the factory for police use. On the outside, the vehicle was a garden-variety Taurus, a plain blue sedan you wouldn't look at twice. On the inside, it was something else. The engine was a thirty-two-valve V-8 with an intercooler and high-lift cams that gave the machine a top of around 150 mph. And to hold it on the road, the suspension featured antisway bars and heavy-duty shocks.

In addition, friends of the lieutenant in the NYPD motor-vehicle unit had added a few more touches, among them bulletproof glass and armor panels in the front doors and behind the driver's seat. Hidden up under the dash in a quick-release scabbard was a 12-gauge pump shotgun with a pistol grip and a twenty-inch barrel. In the trunk was a coil of nylon rope, a length of steel chain, extra ammunition for the Mauser as well as the shotgun, and a number of other useful items, including a complete set of burglar's tools. The car was not exactly designed for calling on a lady, but it would do. And it sure beat Ben's old one, a battered wreck he'd owned for years.

Best of all, the Ford was a hell of a lot of fun to drive. The reason he chose the FDR to go uptown was only partly because it was the quickest way to get there; it also gave him an opportunity to stretch the car's legs. Some guys relaxed by hitting golf balls. Tolliver blew off steam by racing other drivers, which in New York was a blood sport. He made the trip in sixteen minutes—not a record, but close.

The neighborhood surrounding the adjoining buildings in the Cunningham complex was about as tony as you could get, with the Frick museum just down the street. Fifth Avenue was a few steps away in one direction, Park a few more in the other. The buildings themselves were tall and elegant, faced in white stone.

When he arrived, Ben saw that there was no place to park; the block was jammed with vehicles. One of them was an NYPD patrol car and near that was a van with WPIC TV's call letters on it. Two cops were standing in front of the Cunningham mansion and another was at the entrance of the building housing the foundation. A small crowd of what Ben assumed was a mix of reporters and rubbernecks was on the sidewalk. He drove around the corner and left the Ford in a No Parking zone on Fifth Avenue, dropping a police plate onto the dash before getting out and walking back.

Apparently, most of the civilians were from the media. He pushed his way through them to the front door of the foundation building, which was identified only by a small brass sign on the wall beside the entrance, and showed his shield to the cop. The officer stepped aside to let him in, but before he could get through the door, one of the reporters made him.

She grabbed his arm. ''Lieutenant Tolliver. Good morning.''

He recognized her, as well. Shelley Drake was one of those near-perfect blondes the TV news shows seemed to have an inexhaustible supply of, all of them good-looking in a way that suggested inbreeding among Catherine Crier and Leslie Stahl and Diane Sawyer. No wonder Connie Chung stood out.

''What do you hope to learn from this investigation?'' Drake asked.

Before he could answer, he saw her signal to a guy with a video camera. An instant later, the camera was on Ben. Drake moved close to get herself into the shot.

''We're simply looking into the circumstances surrounding the senator's death,'' Ben said.

''Isn't it true the police suspect there was a personal relationship between him and the woman who was with him when he died?''

He chose his words carefully. ''Senator Cunningham was a very prominent citizen. The police department wants to be sure all the facts concerning his unfortunate death are out in the open.''

''Does that mean they're not out in the open now? Certain information is being suppressed? To do with the woman?''

"I don't know of anything being suppressed. We'll make available a complete report just as soon as possible."

"Why haven't the police revealed that the woman is Jessica Silk, a divorcée who claims she was just writing a story?"

That stopped him. He hadn't realized Silk's name had not been released. Nor did he know she was divorced, or anything else about her personal life. "I'm sorry," he said. "That's all I can tell you at the moment."

Drake still had hold of his arm, and he could feel her fingers digging into his bicep. At the same time, she was standing so that the grip on him wouldn't be visible to the camera. He wondered how she'd like a kick in the kneecap.

She moved her face closer to his. "Do you have any information as to how long they'd been seeing each other?"

Getting rid of her was like trying to shed a bad case of flu. Smiling pleasantly, he peeled her hand off his arm and stepped past her to the door. When he went inside, Drake tried to follow him, but the cop blocked her way.

He found himself in a large entrance foyer with a floor paved in black-and-white marble squares and with a high ceiling that had an elaborate brass chandelier hanging from it. On one wall was a life-size portrait of a man with a square jaw and thick black muttonchop whiskers. An inscription at the bottom of the frame identified the subject as Colonel Clayton Cunningham.

"Yes, sir, may I help you?"

Ben turned, to see a husky, bald-headed man approaching from an inner doorway. He was wearing a plain gray suit, with a bulge showing in his left armpit.

"Police," Ben said. He showed the guy his shield. "I'm Lieutenant Tolliver, from the district attorney's office."

"Evan Montrock, head of security."

"I'd like to see Ardis Merritt. Is she here?"

Montrock said he'd check, then went back through the doorway.

Ben turned to the portrait once more. He'd seen pictures of the senator often enough in the newspapers and he'd also seen him on TV. The man on the wall looked a lot like him. Or more accurately, the senator had looked a lot like his grandfather. Big, with an aggressive way of staring out at you from under bushy brows. Except for the whiskers, the two seemed almost like twins.

Montrock was back. "If you'll follow me, please, Miss Merritt will see you."

He led Tolliver through the door and into a reception area. There was a desk and a sofa and chairs, but no one else was in the room. Ben wondered whether members of the staff had been excused for the day, then decided they had been. He followed the guard through the area and into a wide hallway that had old oil paintings of horses and dogs on the walls. When they reached the end, the guard opened another door and stepped aside. Tolliver went past him into the room and the guard shut the door.

This was a sitting room with a grouping of comfortable furniture arranged near a fireplace. A young woman was standing beside one of the tall windows. As Ben walked in, she stepped toward him, extending her hand. "Hello, Lieutenant. I'm Ardis Merritt."

Ben shook the hand. She wasn't at all what he'd imagined she would be. Young, for one thing, which was the biggest surprise. He'd thought somebody heading an organization of the size and importance of the Cunningham Foundation would be old and starchy, and she wasn't at all.

Nor was she very attractive, with her brown hair tied back on her head, her face plain-featured and pale, dark eyes peering at him through heavy black horn-rims. She was wearing a cardigan sweater and a tweed skirt and blocky shoes, and he wondered whether she thought the frumpy clothes made her seem more serious, so as to offset the impression of youthfulness.

He also noticed the flesh around her eyes was swollen, probably from crying. But she was holding herself erect, as if taking pride in her efforts to remain stoic.

"I was sorry to hear about the senator's death," Ben said.

She nodded briefly. "It was a terrible shock. Somehow you think someone of that stature will be with you forever. And then when he's gone, you can't quite comprehend the loss, can't measure it."

"I'm sure that's true." He shifted his feet. "Miss Merritt, the reason I'm here is that I've been assigned to head up an investigation. I understand you were with him when he died?"

"That's correct, I was."

"And that his death occurred in his office here in this building?"

"Yes."

"Which is where?"

"Upstairs, on the second floor."

"Would you mind showing me? That would make it easier for me to learn exactly what happened."

"I've already told the police exactly what happened," she said, "as well as the family and Dr. Phelps."

Ben kept his tone gentle. "Yes, but you see, I have to make out the final, official report." He didn't know whether it would be final or not, or whether it would be labeled official—or, for that matter, just what Oppenheimer would do with it.

Merritt frowned. "Will the report be made public? I mean, there are already all these outrageous rumors flying around. I can't believe the media would say such things."

"That's why the investigation is important. It'll help put an end to the stories. I know all this is unpleasant, but it's just something that has to be done."

"I understand." She squared her shoulders. "I'll lead the way."

They went through a door beside the fireplace, this one opening onto another hallway, with a flight of stairs at one end.

"Excuse me," Ben said.

She turned back to him. "Yes?"

"How did the senator come over here last night? What route did he take—would you know that?"

"I assume the one he always took, which is through that doorway behind you, at the end of the hall."

"The door connects this building to his house?"

"Yes."

"And then he would have gone up these stairs?"

"That's right."

"How is the building laid out?"

"The first two floors are where reception and the sitting rooms are, and the library and a conference room and the kitchen. The senator's suite is on the second floor. His secretary also works there, and so do I. The third and fourth floors are all staff offices. My apartment is on the top floor, the fifth."

"Okay, thanks. Go ahead."

She led him on up the stairs, at the head of which was another hall, this one wide enough to provide a sitting area with a sofa and some chairs in it. More paintings of hunting scenes were hanging on the walls. Merritt went through the area to a door, opening it and showing Ben into the senator's office.

The room was large and handsomely furnished in what obviously were antiques. He couldn't help making a mental comparison to the space District Attorney Oppenheimer occupied in the Criminal Justice Building. The differences were night and day, spare versus luxurious.

For a few moments, he stood in the center of the office, taking in details. For a room where a great deal had taken place the previous night, it seemed remarkably tidy: all in order, everything in its place. Not so much as a speck of dust could be seen on the furniture or the dark red Persian rug. There weren't even any papers visible on the large, old brass-bound mahogany desk.

He turned to Merritt. ''Has this place been cleaned since last night?''

''Yes. The maids were here at eight o'clock, just as they are every morning.''

Which was perfectly proper, Ben reminded himself; this wasn't a crime scene. ''And the senator's secretary?''

''She came in also, for a short time. The poor woman was devastated, of course, as we all are. I sent her home.''

He looked at the wall behind the desk. It was covered with framed photographs showing the senator with other famous people, mostly politicians who'd been in the public eye at various times over the past four decades. In some of the photos, however, he was with show-biz personalities, including Marlene Dietrich and Humphrey Bogart and a woman Ben thought might be Shirley MacLaine, but that seemed unlikely.

''Mind if we sit down?'' he asked.

Merritt appeared reluctant, but he wanted to get her to relax a little, if possible. He indicated a table with two chairs standing against the wall to his left. ''Over here okay?''

Without waiting for an answer, he took off his raincoat and draped it over one of the chairs. Merritt took the other one and they sat facing each other, the young woman eyeing him warily.

Ben rested his arms on the table. ''If you would,'' he said, ''I'd like you to tell me everything you can remember about what occurred.''

She took a deep breath and exhaled. ''I was up in my apartment watching television when the senator came into the building.''

''What time was that?''

''A little after nine.''

''How did you know he'd arrived?''

"The head of security called me. You met him on the way in, Evan Montrock. That's standard procedure after hours. If anyone comes here, a guard lets me know."

"How many men are on at night?"

"Two, besides Montrock. One is always on the door and the other makes rounds through the building. They also go into the house and check on it periodically."

"I imagine there are TV monitors and an alarm system?"

"Oh yes."

"Ever have any trouble?"

"Not in the time I've worked for the foundation."

"How long has that been?"

"Six years."

"Did you come in as the chief administrator?"

"No. For the first two years, I was an assistant to Mr. Welch, and then when he left, I took over."

"And never any trouble in all that time?"

"No, not really. Once or twice there've been people out in the street in the daytime, demonstrating over one thing or another, but they never did any damage or anything like that."

"So security called you at a little after nine and said the senator had come into the building. Was that unusual, in the evening?"

"Not at all. He often came over after dinner. He liked to do that because it was quiet then. No phones ringing, no people running about."

"What happened next?"

"I came down here to see if there was anything he needed."

"Was that also standard procedure?"

"More or less, but not because I was required to. I always wanted to help him in any way I could. He was the kind of man you felt privileged to do things for." Her lower lip trembled. "After all he did for others, all his life."

Ben looked away, giving her time to compose herself.

When he looked back, she said, "I would have done anything for him."

He wondered whether that included covering up a possible scandal. "Then what?"

"Then Miss Silk arrived. She's a writer who was doing an article on him, as I'm sure you know."

"Yes. How long had she been working on it?"

"Quite a while, but I don't know how long exactly."

"A week, a month?"

"A few weeks, I think. The senator was considering expanding it, turning it into a book."

"Was that his idea, or hers?"

"I don't know."

"Was it a biography?"

"He said it was going to be more about his views on different subjects. He was very progressive, you know. Very innovative in his thinking. Not just about politics but about every kind of social issue." A small, sad smile curled the corners of her mouth. "I'm afraid that made problems for him from time to time."

"What kind of problems?"

"A lot of his constituents were old-line conservatives. They found it hard to go along with some of his more liberal proposals for social reform. To them, *liberal* is a dirty word. Equates with Marxist."

"That must have made life difficult at times."

She held him in a steady gaze. "Did you ever meet him?"

"No, I'm afraid not."

"If you had, you'd know he didn't care what such people thought. He did what he knew in his heart was right, no matter what kind of criticism resulted. He stood for things like free higher education and free medical care. You can imagine the battles that caused."

"Uh-huh. Getting back to Miss Silk . . ."

"Yes?"

"What happened when she got here?"

"I brought her up here to the office and they went right to work."

"Where were they sitting?"

"Here, at this table."

"Was she using a tape recorder?"

"No. The senator didn't approve of them. He felt that recordings could be misused. In the wrong hands, the things people say could put them in a bad light. He much preferred to have an interviewer take notes."

"And then he'd review the material later?"

"When that was the agreement, yes."

"Would he agree to being interviewed for an article otherwise?"

"I doubt it."

''Were you here the whole time they were together?''

''All except for a few minutes, when I went out to get some coffee for us.''

''You went down to the kitchen?''

''No. There's a pantry on this floor, just off the hall. There's a coffee maker there. I made a pot of coffee when the senator arrived, and then when Miss Silk got here, I brought it in.''

''What were you doing while the interview was going on?''

''Actually, I was doing some work of my own—reviewing a request for money from the Cancer Society. The only reason I was here was because the senator liked me to be around in case his memory needed a jog or in case there was something he wanted from the library, or from the files or whatever.''

''Work his secretary would have done, in the daytime.''

''Pretty much, yes.''

''And you didn't mind doing those things?''

She stiffened. ''As I said, I always felt it was a privilege to do anything he needed done.''

''Yes, of course. When you were working in here, where were you sitting?''

She gestured. ''Over there, in one of those chairs in front of the desk. The one on the right. When the senator became ill, I didn't realize what was happening. I heard Jessica cry out, and when I looked up, he was slumped over the table. He seemed to be clutching his throat, or his upper chest. His face was very red. I knew right away he was in trouble and that it was bad.'' She bit her lower lip and looked up at the ceiling for a moment.

''I realize this is hard for you,'' Ben said. ''But please go on.''

She shuddered, and then took a tissue out of the sleeve of her sweater and dabbed her eyes. ''I went over to him and put my hand on his shoulder, tried to talk to him. I was asking him what was wrong. At first, I thought he might be choking or something.''

''What was Miss Silk doing at that point?''

''I don't remember, exactly. I think she stood up and was bending over him, too. We were both pretty shaken. Then he just sort of slid out of his chair and fell down onto the floor.''

''Was he conscious?''

''No, not that I could tell. His eyes were half-closed and his face looked as if he was in pain.''

"Then what?"

"Then we tried to get him some air. We took off his tie and unbuttoned his shirt. But I could see that he wasn't breathing, and I was close to panic. We both were. I always thought I was good in an emergency, but seeing him like that really got to me. I tried mouth-to-mouth resuscitation, but he didn't respond to that, either. I also tried to find a pulse, but I couldn't. Then I thought about trying cardiac compression, but I was afraid I might be doing the wrong thing, that I might make him worse."

"The police report said there was a pillow under his head and his shoes were off."

"Jessica got the pillow from the sofa out in the hallway. We wanted to make him more comfortable."

"And the shoes?"

"He must have kicked them off himself when he was sitting at the table. He often did that when he could relax."

"Okay, what happened next?"

"When we couldn't get any response, I finally ran to the phone and called security. One of them came up here, but he couldn't get a reaction, either."

"Was that Montrock?"

"Yes. Then I called nine-one-one—and after that, the family."

"Who did you speak to there?"

"One of the maids answered and I asked for Mrs. Cunningham. When she came on, I said the senator was ill. Then Clay, his son, got on the phone. After that, he and Ingrid came over right away. Ingrid is the senator's daughter. One of them—I think it was Clay—said it looked as if his father had had a heart attack. Ingrid went back to tell the others what had happened."

"Did any of them come over after that?"

"No."

"When did the police arrive?"

"A few minutes later. There were two officers. And then two people from the ambulance crew came and they all worked on him. They gave him oxygen, but that didn't have any effect, either. Finally, Dr. Phelps got here and examined him. He said he was very sorry . . . but . . ." Merritt covered her face with her hands.

Ben looked away again. He let her cry for a few moments and then she got herself together once more, blowing her nose and forcing herself to sit up straight.

"I'm sorry," she said.

"Perfectly all right. Take your time."

She gave her nose another swipe with the tissue. "After that, the ambulance crew put him on a stretcher and took him out."

"Where did they go?"

"To the Manhattan Medical Center. Dr. Phelps said he'd go there, too. Then Clay went back to the house. He asked me to go with him and I did."

"What about Jessica Silk?"

"She left here at the same time. I don't know where she went. Home, I suppose."

"You haven't spoken to her since?"

"No."

"And what happened when you went to the house?"

"The whole family was there, Mrs. Cunningham and the husbands and wives. We were all in the library, trying to console one another. Everybody was in a state of shock, of course."

"I'm sure you were."

"And then the phone calls started. Reporters—can you believe it? I don't know how they got the news so fast."

Ben did. The media monitored the police frequencies around the clock. The address would have tipped them off, and then the cops probably had escorted the ambulance to the hospital. Reporters had no doubt gone there, as well.

"I don't know how they got the number, either," Merritt went on. "It's not listed, of course, but there they were on the phone, demanding to talk to Mrs. Cunningham."

"Did she take any of the calls?"

"Certainly not. She told the maids she wouldn't speak to anyone but Dr. Phelps, if he called."

"And did he?"

"I don't know. I left the house and went back up to my apartment."

"What time was that?"

"Around one. I made myself a drink and went to bed, but I couldn't sleep. I just sort of dozed until six and then I got up."

"Have you spoken to any of the reporters?"

"No. Except to tell them there would be no statement other than the one that had come from the family. I knew there was one, because Clay took care of it. He called someone from the public-relations agency while I was at the house last night. And then this morning, I turned on the TV and I was horrified. I don't know how they got Jessica's name, but they did. They were trying to make it all sound as if she and the senator were lovers. It's just absolutely appalling."

"How about the family—have you spoken to them today?"

"Just to Clay, on the telephone. He said the funeral will be on Friday."

Ben glanced through his notes and then shut his notebook and returned it to his pocket. "Thank you very much," he said. "I appreciate your help with this. And again, I'm sorry."

"It's all right, Lieutenant. I hope this will put a stop to the hateful dirt they've been spreading."

He rose to his feet and put on his raincoat. "Knowing the media, it probably won't. But if nothing more on it turns up, the story will just go away by itself."

"I certainly hope so."

"If you need to reach me for any reason, please call me at the Manhattan district attorney's office. I may not be there, but I'll be checking in. Okay?"

"Yes, of course. Let me show you out."

"If you don't mind, I'd like to use a telephone, please. I want to call the family, stop in and see them."

Her eyes widened. "I don't think they'll be very happy about that."

"I know, but it's necessary."

She shrugged and indicated a telephone on the senator's desk. "Press the first button. It's a direct line to the house."

7

A maid answered the call. Tolliver told her who he was and asked to speak to Mrs. Cunningham. When she came on, he apologized for disturbing her and requested permission to pay a brief visit. She sounded understandably reluctant but said he could have a few minutes. He told her he'd be there shortly.

Ben then went back down to the first floor, where he questioned

Evan Montrock, the head of security. Montrock's account of what had taken place the night before matched Ardis Merritt's.

"There was nothing anybody could do," the security man said. "I knew he was dead the minute I looked at him, but I didn't want to say so. I think the others did, too, the police and the ambulance crew. When we were working on him, it was really just going through the motions to make everybody feel better." He shook his head. "Such a great man."

"I called the family," Ben said. "I want to stop in and see them."

"Sure, come with me." Montrock led the way to the door that opened into the Cunningham mansion. He knocked and a butler answered. The security man left them and Ben followed the butler along a hallway to the library, where the family was gathered.

The room was large, with lofty windows and floor-to-ceiling bookcases. There were several groupings of furniture, where men and women sat talking. An ornate fireplace was at the far end, with another portrait hanging above it, this one of a woman in an old-fashioned high-necked gown. A fire was blazing on the hearth.

Ben was met at the door by a younger version of the senator. It was amazing how much the males in the family resembled one another. This guy had the same square jaw, the same bushy brows. He was tall and robust, dressed casually in a tweed jacket. "I'm Clay Cunningham," he said.

Ben displayed his shield and ID. "Lieutenant Tolliver. I'm sorry to put you through this, but, as I said on the phone, the police department has ordered me to conduct an investigation into the circumstances surrounding your father's death."

Cunningham spoke quietly, but his tone of voice and dour countenance left no doubt as to what he thought of the visit. "Lieutenant, this is ridiculous. My father is dead, and we're all shattered by the loss. What more could you people possibly want to know?"

Good question, Ben thought. "Can you please tell me what happened last night?"

Cunningham took a deep breath and then resignedly gave him a quick rundown of the previous evening's events, starting with the frantic call that had come from Ardis Merritt at about 9:40 P.M. His version also corresponded to Merritt's, picking up with what he and his sister had found when they went to the senator's office. The two women who had been with his father were very distraught, Cunningham said, and he knew almost at once that the senator had suffered a heart attack, probably fatal. He was sure the security man knew it, as well.

Shortly after that, the police and an emergency ambulance crew had arrived. The crew worked on the stricken man, but to no avail. Then Dr. Phelps came and confirmed their fears.

''Who called the doctor?'' Ben asked.

''I did. As soon as I saw what had happened, I called him at his home. He lives not far away, at Park and Seventy-second. He got there about fifteen or twenty minutes later. He said that Dad had died immediately and that no one could have saved him.''

''How was your father's health, would you say, up until then?''

''By and large, I'd say it was good. Although I'd been a little worried about him, to tell you the truth. He worked too hard, refused to slow down. And he also had a few bad habits. Smoked cigars and was fond of wine and brandy.'' He smiled faintly. ''I think it never occurred to him that he was no longer a young man.''

''I see. Was there anything in particular that was bothering him, do you know? Anything that would have put unusual strain on him?''

Cunningham pursed his lips. ''No, nothing out of the ordinary—at least nothing any of us knew about.''

''How about your personal relationships with him?''

''Excellent. He was totally supportive, very proud of all of us. At dinner last night, he remarked how pleased he was that we were doing so well. Living up to the Cunningham tradition, as he put it.''

Tolliver listened carefully. When Cunningham finished, Ben thanked him, again wondering why he was going through all this. He said he wanted to pay his respects to the other members of the family and that as soon as he'd done so, he'd leave.

Cunningham didn't seem overjoyed by the request, but he complied. When he led Tolliver over to where the others were sitting, Ben was surprised to see that, contrary to what he'd expected, they didn't appear that upset. They were chatting amiably and a maid was moving among them serving drinks. Not an Irish wake, exactly, but not a group of sorrowful mourners, either.

Cunningham introduced Tolliver to each of them and Ben mumbled condolences while filing impressions in his memory.

The widow struck him as pleasant but bland. Her name was

Claire and she seemed some years older than the senator's children, perhaps in her early sixties. She was well groomed, wearing a simple dark dress that set off her silver hair. From her manner, you'd think this was just an ordinary get-together of the clan.

Clay's own wife was a surprise; Ben recognized her as the actress Laura Bentley, whose face he'd often seen in old movies on the tube. Her hair was chestnut, her eyes light blue, and the combination was striking. She favored Ben with a nod, then resumed her conversation with Claire. Apparently they were talking about the upcoming season in Palm Beach.

Ingrid, the senator's daughter by his first marriage, didn't look like a Cunningham at all. Her features were much more refined, under a smoothly styled sweep of sandy hair. She was wearing a string of pearls over her red cashmere sweater, drinking a Bloody Mary as she listened to what the other women were saying about plans for the winter in Florida.

The other man in the group was Kurt Kramer, Ingrid's husband. Younger than the others, his close-cropped blond hair confirmed the Teutonic origins Ben had been told about. But you'd never know it from his accent; if anything, his precise speech sounded faintly British.

After the introductions and Tolliver's perfunctory expressions of sympathy, the members of the group ignored him, picking up the threads of their earlier conversations.

"Excuse me," Ben said.

The room grew quiet as the faces turned toward him, registering curiosity. What did this nosy cop want now?

"I'm sorry I had to intrude," he said. "I'm sure you realize this is all to prevent anyone from besmirching Senator Cunningham's fine character and his outstanding record as a political and social leader. If any of you has anything to add or anything you want to say to me, you can reach me through the Manhattan district attorney's office. Please forgive the interruption. And again, my deepest sympathy to all of you."

He turned and walked back to the door, accompanied by Clay Cunningham. The silence continued until Clay opened the door, then the family members went on chatting once more. Clay led him down the hall to the front entrance and wished him a good day. As Ben left the house, he felt a sense of relief to be getting out of there.

You ought to be a politician yourself, he thought. Anybody who could come up with a bullshit speech like that had the gift.

But at least he was doing this the right way, carrying out the mission. He closed the door behind him and was immediately set upon by the media vultures, who'd continued to camp out on the sidewalk.

8

If anything, there seemed to be more reporters here now than there had been earlier. As soon as Ben stepped out the door, they all began yelling at once.

He raised his hands for quiet. "I have nothing to tell you that you don't already know," he said. "Senator Cunningham was being interviewed for a magazine article when he became ill and died of a heart attack. He was a great man and we'll miss him."

All his little announcement did was prompt another barrage of questions, but Ben ignored them. He made his way through the crowd and walked quickly down the sidewalk, toward where he'd left his car on Fifth Avenue.

One more stop, he thought, and that would be it. He'd locate Jessica Silk and interview her, and that would about wrap it up. Although he might talk to Cunningham's doctor as well, just to be sure everything was nailed down. When that was done, he'd write up his report and turn it over to Oppenheimer, after which he could get back to running his squad.

When he reached his car, he got out his keys and unlocked the door.

"Lieutenant?"

He turned, and there was Miss Influenza, the TV reporter Shelley Drake. For a moment, he was tempted to tell her to get lost, but then he remembered the admonition the district attorney had voiced about treating members of the media courteously.

"Yes?"

She grabbed his arm, which apparently was her customary technique. Although at least this time she didn't have a cameraman in tow. She leaned close, her voice low. "Can I talk to you, just for a minute?

Off the record? I can tell you some things I think you'd find interesting."

"About what?"

"About Senator Cunningham. Could we sit here in your car?"

He exhaled and opened the door. "Yeah, okay. Get in."

She scurried around to the passenger side. Ben climbed in behind the wheel, already thinking about how to get rid of her.

Up close, Drake appeared much the same as she did on TV; if anything, her features seemed even more attractive. The expression on her face was also familiar. It looked as if she'd spent hours practicing sincerity in front of a mirror. Her eyes were a deep shade of blue, however, which Ben hadn't noticed before, a color that went well with her long honey blond hair. She had on a trench coat, which he supposed she thought reinforced the image of a hard-driving reporter.

"Okay," he said, "what is it?"

"I don't know how much you know about the senator's personal life."

"All I need to, I suppose."

"Including his penchant for having an affair with any female he could get his hands on? Surely you've heard about that."

"I've heard rumors, but as far as I know, that's all they were."

"And have you also heard he was a sex freak who got his kicks abusing girls?"

"What?"

"Preferably young ones, but any other kind would do."

He stared at her.

"It's true," Drake said. "And I think Jessica Silk knew it, too. I also think what she was writing wasn't just a puff piece about his illustrious career."

"What was it, then?"

"A story that would have been worth a million bucks, maybe more. I have a hunch she talked the old man into doing the article, using herself as bait. But instead of writing what he thought, she was laying out the details of his weird sex habits."

"Where is all this coming from—you have proof?"

"I can't give you proof—at least not yet."

"Then you'll excuse me, but I have work to do."

"You don't believe me, do you?"

"What's to believe? Look, Miss Drake."

"Please, it's Shelley."

"Okay, Shelley. You want to know how I see this? Let me tell you. A prominent old man who did a lot of good things has died. Now you and all the others in your maggoty business are feeding on the corpse. It's not enough for you to put out a lot of crap about how he was screwing this writer. You're also out to smear his reputation every way you can—just so you can get a beat on your competition."

She flushed. "Will you listen to me? Please?"

"For about ten more seconds. Go ahead."

"I'm not making this up. I'm an investigative reporter, and a good one. I was working on the story when the senator died."

"Uh-huh."

"All right, I'll make a deal with you."

"No you won't."

The blue eyes flashed anger. "Have it your way, Lieutenant. But when you find out what I'm saying is true, you can give *me* a ring. Unless, like everybody else, you're just out to hide all this under a rug." She got out of the car and slammed the door.

Ben watched her go, hands thrust into the pockets of the trench coat, long legs striding, blond hair rippling in the autumn breeze.

Jesus—the shit you had to put up with.

9

Peggy Demarest nosed her small yellow Toyota sedan into a space in the parking lot of the Brentwood Treatment Center and got out of the car. As she walked to the entrance of the ivy-covered stone building, she turned up the collar of her coat and hunched her shoulders. The sun was shining, but the air was brisk out here on the eastern end of Long Island, the wind sweeping in off the sea and rustling the pine trees surrounding the hospital.

This was a trip she undertook at least twice a week, but one she felt ambivalent about making. On one hand, she wanted to see Jan, but on the other, it was depressing to find her sister's condition unchanged each time she came here. Jan was two years younger than Peggy, twenty-one her last birthday, and had always been the more outgoing of the two—a bright, sunny girl with auburn hair and a ready laugh.

And the better-looking one as well, Peggy reminded herself. Jan was a good two inches taller, with a fuller bust line, and Peggy had envied her sister's figure as well as her coloring. Both had been so much more glamorous than Peggy's slim shape and her deep red hair that was dull rather than striking, like Jan's.

Yet nowadays, Jan looked like an old woman and recognized no one.

The receptionist greeted Peggy pleasantly and after speaking into a telephone asked her to have a seat, saying Dr. Chenoweth would be with her shortly. Peggy took a chair near a window and picked up a copy of that morning's *New York Times* from a coffee table.

The story of Clayton Cunningham's death was on the front page, along with a photograph of the former senator. Peggy had already heard the news on CBS TV while she was having breakfast, but seeing the piece in the paper sent another pang through her, nevertheless.

If it hadn't been for the generosity of the Cunningham family, Jan wouldn't be receiving the treatment she was getting at Brentwood; the Demarests never could have afforded it. Peggy's salary as a dental hygienist wouldn't cover a tenth of the bills, and her mother had only a small income from the insurance Peggy's father had left when he died. It was the Cunninghams who'd stepped in when the Demarests had been desperate for help.

And now the senator was dead. She felt a wave of sympathy for his wife and his children and a sense of regret that New York—and the world—had lost a fine man.

"Morning, Peggy. How are you?"

She looked up, to see Jay Chenoweth approaching. Despite her feelings of depression over her sister's condition and the death of Clayton Cunningham, she had to smile. The psychiatrist had an invariably pleasant manner, always easygoing and friendly. Today he was as casual as ever, wearing a battered herringbone tweed jacket with leather patches on the elbows, a knitted tie askew on his blue shirt. But his short brown beard was neatly trimmed and his grin was infectious.

How someone could work in a mental hospital and remain so cheerful was beyond her, but optimism probably was vital to survival in such a job. If you didn't have it, you'd be in danger of losing your own sanity.

She stood up and shook his hand. "I'm fine, Doctor. How are you?"

"The way I always am. Upbeat."

"Must be wonderful."

"Better than not, believe me. Come on along and we'll have a chat before you see Jan." He led her down a corridor to his office.

The room was like its occupant: unpretentious. It was small and cluttered, with a metal desk piled high with papers, only one visitor's chair, plus a filing cabinet and a bookcase. A single window gave a view of the grounds.

The framed diplomas were impressive, however, their Latin inscriptions proclaiming that Jay Chenoweth was an alumnus of Columbia College and the Yale University School of Medicine. He'd also been a resident at Massachussetts General and McLean hospitals and was a graduate of the New York State Psychoanalytic Institute.

Peggy sat down and unbuttoned her coat. Then she asked the same question she raised each time she came here. "How is she—any change?"

And Chenoweth gave the same answer. "No, but I'm hopeful. At least she hasn't deteriorated further, and that's a good sign. And she's eating better than she was at first."

"But she's still not able to feed herself."

"No, not yet."

"Not yet? Tell me the truth, Doctor. Do you really feel there's any chance that she'll ever come out of this . . . state she's in?"

"Of course I do. I can't sit here and give you odds or forecast exactly when it might happen. But does she have a chance? You bet she does."

Peggy said nothing. Sometimes she suspected his responses were simply standard phrases he used to console friends and relatives of Brentwood's patients. And then she felt guilty at having thought such a thing.

As if he'd read her mind, he softened his tone. "Peggy, you have to remember we're lucky to have her at all. The injuries she suffered could easily have killed her."

"Oh, God—I know that. But there are times when . . ." Her voice trailed off.

"When you think she might be better off if she had died, right?"

She flushed. "That's terrible, isn't it?"

"No, it's not. It's perfectly normal, in fact. Seeing her the way she is now and not knowing when she might improve imposes great stress on you. I'd be amazed if it didn't. But you mustn't punish yourself for having negative thoughts about her or about her condition. Those reactions are only to be expected.''

Peggy nodded. What he was saying was true, but knowing that didn't help much. The only thing that could really help would be for Jan to get better.

She looked Chenoweth in the eye. ''It's possible that she could stay like this for the rest of her life, isn't it?''

''It's possible, yes. But we can't think in those terms. Instead, we have to continue trying to get her to respond. And for all we know about this catatonic state she's in, the best way to do that is never to lose faith. We have to show her kindness and love, even if she doesn't seem to have any awareness of what we're trying to tell her.''

''But couldn't it be that the physical damage was just too great for her to overcome? The injury to her brain?''

''Yes, that's possible, too. But I don't believe that's the basic problem here. Jan suffered brain damage, yes. But the tests we've made, including the most recent MRI, indicate the neurological trauma wasn't that severe. The psychological damage is what we're dealing with. And that was very grave indeed.''

''You say it's important to show her kindness and love. Do you think any of that registers?''

''Absolutely. I firmly believe she can feel it and sense where it's coming from, even though she makes no response.''

Again Peggy was quiet for a moment.

''Look,'' Chenoweth said. ''Keep in mind that Jan was not only brutally beaten and left for dead, but there was also evidence that she was sexually abused, even tortured. So it's not surprising that although her body has mostly healed, Jan is still in hiding emotionally. She's withdrawn to a safe place where no one can reach her, somewhere deep in her own psyche. But she's there, Peggy. Our job is to bring her back again. And one of the people who can do the most to make that happen is you.''

''Me? I wish I believed that was true.''

''But it is true. You grew up together; you loved each other.''

One corner of Peggy's mouth curled in a small, rueful smile. ''And we were also rivals. Jealous as hell. We had some fights you wouldn't believe. Swiped each other's clothes and other belongings. Once, we even had a tug-of-war over a boyfriend.''

''You mentioned that last time we talked. What happened?''

"It was a couple of years ago. I was dating a guy, brought him to our mother's house for dinner. Jan was there, too, and the next thing I knew, he broke off with me and began seeing her."

"Did it last long?"

"No. I have a hunch she didn't care at all about him, just wanted to show me she could do it."

"And you had a fight about that?"

"Oh sure. But then we more or less got over it—after she dropped him."

"When she broke up with him, was that before the other things happened, before she began the wild period you told me about?"

"Yes, long before. I never did understand that, although I'm sure it's what got her into trouble, eventually."

"You gave the police all the information you could, of course?"

"Yes, as much as I knew—which wasn't a great deal. It was as if she'd become another person. Living in that fancy apartment, all the clothes and the jewelry."

"And she never told you where it was all coming from?"

"No, never. I tried to get her to talk about it, but she wouldn't."

"Did you have any idea, any hunch of your own?"

"Sure. The same one the police had. I thought there were two possibilities. Either somebody was keeping her or she'd become a call girl."

"You say that's what the police thought, too?"

"From the questions they asked me, yes. Although frankly, I don't think they much cared. Their attitude was, so she was a hooker and somebody beat her up—so what? I mean, they didn't say that, but it was pretty clear that was the way they were thinking. One of them did tell me they were sorry, but he also said they were having a tough enough time trying to handle their case load as it was."

"Pretty callous, hmm? And yet you can understand that, too."

"Up to a point. But it was certainly obvious that no one gave a damn. Except my mother and me. And the Cunninghams, of course. I don't know what we would have done without them. Jan didn't even work for them anymore, hadn't for over a year. And yet they stepped right in and gave us all this help."

He nodded. "Very kind of them."

"It's almost saintly, that people could be so generous. Did you hear about the death of Senator Cunningham, by the way?"

"Yes, I read about it in this morning's *Times*. Sad that he's gone."

"A real tragedy." A thought struck her. "God, I hope that won't—"

"Have anything to do with providing support for your sister? It won't, I'm sure. When she came here, I was told the foundation would be taking care of the expenses for however long treatment might be needed."

Peggy shook her head in wonder. "What great people."

"Would you like to see Jan now?"

She got to her feet. "Yes, of course."

Chenoweth led her down a corridor and through two sets of double doors, then down another hallway to the familiar room. On the way, they passed other staff members and also a number of patients, male and female, walking through the halls. Many of the patients seemed quite normal, although some of the older ones showed signs of senility.

The door of Jan's room was open and when Peggy looked in, she saw her sister sitting as always in the same chair beside the window, her eyes staring blankly, hands folded in her lap. She was wearing a blue bathrobe over pajamas and there were slippers on her feet.

"Remember what I told you," Jay said quietly. "Your love can do more than any treatment we could possibly provide." He gave her a reassuring pat on the arm and went on down the corridor. Peggy took a deep breath and stepped into the room.

Despite her resolve, the sight was disheartening. Virtually the only one of her sister's features she'd recognize was the auburn hair. Jan's skin was milky white and there was a vivid red scar that snaked its way down her right cheek. Her face was gaunt, her eyes dull and sunken. It was hard to reconcile this woman's appearance with what Peggy remembered.

But the important thing was to try. She forced herself to speak in a warm tone. "Good morning, Jan. It's so good to see you." She bent over and kissed her sister on the forehead.

She smiled to herself. If Jan could have seen this display of affection before she'd become ill, she would have laughed herself silly. What Peggy had told Dr. Chenoweth about the rivalry between the sisters wasn't the half of it. There'd always been plenty to be jealous about, too; Jan was the more popular, not just the better-looking of the Demarest girls.

Peggy took off her coat and hung it on a hook behind the door. She pulled another chair close and sat down, reaching out to take Jan's hand. The flesh felt waxy and lifeless, as if the hand belonged to a corpse.

"It's a nice fall day outside," Peggy said. She looked out the window to where a nurse was walking with an old man, supporting him with a hand under his arm. He was all bundled up in an overcoat, with a scarf around his neck and a cap pulled down on his head. The wind was still kicking up, gusts bending the pine trees.

"The sun is shining," Peggy continued, feeling somewhat inane, as if she was talking to an inanimate object. "Wouldn't you like to be out there? You used to love to go for walks in the fall, remember?"

Jan continued to stare at nothing. She made no reply.

10

The police report said Jessica Silk's address was on Sutton Place. Under different circumstances, Ben might have called her before going there, but to do that now would only give her a chance to try ducking him. Better to surprise her, have his talk with her and get out. He drove crosstown on Fifty-fourth Street and at the end of the last block before the East River, he turned left.

He remembered reading a piece in the Sunday *Times* about how this locality had been a collection of ramshackle buildings until the early twenties, when the Vanderbilts and the Morgans had moved here from Fifth Avenue to get away from the nouveaux riches. They'd built the elegant apartment buildings and town houses designed by architects like Mott Schmidt and Delano & Aldrich, and today the area remained one of the most exclusive places to live in the city. Ben parked in front of a stately apartment house and went past the green-uniformed doorman into the lobby.

The space seemed more like a large, comfortable living room than a public entrance. There were sofas and chairs upholstered in muted colors, thick green plants in Chinese vases, and a wall mural of what appeared to be a fishing village on the Mediterranean coast. The doorman followed him inside and Ben showed him his shield and told him why he was there.

The man went to a telephone and spoke into it. When he hung up, he said to take the elevator to 22B.

On the way up, Ben thought of his discussion with Ardis Merritt about what had happened in the senator's office the night before. And then he recalled what the TV reporter had tried to peddle to him and felt a jab of anger all over again. He knew whores who had more integrity.

When he stepped off the elevator, Miss Silk was standing in her open doorway, waiting for him. She was tall and dark-haired, wearing black slacks and a black turtleneck sweater. High cheekbones, hazel eyes, a faintly cynical expression on her wide mouth: She was a knockout, no matter which way you looked at her. No wonder the old man had agreed to having her interview him. Or whatever.

"You always just burst in on people, Lieutenant?"

"Sorry, but I have to make out a follow-up report on Senator Cunningham's death. Routine procedure. Shouldn't take more than a few minutes."

"Uh-huh. Come on in."

He followed her through a foyer, thinking he'd been right; she looked great from this angle, as well. She led him into a large room whose windows faced the river and the Queensboro Bridge. The view was similar to the one from his own apartment, only better, because this apartment was on a much higher floor.

He glanced around. The furnishings were contemporary: sofa and chairs in eggshell leather, chocolate carpeting, and wildly abstract paintings on two of the walls.

Silk picked a cigarette out of a box on a glass coffee table and ignited it with a heavy silver lighter. She blew out a cloud of smoke and studied him more openly than he had her. "You want a drink?"

"No thanks."

"It is a little early in the day, isn't it? Against all convention. So I think I'll have one. Take off your coat and sit down. Make yourself comfortable."

He stripped off the raincoat and sank down into the cushions of the sofa. As he did, she went to an ebony-faced bar on the far side of the room and poured whiskey from a decanter into a squat glass, no ice. Watching her, he wondered how a free-lance magazine writer could afford an apartment like this. Or whether there might be another source of income.

''Nice place you have here,'' he said.

She put the stopper back into the decanter. ''Compliments of my ex-husband. Part of our divorce agreement, along with very generous alimony. That answers your question, doesn't it? Even though you didn't ask it?''

He made no reply. Her irritation was understandable, and he wasn't here to rankle her.

Returning with the drink, she sat down across from him in one of the blocky chairs. ''So? What do you want to know? I've already told the police everything that happened. There were two officers and I gave them a statement. You've seen their report?''

''Yes, I have. But there are a few points I want to go over with you.''

''Okay, go ahead.''

He thought about getting out his notebook, then decided against it, not wanting to put her on guard. And anyway, there wasn't much she'd tell him that he was likely to forget. ''I understand you were writing an article on the senator.''

''Yes. I'd been working on it for weeks, off and on. The project kept getting more and more ambitious. We'd even begun to think of turning it into a book.''

''We?''

''The senator and I. The more we talked, the more great material he kept bringing out. He was a fascinating man. I'd never met anyone with so much vitality, so much . . . mental energy. Certainly never anyone with his charisma.''

''How did you get the assignment?''

''I was introduced to him when I was in Palm Beach, working on something else. I told him I was interested in doing an article on him and he said to call him.''

''You must have very good credentials.''

She crossed her legs. ''Outstanding.''

''Have you always worked free-lance?''

''No. I started at *Vogue*. Or *Vague,* as we called it. I was one of those naïve kids they hire right out of college, honored to be working for a famous magazine. As soon as I could, I moved over to *Vanity Fair,* and then eventually I realized I could make a lot more by selling my stuff to the highest bidder.''

''You write an article and then sell it?''

"I usually sell an editor on the subject I have in mind and get an advance on that."

"Was that the arrangement you had for the piece on the senator?"

"No."

"Why was that different?"

She shrugged. "I knew there'd be a market for it, so I just went ahead."

"You mentioned your ex-husband. Is he in the same business?"

She drank some of her whiskey. "He's an investment banker, a vice president with Broderick and Stone."

"How long have you been divorced?"

"It became final in August, but we hadn't lived together for over a year."

"Getting back to the article you were writing on the senator. When you met with him to work on it, was that always in the evening?"

"Most of the time. His office was quiet then, and he could give the subject his full attention. He had quite a remarkable career, you know. Did more in his lifetime than any five or six ordinary men put together. I think he could have run for President and made it." A faint smile passed over her lips. "If he hadn't been so damned stubborn about his ideals, that is."

"Tell me about that, and how you handled it in what you were writing."

She dragged on the cigarette and stubbed it out in an ashtray. Then she began relating how Cunningham had always stuck to his principles, even though that had frequently gotten him into difficulties politically; how he'd struggled not only with his avowed enemies and with one governmental body after another but with members of his own party, as well.

Ben kept his gaze fixed on her, as if he was absorbed in her words, but what he really wanted was simply to keep her talking. It gave him an opportunity to gauge her, to get more of a sense of what she was all about. If there had been an affair going on between her and Cunningham, what he saw made it easy to understand what attracted the old man. She practically radiated sex appeal.

But what would have been the turn-on for her? Was it the senator's power, supposedly the ultimate aphrodisiac? Or something else? Money, maybe?

Or had the relationship been strictly professional, after all? And for that matter, was it really so important? Put an end to the rumors, Oppenheimer had said. Button this thing up.

So why not do just that and forget it?

Because the DA also wanted to know the truth. And because Ben was a highly skilled investigator. Almost twenty years on the job had programmed his nose to work the way it did. He smelled something here, something more than Silk's perfume. And whether he would admit it to himself or not, what the TV reporter had told him had piqued his curiosity. "What happened last night with the senator?"

She sipped her drink. "We were sitting in his office and he was reading a draft of something I'd written from our previous session. The woman who works for the foundation was there, too, Ardis Merritt. She was on the other side of the room, doing something of her own. All of a sudden, he made this awful choking noise."

"As if he was literally choking?"

"Yes, sort of." She shuddered. "It was terrible. I'd never seen anyone die before."

"You knew he was dying?"

"No. That is, not then. I had no idea what was wrong with him. We both jumped up and went to him, but then he fell out of his chair onto the floor. We pulled off his tie and tried to get him some air. Ardis even gave him mouth-to-mouth resuscitation. But nothing seemed to help. We were sort of—well, not hysterical, but pretty upset. Frightened. She called security and the guard came up. Then she called the police, and after that, the family."

"You went out and got a pillow to put under his head. That right?"

"Yes."

"Why did you take his shoes off?"

Her eyes flickered, the movement as quick as a camera's shutter, but Ben caught it.

"Just trying to make him more comfortable," she said.

"You thought he'd be more comfortable without shoes?"

"Sure. So what? I wanted to do anything I could."

"Was that after you got the pillow?"

"I think it was before. What difference does it make?"

He opened the trap wider. "From what I've been able to learn, his clothing was in disarray. It wasn't just that his tie was off . . . and his shoes."

She became exasperated. ''I told you, we were trying to get him some air. Maybe we undid some buttons or whatever. Is that so surprising when somebody's having a heart attack right in front of you?''

''No, but why unzip his pants?''

The eyes flickered again. ''I didn't—I don't know. Maybe Ardis did that.''

He cocked his head, looking at her. ''Your stories don't jibe.''

''What do you mean?''

''Some of the things she told me don't square with what you're saying now.''

''What things? What did she say?''

''She gave me a very detailed description of what went on, and it's different from what you're saying.''

Silk's tone took on a hard edge. ''Maybe she has a better memory than I do.''

''How could that be? You're a trained journalist, aren't you?''

''What are you getting at, Lieutenant?''

''You were having an affair with him, weren't you?''

Her eyes widened. ''What?''

''You heard me. You were, weren't you?''

''How dare you say such a thing?''

''Answer the question.''

She gulped the rest of her whiskey and put the empty glass down on the table beside her chair. ''This is outrageous.''

''Is it?''

''It most certainly is. You come barging in here—''

''I didn't. I asked to see you and you invited me up. And you still haven't told me. Did you have intercourse with him last night?''

Her mouth opened, then snapped shut.

''Come on,'' Ben said. ''What about it? As you've probably gathered by now, I've already picked up a lot of information. Why don't you tell me what really went on?''

She didn't bite. Hazel eyes bright with anger, she said, ''Listen, if you insist on making these wild accusations, I'm going to call my lawyer.''

''Go right ahead.''

She didn't do that, either. Instead, she stood up. ''Get out of here.''

''Sure, I was just leaving. I got the information I wanted, anyway." He rose to his feet and went back through the foyer to the front door, carrying his raincoat.

When he stepped out into the hallway, she slammed the door behind him. Waiting for the elevator, he put on the coat, and as he did, he heard her snap the locks and drop a chain into place on the door.

11

Ben left the lobby and walked back toward his car, thinking maybe this thing wasn't all so cut-and-dried, after all. The lie he'd caught Silk in was a small one, but it had been one she had no reason to tell—if she'd been giving him a truthful account, that is. Instead, she'd made a big deal of the business with the shoes, when all she'd had to do was say she was flustered and didn't remember.

Then when he'd thrown his clumsy curve about the old man's pants being unzipped, she'd flared up. For what reason? Because she was worried that what she said might contradict what Merritt had told him? Why would she care whether it did or didn't?

And when he'd tried bluffing her with his accusation that she'd been having an affair with Cunningham, she hadn't answered directly but had lost her temper instead.

Why?

Only one answer made sense: because she was hiding the truth—and not just about the shoes or the state of Cunningham's fly. Which meant there was indeed something to the innuendos about her relationship with the senator, which in turn would mean that Ardis Merritt had lied, as well.

If all this was an attempt at a cover-up, who else might be in on it? Did the family know? But even if they did, even if the old man and Silk had been having sex and Merritt and the Cunninghams wanted that to remain a secret, was that a crime?

Don't be ridiculous, Ben told himself. Giving a false statement to the police in these circumstances would be nothing more than a misdemeanor, according to the penal code, and adultery was about on the same level as spitting on the sidewalk.

And if the family had taken steps to cover up whatever had gone on before the police arrived, who could blame them? Did they need some tawdry scandal at this point—a smutty story for the media to gorge on?

Nevertheless, Ben had already stumbled across more than he thought he would. What else might he find?

This time, he'd call ahead. He used a pay phone on the west side of the street, across from Silk's apartment house. Dr. Phelps's secretary at the Manhattan Medical Center said the doctor wouldn't be in his office until later in the day, but if Lieutenant Tolliver would call back, she was sure an appointment could be arranged. He thanked her and hung up.

His watch said it was already midafternoon, but he didn't need the watch to know that; his stomach was rumbling. Because he had time and because it wouldn't be too far from the hospital, he decided on a restaurant he knew in Yorkville. Getting back into the Ford, he drove over to First Avenue and north to Seventy-eighth Street, then swung down Second and parked in front of Csarda, one of the last of the old-time Hungarian restaurants left in the city.

The aroma alone was enough to convince you that you were starving. Sweet onions, paprika, garlic, roasting peppers, spiced veal, with a top note of Tokay, the great red wine of Eastern Europe. Even though it was long past lunchtime, a number of patrons were lingering over dessert and coffee.

Ben sat at a table in the dining room and ordered stuffed peppers and chicken paprikash. He'd been promising himself a lunch somewhere up in the country, and this would be the next best thing. In fact, it was one of his better ideas.

As he ate, he tried to recall whether he'd ever been inside the Manhattan Medical Center but decided he hadn't. He knew it well enough by reputation, however, as one of the best private hospitals in New York. It was famous for its excellence in cardiology and cardiac care, the department Phelps headed. And it was also known for obstetrics and gynecology—which made it a favorite place for well-to-do women to have babies.

When he finished, he paid his bill and then called Phelps's office once more. The secretary told him to come ahead but cautioned that he'd have to wait until the doctor finished his rounds. Ben said that would be fine.

After that, he telephoned his office in the Sixth precinct station house and spoke to his second in command, Sgt. Ed Flynn. The sergeant told him Captain Brennan had called to say what Tolliver was working on and also that Chief Houlihan had announced that a special team of detectives was investigating the circumstances surrounding Senator Cunningham's death. Flynn then gave Ben a rundown on cases his squad was dealing with, including the shooting of a gypsy cab-driver on Christopher Street.

The robbery-murder had taken place a week ago and there were no suspects, which meant it was unlikely there ever would be. Fewer than half the homicide cases in the city were ever solved, and of those that were, a suspect most often was arrested within a day. If any more time than that went by, the result would usually be just one more moldering file jacket that would stay open forever.

There was also some good news. A push-in rapist the cops had been after for months was caught in a stakeout, and a street whore had given them a tip on a burglar who'd been operating with great success in the boutiques on Sheridan Square. Flynn said detectives were looking for the guy now. Also George Garrity's wife had had a baby, a boy.

Ben said nice going on the last three counts and to congratulate Garrity. He told the sergeant he'd wrap up what he was doing in another day, two at the most. He'd check in again tomorrow, he said, then hung up.

It was a pleasant fall day and he was in no rush, so he walked to the medical center. It was on Seventy-seventh Street, off Park, a neat brick building that didn't look much different from the surrounding apartment houses. There were even window boxes on the front of it, and although the plane trees lining the street were naked, red geraniums in the boxes had so far survived the autumn frosts.

A receptionist told him where Dr. Phelps's office was and he followed her directions through a maze of corridors. Nurses and residents were scurrying about and now and then he had to step aside as attendants wheeled a gurney past with a patient aboard.

For all that, the place was nothing like some of the other hospitals in the city. Bellevue, for example, always looked as if a bomb had gone off a few minutes earlier, leaving in its wake people who were minus limbs, or eyes, or bowels, and frequently their lives.

Phelps's secretary sat at a desk in a small waiting room outside the physician's inner sanctum. She turned out to be what the sound of her telephone voice had led Ben to picture, red-cheeked and grandmotherly. She invited him to sit down, saying she didn't know how long the doctor would be.

He settled into a chair and began thumbing through well-worn magazines, finally getting hooked on one of *The New Yorker*'s "Annals of Crime" articles, this one about a parole officer being blown away by an ex-mental patient who'd been released after psychiatrists had declared him harmless.

No surprise there, Ben thought. Homicidal psychopaths were hardly ever first-time offenders. They all had long histories of freaky conduct, often torturing animals or people for years before graduating to murder. Moreover, none of the psychos he'd dealt with had ever been cured of their propensity to abuse children or commit rape-murders or carry out whatever their personal specialty might be. Instead, they'd merely learned how to convince doctors and parole boards they were now ready to become model citizens. So they'd been turned loose and then had gone on chalking up scores.

An hour went by, and the secretary announced she was leaving. "But stay right where you are," she told Ben. "Dr. Phelps will be along eventually." She put on her coat and hat and carrying a shopping bag walked out the door, bidding him good night.

After another thirty minutes, he looked at his watch and wondered whether he wasn't wasting his time. Cunningham was dead and his physician had signed the death certificate. Despite Ben's suspicions after talking to Jessica Silk, it was all over but the sobbing, which would conclude a few days from now with the service at Riverside Church, followed by interment in the family plot, wherever that might be.

For a moment, he debated whether to tell Oppenheimer that he now suspected the rumors of what had gone on between the senator and Jessica Silk might be true. Although the basis for his thinking so was admittedly flimsy. And even if the rumors were true, so what? Finally, he decided it would be better to state his suspicion and to recount Silk's furious denial than have it get back to the DA via some other route. Through Silk's lawyer, for example. Therefore Ben would report everything, including his hunch, and let Oppenheimer handle it however he chose.

What Phelps might add, if he ever showed up, was unlikely to be of much value.

So why not get the hell out of here? Ben still might be able to hunt up a female friend he could interest in dinner. Despite the splendid meal he'd consumed a few hours ago, he was getting hungry again. And it would be nice to have some feminine companionship.

A short, stocky man with neatly trimmed white hair entered the office. He was wearing a pale green tunic, with a stethoscope dangling from his neck, and silver-rimmed spectacles were perched on the end of his nose. "I'm Dr. Phelps," he said. "Understand you want to see me."

Ben stood up and shook hands. "Yes, if you have some time." He got out the case containing his ID and shield and flipped it open.

Phelps didn't bother to glance at it. "Been a busy day," he said, "but I can spare a few minutes."

The office was good-sized yet simply furnished, with a desk and chairs and a few filing cabinets. A large light box was mounted on one wall and the usual array of framed diplomas covered most of another. Phelps led Ben to a visitor's chair, then looked briefly through a stack of phone messages before sitting at his desk.

"You're here about the death of Senator Cunningham," the physician said.

"That's correct."

"On whose authority, and for what purpose?"

"The Manhattan district attorney assigned me to head an investigation," Ben said. "There's been quite a bit of public speculation about the case."

"What kind of speculation?"

Where did this guy live, Ben wondered, on the moon? "About what might have been going on at the time of the senator's death. As you know, he wasn't alone when it happened."

Phelps put his head back and looked down his nose at the detective. "That's quite so. Two women were with him. If you're suggesting there was something improper about that, the allegation is absurd."

"I'm not suggesting anything," Ben said. "Nor am I making allegations. All I said was, there's been a lot of public speculation."

Phelps sniffed. "The public should get its collective mind out of the gutter. This was a great tragedy—not only for the Cunninghams but for the entire state. The country, too, for that matter. His family built this hospital, you know."

"Yes, I did know that," Ben said.

"And Lord only knows how many charities they support. We all have to go sometime, but the senator was one of a kind."

Ben was getting a little tired of hearing clichés about Clayton Cunningham. He wondered whether Phelps would now tell him they didn't make them like that anymore.

"I spoke with the police last night, of course," Phelps said. "They were there when I arrived at the senator's office. I assume they issued a report."

"Yes, I've read it."

Phelps folded his hands across his belly. "Then you know all you need to know, Lieutenant."

Maybe, Ben thought, and maybe not. "I understand the senator died of a heart attack."

"That's correct."

"Can you tell me what caused it?"

"What caused it? A coronary thrombosis."

"And what is that, exactly?" Ben knew, but he wanted to get Phelps talking about it.

"A thrombosis is an occlusion of the circulatory system," the doctor said. He sounded as if he was lecturing a class of medical students. "Caused by a clot, or thrombus. In Senator Cunningham's case, it produced a stationary blockage in one of the arteries of his heart."

"And when that happens, the patient dies?"

"Not always. But this one was massive. The occlusion resulted in myocardial infarction." He paused, then continued in the same condescending tone. "Which in turn caused the heart to lose its ability to maintain adequate blood circulation. The result was cardiac failure. The heart stopped beating; he was dead."

"Then I take it death was quite sudden?"

"Almost instantaneous. Blood supply was cut off from his brain, so he was rendered unconscious virtually at once. For all practical purposes, that was the moment of death."

"I see. Then he was dead by the time you got there."

"Quite dead." Phelps was regarding him with a steady gaze through the silver-rimmed spectacles. It must be wonderful, Ben thought, to consider yourself possessed of knowledge ordinary mortals could only marginally understand.

"Did the paramedics undertake emergency procedures?"

The physician was obviously becoming nettled by the insistent questioning. "Yes, of course they did. They attempted defibrillation, which involves shocking the heart with electric paddles held against the chest. But it was much too late and wouldn't have been effective, anyway."

"Why didn't you call a medical examiner?"

"Why?"

"Yes, why? The law says—"

"Don't lecture me on the law, young man. It states that in such an event, an examiner must be notified *unless the deceased was attended by his physician*. I was at the scene, and he had been my patient for twelve years."

"How long had he been having heart problems?"

Phelps's eyebrows raised slightly. "He hadn't. Until this incident, I had seen no evidence of arteriosclerosis, and therefore there was no warning."

"Isn't that unusual? For a patient to die from the first such attack, with no sign of a problem before that?"

The eyebrows came down again, and now Phelps's voice carried a distinct note of annoyance. "No, Lieutenant, it's not. Senator Cunningham was in generally good condition for his age, but he worked much too hard, drove himself relentlessly. And hardening of the arteries in a seventy-two-year-old man is hardly unusual."

"But you said you'd seen no sign of it."

Phelps leaned forward, putting his elbows on the desk. "I said he hadn't had problems with his heart. And now if you'll excuse me, I have a number of matters to attend to. Good night, Lieutenant."

"Sure. Just one more thing."

"What is it?"

"Why no autopsy? Wouldn't that clear up some of these points?"

"There are no points that need clearing up, as you put it. In front of witnesses, Senator Cunningham suffered a fatal heart attack. One of the witnesses attempted CPR, which was ineffectual. Paramedics applied emergency procedures, which didn't work, either. I then examined him and pronounced him dead. The family didn't want an autopsy, because that would only inspire more stupid speculation."

Ben was about to say that it wasn't his speculation, stupid or otherwise, but he bit his tongue. Instead, he asked, "The body was brought here?"

"Yes."

"Where is it now?"

"At the Bennett Funeral Home. It was sent there at the family's request.'' Phelps was on the edge of hostility now. ''What was your name again, Lieutenant?''

Ben got to his feet and smiled. ''Tolliver. Thanks for the chat, Doc.''

He turned and left the office, walking through the hospital corridors toward the front entrance.

Maybe it was because of Phelps's attitude, or maybe because Ben didn't believe a number of the things he'd been told—first by Ardis Merritt and then by Jessica Silk, and now by this haughty dickhead. Or maybe it was because Ben was a stubborn cop who'd finally gotten his back up. Whatever, he'd be damned if he'd simply walk away now—not as long as so many people were working hard to cover this up.

There was one more person he could check who might give him some answers he could rely on. But Ben would have to hurry, before they covered that one up, too.

12

The Bennett Funeral Home featured a chapel the size of a small church. The establishment was on the west side of Madison Avenue, in the low Eighties, blending in nicely with a number of the city's renowned art galleries and boutiques. The area was famed for posh shopping.

Givenchy, for example, was a few blocks down, handy if you didn't have time to zip over to Paris for additions to your wardrobe. So was Gimple & Weitzenhoffer, where you could pick up a Picasso or a Manet for a few million, or a Nikki de Saint Phalle, if you preferred something more contemporary. The Carlyle was also in the neighborhood, Jack Kennedy's favorite Manhattan hotel, back in his sporting days.

Like the other businesses in the area, the mortuary carried out its functions with taste and dignity and was discreet about the people it served. Thus when it came time to depart, sophisticated New Yorkers considered the Bennett Funeral Chapel the only way to go.

For its patrons, Bennett's would do the preparation, which in the genteel jargon of the boneyard industry meant embalming the corpse, and then there would be a viewing and a service in the chapel. Burial or cremation would follow.

But this was for customers who were merely run-of-the-mill rich. The *really* rich, the people with superbucks, used Bennett's for the first stage of a two-stage send-off. First, they would have a private service in the chapel, by invitation only. Like a wedding reception, only more somber. That would be attended by members of the family and a few hundred close friends, including persons of political or business prominence.

After that, the show went on the road, shifting to a suitable church or cathedral, where it would be open to the public. Finally, after everyone from the high to the low had taken a last look and the eulogies had been delivered and the television cameras had covered the notables getting in and out of glossy black limousines, the deceased would be laid to rest. In a mausoleum, or a family plot, or occasionally in a private cemetery, when the individual was so important it would be unseemly to associate with commoners, even after the soul had moved on.

Cremation was out. To members of this class, that whole process was considered gauche, to put it mildly. Especially when it was carried to the extreme of heaving the ashes out of airplanes or dumping them into the ocean. Such ceremonies were thought to be vulgar, on a par with voodoo rites.

Clayton Cunningham would go in a two-stager, Ben knew, and a memorable one, at that. Even among such grand events, his would be an outstanding production. The detective parked in front of Bennett's and went into the lobby.

The place was busy, with evening viewings going on in two of the so-called slumber rooms. Its decor reminded Ben of what he'd seen in the Cunningham Foundation building, quietly understated, with oil paintings in gold frames, dignified drapes and carpeting, the furniture apparently all antiques. Men and women wearing dark clothes and sad expressions were moving through the lobby, and the smell of flowers was so heavy you could slice it.

A patrician-looking gentleman in a cutaway and striped trousers approached, smiling politely as he asked Tolliver which visitation he'd come for. Ben told him neither one and showed the guy his shield and ID, saying he wanted to talk to whoever was in charge.

"I'm Mr. Westover," the man said in a low voice, "one of the directors.'' He drew Tolliver to one side. ''Is there a problem, Officer?''

''No, no problem,'' Ben said. ''I'm in charge of an investigation into the death of Senator Cunningham. I want to see his body.''

That got a reaction. Westover frowned, but then quickly recovered. ''I'm afraid that won't be possible. You see—''

Tolliver knew exactly how to handle a situation like this one. All he had to do was raise his voice. In a loud tone, he said, ''This is a police matter, and it's urgent.''

The funeral director jumped as if he'd been goosed with an icicle. He raised his hands, palms up. ''Please, Lieutenant. The uh, subject is still in preparation. It wouldn't—''

Ben turned up the volume another notch. ''I said this is police business.''

It had the desired effect. Westover glanced quickly from side to side in hopes they hadn't been overheard. ''Come this way,'' he said.

Ben followed him through a door at one end of the lobby and then down a long hallway leading toward the rear of the building. They turned a corner and went down a flight of stairs and Westover stopped before another door.

Before opening it, he turned to the detective. ''Lieutenant, may I at least ask why this is necessary? Is anything wrong?''

''No, there isn't. It's just that the senator was a very important man. I have to do a complete report for the district attorney's office, and this is only one step.''

''I see. And all you want to do is look at the body?''

''That's it.''

''Very well. Forgive me for seeming reluctant, but I'm sure you understand. We're very circumspect about our clientele.''

''Sure,'' Ben said. ''I understand completely.''

Westover opened the door and Tolliver followed him inside.

The room had the appearance of a medical facility. It was about fifteen feet square, its walls and floor surfaced in pale green ceramic tile. There were no windows; light came from overhead fluorescent bars. At one end was a row of cabinets with a stainless-steel sink in the center of the countertop and next to that stood a porcelain table with raised edges.

On the table lay the nude corpse of Clayton Cunningham III, its head resting on a concave block.

A machine mounted on a mobile cart was positioned beside the table. At the top of the device was a transparent cylinder filled with an orangy pink liquid. A tube ran from the apparatus to the cadaver's neck. The machine was chugging steadily, pumping the contents of the cylinder into the senator's body.

Two men were in the room, both wearing surgical masks and rubber aprons and gloves. One appeared to be monitoring gauges at the base of the machine, while the other was putting surgical instruments into a sterilizer.

"This is Lieutenant Tolliver of the police department," Westover said to them. "He's making a routine check on the passing of Senator Cunningham. Lieutenant, this is Mr. Zander and Mr. Potensky."

Both men nodded and went about their business.

Westover gestured toward the table. "We're in the process of injecting embalming fluid at the moment."

"So I see," Ben said.

"The equipment we use is all state-of-the-art. You'll note the machine operates with the same rhythm as the beating of the human heart. It's called a Porti-Boy."

Catchy name, Ben thought. He stepped to the table for a closer look at the body.

To his surprise, Cunningham didn't appear at all peaceful, the way people invariably did when they were laid out prior to burial. The senator's eyes were open and staring hard and his lips were drawn back over his teeth in a rictus, as if he were experiencing severe pain.

The embalmer standing by the machine noticed Tolliver's reaction. "I haven't set his features yet," he said. "An expression like that is common with sudden death."

It had been common in Ben's experience as well, although the circumstances had been different. He'd seen expressions like it often enough, but always on people who'd been knifed, or shot, or bludgeoned with a heavy object.

Westover hastily interjected, "Of course he won't look anything like that when he's fully prepared. We take a great deal of pride in a client's appearance."

The door opened and another guy in a cutaway and striped pants stepped into the room. He whispered something to Westover and the director turned to Ben, saying, ''Sorry, but I'm wanted upstairs. Shall we go back, Lieutenant?''

''You go ahead,'' Ben said. ''I'll just be another minute or two.''

Westover again seemed hesitant, but then he said he'd be back shortly to show the detective out. He and the other man left the room.

Ben resumed his study of the dead man's face. The features were familiar, of course, despite the way they were contorted now. He'd seen the heavy jaw, the prominent nose, the thick shock of black hair countless times in newspaper photographs and on TV. It was also remarkable how much the senator resembled his grandfather in the portrait Tolliver had seen earlier in the day—and how much his son looked like him.

''His color will be better, too,'' Zander said, ''when we get finished with him.'' He inclined his head toward the cylinder atop the steadily chugging machine. ''We use a cosmetic dye in the formula, along with the formaldahyde and the phenol. That's what gives it that pink shade. Stuff's called Lifetone. Makes him look real healthy.''

''I'll bet it does,'' Ben said.

''We also use topical cosmetics on the face and hands as a final touch.''

''Uh-huh.'' Tolliver continued to stare at the twisted countenance. ''Right now, he looks like he was in a lot of pain when he died.''

''Yeah, I'd say he was.''

Ben turned to the embalmer. ''You said an expression like that is common with sudden death. That includes people who've had a heart attack?''

''Sometimes. At least when somebody had a coronary. You also see it with pectoral angina. But not so often if the heart just failed, the way it often does with a very old person.''

''So in this instance, does it look to you like the senator died of a coronary?''

Zander hesitated. ''It could be.''

''It could be?''

''Right.''

''But not necessarily?''

''No, not necessarily.''

''And therefore, it could have been something else. Is that correct?''

''It's possible.''

''I see. So now tell me this. In your opinion—your *opinion,* mind you—did this man die of a heart attack?''

The embalmer's eyes narrowed. ''That's what it says on the death certificate.''

''I know what it says. But that's not what I asked you.''

''I don't know what he died of. I'm not a doctor.''

Tolliver looked at the other man, Potensky. ''And what about you—what's your opinion?''

Potensky returned Ben's gaze and then glanced away. ''I'm not a doctor, either.''

Tolliver folded his arms. ''Come on over here, both of you.''

The two men stepped toward him. They seemed nervous, but it was hard to read their faces with only their eyes showing above the surgical masks.

''Let's get something straight,'' Ben said. ''I know you're not doctors. I know your answers can be only opinions. But that's all I'm asking for.''

For a few moments, neither embalmer spoke. The room was quiet except for the rhythmic chug of the Porti-Boy. Then Zander said, ''Lieutenant, if I tell you anything, could it be just between us?''

''Absolutely. What is it?''

''It won't get back to the management here?''

''You have my word,'' Ben said, ''that I'll protect you. Anything either one of you tells me will stay strictly confidential.''

''Okay,'' Zander said. ''In my opinion, this man did not die from a heart attack. How about it, Dave?''

''No, I don't think so.''

Both men were now holding the detective in a fixed gaze.

Ben stared back at them. ''What makes you say that?''

''We knew it right away,'' Zander said, ''when we drained him.''

''It was obvious,'' Potensky said.

Zander continued: ''See, when there's a clot in one of the major heart arteries, it creates a problem for us. Makes it harder to get the blood out. We have to get it out before we put in the embalming fluid. If we can't get all of it, we have to use a special preinjection formula that's got anticoagulants in it. Otherwise, the clot obstructs the fluid distribution—what we're doing now. But with the senator here, the whole thing's been going like zip. Nothing to it.''

"You're sure? You couldn't be mistaken?"

"Hey, anything's possible. But if I'm wrong, it'd be a surprise. You ask me, there was no heart attack." He again turned to his colleague. "How about it, Dave?"

"That's how I see it," Potensky said. "No clot, no heart attack."

Ben looked at the body and then at Zander. "Then what did he die from?"

The embalmer shrugged. "That, I can't say."

"You didn't see any marks or bruises?"

"No, nothing."

"If there had been any," Potensky said, "we would have spotted them when we washed him down."

"What about poison?" Ben asked.

Zander considered the question. "Possible, but unlikely. I mean, with any kind there is, we see some evidence. Arsenic, for instance, causes hemorrhages, and ulcerations on the tissues. Same thing with cresol . . . or cyanide. We didn't see anything like that here. Even ones that are hard to detect, like the organophosphates, give you clues."

"Such as?"

"Look at his pupils," Zander said.

Ben bent down, peering into the dead man's eyes. They stared back at him dully.

"If he was poisoned, they'd be pinpoints," Potensky said. "That would tell you. But his are dilated, right?"

"Like I said," Zander went on, "poison's possible. But I doubt it."

Tolliver wasn't ready to give up on it. "Barbiturates, maybe?"

The embalmer shook his head. "They depress the central nervous system. Everything relaxes." He pointed. "The face doesn't get all screwed up like that."

"So if it wasn't a blow and it wasn't poison, what could have killed him?"

"Beats me," Zander said.

"You'd have to have an autopsy," Potensky added, "if you wanted to find out."

Ben nodded. "Wouldn't you, though."

"Hard to figure why there wasn't one," Zander said. "Usually with somebody like this, there is. I mean, somebody this well known."

"Yeah," Ben said. "But it's never too late, right?"

"No, it's not," Potensky said. "A lot of times, even years after the body's buried, a good pathologist can find the cause of death. Not always, of course, but often. That's why it's against the law for us to use certain poisonous compounds for embalming. Like mercury, or antimony. They'd hide the truth, or destroy it."

"Say, Lieutenant," Zander said.

"Yes?"

"You'll keep your promise, won't you? It could get us in a lot of trouble, talking out of school."

"Don't worry," Ben said. "I won't mention it."

Another minute passed and then the door opened once more. Westover entered the room, wearing his professionally earnest look. "Well, Lieutenant. Seen enough?"

"Sure. A lot more than I thought I would." Ben took one more look at the senator and then followed Westover out of the room.

13

There was a small restaurant around the corner from the funeral home, French and très chichi. The maître d' greeted Tolliver imperiously. When Ben told him all he wanted was to use the phone, the guy seemed offended. But he pointed toward a rear hallway that led to the rest rooms. Tolliver hurried back there.

The instrument was on the wall, not as private as he would have preferred, but it would do. He looked up the number for the New York City medical examiner's office and called it, half-expecting that at this time of night there'd be nobody on hand who could help him.

But he was in luck; an assistant ME was in the lab. When the pathologist came onto the line, Tolliver identified himself, saying he wanted to verify what he'd been told by embalmers about the condition of a dead body. The ME's name was Marvin Pierce. "Go ahead," he said.

Ben gave him a rundown on the situation he'd encountered at Bennett's, taking care not to reveal either the senator's name or that of the mortuary.

When Tolliver finished, Pierce said, ''And the body's already been embalmed?''

''They were pumping embalming fluid into it when I saw it.''

''Then forget it, Lieutenant.''

''What do you mean, forget it? It's my understanding an autopsy can be performed years later and the cause of death can be determined.''

''Sometimes, but not always. If the guy was shot, or stabbed, something like that, no problem. Or if a truck ran over him, or he died from some disfiguring disease, sure. But that's not what you've got here, right?''

''No, but—''

''Look, let me explain. First of all, you said you wanted to know if this guy died of a coronary thrombosis, is that correct?''

''Yes. And if not from that, from what, then?''

''Okay, one thing at a time. Once he's embalmed, there's no way to tell whether a coronary killed him. Not for sure, anyway. We can see if there's evidence of cardiopathy, like maybe degeneration of the myocardium, or aortostenosis, but—''

''In lay terms.''

''Whether the heart or its major arteries show signs of weakening or damage from a preexisting condition. For instance, we might find scar tissue from previous events. But whether or not that's what he died from, nobody can nail that down. Not now, anyway.''

''So what you're saying is maybe he did and maybe he didn't.''

''Correct. Of course, if we could do a post, we could give you an educated guess. Maybe six-five or better.''

Dear God, Ben thought—I need an ME, I get a horseplayer.

''Where is this guy?'' Pierce asked. ''Maybe if I could at least have a look at him—''

''Not possible,'' Tolliver said. ''What about if he was poisoned? I'm also told you can detect that, as well.''

''Who told you that?''

''The embalmers.''

The ME laughed briefly. In the receiver, it sounded like a bark. ''Embalmers? What the hell do they know?''

''They said certain poisons would show up. Arsenic, for example, and—''

''Very true, Lieutenant. Arsenic, cyanide, strychnine, and a number of others. But I could also name toxins that would have killed him deader than Kelsey's nuts and nobody would find the slightest trace of them—even *before* he was embalmed. Do you follow?"

What a lovely day this had turned into. "Yeah, I follow."

"Let's put this in perspective, all right? You want the best information this office can provide, we need to perform a postmortem before the body's embalmed. Otherwise, the most we could do would be to give you those educated guesses I was talking about. At least when it comes to what you seem to be zeroing in on, death caused by myocardial infarction due to a coronary, or by poisons. Okay?"

"Yeah."

"In fact, you're never going to get anything solid without a post, no matter what he died from. But at least if we did one, you'd have a better idea. Clear?"

"Entirely."

"Give us the body, Lieutenant, and we'll give you the best results we can."

"Thanks a lot," Ben said, and hung up.

14

This is no hot potato," Michael Brennan said. "It's a fucking bomb." The captain was sitting in his office at One Police Plaza, with Tolliver seated across from him.

A beefy man, Brennan had been a boxer in his youth, which explained the broken nose and the scar tissue around his eyes. Like Tolliver, he'd served in the Marine Corps before joining the NYPD, and that was one of the factors that had helped to form a bond between the two men.

"You understand what I'm saying?" Brennan continued. "The thing could turn into big trouble."

"I realize that," Ben said.

"That's why I think what you should do is just give the DA a report that says there was no evidence of wrongdoing. Mark the thing closed and everybody gets on with their business."

"I don't know, Cap," Ben said. "I'm not so sure."

Brennan looked at him. "You're not so sure? What's it amount to? A bunch of ifs and maybes. No proof of anything, and that's what you should report to Oppenheimer. It'd shut him up, so why not give it to him?''

''Suppose I say nothing suspicious happened and then it turns out to have been a homicide?''

''So? It's the DA's baby, isn't it? He's the one who'd take the heat.''

''Maybe. He might also tell the media he asked to have the police investigate the matter and they let everybody down.''

Brennan sighed. ''Yeah, you're right. That's why I said it's a bomb. If it went off, it'd get everybody in the act—including the mayor. We got enough problems without His Honor taking more shots at us. He'd say it's another example why the city needs the Civilian Review Board. Can't trust the cops to do the job the way it should be done.''

''Maybe we ought to tell the DA there were unexplained circumstances. Demand an autopsy.''

''The family already said they don't want one, didn't they? Forcing it would mean getting a court order, and what judge would sign that?''

''Yeah, good point,'' Ben said.

''In fact, even if we did get a post on him, then what? A medical examiner already told you they might not be able to find anything wrong. If that happened, we'd be in a worse light. The Cunninghams have got a lot of clout. They'd accuse us of pushing it for political purposes, trying to smear the senator after he was dead. And if it did show something suspicious, then *all* the burden would be on us. We don't clear the case, you'd see some shake-up.''

''Probably.''

''And who would the commissioner start with? Us, that's who. I say tell the DA there's no evidence of anything suspicious, but then stay on top of the situation. Run down any possibilities, just for insurance.''

''Maybe that's the way to go,'' Ben conceded.

''Sure it is,'' the captain said. ''Look, what have we actually got? The senator was in his office being interviewed by a writer. The writer was legitimate, a journalist who worked for magazines and did a lot of free-lance articles. What's more, another woman says she was right there in the office with them and everything was on the up-and-up. Of course it's possible this other woman wasn't there and her story was just a cover-up. Everybody says the old boy was a swinger, true?''

''So I've heard.''

''Okay, then maybe—but *only* maybe—he was humping this writer, after all. And even if he was, who gives a shit, except the media? The point is, there's no substantiation. Anyway, he died, and a prominent medical authority pronounced him dead. Cause of death, a heart attack. Then the embalmers said they didn't think there was a clot in his arteries. Only there's no proof of that, either. And this ME says that now he's embalmed, a postmortem might not prove anything. What does it all add up to? A big nothing. Let's keep it that way. When's the funeral?''

''Day after tomorrow.''

''Okay. Tell Oppenheimer you think there were certain unresolved questions but no proof. That way, it's up to him to decide if he wants to push this any further, and I'm pretty sure he won't. Now what about the guy that was assigned to work with you—would he go along with that?''

''Oh yeah. He knows the political situation. He was in the job himself, retired on a medical. Name's Mulloy.''

''Is that Jack Mulloy?''

''Yes.''

''I remember him,'' Brennan said. ''He was a good cop. Shot a druggie in East Harlem a few years back.''

''Is that so?''

''Sure. That's when he got hurt. You said he's working on an investigation into Cunningham Securities? How's that going?''

''The prosecutors've put together a lot of information, but they still don't have a case.''

''Keep your eyes and ears open on that, too,'' Brennan said.

''Okay, I will.''

''That's all, Lieutenant, for the moment.''

15

At a little past noon, Orcus got out of the taxi on the corner of Fifty-seventh Street and walked back toward the apartment house. He noticed that the sky had clouded over and the breeze had stiffened.

With a scarf high around his neck and the collar of his topcoat turned up, wearing a felt hat and dark glasses, he was sure it would be all but impossible for anyone to recognize him. He maintained a steady but unhurried gait, just an average, unremarkable man out for a stroll down Sutton Place.

The building was on the east side of the street, the side toward the river. It wasn't quite as ornate as some of the others along here, but it was stately nevertheless, faced in beige brick and with a dark green-and-white awning over the entrance. The large glass doors had fixtures of gleaming brass, and there were shrubs in stone pots on either side of the walk. A doorman was standing out front, wearing a uniform of the same color scheme as the awning.

Looking through the doors, Orcus could get a glimpse of the lobby interior. It was decorated with sumptuous furniture and tall plants in Oriental vases and there was a mural on the wall beside the elevators. He walked on by, taking in details.

On the north side, the building abutted its neighbor. But on the other side, there was a narrow alley between the apartment house and the next building. Orcus knew the alley would be for use by service people; it was what he'd been hoping to see.

There was a public phone diagonally across from the building, a semienclosed glass booth on Fifty-third Street. He crossed Sutton Place and went to the phone, dropping a coin into the box and then punching the buttons.

She answered on the first ring.

"It's me," Orcus said. "I just got here."

"Good. What's it look like?"

"Like a secure building. But don't worry about it, I can handle it okay. You find out which apartment?"

"Twenty-two B."

"All right, I'll call you later."

"Be sure you don't miss any of it."

He didn't bother to reply to that. Holding the phone in one hand, he cut off the call with his other. Then he dug into his trouser pocket for a slip of paper with a different number on it. After dropping another coin into the slot, he called the second one.

This time, he listened to ring after ring without getting an answer, feeling a growing sense of disappointment. She must have gone out, and he couldn't wait around here for her to come back. He'd have to try again another time. Shit.

He was about to hang up when at last she answered. Her voice was low and throaty. "Hello?"

"Miss Silk," he said, "this is Mr. Orcus calling. I'm with the law firm of Wellington, Baker and Marsh. I've been instructed to tell you we're prepared to meet your terms."

There was a pause and then she said, "How do you want to proceed?"

"You can come to my office, if you wish."

Her reply was what he'd known it would be. "No, I don't want to do that."

"Would you prefer to have me come to your place?"

"Absolutely not."

He smiled to himself. That would have been too much to hope for. "Perhaps we can meet somewhere."

"Much better. How about the bar in the Regency?"

"Fine. How soon can you be there? Our client feels it's urgent for this to be settled. I'm sure you can understand that."

"Yeah, I can. Let's say in an hour?"

"Very well, I'll be waiting for you. You'll bring the material with you?"

"No. But I will bring a sample. What you're to bring is a hundred thousand dollars in cash, all in hundreds. When I'm satisfied we have a deal, I'll tell you how I want the rest of the money transferred to me. Is that clear?"

"Quite clear. And acceptable. I'll see you at the Regency bar in one hour." He hung up but continued to hold the phone to his mouth, using the instrument for cover as he looked over at the apartment house, watching the doorman.

He'd been standing there for about five minutes when a taxi drew up to the sidewalk in front of the building and an elderly woman got out, dressed in furs and carrying a shopping bag. The doorman tipped his cap and opened one of the doors for her as she stepped past him into the lobby, and then he followed her inside. The two began talking.

Orcus put the phone back on its hook and again crossed the street, striding through the alley between the apartment building and its neighbor to the south. At the end of the alley, there was a flight of stairs leading down to a metal door. He went down the stairs, and when he reached the bottom, he was out of sight from the sidewalk.

The lock was a Schlage. It was large and flush-mounted, of

excellent quality. And for a man with Orcus's skills, a piece of cake. He took two small tools from his inside jacket pocket and went to work.

The first tool was a torsion wrench, a slim, flat length of steel with an L-shaped end. He inserted the wrench into the keyway and exerted pressure counterclockwise, the direction a key would be turned to open the lock. Then he slid the second tool, a thin pick, into the keyway and began probing for the tumbler pins.

There would be five of them, he knew, in this type of lock. He had the first one in less than a minute, feeling it drop into place and at the same time getting an infinitesimal further yield from the torsion wrench, perhaps a thousandth of an inch. He went on probing and the other four pins followed in short order. Orcus gave the wrench one last twist and the lock opened. He slipped through the door and closed it softly behind him, returning the tools to his pocket.

The basement was in keeping with what he'd seen of the rest of the building; it was spotlessly clean, the walls and floor painted battleship gray. He followed overhead lights around a corner and past the furnace room, and directly ahead of him were the doors to two elevators.

There would be a superintendent around here someplace; Orcus could only hope he wouldn't accidentally run into him, or that the man wouldn't notice an elevator going to the basement and wonder who was using it. There would also be TV cameras, but he knew that with only one doorman on duty, the monitor would not be closely watched, if at all. He pressed the button and waited, and when the car finally arrived, he stepped inside and touched the lighted panel marked 22.

The elevator rose without stopping and deposited him on the twenty-second floor, and when he entered the hallway, it was deserted.

There were four apartment doors up here; he located the one marked B. Using the tools on the lock in that door was out of the question; he knew she'd also have a dead bolt on the inside. Instead, he went to the door leading into the emergency stairway and stepped through onto the landing. Wedging the door open a crack with a matchbook, he kept his eye on the entrance to her apartment.

As he stood there, he pulled the scarf up over his nose and mouth, to a point just under the dark glasses. His face was now entirely obscured. Then he took a pair of rubber gloves out of his topcoat pocket and drew them on.

Lastly, he got out the Browning semiautomatic and jacked a shell into the chamber. He put the pistol back into his pocket, keeping his right hand curled around the grip.

For more than forty minutes, he hardly moved, his gaze fixed on the apartment door. During that time, no one else set foot in the hallway, which was understandable in the middle of the day; most tenants would be in their places of business now—except for a few like the old lady who'd been chatting with the doorman.

And Jessica Silk.

The air in the stairwell was warm and sweat was trickling from his armpits and running down his sides. He could feel his nerves tightening, his mouth getting dry. It was always like this; waiting was the hardest part.

At last, he heard the sound of a bolt being thrown back. Moving quickly, he stepped out of the stairwell and went to the elevators, standing in front of the doors as if waiting for a car to arrive. Behind him, he heard her open her apartment door and close it again, heard her double-lock it before joining him at the elevators. He kept his head down, his hands in his pockets.

Until she was beside him.

Suddenly, he whirled toward her. He shoved the pistol into her face, holding the muzzle an inch from her nose.

For an instant, he thought she might faint. Her knees sagged and she gasped, her eyes popping as she stared into the barrel.

"You want to see God?" Orcus said.

Her lips trembled; the color drained from her cheeks. Her voice was a whisper. "No."

"Then turn around and keep quiet. Go back to your door and open it. I'll be right behind you. Make one wrong move and I'll blow your fucking head off. You understand?"

She nodded and walked unsteadily back to the door, fumbling in her purse and getting out a key ring.

There was more fumbling, and Orcus realized her hands were shaking so much, she couldn't get the key into the lock. He was about to snatch the key away from her when she finally managed to get the lock undone.

He followed her into the apartment and closed the door behind them, shoving the bolt home. Nudging her ahead of him with the Browning, he moved with her through the foyer and into the living room.

She turned to face him. Her face was white and her lips continued to tremble. She was wearing a tan cashmere coat that only partly disguised her lush figure, holding on to the purse with both hands. Her hazel eyes were full of fear.

"What do you want?"

"You."

She began backing away. "No. No—get out."

He raised the pistol once more, pointing it at her face.

"No—please." She stopped moving. "Oh, Jesus, please don't."

"Do exactly what I tell you, or I'll kill you."

"All right, I will. I'll do anything you say."

"That's better." He glanced around the room. The furniture was modern, all done in pale leather, and there was a bar with bottles and decanters standing on it. Across from him, covering the entire east wall, was a bank of windows. The drapes were open, revealing a terrace with a view of Roosevelt Island and the river.

He indicated a nearby sofa. "Get over there."

She went to it, standing beside the sofa and looking back at him apprehensively.

"Drop your purse on the floor," he ordered. "And take off your coat. Put that on the floor, too."

She complied, again looking at him.

"Now your shoes and your panty hose."

"Listen, couldn't we—"

"Do it."

She glanced at the pistol and her shoulders slumped. Resignedly, she kicked off her shoes, then turned away from him and began hauling down the panty hose. She had on a simple blue dress, no jewelry. She steadied herself by holding on to the sofa, and when she got the garment off, she dropped it beside her coat and purse.

Orcus gestured with the pistol. "Lie down."

She did, looking up at him from the sofa, her eyes wide.

He shoved the pistol into his coat pocket, unbuttoned the coat and unzipped his fly, then dropped his pants.

It was over in seconds. He pulled up her dress and spread her legs, then rammed himself into her, not caring that her passage was dry, that there was no response from her whatever.

Afterward, he lay atop her for a few moments, breathing hard, before he withdrew and stood up. Silk continued to stare at him as he rearranged his clothing.

"Get up," he said. "Put your stuff back on."

"Then will you go? I promise I won't tell anybody, or anything."

"Sure."

She moved slowly, cautiously, as if hurrying would cause him to change his mind. Retrieving her panty hose from the floor, she sat on the sofa and put them on. Now she avoided his gaze, and he knew that was because she was praying he'd simply get out, that he'd leave her alone.

He waited until she got her shoes back on and stood up and then he took a half step to the side, which put him behind her.

As quickly as a darting snake, he slipped his arms under hers and gripped the back of her head with both hands. She tried to cry out, but the sound was little more than a choking gurgle as he heaved downward with all his strength.

Her neck broke with a sharp crack.

She collapsed, instantly limp. He let go and stepped back and her body fell to the floor in a heap. Her hands and feet twitched convulsively for a few moments and then were still. She was lying on her belly, with her head at an odd angle, and he could see her right eye open and staring, froth forming on her lips.

Bending down, he picked up her purse and sat on the sofa. He pulled the scarf down to make breathing easier, then went through the contents of the purse.

What he found was an assortment of the usual junk women carried: a wallet with a change compartment, lipstick, mirror, eyebrow pencil, a book of stamps, ticket stubs from a movie theater, a package of cigarettes, a silver lighter engraved with the initials JS, a package of Kleenex, a leather-bound address book, a ballpoint.

There was also what he was looking for: a plain white letter-sized envelope. He opened the envelope and took out a single glossy photograph.

The photo was in sharp focus, with bright colors and excellent detail—altogether, an admirable piece of work. He wondered how Silk had gotten it. Certainly it was worth the hundred grand she was asking for it. And if the balance of the material was this good, her price was quite reasonable. In the long run, it would bring far more than the million the silly bitch had demanded for the whole works.

He put the photo back into the envelope, then took Silk's address book from her purse. Getting to his feet, he stuffed the envelope and the address book into his coat pocket, then began a systematic search of the apartment.

It didn't take long—just over an hour. In part, that was because there were only five rooms and in part because Orcus knew his business. He found Silk's stash within the first few minutes. It was in a black leather attaché case that had been placed behind some pots and pans in one of the lower kitchen cabinets. He took the case into the living room and unlocked it with one of her keys.

The collection was impressive. Museum quality, Orcus thought, smiling at his humor. There were dozens of photos, all in vivid color. Some were three-by-fives, others were eight-by-tens—which was curious, and yet at the moment he couldn't waste time trying to figure it out.

The important thing was that he had the material. Now what he had to do was to make sure this was all of it and then finish his task and get out of here without being seen.

He continued his search, poking through dresser drawers, looking under mattresses, exploring shelves, feeling garments, going through cabinets, and found nothing more of importance until he hit what appeared to be Silk's study.

There was an IBM PC on the desk. He switched it on, then called up her files. There were dozens of them, ranging from correspondence to Silk's personal financial data. He checked every one, spending a few seconds with each, until he found the subject. The Cunningham story would print out to more than a hundred pages.

Next he leafed through a box of diskettes, locating one labeled CC. He put that into the computer and looked at its contents. Satisfied it was a copy, he took it out of the machine and put it aside. Then he erased the original from the hard disc. When that was done, he switched off the machine.

Her notebooks were lined up in a bookcase beside the desk. Three of them contained notes on Cunningham. He took those with him, along with the diskette.

Returning to the living room, he put the materials into the attaché case and locked it. Her coat was still lying on the floor. He picked it up and hung it in the front-hall closet.

He also noticed that a telephone on an end table was hooked up to an answering machine. Opening the machine, he took out the tape and pocketed it.

Next, he went to the bar and poured himself three fingers of Scotch, knocking it back in one gulp. The whiskey burned like fire until it hit bottom, and then it spread soothing warmth through him.

Now there was only the body to deal with.

French doors led onto the terrace. He opened them and stepped outside. There was a lot of noise out here: the rumble of traffic from the FDR Drive, the bleat of horns, other distant sounds rising from the city. Also the wind was stiffer at this height. After drinking the whiskey and spending time in the apartment wearing his hat and coat, the air felt fresh and cool on his face.

He went to the railing and looked down. There was some sort of low building directly behind the apartment house, abutting the rear wall. Its roof was green, probably corroded copper, about twenty floors below where he was standing.

Perfect.

Glancing quickly left and right, he was confident he wouldn't be seen. He returned to the living room and picked up Silk's body, heaving it onto his shoulder as if he was carrying a sack of flour. Stepping back out onto the terrace, he dumped the corpse over the railing.

When he was again inside, he deliberately left the French doors ajar. Then he picked up the attaché case and left the apartment.

Three minutes later, he stepped into the alley. He paused to strip off the rubber gloves and put them into his pocket, then walked out to the sidewalk and once more crossed Sutton Place. Out of the corner of his eye, he saw the doorman standing in the street, waving for a taxi. The doorman paid no attention to him.

Orcus strode along at his same unhurried pace, going west until he reached Second Avenue, where he stopped at another public phone. Again he called the number and again she answered on the first ring.

"Done," Orcus said.

"You get everything?"

"Yes."

"All smooth, no hitches?"

There were times when she gave him a pain in the ass. "You think I'm an amateur?"

"I just wanted to make sure it went all right."

"It did. Talk to you later." He hung up.

A heavy stream of traffic was moving south. Orcus stepped off the curb and hailed a taxi. He gave the driver an address and settled back on the seat, holding the attaché case on his lap.

Did he get everything? Damn right he did. Including a little piece of Jessica Silk, which nobody had to know about.

Oddly, that hadn't been very satisfying. Not nearly as exciting as breaking her neck. Or throwing her off the terrace, seeing her body whirl down through the air and crash onto the roof far below, bursting red when it hit.

That was *real* excitement. Thinking about it, Orcus again produced an erection. And behind the dark glasses, he smiled to himself as he recreated the scene in his mind.

16

Peggy Demarest took off her coat and hung it on the back of the door, then gave her sister a perfunctory kiss on the forehead before sitting down beside her.

This was a gray day, raw and cold, and no one was walking on the paths that wound through the pine trees on the hospital grounds. Looking through the window, all Peggy saw was the leaden sky and the tree limbs bending under the force of the wind gusts. It made the visit seem even more depressing than usual. And Jan's condition seem more hopeless.

But she had to try. Dr. Chenoweth had given her his customary pep talk, urging her to keep up an agreeable line of chatter, as if Jan was eager to hear every word. "Some of it is bound to get through to her," he'd said, "whether it appears to or not. Even if she doesn't understand the words, conveying warmth and affection is what counts."

Still, it felt ridiculous, babbling away about nothing and getting no response—like talking to a statue. Jan looked like one, too, her skin the color of marble, except for the angry red scar on her cheek. As she did each time Peggy visited, Jan simply sat with her hands curled like claws in her lap, her head bent forward slightly, her eyes dull and vacant, giving no sign she was aware of Peggy's presence or of anything else.

And yet Peggy was expected to be cheerful? She felt more like crying.

Nevertheless, she made a brave attempt. "Not so pleasant out there today, Jan. Cold, damp, and dreary. The wind's out of the northeast, and you know what that means—a storm is coming. Supposed to rain by tonight. Good day to be right here inside, where it's snug and warm."

No reaction. Not that Peggy had expected one.

She went on: "We've been busy in the office. So many patients now, Dr. Friedman is planning to take in a partner. There are a couple of people he's considering. One of them is a nice young guy who graduated from Tufts in June and wants to move down here. I hope he's the one who joins us; he's cute. Not that I'm getting bored with Don, far from it. We have some really good times together. He wants me to marry him, but I'm not so sure."

She paused, thinking about it. "Maybe I'm old-fashioned, but I'm a little hesitant, uncomfortable maybe, about the business he's in. He sells cars. Did I tell you that? At Miller Chevrolet. That isn't the most secure job in the world right now."

She paused again for a moment, seeing her boyfriend in her mind's eye: carefree, happy-go-lucky Don.

"That might seem like a terrible attitude," she continued, "but I can't help it. Look at all the problems Mom and Dad had—especially after he got laid off. All he did then was sit around and drink, with Mom yelling at him. The more she yelled, the more he drank. No wonder you couldn't wait to get out of there. I couldn't, either, but I wasn't as gutsy as you. Took my kid sister to show the way. And then when Dad finally died, Mom was just about helpless. Married all those years, and look at how it ended. Mom having to sell the house, and living now in that dingy little apartment."

God, Peggy thought, what am I doing? This is supposed to be a happy visit, and listen to me. And even if it isn't really happy, I have to sound as if it is.

Taking a breath, she tried again. "I'm probably just being overcautious, right? Don's a great guy and I love him—at least I think I do. He's kind to me and generous, and just between you and me, he's terrific in bed. He wants us to move in together, sort of a trial marriage.

Maybe I'll do it. Certainly that'd be better than going through the formalities and then finding out you've made an awful mistake. Remember Sally Dawkins? Jed Halaby got her pregnant and married her, and it only lasted a little over a year. Jed was really mean. He's in some kind of trouble with the law now, too.''

Damn, she thought. There I go again.

''Speaking of cars, my Toyota's been giving me fits. First the front end developed a shimmy and then the transmission needed overhauling. Don says that's what you have to expect from Japanese cars, that they're all shit. But he's prejudiced, right? Maybe I should get a new one, especially now that Dr. Friedman's given me a raise. I don't want to be foolish, and yet it's dumb to keep this one if I have to be pouring money into it.''

Peggy looked at her sister. In all this time, she thought, with me going on like an idiot, she hasn't given the slightest sign she's heard a word. I wonder if Dr. Chenoweth is having pipe dreams or if he's just telling me to do this because it's something that'll give me hope. Keep me occupied, believing I'm doing some good. I might just as well recite the alphabet, or say nothing at all.

Instantly, she felt ashamed. Come on, Peggy, she told herself. If there's even the slightest chance it might help, you've got to give it your best effort. And anyway, in a few more minutes you've got to go back to work.

Another thought occurred to her and she didn't stop to weigh its negative implications before speaking. ''One sad thing that's happened, Jan. Senator Cunningham died. I know you thought a lot of him—I remember your talking about him when you worked at their place out here. He didn't die there, though. He was in his house in New York when it happened. His heart gave out. Too bad, but it said on TV he was seventy-two. I didn't realize he was that old. But still it's tragic, isn't it?''

For an instant, she thought she'd imagined it. Or maybe the light coming through the window had changed slightly. But she could have sworn one of Jan's eyes twitched—her right one. There seemed to be the merest flicker and then it was gone.

Peggy leaned forward until her face was no more than a foot away from her sister's blank counrenance. ''Jan? Did you hear me, Jan?''

Don't be silly, she told herself. This is a prime example of wishful thinking. You're seeing things because you want to see them, not because they're actually there.

And yet, she was almost certain something had occurred. But what? And what could have caused it? If there had been a reaction, what could have been the trigger? What had she been talking about? Senator Cunningham's death, that was it. Had Jan responded to the news ever so slightly?

Keeping her gaze locked on her sister's lackluster eyes, she said, "Jan, I said Senator Cunningham is dead. He died a few days ago, and I think the funeral is tomorrow. Did you hear that, Jan? Senator Cunningham is dead. Isn't that sad?"

What she saw now was no figment of an overworked imagination. It was real, and to Peggy it was like a miracle.

In the corner of that same right eye, a tear formed. A tiny bit of moisture welled up and then the drop rolled down Jan's cheek.

Peggy's jaw dropped. She moved even closer and then she saw a shimmer in Jan's left eye, as well. She grabbed her sister's arm. "Jan! Jan—can you hear me?"

As usual, there was no response. Her sister's features appeared to be as insensible and uncomprehending as they had on all the other days since she'd come here.

But she *had* responded. Peggy had seen it, had seen the tear with her own eyes.

Jumping to her feet, she ran out into the hall. She had to find Dr. Chenoweth, *now*.

17

When Tolliver walked into the investigators' squad room, Jack Mulloy was half-sitting on the desk next to his, talking to another detective. When he caught sight of Ben, he stepped over to greet him, moving as quickly as the bad leg would permit.

"Hey, Ben—I've been waiting for you. You heard the latest?"

"What is it?"

"That writer, Silk. The one who was with the senator when he died? She went out the window."

"When?"

"Sometime earlier today. Jimmy Collins called, from the One-seven. He figured since you were working on the senator's death, you'd want to know right away. Somebody spotted the body and called it in."

"Was this at her apartment?"

"He said on Sutton Place."

"Yeah, that's it. What else did Collins tell you?"

"So far, they haven't found a note. They were still looking for one when he called."

"Then they don't know why she did it."

"Who knows?" Mulloy said. "Maybe it was grief . . . over the senator. Or maybe all the pressure got to her. You want the number? They're probably still there."

"Yeah, give it to me."

They went to Mulloy's desk and the detective handed him a slip of paper with Jessica Silk's phone number scrawled on it. Tolliver picked up a phone and called it. When a cop answered, he asked for Collins, a homicide detective he'd known for a long time. A moment later, Collins came onto the line.

"Jimmy, Ben Tolliver."

"Hey, Ben. The lady did a swan."

"Mulloy said earlier today?"

"Right. The ME's looking at her now."

"And no note?"

"None we could find so far. You know if they leave one, they usually put it in a place where somebody'll see it."

"You run across anything else?"

"Nothing that'd tell us why she jumped. Maybe the uproar over her and the senator. You talk to her after he died?"

"Yes. In that apartment. You gonna be there a while?"

"Oh, yeah—we'll be combing it pretty good. This one'll get a lot of attention, and I don't want to give anybody a reason to second-guess us. You want to have a look?"

"Sure. I'll be there in a few minutes." He hung up.

"You want me to come along?" Mulloy asked.

"Yeah, come on." Ben turned and left the room, the other detective pulling on his suit jacket and struggling to keep up.

They took the FDR, Ben pushing the Ford at his customary

breakneck pace. He whipped in and out of the lines of traffic, slipping over to the extreme right when they ran into the inevitable jam-up near the UN exit.

''You could make a lot of money,'' Mulloy said, ''in the south.''

''How do you figure?''

''Stock-car races. Those rednecks got nothing on you.''

Tolliver blew his horn at some asshole in a Mercedes who apparently thought he rated two lanes. A gap developed when the guy finally gave ground, and Ben shot through it.

''Not leaving a note bothers me,'' he said.

''Me, too,'' Mulloy said. ''You think maybe somebody shoved her?''

''It's possible. Anything's possible—especially after what those embalmers who worked on Cunningham told me. Even the ME admitted nobody knows for sure what killed the old man. And now this?''

''Sure. But remember the Mulloy rule for survival.''

''Which is?''

''Do not step in shit.''

''I'll write that down.''

''You should. You didn't see the brass pick up on it, did you? About the embalmers, or what the ME told you? You said Brennan acted like he wished you hadn't brought it up.''

''Can't altogether blame him. Everybody knows that without an autopsy, it's all just conjecture. The embalmers admitted that. And the ME confirmed it.''

''Yeah, but maybe now with the writer dead, it'll change a few minds. Might be a good time to push for a post on the senator.''

''Maybe. But I doubt it.''

''Worth a try,'' Mulloy said. ''Better than our just sniffing around with nothing solid to go on.''

''True enough. You want to talk to the DA about it? Make the suggestion?''

''Not me. But you can bet this suicide won't just get filed away. The media'll go apeshit.''

''I'm sure they will.''

This time, cops had blocked off the area. Reporters had already gathered outside the barricades and were complaining about not being admitted. Tolliver showed a uniform his shield and the officer moved one of the blue-painted sawhorses aside for the Ford to pass. A number of police cars and an ambulance were at the curb in front of Silk's apartment house, and also a CSU van. Ben parked in the street, two doors up from the building, and he and Mulloy walked back.

As the pair of detectives approached the entrance, white-clad ambulance attendants rolled a gurney with a body bag strapped to it out the front doors. The doorman was standing nearby, looking stricken, and farther down the street another barricade held back a handful of gawkers. Ben and Mulloy watched the crew load the body into the ambulance and then they went into the building.

Inside apartment 22B, the scene was more like what you'd see at a homicide. Cops were everywhere, including Lt. Ralph Watts, who headed the Seventeenth Precinct detective squad. The lieutenant was standing around looking important, watching the activity as the CSU detectives continued to go through the apartment. A heavyset man with freckles dotting his pale skin, Watts belonged to the snappy-dresser school of police officer. In his glen plaid and foulard tie, he could have been a bond salesman.

Watts said hello to Tolliver and Mulloy, remarking that everybody was just about to pack up. Pretty much open and shut, he said, nothing complicated about what they'd found.

Jimmy Collins was on the terrace. Ben went out there, Mulloy trailing.

Even under the pewter-colored November sky, the view was breathtaking. To the left, the Queensboro Bridge spanned the river, connecting Manhattan with the grimy industrial sections beyond Vernon Avenue in Queens, and straight ahead was Roosevelt Island and the Goldwater Memorial Hospital. Visible downstream were the water sculpture and the Pepsi bottling plant on the far side, the Williamsburg Bridge arcing over into Brooklyn.

A strong breeze was blowing, kicking up tiny swirls of dust around the few pieces of outdoor furniture that stood forlornly on the tiled floor. Collins was leaning against the railing, writing something in a small pocket notebook. He turned as the two detectives came out the French doors. The wind had rumpled his short brown hair.

"That was quick," Collins said.

"He thinks he's Richard Petty," Mulloy said.

Tolliver stepped to the railing. "This where she went?"

Collins pointed. "*X* marks the spot."

Ben looked down. Far below was a much smaller building with a green roof. In the center of the roof was a red smear.

Mulloy joined him at the railing. "Heights make me dizzy. Every time I see one of these, I'm afraid of falling off myself. She must have been a mess."

"She was," Collins said. "That roof is twenty floors down."

"You said a neighbor spotted her?" Ben asked.

"Yeah, a lady who lives in the building. She's in Five B, so her apartment faces the same way as this one. She went out on her terrace and looked down, and there it was."

"When?"

"Two-thirty-six, the call came in."

"The ME still here?"

"He left a few minutes ago," Collins said. "Soon as they put her in the bag."

"He fix the time?"

"From the temperature of the body, he thought maybe an hour before she was discovered."

Ben nodded. In this instance, he wouldn't have to wonder what an autopsy might show; New York State law mandated a postmortem in a suicide, just as in a murder case. Whatever secrets the body might hold, the post would reveal them.

"Patrol car here first?" he asked.

"Yeah, they called it in," Collins said. "Soon as I heard the name, I asked for a crime-scene unit. Then I came right over here. Body was fully clothed, except for her shoes. They came off when she hit."

"Still no note?"

"Never found one. And we really went through this place. Her purse was on a table in the living room. Nothing in that, either. I did locate her ex-husband, though. His name was on a card in her wallet. I called him at his office. He said he hadn't talked to her in months but that maybe she'd been depressed over their divorce."

"You pick up anything else?"

"One thing. The super let the cops in with a passkey. But the dead bolt wasn't in place."

"That's strange," Mulloy said. "Specially when a woman's alone."

"Maybe she just didn't bother," Ben said, "because she knew what she planned to do."

Collins considered that. "Could be. The terrace doors were open, too. But she was alone up here, nobody had come to the apartment. I checked the doorman; he's been on since eight o'clock this morning."

Behind them a voice said, "Say, Jimmy?"

The detectives turned, to see Hi Goldstein approaching, the sergeant in charge of the CSU. He was a guy Ben had run into on other cases, thin-faced and intense, respected in the NYPD for his painstaking ways.

Goldstein smiled when he saw Tolliver and Mulloy. "Word gets around, huh?"

"On this one, it does," Ben said. "How've you been, Hi?"

"Keeping busy."

"What've you got?" Collins asked him.

"Nothing unusual," Goldstein said. "Except there weren't many prints. Looks as if the place was cleaned recently. But we did get a few, plus some latents. And some fibers. I'll send you a lab report soon as possible. Probably want a rush on this one, huh?"

"Yeah," Collins said. "I'd appreciate it."

"We'll be out of here in a few more minutes," the sergeant said. He went back inside and the others followed.

Tolliver glanced around the living room. As he caught sight of the bar with its sleek ebony paneling and the array of bottles resting on the surface, he recalled the last time he'd seen Jessica Silk, how she'd looked standing there—pouring herself a drink, smoke curling from her cigarette.

He wished he could have that instant back, wished he'd tried harder to find out what was going on with her. If he had, maybe she'd be alive now. Hindsight, he thought. There were so many moments in a lifetime you'd like to live over again.

Across the room, Silk's purse lay on a table, where the detectives had dumped its contents. One of the CSU men was making an inventory of the articles. Ben went over there and watched the process. The only thing of interest was her wallet; it contained a little over two hundred dollars in cash and some small change, along with the usual assortment of credit cards and her driver's license. The rest of the items were more or less standard.

But there was no address book in the purse, which struck him as odd—contacts were vitally important to somebody like her. Where were the names and phone numbers of people she did business with or used for sources?

His curiosity growing, Ben nosed around in the other rooms but found nothing like what he was looking for. The only list he ran across was one of grocery items, on a wall-mounted pad next to the telephone in the kitchen. That one, Silk apparently had written to herself, a reminder of things she wanted to buy: tuna, lettuce, mushrooms, wine, and so on.

He was about to turn away when he noticed the last entry. Orkis, it said. Orkis? What was an orkis? Had she meant orchids? Seemed unlikely. Whatever, it was an odd word. Or was it somebody's name?

He continued to poke around, but it wasn't until he went into her study that he felt he might find what he was looking for; an IBM 30 was sitting on the desk. He asked one of Goldstein's technicians if the computer keys had been dusted and was assured they had been.

Sitting down at the desk, Tolliver switched on the machine and called up Silk's files. The data included everything from drafts of articles to notes on a wide variety of subjects. But none of the names and addresses and phone numbers he'd wondered about were listed.

She couldn't have carried all that information around in her head; there had to be a book someplace. Where was it?

Another thought occurred to him, and he silently cursed himself for not having picked it up sooner. Nowhere had he seen a word of the article Silk supposedly had been writing on Senator Cunningham. He went back into the computer files, checking and rechecking them, but there was not a single entry on the subject.

A box on the desk contained storage diskettes. He looked through those and found that they contained no reference to the senator, either. Nor did the notebooks that were neatly lined up on the shelf of a nearby bookcase. He leafed through the pages, coming across notes and roughs of other pieces she'd been working on, some of them going back a couple of years.

Nowhere was there so much as a mention of former Senator Clayton Cunningham III.

He sat there for a few minutes, thinking. Maybe there'd never been an article in the works; that could have been just a cover for her meetings with the senator.

And maybe Silk's ex-husband had guessed correctly; she'd been so depressed by their divorce, she'd taken her life. Or maybe Jack Mulloy's joke had hit the truth: She'd been driven to it by grief over the senator's death.

And maybe the answer was none of those. He turned off the machine and left the study.

Back in the living room, the CSU detectives were still at it, but Lieutenant Watts had gone, returning to his office in the Seventeenth Precinct. Mulloy was standing near the bar, talking to Jimmy Collins. Tolliver joined them.

"So—how about it?" Collins asked Ben. "You got any other theories why she did it?"

"Not at the moment."

"She could have had a lot of things bothering her," Collins said, "besides the divorce. Stuff we wouldn't know about—health problems, for instance. Or financial, whatever. And then on top of everything else, all that pressure, all the stories about her and the senator."

"Tell me," Ben said. "You run across an address book, list of her phone numbers, anything like that?"

"No. I asked Al to look for one, too. There wasn't any here."

"Odd, somebody in her business."

"Yeah, I thought so," Collins said. "You want me to send you a copy of the lab report when I get it?"

"Yeah, if you would. Thanks."

Tolliver and Mulloy left the apartment. Down on the street, the crowd had grown larger and the inevitable TV cameras were taping as the detectives went out through the front entrance.

Ben looked up at the building. Simple suicide, nothing out of line. Silk was depressed for a number of good reasons. The pressure had been too much for her. So she'd decided to end it by going over that railing.

The more he thought about it, the less he believed it.

18

Don't mess with it,'' Brennan said.

Ben stared at their reflections in the back-bar mirror. He and the zone commander were in the Shamrock, a cop's hangout a few blocks from One Police Plaza. Both men were drinking Jack Daniel's on the rocks.

''What am I supposed to do,'' Ben said, ''look the other way?''

''Look any way you want. But this suicide puts an end to it.''

''Puts an end to it? You see the papers, watch TV? The town's going crazy.''

''That's just the media, getting as much out of it as they can. The whole thing was a terrible tragedy and now it's over, see? The senator died. The writer killed herself—partly because of the situation she was in, but also because she was probably a little nuts.''

''Maybe she was and maybe she wasn't. Who knows what was really going on with her?''

''And who cares? What you do is cool it. The suicide's not yours anyway, belongs to the One-seven. Collins and Watts said there was nothing suspicious, and so did Hi Goldstein. She was alone in her apartment; the door was locked. Nothing missing, nothing out of line. Typical jumper, busted all to pieces when she hit that roof. End of the story.''

''Come on, Cap. You mean it's the end except for the things that don't add up. Like what she told me happened that night in the senator's office. And what Cunningham did or didn't die from. Now she's dead, too, and nobody really knows why she killed herself—if that's what she did.''

Brennan's tone was mild. ''Not much of a mystery, when you think about it. The lady was distraught for a lot of reasons. She had personal problems, and when the senator died, she flipped out. Then the media put out all that garbage about her and she couldn't stand it. So she jumped. People commit suicide every day, if you haven't noticed. Only reason this one's getting so much attention is because of Cunningham and all the publicity about how she was with him when he died.''

Ben swallowed some of his bourbon. ''I don't buy it. I'm telling you, neither one of them was what they looked like on the surface.''

''Uh-huh. And now let me tell you something, Lieutenant. There's a lot happening you don't know about. Certain people are interested in making this whole fucking thing go away, and the sooner the better. Not just people in the department, either. Chief Houlihan told me the commissioner's been getting calls on it, and some of them were about you.''

''About me?''

''Right. Inquiring about your background and your record, things like that.''

''Who from?''

''I don't know.''

''You don't know?''

''That's correct. At least as far as you're concerned, it is. I'm doing you a favor to tell you even that much.''

''But—''

''Listen to me, will you? You want your career to stay on track? Then pay attention. The senator's funeral is tomorrow. After that, you wrap it up, give Oppenheimer his report, and that's it.''

''Who says Oppenheimer'll be satisfied? He's not stupid, you know. He just might throw it back in my face.''

''No he won't. There's pressure on him, too. So handle it the way I'm telling you. You gonna have another drink?''

Tolliver drained his glass. ''Yeah, I think I'd better.''

19

The senator's funeral was grander than any New York had seen in years. As Tolliver had expected, it went off in two stages: first, a private ceremony in the Bennett Chapel that was attended by civic leaders, friends of the family, and persons of importance; and second, the public presentation, which was held at Riverside Church.

Although the church was one of the largest in the city, it was jammed to the last pew with mourners, and with people who knew history in the making when they saw it. The choice of the church was appropriate; built in 1930, it had been funded by Colonel Cunningham's idol, John D. Rockefeller, Sr. Its massive tower loomed twenty-one stories above Riverside Drive and offered a splendid view of the Hudson, and its seventy-four-bell carillon was bigger than any other in the world.

The cortege, led by a phalanx of mounted police, stretched for several blocks and included more Rolls-Royce and Mercedes limousines than it did Cadillacs. Four flower cars followed the hearse, which in turn was followed by eight more vehicles containing various members of the Cunningham family.

As a media event, the funeral was unsurpassed. Because of the implications of scandal stirred up by the tabloids and TV, especially with Jessica Silk's suicide coming on the heels of the senator's death, audiences couldn't get enough of the story. Not since Crazy Joey Gallo was gunned down in Umberto's Clam House while celebrating his forty-third birthday had the public imagination been so aroused.

The newspapers led the attack. Especially the *Post,* which outdid even its own rabid approach to reporting, mixing the weird with the bizarre. One article quoted an unnamed source who said the senator had been planning to divorce his wife and marry Jessica, after learning the writer was pregnant. Upon Cunningham's death, according to the piece, Silk was so depressed, she leapt off her terrace.

Not to be outdone, the *Daily News* interviewed a female psychic who claimed the senator had been running a ménage à trois with Silk and Ardis Merritt and that the exertion was the cause of his fatal heart attack. Silk jumped, the psychic said, when she learned she wouldn't be named a beneficiary in the senator's will.

Meantime, TV dredged up its own shticks, including asking people in the streets what they thought. Only the most outlandish opinions were aired, including one expressed by a guy in Queens who said he'd heard Cunningham wasn't dead at all but was shacked up in Hollywood under an assumed name.

As a result of all this, Riverside was packed. The service was conducted by the bishop and the eulogy was delivered by the mayor, even though he and the senator had personally despised each other. His Honor spoke glowingly of Clayton Cunningham and of his works for the people of New York, going on for almost an hour.

Tolliver watched quietly from the extreme rear of the church, sitting among a number of lesser city officials. Many of the NYPD brass were also in attendance, but Ben steered clear of them. He hated funerals and had rarely been to one at which he believed a word that was said about the departed. The only reason he attended this one was because experience had taught him you could sometimes learn things that would help you with what you were working on.

Which was another problem he was struggling with. He'd been told how to handle this case in no uncertain terms: back off. Let both Cunningham and Silk rest in peace. Yet he still had to live with himself. Was a promotion that important? Was the job?

He looked over the audience, making mental notes of what he saw. Clay Cunningham, the senator's son, was sitting in a front pew. His father's widow was on one side of him and his actress wife on the other. Even in a black hat with a veil, Laura Bentley was stunning.

Rounding out the group were Ingrid, not as showy as Laura but just as lovely, and her German husband. A sprinkling of teenaged children sat among them, but Ben didn't know which kids belonged to what set of parents.

Behind the immediate family was a large number of what he assumed were relatives, males and females of all ages. Sitting with them were Ardis Merritt, the administrator of the Cunningham Foundation, and a few places away, the security chief, Evan Montrock. Ben supposed other members of the staff were here as well, but the only one he recognized was the butler he'd seen on the morning he'd gone into the mansion.

When the service was concluded, pallbearers who had all been political allies of the senator bore the casket out to the waiting hearse. The family members then filed from the church, got into their cars, and were whisked away. Interment, Tolliver had learned, would be at the Cunningham estate on Long Island. Stepping outside, Ben continued to look over the crowd, recognizing many prominent people who had come to see and to be seen.

The media was also in attendance, of course, but a cordon of police was keeping them at bay. As Tolliver walked toward the spot where he'd left the Ford, he heard one of the reporters call his name.

Turning, he saw that the voice belonged to the newscaster from WPIC TV, Shelley Drake. For a moment, he was tempted to keep going, but then he thought again of their last conversation. He stepped over to where she was standing. A cameraman was with her, shooting tape of the scene. He paid no attention to Ben.

Drake had on the trench coat again, and the breeze was stirring her honey blond hair. This time, she wasn't at all aggressive. "Hello, Lieutenant."

Ben nodded.

"I saw you when you came out of Jessica Silk's apartment," she said, "on Sutton Place."

"Is that so?"

"Yes, but I didn't get a chance to talk to you. Before I could catch up, you were in your car and gone. I was hoping you were ready to hear what I could tell you."

"You're still trying to make a deal?"

"Of course. And if you'd only listen, I think you'd agree what I'm offering is fair."

"Okay, what is it?"

"If I can help you, all I'd ask is that you give me a little information in return—and only if my help is as valuable as I say it is."

"You that confident?"

"Yes."

He glanced again at the throng that continued to flow out of the church, a vast stream of people dressed mostly in black. "I'll think about it."

"You do that." She handed him a card. "Call me anytime."

He put the card into a pocket of his raincoat and walked away. Getting chummy with a member of the press was something he'd always assiduously avoided. But now he wasn't so sure. Maybe it was time to forget about his rules and grab anything that came his way.

At the moment, however, there was another lady he wanted to call on. But whether he'd learn anything from her was questionable. Twenty stories was a long way to fall.

20

The morgue was in the basement of one of the seven brick buildings in the Bellevue Hospital Center on First Avenue, the oldest general hospital in the United States. Tolliver went down the steps into the dank, chilly corridors, following the passageway to the autopsy room. He showed his shield to the cop on the door and walked inside.

Jessica Silk looked nothing like the way she had the last time Ben had seen her. Now she was naked, lying on her back on one of the tables, her abdomen laid open from crotch to sternum. There were gaping ruptures in her flesh and the top of her skull had been removed, exposing her brain.

Two white-coated medical examiners were working on the cadaver. One of them was speaking into a microphone, recording his procedures as he removed each organ, then examined and weighed it. He glanced up as Ben entered the room. "Hey, Lieutenant. You do have an eye for pretty girls."

"Hello, Ed," Tolliver said. "You still trying to become a doctor?"

The ME grinned. He had red hair and a beaklike nose that always put Ben in mind of an oversized woodpecker. His name was Edgar Feldman. Tolliver had worked with him on a number of homicide cases.

"Anybody can be a pill-pusher," Feldman said. "Pathology requires a real virtuoso. And besides, you'll note that when it comes to autopsying somebody important, they turn to the old master himself."

"I hadn't noticed."

"It's true. This was Senator Cunningham's girlfriend, right? Our celebrity of the week."

"She knew him," Tolliver said.

"Knew him? Hey, Ben—you of all people wouldn't buy that shit about her interviewing him, would you? Unless interviewing is a polite way of saying she was shtupping the old boy. I think the papers and the TV got it right."

"Don't believe everything you see or read," Ben said.

"Okay, but that's why you're here, isn't it?"

"Possibly."

"I thought so. At least you cared enough to attend our little party. None of your fellow officers bothered, as you can see. Say hello to my assistant, Dave Wilkison."

The second ME raised a gloved hand in greeting, the latex smeared crimson. Ben nodded and then stepped closer to the table, peering down at the corpse.

Silk's appearance was also very different from that of the last dead body he'd seen. Among other things, her color was chalk white—except for the yawning abdominal cavity and the many places where her flesh had burst open. Those areas were purplish red.

Maybe the embalmers had been right; the senator's countenance had been considerably improved by Lifetone. Certainly he'd looked better than Silk did now. Even his expression of pained horror was preferable to the way the skin of her forehead had been rolled down over her face and the way her body had split apart, as if her life had leaked out of the holes.

The ME was watching Tolliver's reaction. "That's the thing about jumpers," he said. "When they hit, it all hangs out."

"Uh-huh. What've you found?"

"Several points of interest." Feldman gestured with a scalpel. "One, she landed flat on her back, which is unusual."

"What's unusual about it?"

"Because when somebody jumps, they almost always go feet-first, like kids hopping into a pool. Don't ask me why, they just do. I've done posts on dozens of them, and I'd say over ninety percent hit that way. You can't miss it, because it drives the femurs, the thigh-bones, all the way up into the abdomen."

Ben had seen a few himself. The picture wasn't pleasant.

"This lady, however, didn't land that way. She did a back whopper, I guess you could call it. When she hit, she popped open, which is to be expected. Like dropping a paper sack filled with water from a height."

"And I suppose the fall also broke a lot of her bones?"

"A lot? All of them, just about. She would have been doing around a hundred-thirty miles an hour when she smacked that roof. It was made of copper, and she put a dent in the surface."

Ben tried to envision Silk climbing over the railing, making her leap. "I wonder how she went off. That is, if she landed on her back, she must have had her body turned around and facing the terrace before she let go."

"It would seem that way. Odd, isn't it?"

"Yeah, it is."

"But not the oddest, not by a long shot."

"Oh?"

"I've been saving the best parts."

"Okay, what are they?"

"Take a good close look at her neck and her shoulders. See the bruises?"

Tolliver bent over the body. Just as Feldman had said, there were small bluish marks in her flesh, many of them. Because of the way her skin had ruptured, Ben might well have overlooked them or ascribed them to injuries caused by her fall.

The ME pointed. "Some of these are from pinches, I would say, somebody grabbing hold of her and twisting. But some of them were made by teeth. Love bites, the kind of thing you see when people have been involved in what we so delicately describe as rough sex."

"Yeah," Ben said. "I do see them." He also saw an image in his mind's eye of Jessica standing in her doorway when he'd gone to her apartment, looking tall and beautiful in black slacks and a black turtleneck. The sweater would have covered the marks on her neck. Was that why she'd been wearing it?

"And that's still not all," Feldman said. "Look at these." He brought the point of the scalpel close to Silk's right thigh. Clearly visible in the skin were a number of small red sores. Some of them apparently were fresh, seeming raw and angry. Others were scabbed over.

Tolliver stared at the wounds. "What caused them, do you know? They look like burns."

The ME beamed. "Spoken like a true detective. That's exactly what they are. Some are recent; some are weeks old. And there are more of them on her buttocks."

"So what caused them?"

"In my opinion, they were made by somebody touching her with something very hot. Not a cigarette—the burns are too big for that. Best bet? A lighted cigar."

"I'll be damned."

Feldman shook his head. "What some people won't do for pleasure. Ay, Lieutenant?"

"Couldn't have been very pleasurable for her," Ben said.

"Oh? And why not? Has masochism gone out of style? Maybe she loved it. Wouldn't be the first time a man and woman had a weird relationship . . . or the last."

"No, I suppose not."

"Spices up the story, too, right? Could be that she and the senator liked to work each other over."

"Come on, Ed, don't get carried away. You sound like you should be writing for the *Daily News.*"

"Just trying to be helpful."

"Yeah. What else?"

"Turns out she was a heavy smoker herself; lung tissue was in bad shape. Probably would have died of cancer in a few more years. Also she drank more than she should have. Blood-alcohol level was point-oh-nine at the time of death, and there was some evidence of liver damage."

Once again a picture of Jessica Silk formed in Ben's mind—the one of her standing at the bar in her apartment, smoking a cigarette and pouring herself a drink.

"Worried a lot, too," Feldman went on.

"What makes you say that?"

"I found an incipient ulcer in her duodenum."

"Interesting."

"Isn't it, though. I said this was a fascinating branch of medicine, didn't I?"

"That you did. What more can you tell me?"

"What more do you want? The brand of cigar that caused those burns? You should be grateful for all I've given you as it is."

"I am. But let me tell you about why I came here. First, however, I want to point out that this is not my case. So I'd appreciate it if you didn't mention that I dropped by."

"Okay, done."

"I came because I'm not convinced this was a suicide—even though no evidence turned up at the scene to suggest it wasn't."

"Ah. I thought that might be what was on your mind."

"What I want you to do is this. Look for *anything* that could be labeled suspicious. Those burns, for instance, have some meaning, I feel sure. See if there might be something else, something that could support the theory that she didn't go off the terrace of her own accord."

"Sure, will do."

"You scrape her nails?"

"No."

"Do it. Maybe there was a struggle and she scratched somebody."

"Yeah, okay."

"And keep an eye out for anything else you might come across. Any other injuries, for instance, that weren't from the fall."

Feldman glanced down at the cadaver. "That one's a little tougher. Look at her."

''Yeah, I know. But try, anyway. You just might come up with something I can use. Okay?''

''I'll do my best, Lieutenant.''

''Thanks, Ed. You've already been a terrific help.''

Feldman bowed. ''Where shall I send my bill?''

''Try the mayor.'' Ben turned and left the room.

21

Wanted to stop by and say hello,'' Tolliver said. He was standing in the doorway of Capt. Daniel Brannigan's office. ''Appreciate the hospitality.''

The captain was another one-time detective in the NYPD, according to Mulloy. He struck Ben as much like a lot of other senior officers, men who'd built their careers by establishing connections, playing the game. They traded favors, looked the other way when there were things they chose not to see. Brannigan had that same well-fed sleekness, same laid-back style. With his prominent nose and thinning hair, his dark blue suit, he might have been a city councilman or the head of some minor agency. But a bureaucrat, without question.

''Don't mention it,'' Brannigan said. ''Glad to have you aboard. Little different operation from what you're used to, though, right? The kind of things my people work on are more cerebral.''

''More cerebral?''

''Sure. White-collar crime requires brains—which puts it on a higher plane. Not as exciting, probably, to somebody who's been running a precinct squad. The guys we chase steal with greater finesse.''

''And get away with more money.''

''A lot more. It's what makes the work so challenging. Our bad guys are well educated, know more loopholes than most lawyers. That's why it takes special skills to nail them. When we do, the money we recover is about a million times what one of your street punks runs off with.''

Tolliver wasn't about to get into a pissing contest over who was doing more to protect New York from the criminal hordes. ''Yeah, well. Thanks anyway, for your help.''

"Glad we could lend a hand. Mulloy giving you everything you need?"

"Yes, so far."

"He's swamped, you know, with the investigation he's working on. I wouldn't want him to get sidetracked. So if you're gonna need much more assistance, see me. I'll assign somebody else."

"All right, fine."

Brannigan sat back in his chair. "How's it going, by the way?"

"Well enough, I guess. Few loose ends."

"This latest thing was some wrinkle, huh? The woman killing herself? Whatever went on with her and the senator, she sure paid for it. All those stories—no wonder she jumped."

"Yeah."

"I was saying to the DA, it was a lousy way for Cunningham to go out, too. Poor guy couldn't even die in peace. But that's to be expected, under the circumstances. Same kind of thing happened when Nelson Rockefeller died."

"Uh-huh."

"It's like Oppenheimer says, everything gets tried in the media nowadays. Nobody knows better than him how much trouble they can make."

And what you're really telling me, Ben thought, is that you and the DA are very close. Chat together regularly about various matters.

Brannigan was elaborately casual. "So how long you figure it'll take you to get this finished up?"

"Hard to say. But not too long, I hope."

"Anytime you want to talk about it, bounce some ideas, don't hesitate. By the way, I have a spare office you can use while you're here. Mulloy will show you."

"Okay, sounds fine."

"Good morning," a voice behind Tolliver said.

Ben turned to see a tall man step into the room. He was slim and urbane in a gray pinstripe and a paisley tie, his dark hair brushed straight back.

Brannigan stood up. "Morning, Fletcher. Say hello to Lt. Ben Tolliver. Ben, this is Fletcher Shackley, the senior prosecutor who's handling the Cunningham case."

They shook hands and Shackley said, "Understand you're doing a report on the senator's death. Is that right, Lieutenant?"

''I'm investigating it, yes.''

''Have you been making progress?''

''Some.''

''Very unfortunate turn of events. Not only for the senator and that poor woman who committed suicide; it's also upset our work, ironically.''

''Why is that?''

''Why? All the publicity, of course. Focuses too much attention on the family. And their business.''

Shackley had a way of speaking that suggested he was explaining arithmetic to a retarded child. It occurred to Ben that listening to it could get on his nerves in a hurry.

''What's more,'' the prosecutor went on, ''it removed what would have been a valuable source of information. We certainly would have questioned the senator, at an appropriate time.''

''I see.''

Shackley went to a chair and sat down. ''Nice to meet you, Lieutenant. Good luck with your work.''

It was a clear note of dismissal. ''Thanks,'' Ben said. ''See you later, Captain.''

''Sure, drop in again.''

Tolliver turned and walked out into the area where Jack Mulloy was working at his desk. When the detective saw Ben, he rose to his feet, saying, ''Hey, we got some space for you.''

''So I'm told.''

''Come on, I'll take you over there.''

Ben followed him across the crowded floor, where male and female plainclothes cops sat typing and talking on telephones, to one of the glass-enclosed cubicles on the outer wall. The furnishings were standard issue: a gray metal desk, a swivel chair with a vinyl seat, a couple of straight-backed visitor's chairs, a gray metal filing cabinet. A stand supported a beat-up typewriter. On the desk were a telephone, an in-box, and a couple of scratch pads.

Mulloy smiled. ''Not bad, huh? Even got a window.''

This was true enough. A grimy double-hung window faced an air shaft, giving a view of the neighboring brick wall. If you stood on your head near the window and looked up, you might be able to see a small patch of sky.

Tolliver took off his raincoat and hung it on a wall hook. Then he sat down at the desk and surveyed his surroundings. The office wasn't much different from the one he occupied as a squad commander in the Sixth Precinct, although that one at least looked out onto Tenth Street. Thinking of it made him feel nostalgic.

Mulloy folded his arms and leaned against the glass partition. "How'd the funeral go?"

Ben glanced up. "How'd it go? It was a big deal, of course. You should have been there, Jack. You would've loved it."

"I doubt it. Funerals depress me."

"That's what they're supposed to do. After that, I went to the Silk autopsy. That was some show, too."

"I can imagine."

"The ME found something interesting."

"What was it?"

"There were marks on her body that didn't come from the fall. Bruises and love bites. And burns."

"Burns?"

"From a cigar, he said. And Senator Cunningham smoked cigars."

"Holy Christ. You sure about that?"

"Yeah, I am. His son mentioned it when I went to the house, and there was a humidor in his office."

"Sounds like he had something going with her, after all. Something freaky. Right?"

"Maybe, maybe not. Like everything else with this thing, there's no way to prove where the marks came from—or who put them there."

"You told anybody this?"

"No. Keep it buttoned up."

"Don't worry, I will. Need anything more from me?"

"Yes. I want to see the files on the Cunningham brokerage case."

"Okay, sure. But remember, the stuff is supersecret. I'm not supposed to let those files out of my hands. If Shackley knew I turned them over to you, he'd have a shit fit."

"I'll take responsibility. Give me everything, including whatever you have on any of the other family activities, as well. You said there was information on the commercial real estate company, too, didn't you?"

"Yeah, some. Just be very careful with the material."

"I don't intend to pass it around," Ben said.

''Okay, be right back.'' The detective limped off toward his desk.

Ben rifled through the phone messages. One of them was from his zone commander, Michael Brennan, telling Ben to call. He picked up the phone and dialed the number, but the cop who answered told him the captain was out. Which was a good thing. Brennan would want to know what was going on, and Tolliver had no desire to be told again to let things rest.

Another of the calls had come from the medical examiner, Edgar Feldman. Ben returned that one next, and when the ME answered, Ben said, ''It's Tolliver, Ed. You come up with anything?''

''There was nothing under her nails, but I did find something else. What you might call a romantic footnote.''

''How so?''

''Just before her exit, the lady made love.''

''She what?''

''There was semen in her vaginal tract. When I looked at it under a microscope, some of the spermatazoa were still active.''

''I'll be damned.''

''Fascinating, right? Sort of a Romeo and Juliet ending. I knew you'd be pleased.''

''Any way of fixing the time? When it got there?''

''Come on, Ben. I'm only a genius, not a wizard. But I will say it probably wasn't long before she took her big jump. Maybe she found the guy a disappointing lover. Premature ejaculation, or something. You know how women are.''

''Have it analyzed, will you? I want the DNA.''

''It's already at the lab.''

''Good work.''

''A pleasure, Lieutenant.''

''Say, Ed?''

''Yes?''

''You plan to put this in your report?''

''Of course.''

''What if I asked you not to?''

''Sure, I could leave it out. If I wanted to lose my license. Which I don't. The One-seven has jurisdiction, so I have to send it up there. Anyway, the report's confidential, as you know.''

''Yeah, but things have a way of leaking. If what you told me got around, it could louse up my investigation. At the moment, there's only one other guy besides us who knows this."

"Meaning the one who deposited the semen."

"Exactly."

"I see what you mean. Look, how's this? I'll put it in the report, only I'll tuck it into a reference to the chemistry in her body, okay? That way, I can practically guarantee nobody will pick it up. That help you?"

"A lot. Thanks, Ed."

"What are friends for? Just remember, you owe me one."

"I sure do." Ben put the phone down and sat back in his chair, thinking about what the ME had told him.

Silk had had intercourse not long before she went off that terrace? For once, he wasn't dealing with conjecture. Or with conclusions based on hunches. What this almost surely meant was that she hadn't been alone in her apartment before she died.

But what else did it mean—that nothing about her death was what it seemed to be? Who had been there with her? Why would she have sex with him and then jump? Or was she pushed? Did her lover push her? Did someone else?

Supposedly she'd been writing an article about the senator. If that was true, where were her notes, and where was the manuscript?

Had the witnesses told the truth about what had happened in the senator's study that night? Apparently not; Tolliver had caught Silk in a lie about it. Had there been other lies?

What about the administrator, Ardis Merritt—had she lied, as well?

And the family—how much did they know? The signs of physical abuse on Silk's body—the bruises and the burns—where had they come from? Maybe the senator had put them there, but he certainly hadn't deposited the semen the ME found; by that time, he was already dead himself. Also under circumstances that might not be what they seemed.

Everywhere Ben looked, he saw only shadows.

Mulloy returned with an armful of thickly packed manila folders. He plopped the load down onto Tolliver's desk. "Be sure you keep this stuff locked up."

"I will."

"Anything you want more information on, just let me know.

Like I said, the ADAs are doing most of this, but I know everything that's going on."

"Okay, thanks." For a moment, Ben was tempted to tell him about the call from the medical examiner, but then he decided against it. As he'd said to Feldman, the fewer the people who knew about that, the better.

"The family is some outfit," Mulloy said. "It's one thing about all the good they do. But then when you start poking around in their business deals, it's a whole other thing."

"So I gather."

"Anything else?"

"Yeah, let me ask you something. You ever hear of an orkis?"

"Of a what?"

"An orkis. O-r-k-i-s."

Mulloy grinned. "What's this, a gag? It's a female dick, right? The thing in front?"

"That's a clitoris, Jack."

"Oh. Must be something else, then."

"It's not in the dictionary; I looked. So then I thought maybe it's somebody's name. But there's no listing for it in the phone book. Not in the Manhattan directory, or the ones for the other four boroughs."

"So what's the point?"

"I saw it written on a pad in Silk's kitchen when we were in her apartment."

"Damn, I missed that."

"The pad had that day's date printed on it. So she must have written it sometime before she jumped."

"Orkis, huh? Beats me."

"Still could be a name." Ben looked at the pile of material in front of him. "You never ran across it in any of the work that's been done on the Cunninghams?"

"Not that I remember. But I'll keep an eye out. Maybe I should check Albany's records and VICAP."

"Good idea. They might have something."

"Sure. About these files," Mulloy said.

"Yes?"

"Shackley's one of the top guns around here. But some of what you'll find is gonna make you curious. You might want to look into his approach. Okay?"

"Yeah, I'll bear that in mind. I'm sure I'll have questions later."

Mulloy left the office, and Ben picked up the first of the file folders. It would take hours to go through it all, but he wanted to get started. At least the material would give him insights into what the Cunningham family business was about.

As he began leafing through the investigator's reports, he thought once more of what Feldman had told him he'd found in Silk's body; and about what he'd seen when he watched the ME conduct the post-mortem—the bruises on her neck and shoulders—and about the burns Feldman said had most likely been made by someone pressing a lighted cigar against her flesh.

From the beginning of this assignment, only one person had claimed to know anything about the senator's sex life. And when she'd tried to talk to him about it, he told her to get lost.

Getting up from the desk, he went to his raincoat and dug out the card that had been given him by the TV reporter, Shelley Drake. Then he picked up the phone and called Drake's number at WPIC TV.

When she answered, he said, "Lieutenant Tolliver."

"Hello, Lieutenant. I was hoping I'd hear from you."

"I've been thinking over what you told me."

"That mean you accept my offer?"

"It means I'm willing to discuss it."

"Wonderful. I'll buy you a drink."

"Wrong."

"Don't you want to get together?"

"Yeah, but I'll buy. You're on Forty-second Street, right? See you at Christ Cella at six o'clock."

22

I'm sure there was a reaction," Peggy Demarest said. "I know there was. I saw it."

She was sitting in Dr. Chenoweth's office, feeling disappointed and frustrated. On successive days, she and the psychiatrist had spent hours with Jan in her room, but there had been no repetition of the response Jan had shown earlier.

Peggy twisted her fingers together. "You do believe me, don't you?"

"Of course I do," Chenoweth said. "And I take it as a very positive sign."

"But why would she go back into her shell afterward? She actually cried tears when I told her Senator Cunningham had died. But now each time I go to see her with you, it's as if nothing ever happened. She's just the same as always, sitting there not moving, not hearing anything we say to her."

"Let's be grateful that she did respond," Chenoweth said. "That's the first indication since she's been here that something might have gotten through to her."

"Yes, but here's another thing I thought of. Do you suppose it was the wrong kind of response? I mean, that by telling her something sad, all I did was make her worse? Cause her to withdraw even further? After all, when she heard about the senator's death, that must have been a shock."

"If she comprehended what you were saying, I'm sure it was."

"*If* she did? I'm telling you, it was when I talked about the senator dying that she cried. So she must have understood me. When I mentioned it the first time, I thought I saw a reaction, but I wasn't sure. Then I said it again, slowly, while I watched her. I said Senator Cunningham was dead. And that time, there was no mistaking that she heard. There were tears in her eyes. I got so excited, I ran down here right away, looking for you. You can imagine how I felt, can't you?"

"Of course I can."

"But now she's right back in that awful blank state again, as if she's in another world. Even when you mention the senator to her, it just doesn't register. Or if it does, she certainly doesn't give any indication that she understands."

"No, she doesn't."

"So isn't it possible that what I said to her might have had a bad effect? That maybe it would be better for her if I'd never said it?"

Chenoweth took a deep breath. "Peggy, let me be very frank with you. The answer to your question is that at this point, I don't know. There simply isn't enough to go on. But all my experience tells me that even though her reaction was one of sadness at hearing that news, we have to take it as a hopeful development. As far as the possibility of her withdrawing further as a result of this is concerned, I don't think that's very likely.''

''Then what do you think?''

''I think that what happened was, Jan responded because what you told her caused a strong jolt to her emotions. She probably had a great affection for Senator Cunningham, undoubtedly knew him quite well from the time she worked for the family. Therefore, when she learned he was dead, she reacted in the most natural way possible. She cried.''

Hearing this, Peggy felt tears form in her own eyes. She brushed them away. ''So you don't think it did her any harm to hear that?''

''No, I don't. I think we should only be encouraged. In a way, this was as if she was telling us to keep on working with her, to keep on trying. You see, sometimes a reaction to bad news can be stronger than hearing about something joyful. It can exert a deeper tug on the emotions, even in a healthy person. But the most important thing is, a sorrowful reaction is better than no reaction at all. Remember that.''

''I will,'' Peggy said. ''And I'm going to keep on talking to her about the Cunninghams. That was what triggered the response, so maybe it'll do the same thing again.''

''Good idea,'' Chenoweth said. ''It could have just the effect we're looking for. Although this time I'd suggest you try to steer clear of anything that might upset her. Meantime, I want to conduct some tests. There are ways we can measure response to mental stimuli, and that will enable us to determine the level of cognition. In other words, we'll have a better idea of whether she actually grasps what's being said to her. So go right on talking about the Cunninghams, but keep it upbeat.''

Peggy nodded. ''Fine, Doctor. I'll do that.''

23

Tolliver spent the rest of the afternoon struggling with the mountain of paper that had been collected in the files on the Cunningham investigation. He began by reading background material on the family's various enterprises, then moved on to the companies themselves.

Most of the data concerned the brokerage operation, but there was also information concerning the holding company, Cunningham Mining, and the family's real estate company, which was headed by the senator's daughter, Ingrid.

The reports on the brokerage, Cunningham Securities, were voluminous. They ranged from the history of the firm to accounts of its recent dealings, including detailed studies of trading activity.

Yet the more Ben read, the more baffled he became. There were clear signs of insider trading, most of it centering around mergers and acquisitions that involved a number of companies over the past two years. In each instance, Clay Cunningham and his clients had made millions of dollars when the deals were done.

But for all the investigators' efforts, none of the attempts to fix blame had been fruitful. Not so much as a single indictment had been achieved, either by federal prosecutors acting on recommendations of the SEC or by Shackley's group in the Manhattan district attorney's office.

Much of the investigation by both the feds and the New York prosecutors had focused on the lawyers representing the acquiring company and its prey, as well as on the management of Cunningham Securities. Despite court-ordered wiretaps and endless questioning of attorneys and stockbrokers, including Clay Cunningham himself, there was never enough evidence to take to a grand jury.

But certain events hoisted flags in Ben's head. In one situation, an associate in the law firm of Fowler, Patten, Callaway and Dugan had begun cooperating with investigators. This was after a deal in which Morris Frozen Foods had been swallowed by Grenzle, the giant conglomerate based in Geneva. Morris, listed on the New York Stock Exchange, had been trading at eleven before the action began. When its management folded eight weeks later, Grenzle paid forty-three dollars a share to take over the company.

Cunningham and several of his clients had begun buying Morris stock exactly one month before the first indication of Grenzle's intentions came to light. They made millions on the deal.

The lawyer who'd been induced to talk to the investigators was a thirty-three-year-old named Jonas Darment, who'd joined his firm as a clerk fresh out of Columbia Law School and who had twice been passed over as a candidate for partner. Darment had failed to explain why he'd been making visits to Liechtenstein, a tiny country in the

Alps where secrecy in banking laws was even tighter than those in Switzerland, or how he'd recently bought a Jaguar and a summer house in the Hamptons.

Unfortunately, prosecutors had been unable to pursue the matter further. The lawyer met with an accident while driving home to Scarsdale on the Hutchinson River Parkway, and a Westchester emergency squad had had to use acetylene torches to cut what was left of him out of the Jag.

In another instance, a broker employed by Cunningham Securities had drowned while vacationing in Maine. And a female assistant in the company had fallen from the platform of the Union Square IRT station one evening at rush hour, smack in front of the Lexington Avenue express.

On the surface, Shackley's team seemed to be pursuing the investigation vigorously. The stacks of manila folders on Tolliver's desk contained several thousand pages of security-transaction records, transcripts of interviews, investigators' reports, summary findings. But the bottom line was that for all the countless man-hours spent on the case, nothing positive had been accomplished. There'd been no arrests, no trials, no convictions.

The closest the prosecutors had come to tying possibly illegal activities to Cunningham Securities involved questioning two employees of the brokerage. But even that had fizzled. Nothing was ever proven, and both men had been fired by the firm. Follow-up interrogations had gone nowhere.

When Ben finished reading, he stood up and stretched. He still hadn't gone through everything, but he'd seen enough to understand why Mulloy was so frustrated. He opened his door and called the detective back into his office.

Mulloy sat in one of the visitor's chairs and fixed Tolliver in a steady gaze. "Well? You see what I mean?"

"I see it," Ben said, "but I can't explain it. Where was the DA while all this was going on?"

"You remember what I was telling you, about how he's a politician? Okay, that's your answer. Whenever you got a high-profile case, one that's getting a lot of attention in the media, that's where you'll see Oppenheimer. The thing with the judge who went nuts and tried to extort money from his girlfriend? The phony bank the Arabs were running? In one of those, he's all over the tube, all over the front page of the newspapers. But with something like this, he assigns a senior prosecutor and a bunch of ADAs and stays out of it—until it gets hot, if it ever does. Once there's a strong case and a chance for an indictment, then watch him lead the charge."

"Okay, but what's with Shackley? You look at this stuff and you have to wonder."

"Exactly. I told you it'd make you curious."

"And what about the feds? Why haven't they gotten anywhere?"

"They claim they've got the same problem, lack of evidence. But also, Oppenheimer holds 'em at arm's length. He's a master at defending his territory, as you might know."

Ben sat at his desk and gestured at the stack of folders. "From what I can see, there's plenty of evidence. What there's a lack of is substantiation. How do you explain these accidents happening to people who could be key witnesses?"

"I can't. But now let me ask you something, okay?"

"Sure, go ahead."

Mulloy reached behind him and swung the door shut. "How come you're messing around with this? It's not what you were brought in here for, right?"

"No, it's not. But I've got a gut feeling all of it ties together."

"What makes you think that?"

"First of all, I don't believe the senator died because he got old and his heart gave out—regardless of what he might have been doing with the Silk woman that night. And I don't believe Silk jumped, either. With two suspicious deaths and holdings worth hundreds of millions of dollars, there's got to be a connection someplace."

"You think both of them were homicides?"

"I think it's possible. Don't you?"

Mulloy looked at the ceiling and then back at Tolliver. "I don't know whether they were or not. But there's one thing I do know."

"Which is?"

"Which is, I'd give my soul to have this investigation go someplace. I've spent two years sitting on my ass—half cop, half clerk—and I've got nothing to show for it but that pile of crap in front of you. Personally, I think you're nuts to stick your neck out by getting into it, but if you're willing to do it, you got a friend for life."

Ben leaned forward, placing his elbows on his desk. "I'm willing, Jack, if you'll help me. What do you say?"

Mulloy nodded. ''I say let's go, Lieutenant. Whatever you need, you got it.''

''Good. Although I'd play it close if I were you. Brannigan's already told me you were swamped and that if I needed more help, he'd assign somebody else.''

''Fuck him,'' Mulloy said. ''What do you want me to do?''

''First, look for a pattern among the deals. See whether the same clients are benefiting each time. There may be some pooling of information going on. Meantime, I want to keep studying this material. There are questions I have about some of the figures. When I finish, we'll talk.''

''Okay, great. Any way I can help, just say the word.''

''I will.''

''You met Shackley yet?''

''Yeah, this morning in Brannigan's office. I plan to take a hard look at how he operates.''

''Okay, but remember Mulloy's law.''

''About not getting shit on your shoes?''

''That's the one. Watch yourself. Shackley has friends in high places.''

''I'll be careful.''

Mulloy stood up. He turned to go, then turned back. ''Say, Ben?''

''Yeah?''

''Thanks. I haven't felt this good in a long time.'' He left the office.

Tolliver worked on, making notes on the figures involving the deals. He borrowed a calculator and ran the figures, checking and rechecking them. He also called several publicly traded brokerages for information on their operating costs so he'd have a basis for comparison. The deeper he went into the situation, the more puzzling it seemed.

Suddenly, he realized it had gotten dark outside. At least his window could reveal that much. He glanced at his watch, then shoveled the papers and his notes back into the folders and locked the files in a drawer of his desk. He'd have to hurry to keep his date with the reporter.

24

Jack Mulloy was elated. He felt even better than he'd let on to Tolliver. Having the lieutenant come into the case was a real break, more than he'd ever hoped for. Now things would really begin to jump.

Driving home over the Brooklyn Bridge, he tuned in WNEW and sang along with Linda Rondstadt on ''Blue Bayou.'' Beautiful, especially when she went up for that high note at the end. Mulloy didn't try to stay with her then; he knew if he did, he'd pop his vocal cords.

Hearing the record reminded him of the days when he was a young cop in a patrol car, full of piss and vinegar and proud to have joined the thin blue line that stood between the city and the forces of evil.

But that was before he began to realize how many of his fellow officers were on the pad. Some guys were making more on bribes and payoffs in a month than they could on a policeman's salary in a year.

Mulloy's partner in those days was a veteran named Mike Zabriskie who'd been busted down from sergeant twice and was now simply putting in his time until he retired. Mike was the guy responsible for Mulloy's education.

Zabriskie allowed that most cops were basically honest, and, in fact, some of them wouldn't take anything even if it fell in their laps. Those were the Boy Scouts, Mike said, and in his opinion they were assholes. After them came the guys who took only nickel-and-dime stuff, freebies like a sandwich and a cup of coffee, or maybe a bag of fruit. They were suckers, too.

But then there were cops who took because they were smart. So brazen that they made it a business, and they were the ones who cleaned up. They didn't wait for the money to come their way; they went after it.

From that point on, Mulloy learned of schemes that were highly profitable, and often ingenious. He'd personally known a number of cops who worked stolen goods. Some of it they fenced for burglars, some they appropriated from collars. And some of it they stole themselves, from stores, warehouses, private homes. The best organized among them was a ring that had its own storage lockers, right off Ditmars Boulevard in Queens. They'd take anything—TVs, jewelry, fur coats. If the merchandise had value, they grabbed it.

Another group Mulloy knew of ran a car-theft operation in the Bronx. They had teenagers working for them who hot-wired cars and drove them into a chop shop not far from Yankee Stadium. The shop was owned by the brother-in-law of one of the cops. Once inside, the cars would be cut up and sold for parts. Or else the serial numbers would be changed, the bodies would be painted different colors, and then they'd be sold and shipped elsewhere, some of them as far as South America.

Whores also paid. Not just the poor, broken-down street bitches or the kids who got off buses from Minneapolis and Milwaukee with their blond hair and their stupidity, easy meat for black pimps looking to build their stables. Cops took from them, too, but that wasn't where the big money was. The real bread was in the houses and the escort services and the call-girl networks. That was the industry, and the people who ran it bribed police officers in droves.

Gambling was also lucrative. So were loan-sharking and union racketeering. Every one of those activities needed police protection of one kind or another.

And then there was drugs. Which made everything else seem paltry. There were cops who didn't merely live well off narcotics but who became rich. Nick Feracci and Mike Halloran, to name just two. Or Joey Esposito, who now owned a big house in Miami and drove a Mercedes.

In fact, police officers could rake in more money from drugs than from any other source—while they were using the shit themselves, living like kings, with all the broads they could handle.

Not that some cops weren't brought down from time to time. Dismissed from the force, even imprisoned. Which could be a death sentence. A former New York City police officer sent to Attica or Elmira had only a slim chance of making it to parole. More likely, the COs would find him in the shower with his throat cut, or with a shank buried in his skull.

But that was something else you learned: Nothing in life was free.

So by and large, Mulloy had resisted temptation. He took, but nothing big. Only what was due him, more or less, in return for what he was giving the civilians. A few bucks here and there, a turkey, a bottle of whiskey.

The rationalization was easy. As a cop, you went out there and put your life on the line every day. For that, they paid you less than a garbage collector, less than a school janitor—while the civilians sneered at you and thought of you as their enemy.

Meantime, his wife complained about every aspect of their lives, from their lousy little house in Flatbush to his miserable income, grousing that it wasn't enough for one person to live on, let alone a married couple with a child. Why the hell didn't he quit the cops? Ethel wanted to know. Get into something with a future, like her sister Jean's husband, Harry Hunsacker. Harry had his own TV-repair business. They owned a nice house in Oceanside and Harry was getting them a maid.

There was one other thing Mulloy would like to see Harry get: cancer.

But for all his problems, things hadn't gone too badly in Mulloy's career as a police officer. He loved being a detective, loved wearing the sharp suits he bought at Rothman's, loved carrying the gold shield. He'd won himself a number of citations and twice had killed people in the line of duty.

The first time was when he and a partner had gone to a fifth-floor walk-up on 117th Street to question a woman about the whereabouts of her boyfriend, who was wanted for boosting dresses from shops on Madison Avenue.

The guy had a clever MO, Mulloy thought. He wore neatly pressed blue coveralls that had the logo of an electrician on them and carried a large toolbox. He'd tell the proprietor the landlord had sent him, and when nobody was watching, he'd pack the toolbox with merchandise and walk out.

The woman who came to the door was nursing a baby. She couldn't have been more than eighteen, with skin the color of brown sugar and her hair done up in cornrows, really quite pretty. She told the cops she hadn't seen her boyfriend in two weeks.

They were about to leave when Mulloy's partner, Ed Gillotti, noticed a metal box sitting on the floor next to a sofa. He pointed to it. "What's that?"

"What's what?"

"On the floor there."

"Linoleum."

"I mean the box. What is it?"

"I dunno."

"You got a toolbox in your apartment and you don't know what it is?"

She made no reply, but Mulloy noticed her breathing had picked up a little.

"Mind if we have a look?" Gillotti said.

She started to protest, but they pushed past her. The room was a mess, with bits of clothing and newspapers scattered about, a bottle of Ripple and two glasses standing on a table. There was an ashtray on the table as well, with a roach still smoldering in it.

Gillotti went over to the box and squatted beside it. "This thing is locked. You got a key?"

She shook her head defiantly. "No. Get the fuck outta here."

Mulloy glanced about. There was a tiny kitchen off this room and beside the entrance to it was a closed door. "What's in there?" he asked.

"Nothin'. I told you motherfuckers to get out!"

Gillotti straightened up. "Think I'll just take a peek."

The girl's chest was really moving now, heaving with each breath. Mulloy drew his snub-nosed Colt as Gillotti stepped over the box and reached toward the door.

What happened next was a blur. The door burst open and a tall, skinny black man charged into the room, howling at the top of his lungs and swinging a machete. Gillotti went over backward, tripping on the toolbox and falling heavily to the floor. The blade missed his face by an inch.

Mulloy didn't think; he shot. Six times. The first round caught the guy in the chest and straightened him up, the second and third spun him around and knocked him down. The last three went in as he lay there, but they were unnecessary; he was already dead.

Afterward, Mulloy was put on restricted duty while the case was perfunctorily presented to a grand jury and he was perfunctorily exonerated. Some schmuck of an ADA made noises about violation of the woman's Fourth Amendment rights, but nothing ever came of it. Then in a ceremony at One Police Plaza, the commissioner pinned a decoration on Mulloy's chest.

Best of all, he got thirty-six seconds on the evening news. He had a video of the newsbreak showing him answering questions put to him by a reporter as he left the scene of the shooting, and for years afterward, he'd pop it into the VCR, usually when he'd had a few bombs.

Jack Mulloy, a brave officer whose quick thinking in the face of danger saved his partner's life. Hot shit.

The second time he used his gun in combat hadn't been nearly as satisfying. It had been the opposite, in fact, because it marked the beginning of the end of his career.

The scene was a tenement in Spanish Harlem, a burned-out hulk where dealers operated a druggies' flea market. It wasn't even Mulloy's operation. He'd gotten mixed up in it because he was working on a homicide out of Midtown South and a tip had come in on a guy wanted in the case. The suspect was a Dominican, part of the crew that did business in the building. The cops raided the place and Mulloy went along.

Ordinarily, he would have stayed as far away as possible. Dealers sometimes got high on their own wares, and there was nothing worse than some wild-assed Hispanic who'd been running dope in his arm. Even clean, they were bad enough.

But the taste of glory had been wonderful the first time, and it had also been years since he'd made a big score. He was sure that this one could bump him up a grade, which would mean more money and maybe even another spot on TV. Worth it.

But it wasn't.

The thing was a total fuckup, from the minute the cops went in. They were all in vests and helmets, some of them carrying shields; heavily armed with pistols and shotguns. The trouble was, so were the bad guys.

Mulloy was on the ground floor, behind the others. He was wearing a vest but carrying nothing but the Colt. His plan was to wait for the action to die down and then claim his man if the suspect was there.

Instead, he was caught in a crossfire, deafened by the roar of gunshots, cordite burning his nostrils, his eyes filled with tears from the thick smoke. He fired his pistol at a dim form and the target went down. Mulloy stepped back, and that was when he went through the floor.

For an instant, he was weightless, floating in the darkness. Then came the tremendous shock as he hit.

The pain was incredible. He was in the cellar, lying on his back in a pool of filthy water, and somebody was screaming. After a time, he realized the cries were his own, and he clamped his jaws together to shut off the sound. From above him came the rattle of more gunfire. He put his hand down onto his right leg and felt torn cloth, touched the jagged ends of bone. After that he passed out.

This time, he didn't make TV. He spent four months in Bellevue and over the following year underwent two lengthy operations to repair the damage to his leg. By the time he was able to hobble around, the shoot-out had long been forgotten, at least by the public and the media. Other drug busts had taken place, other shootings had occurred, other perpetrators had been killed. Mulloy did pick up another citation, but he stayed in grade.

That was when he'd made his decision. He turned down a generous job offer from his brother-in-law, the prick, and moved into a rubber-gun assignment in the DA's office. Because the way he saw it, being half a detective was better than being none at all.

And now? He couldn't believe his good fortune. This guy Tolliver had come out of nowhere. The lieutenant was a straight arrow, with a big rep—a tough cop who wouldn't be pushed around by Captain Brannigan or Fletcher Shackley or anyone else. Not only was he looking into the deaths of the senator and the Silk woman, but he was also determined to dig deep into the Cunningham investigation and to root out the answers.

Tolliver was smart, too. He'd already put his finger on a number of key questions concerning the brokerage.

Would Mulloy help? Goddamn right he would. It'd be risky, of course—Brannigan would destroy him if what he was doing came to light. But what an opportunity. If he played it right, he could be rolling again.

The Dead were on now, doing "Sugar Magnolia." Mulloy sang along with that one, too, suddenly realizing he was almost home.

25

The trip uptown was worse than during midday because it was now rush hour—which was a misnomer: The traffic crawled. Nevertheless, Tolliver arrived at Christ Cella before Shelley Drake did, taking a seat at the small bar and ordering bourbon on the rocks.

This was a man's joint, and he wondered whether that had been a subconscious reason for his choosing it. The restaurant had bare wood floors, dark walls, snotty waiters, and the best steaks in New York. But the food wasn't important; he'd have a drink with the reporter, find out whether she could tell him anything of value, and leave.

When she showed up, however, his attitude eased—considerably. As she checked the trench coat, he saw that instead of one of the business suits she'd invariably worn when he saw her on TV, she had on a frilly blue dress that hugged her body and revealed gentle curves. Her face seemed softer, too, the blue of the dress complementing her eyes. She joined him at the bar, saying she'd have whatever he was drinking.

Evidently, she made an impression on some of the other patrons, as well. Men stared as they recognized her, taking in the familiar mane of honey blond hair and the wide mouth. Tolliver didn't blame them; she'd stand out anywhere, on or off the tube. He told the bartender to bring her a Jack Daniel's over ice.

When the drink was placed in front of her, she raised her glass. "Cheers. I'm glad we could get together. May I call you Ben?"

"Sure."

"I'm Shelley."

They touched glasses and drank.

"I told you I could give you some valuable information," she said.

"We'll see."

"Hey, come on. You made your feelings clear the first time we talked. You thought I was just out to make the story on the senator as sensational as I possibly could. But that's not true."

"No?"

"No, it isn't. I want the facts on all this as much as you do."

"Then what is it you can tell me?"

"First, what about my offer? If I can help you with your investigation, will you give me stuff in return?"

"Hey, you know how it works. The department has its own public-information unit. And the rule is, everybody in the media gets the same material at once. If it ever got out that I had a side deal with a reporter, I'd be patrolling the beach on Coney Island."

"Yes, but nobody needs to know about it. I promise it'll stay between us. So will you give me things, if what I tell you turns out to be valuable? That's fair, isn't it—quid pro quo?"

"Maybe."

"Then we have a deal?"

"It depends on what you've got. And here's the kicker. If I do give you anything, you're not to break it unless I say so."

She chewed her lower lip, thinking about it. Finally, she nodded. "Agreed."

"So what do you have?"

"Remember what I said that day in your car, about the senator's weird sex habits?"

"That's why I'm here."

"Okay. The way this got started was, I had a tip. On Senator Cunningham and his involvement with Jessica Silk. Everybody knew his reputation as a womanizer, so I talked my news editor into letting me work on an exposé. I went to the offices in the foundation, said I wanted to do a story on the senator. But I never could get to talk to him. His secretary gave me a runaround, kept fobbing me off on the administrator."

"Ardis Merritt."

"Right. Merritt was polite enough, but she wouldn't let me near Cunningham, either. Every time I went there, she said she'd be happy to answer my questions, give me any information I needed."

"So what you had was nothing."

"That's what my editor said. I had to fight like hell to keep going on it. The thing was about to get canned when the senator died. But the minute I heard he was with Silk at the time, I knew for sure there was something there. It still wasn't anything solid, but what saved it was the notoriety surrounding his death. And now Silk's dead, too. Which makes me all the more sure."

"What was the tip you had?"

"It came from a writer I know. She'd heard Silk was not only having an affair with the senator but at the same time she was also working on a dynamite story about his abusing young women. He didn't realize what she was up to, of course. I thought, Wow, wouldn't that be a shocker? That's why I went to my editor and got him to let me go back to work on it."

"What did you know about Silk?"

"Only what I'd heard in the business. She had a reputation not just for writing juicy stories about well-known people but for putting herself into the situation."

"Making the news as well as writing it."

"Right. *Vanity Fair* loved her. So did *New York* magazine. Did you see the article she wrote on the William Kennedy Smith rape trial?"

"No, what about it?"

"She went to Palm Beach and got herself involved with that crowd of yo-yos who hung around Au Bar and Bradley's. She was sleeping with one of them while she was writing the piece. Supposedly, it was in Palm Beach that she first met the senator. The family has a winter home there."

"And that's why you figured the story on her and the senator could be true."

"Yes. I don't know what went on in his office that night, but I'd bet my life it wasn't what the family said."

"Ardis Merritt claims she was in the office, too, at the time. That would make her the only one still alive who actually saw what happened."

"You think she told the truth?"

"I don't know."

"Neither do I. But I think it was all just a cover-up, concocted by the family to shield the old man."

"That's possible." Shelley Drake was turning out to be not only beautiful but smart. He decided to let her in a little further on what he'd learned. "There were some holes in Merritt's story, and in Silk's."

"Like what?"

"They said that when Cunningham was stricken, they loosened his clothing to get him some air."

"Okay, so? Oh wait—I get it. Maybe what they actually were

doing wasn't loosening his clothes but trying to get them back on. Right?''

''Exactly.''

Shelley continued to stare at him for a few seconds, then raised her gaze to a point somewhere above his head.

''Forget it,'' Ben said.

''Forget what?''

''Doing anything with that.''

''Yeah, but—''

''But nothing. I can't prove it. And that's been the whole problem with this, from the beginning. No proof.''

''It fits, though. No wonder the family wanted to hush it up.''

''Uh-huh.''

She was looking at him with those large, serious blue eyes. ''So what do you think, Lieutenant?''

Ben drained his glass. ''I think we better have another drink, and then I'm going to buy you a steak.''

26

They sat upstairs, at a corner table. The room was just as gloomy as the ones on the first floor, but apparently the customers didn't mind. They seemed to take the restaurant's less-is-more attitude in stride, putting up with the dingy decor and the quaint no-menu service as long as the slabs of beef were the thickest and juiciest you could find in the city. The ratio of men to women was about three to one, and Tolliver began to wish he'd suggested a place with less of a saloonlike atmosphere.

The lack of grace didn't appear to bother Shelley, however. She waded into her medium-rare sirloin with baked potato and broccoli au gratin like a starved lumberjack. ''Amazing, isn't it,'' she said, ''that the senator could be getting away with it? An important public figure like him?''

''Not so amazing,'' Ben replied. ''If it's true. People with money and political power often decide they can make up their own rules.''

''Good point. As a matter of fact, look at what's been going on in Washington. Not only were a bunch of those characters forcing themselves on women but Congress actually passed a law exempting its members from being accused of sexual harassment."

"Sure. Their attitude is, they don't work for the government, they own it. But that's not where Cunningham developed his habits, if what you're speculating is correct."

"No, it has to go back a lot further than that. From what I've read, there are two schools of thought as to just how far."

"Freud, and the geneticists."

"Which side are you on?"

"Both. You care for some wine?"

"I'd love some."

Ben signaled a waiter, and when the man came to their table, he ordered a bottle of Burgundy.

After the waiter had departed, Shelley said, "You're on both sides? Now you're the one who sounds like a politician."

"Maybe I do, but there's plenty of evidence that genes have more to do with sex than just determining whether we're male or female. They also influence sexuality—whether we turn out to be straight, gay, or psychopathic. The genes provide the raw material, which has to be there first. And then environmental factors influence the direction we follow after that. So Freud was also right. But it takes both."

"Then you can imagine what traits the senator inherited and what kind of upbringing he had."

Ben thought of the background material he'd read. "I don't know much about that, except that his grandfather started the family fortune. The Colonel was one of the robber barons, along with people like Jay Gould and John D. Rockefeller and Cornelius Vanderbilt. He cheated people out of their deeds on gold and silver mines in Colorado, and then he came to New York and bought acres of Manhattan real estate. That's why the holding company is still called Cunningham Mining Corporation."

"Fascinating."

"Isn't it? He was one of the biggest slumlords in the city at one time."

"Is that so?"

"Sure. After he bought all that land he owned in Manhattan, he put up tenements, tracts of them. They were terrible places, many even without plumbing. Then he packed the buildings full of immigrants, with whole families living in one or two rooms. He charged them exorbitant rents, but they couldn't complain, because there was no one to complain to. No rent commission existed, and everybody in the administration was for sale."

"And that's what the real estate company grew out of?"

"Right. Eventually, all the tenements were sold off at tremendous profits because of the value of the land. Some of the money went into other developments, mostly office towers. And the profits from those operations are what funded projects like the Manhattan Medical Center. The Cunningham PR machine is always beating the drum about how wonderful the family was to build it, but what they don't mention is that as a private hospital, it's free to make as much money as possible. So it's always been a cash cow, and now more than ever. If you've followed what's been going on with medical costs, you know they've gone through the roof."

Shelley shook her head. "I think it's all amazing. When you dig into the Cunninghams, you find so many skeletons. The family is nothing like what they'd have you believe. There've been stories about every one of them."

"Such as?"

"Such as Clay, the senator's son. He's been in a string of scandals, but the senator's influence kept most of them quiet. His first wife divorced him years ago. Now he's married to Laura Bentley, the actress."

"Yes, I know."

"His sister, Ingrid, who runs the real estate company? When she was a student at Foxcroft, she ran away with a guy twice her age. The old man tracked her down and then sent her to Switzerland, supposedly to a private school, but I hear it was actually a sanitarium. She's been married three times, and the first two ended in very messy divorces. Her current husband is a con man who calls himself a financier. He skipped out of Munich after running a Ponzi scheme on investors."

"I'm familiar with him, too. What do you know about the senator's widow, Claire?"

"Heavy drinker . . . but then, all of them are. She was married to someone else when the senator first knew her. Supposedly, she was after his money. Altogether, the Cunninghams make quite a group."

"Just your typical all-American family."

"It's a little different from their image, isn't it? Even now, most people have no idea about what they're really like—or what the truth about the senator was.''

The waiter returned with the wine, and as he opened the bottle and poured some for Tolliver to taste, Ben thought about what Shelley had told him. It was true; even after his death, Cunningham was protected by his power and his wealth.

When their glasses had been filled and the waiter again left them, Ben said, ''But whatever has gone on in the past is nothing compared with what's coming up. With the old man dead, there'll be a struggle to get control of the family fortune. No matter how the senator's will locks money up in trusts, they'll all be at each other's throats.''

''No doubt.''

He thought again of what he'd seen in the files. ''What else do you know?''

''That's about it. Getting anything more than public information on the family is tough. It's like there's a wall around them.''

''So I've seen.''

''They've got their own security force, you know. Headed by a man named Evan Montrock.''

''I've met him.''

''From what I could learn, they have an estate on Long Island. The family goes out there on weekends, although Ingrid spends most of her time in Connecticut at her horse farm.''

''But Clay and Laura usually go to the house on Long Island?''

''Right. And Claire, of course. The place is huge, from what I can gather. I'd love to know what goes on out there, but Montrock and his troops keep people from getting near it.''

''Where is it?''

''Way out, in a small town called Farmington. Ever been in that area?''

''I don't think so.''

''Senator Cunningham grew up on the estate, spent all his boyhood there, except for when he was away at school. Which is another odd thing. For all his time in the public eye, it's still hard to learn much about what his early life was like.''

''I understand his father died when he was quite young.''

''Both parents did. According to the obit that was in the *Times,* they were skiing in Austria, got caught in a spring avalanche. Clayton was their only son. He was eleven at the time. After that, the Colonel raised him."

The waiter was back to refill their glasses. When they were alone again, Shelley said, "Now tell me what you've found out about Jessica Silk's death. You really believe she committed suicide?"

He sidestepped the question. "What else could it have been?"

"Maybe somebody didn't want that story of hers to get out."

A series of impressions flashed through Ben's mind: the absence of material on the article Silk had been writing, the marks he'd seen on her body when he went to the morgue, what the ME said he'd discovered in the postmortem.

Shelley was watching him. "Well? Couldn't somebody have given her a push?"

He sliced into his steak. It was so tender he could have cut it with a fork. "No evidence of anything like that."

She was too bright to let it go by. "Come on, Lieutenant. This is a two-way street."

"Who says so?"

"I do. How can I help you if you don't trust me enough to tell me everything?"

"Everything? That wasn't our agreement."

"But that's what I want. It has to be like that if it's really going to work. Come on, what did you find out about how she died?"

"The doorman said no one had gone to her apartment. When the police got there, the door was locked."

She drank some more of her wine. "This is delicious."

"Glad you like it."

"Did you go to the autopsy?"

He looked at her and shook his head in wonderment. "You're too much."

"Is that a compliment?"

"I guess so."

"Good. Now what did you learn?"

He had to smile. She was showing more intelligence than any of the detectives who'd conducted the investigation, and more drive. None of them had spotted the abrasions and burns on Silk's body at the site of her fall and they hadn't bothered to attend the postmortem. Maybe Shelley could be useful, at that. He decided to test her a little. "Anything I tell you is in absolute confidence?"

"So help me."

"There were some marks on her that weren't the result of her falling."

"What kind of marks?"

"Bruises that might have been from rough sex."

Shelley put her fork down. "Then what I'd heard about the senator was true, wasn't it? He put those marks there. They were having sex and he was knocking her around."

"Maybe."

"Maybe again? How can you sit there and say that?"

He leaned forward. "Because I'm a cop. In your business, you can get away with saying almost anything. But in mine, I have to have indisputable proof—evidence that will be accepted by a prosecutor, so he can use it to convince a grand jury to bring an indictment. No matter what I think went on, I don't have evidence. A hunch isn't good enough."

"But that's what you think, isn't it? You just said it was."

"So? Whatever occurred between Silk and the senator, it could have been consensual, nevertheless."

"Sure, but it's still all the more reason to be suspicious of how she died. And you haven't answered my question. Isn't it possible that she didn't jump off her balcony, that somebody shoved her?"

"I told you, we don't have any proof of that, either."

"Nothing to suggest that's what happened?"

Ben looked at her. If he told her about the burns or the semen the ME had found in Silk's body, she'd probably leap up and start hollering. "I said there was no proof."

"Okay, I get the message."

"But now let me ask you something. You ever hear of someone named Orkis?"

"Orkis? No, but it sounds sort of familiar. Who is it?"

"I don't know."

"Somebody connected to what you're working on?"

"I don't know that, either. It's possible."

"Offhand, the name doesn't ring any bells. But if I run across it anywhere, I'll tell you."

"Good."

"How does it figure in this?"

"You want some dessert?"

"You're trying to change the subject again, aren't you?"

"Sure. Do you?"

"Yes, but I'm not going to have any. That's another thing about my job. If I don't stay in shape, I lose it."

"How about some coffee, then?"

"Fine."

"We can have it at my place, if that's okay with you." He didn't know why he'd said it; he hadn't planned to, and he wasn't trying to make a move on her. It had just popped out.

But then she made him glad he'd offered. She smiled and said, "That sounds lovely."

27

Hey, I really like this," Shelley said. She was standing at the windows in Ben's apartment, looking down at the South Street Seaport. The night had turned cold and a brisk autumn wind was blowing, but throngs of people were strolling in the area, visiting the shops and the bars and the restaurants. There were lights on the docks and the ancient sailing ships and more lights twinkled from the spidery cables of the Brooklyn Bridge and from the buildings on the far side of the East River.

Ben came out of the kitchen, carrying two china mugs of coffee. "I like it, too. Should be downright homey, if I ever get it furnished."

She took a mug from him and looked around at the living room. "You could use some help, at that."

"You volunteering?"

"Sure, if you want me to."

"Okay, what would you do?"

She studied the plain white walls, the blocky green sofa he'd bought on sale at Bloomingdale's, the bench he was using for a coffee table, the fake Persian rug. "For one thing, I'd get rid of that sofa."

"That would leave no place in here to sit down."

"Buy some new stuff first. When it's delivered, have them haul that one away."

"I don't have time to do a lot of shopping."

"I said I'd help, right? You give me the word, I'll do the shopping for you. New York is full of bargains, if you know where to find them. I could make this place look sensational, and it wouldn't cost much at all."

"You mean it?"

"Sure. If your girlfriend wouldn't get jealous."

He grinned. "That a probe?"

"Of course."

"I don't have a girlfriend. That is, I have some friends, but I'm not involved with anybody special. Are you?"

"No. I was, for a while. With a VP of the company that owns the station. But there was a problem."

"Which was?"

"He was cheating on me. We weren't even married yet, and he had all these things going on the side. I'd be doing the eleven o'clock news and he'd be doing something else. Took me a year to catch on. Pretty stupid, huh?"

Ben stood beside her and looked out at the river. The lights from the buildings and the bridge were reflecting from the fast-moving black waters. "Happens sometimes. At least you found out in time."

"Yeah, but even then I didn't want to believe it. I should have known better. He kept telling me he'd reform, if only I'd give him another chance."

"So you gave him one?"

"I gave him lots of them. It just made him more careful, or more inventive. I finally came to my senses, and then he left for a job at NBC. That was the end of it."

"And now you're sadder but wiser."

"I'm not sad. Wiser, maybe, but not sad. Were you ever married?"

"Nope. The ladies I've known all got tired of my lifestyle in a hurry. Crazy hours, too much pressure."

"Sounds like broadcasting."

"Does it?"

"Uh-huh. For every Paula Zahn, there are all the nameless nobodies like me. We break our buns hoping for the big break, but then in a couple of years we burn out."

"Is it that bad?"

"Watch the tube. We come and go, in case you haven't noticed. Management's position is, they have to give the audience fresh faces."

"So why stick with it?"

"Because I'm determined, that's why. I don't quit."

"So I've seen."

"Touché, Lieutenant."

He went over to the sofa and sat down, while she stayed at the window for a few more moments, looking out at the lights. Then she joined him, kicking off her shoes and curling her legs under her. "At least this thing is comfortable."

"That's why I bought it. How's your coffee—need a refill?"

"No thanks, this is fine."

It was funny, but she was turning out to be the direct opposite of what he'd thought the first time he'd seen her. She was strong-minded and persistent, but she was also straightforward, honest about herself, not afraid to admit her mistakes. Didn't waste time feeling sorry for herself, either.

"Did you grow up in New York, Ben?"

"Oh yeah. Born here. My father died when I was a baby. We lived in the Bronx, not far from Yankee Stadium. I used to dream of playing there, but the closest I ever got was selling popcorn in the bleachers."

"You were a baseball player?"

"Uh-huh. An outfielder. When I realized I'd never be able to hit a big-league curveball, I adjusted my ambitions."

She finished her coffee and put the mug down on the bench coffee table. "To becoming a police officer?"

"Yes. My mother died while I was in the Marine Corps. When I got out, I went into the Academy."

"But you went to college, too, didn't you? You didn't learn all that stuff about genetics and psychological development just by reading."

"NYU. On a catch-as-catch-can basis, mostly at night. Took me eight years to get a degree."

"Must have been a grind."

"It was."

"But worth it, right?"

"I hope so. How about you? You're not a New Yorker, are you?"

"Lord, no—I'm a real hayseed. Came here from Haven, Kansas. Bet you never heard of it."

"True."

"It's about sixty miles northwest of Wichita. My father owns a drugstore there. I have one sister, who's married with three kids and living in Salina. That's an exciting place, too."

"I'll bet."

"In some ways, I envy her. She's married to a dentist who has a successful practice. She's very happy."

"You wish you were married to a dentist?"

She smiled. "You know what I mean. I wish I was happy. Or contented, I should say."

"What would that take?"

"Same thing most people want most—fulfillment. I'd like to do something worthwhile in television, be more than just one more blonde doing news spots on a local station. Maybe have a program of my own. Have guests on but deal with subjects worth talking about."

"So a successful career would fulfill you?"

"Partly. But I want to make something good out of my personal life, as well."

"Such as a husband and kids?"

"Absolutely. My memories of my own childhood are great. My parents got along well, which was a rarity."

"She must have given him a long leash."

"Spoken like a true chauvinist. But I'll admit it, she did. At least she didn't mind when he went off with his buddies a couple of times a year on fishing trips or hunting deer or pheasant."

"So long as that was all he hunted."

She laughed. "That's right."

He was quiet for a time. Sitting here with her, the two of them relaxed and comfortable, was more than just pleasant. He was conscious of her closeness, of the animal attraction he felt coming from her. She was beautiful and sexy and he liked her very much. And from what he could tell, she seemed to respond to him the same way.

Yet he didn't want to make a pass at her. He wondered why. Probably because he felt she might rebuff him, and that would cheapen whatever existed between them, turn it into something else before it ever had a chance to get started. The truth was, he was sick of one-night stands, relationships with women that were based on sex and not much else.

He put his mug down. "I have a bottle of brandy, if you'd like some."

"No thanks. I've had enough to drink for one evening."

"Speaking of the eleven o'clock news, do you have to get back?"

"No, I'm off tonight." She looked at him. "If I tell you something, I hope you won't get the wrong idea about me."

"I won't. What is it?"

The blue eyes were very steady. "I like you a lot, Ben. And I don't want to leave here tonight. I'd love it if you asked me to stay."

He felt like a kid on Christmas morning, maybe even better than that. Taking her into his arms, he said, "I was worried you'd get the wrong idea, too."

She smiled. "I think it's the right idea. We're on the same team, aren't we?"

"We are now," he said.

28

In the morning, Ben woke up feeling wonderful. Better than he had in weeks. He was alone in his bed, but a tantalizing aroma of coffee was drifting in from the kitchen, which meant Shelley had been busy. He got up and went into the bathroom. After brushing his teeth and splashing cold water on his face, he put on a robe and followed his nose to the coffee.

A fresh-brewed pot was sitting on the counter. But to his disappointment, he saw that she'd left the apartment. A note on the refrigerator said she had work to do and would call him later. The note was signed, "Your partner in crime."

He yawned and looked at his watch. Christ—after eight o'clock. Sleeping this late was another thing he hadn't done in a long time. He had a quick mug of the coffee and after that he showered, shaved, and dressed.

Back in the kitchen, he poured himself another mugful and, while he drank it, thought about what his next moves should be, continuing to run over the case in his mind. Clay Cunningham was high on the list of people he wanted to talk to further, and so was the sister, Ingrid. He wasn't through with Ardis Merritt, either.

There was also something strange about the brokerage investigation, and not merely that the prosecutors hadn't come up with proof of what was obviously illegal trading. Ben was no CPA, but he'd taken courses in finance and accounting, and he was curious about the numbers. When he'd checked through them, he found they raised more questions than they answered. He made a mental note to take another hard look.

Then he rinsed out the mug and the pot and left the apartment. He'd catch up with some breakfast later.

There was a garage in the basement of the building, which was a good thing—leave a car on the street and you might never see it again, even though this area was better than a lot of others. He took the elevator down to the garage, got into the Taurus, and drove to the Criminal Justice Building. The trip took less than fifteen minutes.

When he walked into the investigators' area, Jack Mulloy was already at work. The detective jumped up and followed Ben into his office.

"You seen the papers?" Mulloy asked.

Ben took off his coat and hung it on the wall hook, then sat at his desk. "No, why?"

"Today's story on the senator is on page five. Another couple days and it'll be gone altogether."

"Fame is fleeting, Jack. You get a reply on Orkis?"

Mulloy took one of the visitor's chairs. "Albany didn't have anything; neither did VICAP. But I'll keep looking. Right now, I'm tabulating copies of trading confirmations from the brokerage. How'd you make out with the files?"

"Okay, but the more I see, the more I wonder. Cunningham Securities has made profits that weren't just big, they were obscene. Yet a large part of that money was swallowed up, fell in a black hole. Let me show you what I mean."

Ben unlocked a drawer in his desk and took out the stack of files. He laid out sheets on which he'd penciled figures, and Mulloy came around the desk and peered over his shoulder.

"I ran the numbers on the amounts involved in the acquisitions and then I went through the company's financials. According to the statements, the company's core business is in two areas. One is the buying and selling of securities, option contracts, futures, and mutual funds, for both individual and institutional clients. The income from that business is commissions. Correct, so far?"

"Sure. Go on."

"The other area is investment banking, which entails direct investment and underwriting. Plus arbitrage. That's where the acquisition deals were made and where the bulk of the company's profits came from. Total revenues were just over eight hundred million last year. Deduct operating expenses and the brokerage showed a pretax profit of two hundred twenty million." He pointed. "Net earnings were a hundred fourteen million bucks."

"Also right. So?"

"I spoke to several publicly traded brokerage houses. Merrill Lynch, Morgan Stanley, some others. I took the figures they gave me and compared them to Cunningham's. What I found was that Cunningham's profits were more than twice the average, as a percentage of revenues."

"Okay, but we already know the reasons for it. Our problem is not being able to prove it."

"Very true. But it also occurred to me that if we knew where that money wound up, it might lead us to something the prosecutors could take to a grand jury."

"Yeah, I see where you're going."

"According to the records, some of the money stayed in play, was used for other deals. But big chunks of it went to the holding company, Cunningham Mining. It was transferred through their bank, Fidelity Trust, where Cunningham's a director, by the way, and so's his sister. The senator was, too, before he died."

"I know."

"What I want to find out is, what happened to the money after it went to the holding company?"

Mulloy gestured toward the papers on Tolliver's desk. "According to the reports, the biggest stake is in the family's real estate company. But there's also a whole range of investments. They're in cable TV companies, insurance underwriters—the list is as long as your arm, and they're all legitimate. So I would guess the dough went into more of the same."

"Maybe. But that's why I want to see Cunningham Mining's records. It's the only way we can get a complete picture."

"And right there you run into a brick wall."

"Why?"

"Because you couldn't get those records without a subpoena, that's why. Where's probable cause? Any judge'd know it wouldn't be like dicking around with some guy who sells bagels. Unless there were solid reasons, he wouldn't touch it.''

Tolliver thought about that. ''Yeah, I guess you're right. But has Shackley ever gone for one?''

''Not as far as I know.'' Mulloy returned to his chair. ''The trouble is, there's no basis to force the holding company to open up. They filed tax returns and the IRS accepted them. Same with the brokerage, for that matter. The agents went over all of it like ants at a picnic and found nothing wrong.''

''Then it looks like Cunningham Mining is clean.''

''Far as anybody can tell, yes. So where do we go from here?''

''I want to noodle around with this some more, and meantime you think about it, too. How're you doing with what I asked for, by the way—you find anything unusual in the trading patterns?''

''Not yet. But I'll stay after it.''

''Okay, we'll talk again, when you're ready.''

''Sure. It's a bitch, though, isn't it? Makes me think of one of those gag boxes. You open it up and there's another box inside, and then another one inside that.'' He went back to his desk, shaking his head.

The phone rang and Ben answered it. The district attorney's secretary was on the line, asking the lieutenant to come to Mr. Oppenheimer's office. Tolliver said he'd be there right away.

29

Oppenheimer wasn't nearly as affable as he had been the first time Tolliver had visited him. When Ben was led into his office, the DA was sitting at his desk, talking with two young men who were standing in front of him. Remonstrating with them, actually. Tolliver assumed the men were ADAs. Oppenheimer paid no attention to Ben, who stood nearby waiting to be acknowledged.

Tolliver had heard the DA had a temper, but it was something else to see it in action. Under the wreath of white hair, Oppenheimer's face looked not so much ruddy now as livid. In fact, it looked as if he was about to blow an artery.

''But sir,'' one of the young guys was saying, ''we have more than enough evidence to take to a grand jury. Two witnesses saw the accused pull the driver out of the truck and beat him with a baseball bat. We have sworn statements from both of them.''

''Goddamn it,'' Oppenheimer said, ''that's nothing but a charge of aggravated assault. Not even assault with a deadly weapon. What I want is a proven link between the perpetrator and the Gambinos. Otherwise, we're throwing away a chance to nail those bastards. Is that so difficult for you to grasp?''

''No, sir. But—''

''No buts,'' the DA said. ''Get me what I'm asking for, and get it fast. Otherwise, this isn't going before a grand jury or anywhere else.''

Ben realized what this was about. One of Oppenheimer's pet projects was to break the mob's stranglehold on the drivers of delivery trucks. No previous DA had ever taken the problem on, but no previous DA had shown Oppenheimer's courage and tenacity, either.

The two young guys gathered up their papers from the desk and hurried out of the room.

The DA looked at Tolliver. His face was still red, but at the sight of his visitor, his tone grew less strident. ''Morning, Lieutenant. I've been waiting to hear from you.''

''I'm still working on my investigation,'' Ben said.

''And what progress have you made?''

Ben had already decided to level. He gave Oppenheimer a briefing on what he'd seen and learned, including what the embalmers had told him about the condition of the senator's body and their convictions, along with the pathologist's remarks. He also gave him an account of how he'd gone to Jessica Silk's apartment after her death. Lastly, he related what he'd seen at the postmortem and what he'd been told later by Dr. Feldman.

There were a few things Ben didn't mention, such as the attitude of his superiors in the NYPD and his examination of the files on the Cunningham brokerage investigation. Everything else, however, he laid out in detail.

Oppenheimer never took his eyes off Tolliver's face, listening intently to every word of the recap. He didn't ask Ben to sit down, but kept him standing in front of the desk throughout the recitation.

When Tolliver finished, the DA said, ''So there's no hard evidence of any wrongdoing. Is that right, Lieutenant?''

''Depends on how you look at it,'' Ben said. ''I've seen a lot of things that make me suspicious. No matter what's been said, I don't believe we know the truth about Senator Cunningham's death. Or about Jessica Silk's, either.''

''That may be. But suspicions don't constitute evidence. As far as the senator is concerned, I'm sure you'll agree with what that medical examiner told you. Without an autopsy, speculation on the part of morticians is of no value, except to fuel your curiosity. And you have nothing that would discredit the statements of the two women who say they were with the senator at the time he died.''

''Nothing except the discrepancies in their stories.''

''Which amount to very little. They told you they were flustered at the time, which is certainly understandable. Anybody could make a mistake under those circumstances.''

''But Silk's death was even more suspicious,'' Ben said. ''Especially when you consider what the ME found when he did the post. There was evidence of physical abuse, and also what he discovered in her vagina. That's proof she wasn't alone before she went off that terrace.''

The white eyebrows went up a notch. ''Proof? What proof? All you have is his report that semen was present in the body of the deceased. What that proves is that she had sexual intercourse at some point before she died.''

''Feldman said he thought shortly before,'' Ben said.

''But isn't it possible that he could have been wrong? That another medical expert might offer a different opinion? That he might say the woman had intercourse the night before?''

Ben shifted his weight from one foot to the other. ''Yes, that's possible.'' Jesus, this was the same kind of lecture he'd given Shelley, about the need to have concrete evidence. Maybe Jack Mulloy was right; the criminal-justice system today was hopelessly mired in procedures intended to protect criminals, not apprehend them.

The DA wasn't through. ''And the marks on her body. Bruises, you said. And burns that might have been caused by a lighted cigar, or might not. None of those wounds were life-threatening, and there is no way they could be traced to the person who inflicted them. Is that right?''

''I—yes, it is.''

Oppenheimer shook his head. ''Lieutenant, you've been around long enough to know that what you have so far amounts to little more than hypothesis. What you don't have are reasons for you to challenge Dr. Phelps's conclusions as to the cause of the senator's death, nor to challenge the judgment of the officers who investigated Miss Silk's suicide—Lieutenant Watts and Detective Collins. So why not put that in writing and go back to your squad?"

Tolliver should have kept quiet. It was time to fold his hand and get out of here.

But he didn't. "I think I have some very good reasons."

Oppenheimer surprised him. Instead of showing annoyance, the old man sat back in his chair and studied him intently. Then he said, "You'll recall that when I first gave you this assignment, I let you know there were weighty political implications involved in the case. That it could be highly charged and sensitive. Do you remember that?"

"Yes, sir."

"And since then, you've no doubt also become aware that a fair amount of pressure has been exerted to close this up and move on. True?"

"Yes."

"Yet you persist in shaking the situation like a terrier with a rat. In doing so, you put your own career at risk, not to mention the negative effect your actions could have on this office. Do you understand?"

"Yes, I do."

"And?"

"And I want to finish the job I set out to do."

"Even though the more prudent course, or at least the more expedient one, would be to take the out I'm giving you? Think hard, Lieutenant, before you answer that."

Why the fuck, Ben thought, did this have to come down on me?

"Well?"

"I want to stay with it."

Oppenheimer remained impassive, his eyes revealing not so much as a hint of what he was thinking. "All right, Lieutenant, I'll tell you what I'm willing to do. I'll give you a little more time, to see if you can come up with something substantial. If you can, fine. If you can't, I think we can put this to bed. I'll make an announcement that after a full investigation into the senator's death, it was determined that he died of a heart attack, period. There was nothing to indicate that anything out of the way went on, and there was no cover-up.''

''What about the Silk woman?''

''What about her? Your own department has already concluded her death was a suicide. And you admit you've discovered no evidence to the contrary. Is that correct?''

''Yes, sir.''

''All right, then. Get back to me in a few more days, and I'll make a decision at that time.''

Ben returned to the investigators' offices, feeling thwarted and angry. Captain Brennan had called the shot on this, after all. Let it go, he'd said. Give the DA what he wants and that's the end of it. Don't go messing with a political bomb; it just might go off.

So why not pack it in? Wouldn't that have been the smart thing to do, and hadn't Ben thought so himself, right from the start? And what about his own situation? Was he going to blow his chances for promotion when common sense was telling him to put this thing behind him and move on? Could he really be that stubborn?

Yeah, he could. Everything he'd ever learned about police work, to say nothing of what he'd seen from the moment he'd been handed this thing, told him something very wrong was going on here. And not only to do with how and why the senator and Silk had died, either. A number of people were pushing for this case to be buried along with the senator and Silk, for the DA to put out the expedient announcement he'd talked about.

Then why not let it go?

Because Tolliver would be damned if he'd just knuckle under. Instead, what he had to do now was hurry. A few days wasn't much time.

30

A key question was what actually had happened that night in the senator's office. Tolliver decided that if he could answer that, he could track down whatever else there was, including what had caused Jennifer Silk to go off her terrace. He left the Criminal Justice Building and drove up to East Seventieth Street.

When he arrived, there was only one uniformed officer on the sidewalk, patrolling back and forth along the stretch in front of the mansion and its neighbor. No media people were present; they'd moved on to the scenes of other disasters. Tolliver identified himself and went into the stately building where the foundation offices were located.

This was a routine business day; people were sitting in the reception area and he saw others going into one of the meeting rooms on the first floor. He told the receptionist who he was and said he wanted to see Ardis Merritt. She spoke into a telephone and then asked him to be seated.

A minute later the security chief, Evan Montrock, walked into the area; apparently he'd been summoned. "Hello, Lieutenant. Want to follow me, please?"

Ben did, through a door and down a corridor to a room that contained a desk and no windows, evidently Montrock's station. There was a bank of TV monitors over the desk, showing that the cameras were trained on different areas of the building.

"Miss Merritt is in a meeting," Montrock said. He was bulky in the gray suit, lamplight shining on his bald head. "But she won't be long. Said she can give you a few minutes when she gets out. How about a cup of coffee?"

"No thanks."

Ben glanced at the monitors. On one of them, he could see people sitting around a conference table. Other pictures showed the interiors of offices, hallways, sitting rooms. In nearly all of them, the images revealed industrious goings-on.

Montrock's tone was affable. "How's life in your department? This isn't the best town to be doing police work these days, is it?"

"There are worse places," Ben said.

The security man smiled. "I know. I was a cop myself for over twenty years—in D.C. That's a worse place."

"Uh-huh. That where you met the senator?"

"Yep. I was on a guard detail and he got to know me, took a liking to me. Eventually, he said if I ever wanted to quit the force, I could go to work for him."

"And so you did."

"Signed on right away. Best thing ever happened to me."

"Shame that he died."

"Terrible. Never was a better man. At least none I ever knew."

"But you're able to stay on here."

"Oh yeah. I'm like part of the family now. During the week I'm here, of course, but then on weekends I go out to the estate on Long Island. Then during the winter season, I go to the house in Palm Beach."

"Sounds like a nice life."

"It's great. I have men assigned in each of the places, but I personally go where the family is at the moment."

"What about the other homes?" Ben asked. "Where the senator's son and daughter live? What happens when they're not all together?"

"They all have their own security."

"Also part of your organization?"

"Right."

Tolliver indicated the television monitors. "You can see into every room in this building, right?"

"Not all, but most of them. The public rooms and the hallways. The cameras sweep automatically, you know, like they're doing now. If there's a particular place I want to look at, I just punch it in."

"That include the senator's office?"

"No. That's off limits."

"What about Miss Merritt's apartment on the top floor?"

"Also private."

"The night the senator died," Tolliver said, "you let Miss Silk in, didn't you? Took her up to his office. Isn't that what you told me?"

"Yes."

"What was she carrying with her?"

"Carrying? A purse and a black case."

"Like an attaché case?"

"Yes."

There had been no black attaché case in Silk's apartment when Ben had gone there after her death. "She always have that along when she came here?"

"Far as I remember, yes."

"She take the case with her when she left here that night?"

"Yes, I believe she did."

"Where were you while she was in visiting the senator?"

"Right here at my desk, most of the time."

"But not all the time?"

"I don't think so. Might have walked around a little. Checked on the other guards, taken a leak, whatever."

"But you were here when the call for help came in?"

"Yes."

"It was Miss Merritt who called you?"

"That's right."

"What if you hadn't been here when she called?"

Montrock pointed to the radio attached to his belt. "She still would have reached me. This operates as a cordless phone as well as a walkie-talkie."

"So you can make calls, receive them, and talk to other frequencies if you want to."

"Correct."

"There was a total of five people here that night, in addition to the senator. Is that right?"

"Yes. The two women, two of my guards, and myself."

"Suppose someone other than you five had been here and you weren't in this office to see the monitors. Then you would have missed seeing that person, true?"

"Very unlikely, Lieutenant. I wouldn't have been gone for more than a couple of minutes at the most. And we have a very sophisticated system here. No one could get in without my opening a door for them."

"The senator did. Isn't that so?"

"He came in from his home, which is connected by the door I showed you. I took you into the house that way, the morning you came here after he died. Even so, whenever he used that door, he had to punch in a combination in an electronic lock."

"I see. Anybody else know that combination?"

"Only the members of the family."

The telephone rang and Montrock picked it up and spoke briefly to the caller before hanging up. "That was Miss Merritt. She can see you now. Come on, I'll take you up there."

31

I had a talk with Jessica Silk,'' Tolliver said. ''The day after Senator Cunningham's death. Not long after I spoke to you.''

Ardis Merritt surveyed him coolly. She had on the usual stodgy outfit, a plain blouse with a mouse-colored sweater over it, her brown hair tied back in a bun. Ben wondered why she seemed to go out of her way to look unattractive. They were in her office, just down the hall from the senator's, and she was making him feel about as welcome as herpes.

''How well did you know her?'' he asked.

''Not well at all. Only through the work she was doing with the senator.''

''When did you first meet her?''

''When she approached him about doing the article.''

''That was in Florida, wasn't it—in Palm Beach?''

She hesitated. ''Yes. I was down there on business for the foundation.''

''Some of the things she told me,'' he went on, ''didn't square with your account of what happened the night the senator died.''

''Really? Such as what?''

''Such as the fact that the two of you had a tough time getting his clothes back together when you realized he was dead. Zipping up his pants, for instance.''

Her lips compressed, until the skin around them was white. Then she said, ''What are you suggesting, Lieutenant?''

''That you didn't tell me the truth about what actually went on that night.''

''What I told you is precisely what happened—in every respect.''

''Except for a few minor details. Were you actually in the room when he died or just before he did?''

''Of course I was.''

''Or maybe that's stretching things a bit? Maybe you came in shortly afterward? And maybe the senator was already in trouble, or dead?''

Spots of color appeared in her cheeks. ''How dare you make these accusations?''

''I'm making them because I keep uncovering conflicts in your stories—yours and Silk's. If you were in the room, then what went on wasn't what you described the first time we talked—the version you gave the police officers who came to the house.''

She stared at him, eyes glinting with anger.

''And if you weren't in the room, why say that you were? What were you trying to hide? Silk admitted to me you had the problem with the senator's pants before you called for help. Why was that? And why did you lie about it? What were your reasons for not wanting the truth to come out?''

''The truth did come out. We tried to loosen his clothing so that it would be easier for him to breathe. As I've already told you, we were both terribly upset. It was an emergency situation, and I'll admit we were panicky. But what you're implying is absurd.''

''Is it? What was the relationship between the senator and Miss Silk? It wasn't just a writer interviewing an important figure, was it? There was something going on between them, isn't that so? And you knew it.''

''I knew nothing of the kind. You're as bad as those ghouls from the media. Running a bunch of hideous lies without a scrap of evidence to back them up.''

''And now you're fishing, trying to find out what I've got.''

Behind the heavy horn-rims, her eyes flashed. ''Let me assure you, Lieutenant, I don't *care* what you've got or haven't got. It's apparent that this is nothing but one more attempt to smear the memory of a great man. And as far as Jessica Silk is concerned, it's quite convenient, isn't it, that the poor woman can't be here to defend herself?''

''Whether she's here or not, she gave me a statement.''

''Then you don't need one from me, do you?''

''Oh, I think you'll tell me the truth about what happened, sooner or later. I hope you realize you could be charged with obstructing justice if you don't.'' Which was bullshit, but he wanted to see how far he could push her.

Not far, as it turned out. ''Then why don't you charge me? You'll have to if you expect me to answer any more of these outrageous questions about Senator Cunningham's death.''

''Maybe I'll do just that. And by the way, there are a few other things I want to ask about, as well. What does the name Orkis mean to you?''

"It means nothing. I don't know anyone by that name."

"You're sure?"

"Quite sure."

"But of course you can't remember everything, can you? Not every detail—that's what records are for. Which is why I'd like to see a list of the foundation's disbursements—if you don't mind."

"Of course I don't mind. We're a charitable organization and our activities are a matter of public record. They're closely monitored by the federal authorities, as well as by those of the city and the state."

She opened a drawer in her desk and took out a binder with a green cover, handing it to him. Gold letters on the cover read "The Cunningham Foundation."

Tolliver leafed through it. "Okay if I keep this?"

"Yes. Although I can see no reason for you to go prying into our business."

"I have a number of reasons. All of them to do with my investigation."

"Your investigation seems to be little more than a shabby effort to disparage Senator Cunningham. And now if you'll excuse me, I'm very busy. I'm not used to having people simply pop in on me without at least showing the courtesy of calling for an appointment. People are waiting for me. There are many important things I'm involved in."

"I'm sure there are," Ben said. He rolled up the binder and put it into his raincoat pocket, then got up to go, saying, "Don't bother to see me out. I know the way."

32

Out on the sidewalk, the same bored cop was slowly parading back and forth. Tolliver walked next door and rang the bell of the Cunningham mansion. A moment later, the door swung open and the butler he'd seen last time he was here peered out at him.

Ben displayed his shield. "Lieutenant Tolliver. Would you please tell Mrs. Cunningham I'd like to speak with her for a few minutes?"

"Is madam expecting you, sir?"

"No, she isn't. But it's important that I see her."

''Yes, sir. I'll see if she's in.'' He shut the door.

The cop glanced over this way but continued to walk, exhibiting no curiosity. Ben noticed that the traffic along here was light, although looking down the street toward the park he could see taxis whizzing south on Fifth Avenue. The breeze was bending the naked branches of the trees.

The butler returned. ''Madam will see you, Lieutenant. Please come this way.''

Tolliver followed him into a domed rotunda and, through it, down a long hallway. The butler opened another door and showed the visitor into a study. He took Ben's raincoat and asked him to be seated, saying that Mrs. Cunningham would join him shortly. Then he backed out and closed the door.

The room was smaller than the one Ben had been in the morning after the senator's death, when he'd met the family. This was cozy and intimate, with comfortable furniture covered in bright prints and with paintings he recognized as those of French Impressionists hanging on the walls. The paintings showed gauzy landscapes and gardens bursting with flowers. There was a delicate writing desk near a tall window and a corner fireplace with logs crackling on the hearth. It was a woman's room, he realized, probably Mrs. Cunningham's sanctuary.

The door opened and she walked into the room.

Ben stood up. ''Sorry to barge in on you, ma'am. I appreciate your seeing me.''

''That's all right, Lieutenant. Please sit down.'' Clayton Cunningham's widow was smartly dressed in a dark red wool suit, her silver hair carefully styled. But despite makeup, wrinkles were visible around her eyes and at the corners of her mouth. Ben also noticed she was heavy in the hips. Overall, she seemed the direct opposite of Jessica Silk, which probably had a lot to do with the senator's interest in the journalist.

She took a chair facing him, crossing her legs. ''I would have expected your investigation to be finished long ago.''

He sank back into his seat. ''I still have questions about what happened the night of your husband's death. There were conflicts in the account given me by Ardis Merritt.''

''Conflicts?''

''Yes. I also spoke to Jessica Silk, the writer who—''

She stiffened. "I know who she is—or was. What are your questions?"

"The two women's stories don't match. I'm not convinced Miss Merritt has been telling me the truth."

"Then why don't you discuss that with her?"

"I did, just a few minutes ago."

"And?"

"She was less than cooperative. Nevertheless, I need to file a report. I don't want to embarrass anyone, but I want to find out what happened."

"We're already embarrassed, Lieutenant. Or at least I am. The publicity has been unspeakable."

"I'm sure it's been very painful for you. Losing your husband and then having to put up with all that churning by the media."

She bit her lip and looked away.

"If you don't mind, I'd like to ask you a few things."

Her gaze swung back to him. "I do mind. But I'll answer if I can."

"How well do you know Miss Merritt?"

"Well enough, I suppose. My husband thought she was quite capable. She sometimes helped him in matters that were outside her duties with the foundation."

"What matters were they?"

"Advice on what committees to serve on, the importance of various functions he was asked to attend. She also made many of his appointments, helped direct the public-relations agency, and so on."

"Why didn't his secretary handle those things?"

"She did, but with Ardis telling her what to do."

"Wasn't that rather unusual?"

"Ardis is an unusual person. Very determined, very efficient."

"And very loyal."

"Yes."

"So of course she wouldn't want to see his reputation harmed, would she?"

"Are you suggesting she deliberately attempted to mislead you? That she lied in order protect him—and the family?"

"I think it's possible. Did you speak to her that night?"

"Yes, of course I did. She came to the house afterward to express her sympathy and to ask if there was anything she could do. I told her there wasn't, and after she stayed with us for a time, she went back to her apartment in the foundation building.''

''What about the others? Did Clay speak to her—or Ingrid or anyone else—about what had happened?''

''We all did. We were stunned, couldn't believe he was dead. He always seemed so strong, so vigorous. At dinner, he'd been his normal self, enjoying everyone's company.''

''Were you present the whole time Miss Merritt was here?''

For the first time, Claire Cunningham showed a touch of annoyance. ''Look, Lieutenant. I'm telling you that I have no knowledge of any attempt to distort or obscure the facts. Not by Ardis or by any member of the family.''

He decided to give her another jab, harder this time. ''Did you know Jessica Silk?''

Her eyes narrowed. ''Don't try to get me into a discussion of my husband's personal life. I'll admit it was difficult at times to be the wife of Clayton Cunningham. But that's over now. He's gone, and whatever he did or didn't do will no longer trouble me.''

''Has the family been supportive to you?''

He didn't really expect her to answer that, but apparently she'd become just angry enough to snap out a reply. ''As much as I would have expected, which isn't very much. As it is now, I no longer have a family. Either his or mine.''

''Excuse me?''

''I divorced my first husband to marry the senator, as you probably know. It was considered a scandal at the time. At least that's what the newspapers made of it. My own children have never spoken to me since.''

''That must have been painful too.''

''I made my bed and now I'm forced to lie in it. Fortunately, it's a very comfortable bed, thanks to the trusts that were set up for me when I married him. As far as my share of the estate is concerned, I'm quite sure I'll come out very well, in spite of efforts by Clay and Ingrid to prevent that from happening.''

''They're disputing your interest in the estate?''

''You can't be surprised, Lieutenant. By now, you must have a good idea of what they're like. But in the end, they won't succeed. They wouldn't dare push me too hard—I'm on the board of Cunningham Mining. I know far too much.''

"About what?"

Her mouth opened as she seemed to realize what she'd said. But she recovered quickly. "I have no further comments, Lieutenant. You came here to ask about Ardis Merritt, and if you have any other questions, they should be directed to her. But you'd better hurry, because she'll be leaving soon."

"She's leaving the foundation?"

"Yes, in a few more weeks."

"Because of the senator's death?"

"In part. But also because her term was up, anyway. The foundation's bylaws call for a new administrator to be appointed every four years."

"I see."

She moved her foot, and Ben wondered whether she'd touched a button concealed underneath the small Oriental rug that lay between her chair and his.

He was correct; a few seconds later, there was a knock at the door and then the butler entered the room. "Yes, madam?"

"We've finished our discussion, Raymond. Please show the lieutenant out."

33

"I don't want you to get your hopes too high," Dr. Chenoweth said. "Although she is definitely responding. The tests all show it."

"I know that," Peggy replied. "I saw it myself. But you don't sound very encouraged. It is good news, isn't it?"

The psychiatrist didn't answer immediately. He seemed hesitant, which wasn't like him. Nor was it in character for him to be anything but cheerful. Yet lately when he'd spoken with her, there were times when he sounded almost gloomy.

What was it that he seemed reluctant to share with her?

He glanced at the papers spread out before him, rubbing his short brown beard thoughtfully. Then he leaned forward, resting his elbows on the desk. "Peggy, when you came running in here the other day to tell me Jan seemed to understand what you'd been saying to her, I was as excited as you were. Since then, I've worked with her extensively, and yes, there are signs of cognition."

"Then what's wrong?"

"It's hard to say. I have mixed reactions to what I see. We've made progress, yes. But I also see danger signals."

"I don't understand."

"Okay, let me explain. You'll recall that when we went back into her room and spoke to her, she'd withdrawn again. She didn't seem to be aware of anything we said to her."

"Yes, but I certainly saw those tears. I know I did."

"I don't doubt that. Over the past few days, I've been running tests that confirm awareness. Yet what I've seen troubles me."

"Why?"

"Because it seems as if your sister is making a conscious effort to hide her emotions."

Peggy shook her head, perplexed. "Hide them? Why would she do such a thing?"

"I don't know. But I'm reasonably sure that's what's going on. You see, we have ways of measuring her responses. We check pulse rate, skin temperature, even minute changes in pupil dilation. So we know she's hearing us and that certain words are triggering reactions. The words that cause the greatest changes are all negative."

"Such as?"

"Hurt, damage, injury, that kind of thing. Which is to be expected after what she's been through. But the one that causes the strongest reaction of all is Cunningham."

"Of course—that's what happened when I told her the senator had died. She was saddened to hear the news and that made her cry."

Chenoweth regarded her steadily. "You may be right, but now she's doing the same thing as when she first came here—withdrawing deeper and deeper into herself. Hiding from the world, as it were. As far as her reaction to names or words is concerned, there is a measurable reaction, yes. But just what that is, I can't tell. All the signs point to a phobic disorder that might lead to further withdrawal. In other words, whatever the basis for her anxiety, it might cause her to sink into a deeper state of catatonia."

"Do you really think that could happen?"

"I think it's possible, yes. My concern is that she may go so far back into the recesses of her mind that we'd be unable to reach her again."

"Because of this disturbance, or whatever it is?"

"Yes. What she's doing is making an effort to escape."

Peggy was silent for a few moments as she tried to digest what she'd been told. When she again spoke, she had to struggle to keep her voice from trembling. "What are you going to do about it, Doctor?"

"Everything I can to reassure her."

34

Ben walked west to Fifth Avenue. There was a public phone on the corner and he went to it and asked information for the number of Cunningham Securities. He called the number, telling the switchboard he wanted to speak to Mr. Cunningham. Getting past the secretary took some doing, but eventually he was put through.

The voice on the telephone was smooth and unruffled. Tolliver could picture its owner, handling the bumptious cop courteously but at the same time with thinly disguised condescension. "What can I do for you, Lieutenant?"

"I want to stop in at your office," Ben said. "Like to have another talk."

"About what? My father is gone, the funeral is over. I think it's time for all of us to get on with our lives."

"That may be. But I haven't finished my investigation."

"Haven't finished? Good Lord, what else is there to say or do? Anything more will just add grist for the media mills."

"No reason for the media to be aware of my visit," Ben said. "And anyway, this only partly relates to your father's death. As you know, I'm attached to the district attorney's office."

There was a pause and then Cunningham said, "Yes, so I recall. Well, perhaps I could spare some time. Tell you what. If it's agreeable to you, why don't we have a bite of lunch together? Then it won't cut into the business day. That sound all right?"

"Sure," Ben said. He looked at his watch. "I'll be there at twelve."

"Fine. See you then."

The offices of Cunningham Securities were on Wall Street, a few steps from the New York Stock Exchange. Ben left the Ford in a parking garage and walked back to the address. The streets here were narrow and winding, as they'd been ever since the Dutch owned the island. And at this time of day, the sidewalks were overflowing with pedestrians, the lofty old buildings disgorging armies of workers en route to lunch.

He wondered why Cunningham would maintain his offices here rather than in midtown. Most of the firm's business would be done by telephone and fax; physical proximity to the stock exchange was unnecessary. Certainly a Park Avenue location would be more to Cunningham's liking. The restaurants were better, the shops and clubs handier, the streets wider and less congested. And it would be closer to his apartment, which was about ten blocks to the north of the Waldorf.

The brokerage occupied several floors of a building clad in polished dark gray granite. Tolliver arrived at twelve on the dot. He found the reception area tastefully decorated with contemporary furniture, the floor covered in deep sound-absorbing carpeting. There were fresh flowers on the receptionist's desk and a bright smile on her face. Ben told her he was there to see Mr. Cunningham and she telephoned inside. A moment later, a secretary appeared and led him through a door into the operations area.

This was where the trading took place, and it was the opposite in character from the room he'd just left. Tiny desks were jammed together across the huge space, and at each one a man or woman sat jabbering on the telephone while staring at the screen of a Quotron and punching the keys. The noise level and the confusion reminded him of the Chinese laundry where he took his shirts. How anybody could make sense of what they were doing in this atmosphere was a mystery, and maybe they couldn't.

Cunningham's office was another reversal. Ben was shown into a room that was spacious and eerily quiet, situated on the southwest corner of the floor. Sofas and chairs were upholstered in a soothing shade of gray and at various points in the room stood pieces of ancient statuary. Windows covered two of the walls. Through them, he could see across other business towers to the harbor. The Statue of Liberty was visible, and a ferry was slowly making its way toward Staten Island.

Cunningham himself was ensconsed behind a wide desk with stainless-steel legs and a surface of black granite. He was in shirt sleeves, wearing gold cuff links and red suspenders, a figured tie. He got up when Ben entered and extended his hand. "Greetings, Lieutenant."

Ben shook the hand. "Hello, Mr. Cunningham."

"Take your coat?"

"I'll keep it on, as long as we'll be leaving soon."

"As you wish. Please sit down," the broker said. "And call me Clay. Everyone does."

Tolliver sank into the depths of a sofa and Cunningham sat facing him in a nearby chair.

"Nice office," Ben said. "Interesting statues."

Cunningham smiled. "I'm an incurable collector. Although getting pieces like these out of Italy has been a bit more difficult lately. The Italian government frowns on it."

"That so?"

"Oh yes. They consider Roman relics to be national treasures, and so on. But the statues come in handy, for reminding me of what a brief time we have on earth. Some of them are two thousand years old. Thinking about that makes trading stocks seem a little less important than it might otherwise."

"Uh-huh."

"Been a strange day so far," Cunningham said. "The market's been bobbing up and down, doesn't seem to know where it wants to go. I don't think the President's economic policies are helping very much. That's just one factor, of course."

Ben wasn't here to chitchat about vagaries in the securities business. "I noted in the files that two people who worked for your company were questioned about leaking inside information."

The broker waved a hand dismissively. "Lieutenant, you must know they don't work for us any longer. As soon as that suspicion arose, we asked both of them to leave. I'd be as happy as anyone to see them prosecuted if the facts warrant it."

"If you didn't think there was evidence, why did you fire them?"

"It's like Caesar's wife. A brokerage has to be above reproach—or suspicion. I wouldn't welcome the publicity, of course, but if those guys did what your office apparently thought they did, they both ought to be sent to jail. How's that going, by the way?"

"It's moving along," Ben said.

"Frankly, I don't see how. The SEC has dropped their investigation, as I'm sure you're aware."

"Yes, I know they have. But we won't drop ours. Not until we're completely satisfied." If Shackley could hear what I'm saying, he'd go up the wall, Ben thought.

"That's good to hear," Cunningham said. "I believe there's no substitute for thoroughness. Although I must say I have no illusions as to why it's dragged on the way it has. My father had many political enemies, and they thought that attacking our family businesses was a way to get at him. Terrible, but that's the way things are done sometimes. Perhaps now that he's dead, they'll go on to more important matters and leave us alone."

"You're also on the board of the Cunningham Foundation, aren't you?"

"Yes, of course."

"I spoke again with the administrator, Ardis Merritt."

"Oh?"

"I don't think she told the truth about what happened the night your father died."

Cunningham's eyebrows rose. "Ardis? Impossible. She's one of the most honest people I've ever known."

"And loyal?"

"Of course."

"To the extent she'd be willing to cover up a few facts so as not to cause trouble for the family?"

"That's absurd. Ardis wouldn't lie, I assure you. And anyway, there was nothing to lie about. Whatever gave you such an idea?"

"I also spoke with Jessica Silk before she died. Her version didn't square with Miss Merritt's."

"Is that so surprising? People often get confused in stressful situations. You of all people would know that."

"Nevertheless, I believe your father and the Silk woman were having an affair. And that Ardis Merritt knew about it and was trying to cover it up. Did you discuss that with her? Maybe suggest it would be better for everybody if it never got out?"

"Certainly not. What you're implying is preposterous. And as far as Jessica Silk is concerned, I was desperately sorry for her. Poor miserable creature—she must have been terribly distresed. I, don't think suicide is ever justifiable, yet I can imagine how she felt."

"Can you?"

"Good Lord, yes. Working so closely with my father and then having him die while she was with him. And after that, being pilloried by the media. Ghastly."

"Did you know her?"

"Personally, you mean?"

"Yes. Did you?"

"I met her a few times, yes."

"Under what circumstances?"

"I was with my father one evening when she came to his office to work on the article she was writing. And she also came out to the estate for the same purpose."

"That the family place on Long Island?"

"Yes."

"It was taking her quite some time to get the piece written, wasn't it?"

"I suppose. But maybe she was hoping to turn it into a book. We were all saddened when she died."

"Your sister knew her, as well?"

"Yes. At least Ingrid was acquainted with her, just as I was."

"You must see a lot of your sister. You two work on a number of deals together?"

"Sometimes. She runs our commercial real estate operation. And I'm sorry to say she doesn't run it very well. I'm quite disappointed with what's been going on there. Ingrid doesn't have much business sense."

"Doesn't she sit on several of your boards?"

"Yes, at the moment. But that may change, in time. I'll be taking over as chairman and CEO of our holding company, Cunningham Mining. Replacing my father."

Just as Ben had suspected, a struggle was taking place inside the family. Instead of the united front the Cunninghams were always believed to form, it seemed Clay was preparing to shove his sister aside. And then there was what the senator's widow had said about the pair attempting to screw her out of her share of the estate.

Cunningham got to his feet. "Well, let's get some lunch, shall we? Don't know about you, but by the time midday rolls around, I'm usually starved."

"Sure," Ben said, "let's go."

The broker went to a closet, getting out his suit jacket and putting it on. "We'll go to my club, if that's agreeable. The car will be waiting out front."

35

On the drive uptown, Cunningham chatted amiably. But each time Ben asked a question about the brokerage's operations, Cunningham offhandedly deflected it, as if they were discussing nothing more important than ball scores or the weather.

When they arrived at their destination, the broker asked if he'd been here before.

From his seat in the limousine, Ben looked up at the building housing the Metropolitan Club, an ornate structure at 1 East Sixtieth Street. "No. Not inside, anyway."

The chauffeur ran around to the curb and opened the door for them. They got out, and as he stepped onto the sidewalk, Cunningham said, "Interesting old place. Stanford White designed it. A little extravagant for my taste, but it's a good example of what New York thought was elegant around the turn of the century."

Ben wasn't taken in by the remark. Cunningham might have thought he sounded humble, but in fact he came off as smug. This was one of the most exclusive private clubs in the city.

The broker led the way past the elaborate gates and the colonnaded carriage entrance. "J. P. Morgan founded it," he went on. "Wanted to have a quiet spot where he and his friends could get together. One of them was my great-grandfather, Colonel Clayton Cunningham. They used to meet here regularly, and a lot of ambitious plans were hatched in the dining room. Some of them in the bar, too, I imagine. Political as well as financial. It's all been well preserved, so that its furnishings are just as they were at that time."

Tolliver had to admit the interior was splendid. Soaring ceilings, intricately carved mahogany paneling, dark paintings in gilded frames. He could imagine a number of the city's former leaders strutting around in here, potbellied and mustachioed. Today's members seemed to take themselves just as seriously.

The dining room was no less grand. The tables were set far apart, with snowy napery and gleaming silver, waiters in black uniforms serving the lunch crowd. With so much space, the conversations produced only a gentle murmur—nothing like the restaurants in the neighborhood, where the sound was a constant roar.

Surprisingly, most of the diners were male. After all the screaming and bitching women had done to force clubs in the city to open membership to them, you had to look hard to find a female in the room. Must have been only the principle that was important to them, Ben thought. Having won that battle, they apparently had taken up the next.

"Care for a drink?" Cunningham asked.

They were sitting beside one of the tall windows, filtered sunlight casting a pale glow across the table. Tolliver was about to say no; he usually avoided booze at lunch. But today was different. "Sounds fine. Bourbon on the rocks."

Cunningham ordered Scotch. The waiter moved off, and Ben said, "Nice place."

"Yes, it is. And not really as fancy as it looks. Nothing stuffy. Everyone is quite congenial."

Could have fooled me, Ben thought. Aloud he said, "Little different from what I'm used to."

Cunningham was watching him with interest. "How long have you been with the police department?"

"Almost twenty years."

"Ever think about leaving, doing something else?"

"Sure, now and then. But this is all I've ever done—except for a hitch in the Marine Corps."

The waiter returned with their drinks. When he'd moved off again, Cunningham raised his glass. "Cheers."

"Cheers," Ben said. The bourbon was aged and very smooth, and he was glad he'd decided to have it. "You come here often?"

"Oh, once or twice a week, I guess."

"Probably belong to other clubs, as well, right?"

"A few. The Union, the New York Yacht Club. And the Dartmouth Club, of course. Dartmouth is a family tradition."

"How about a country club—you must play golf, don't you?"

"No, I prefer tennis."

"Where do you play?"

"At our place on Long Island. The estate's another legacy from my great-grandfather. And then my father expanded it. He liked to have the family around, you see, so it's sort of a self-contained compound. There's a stable and riding trails, and tennis courts and a pool, of course. Also a cottage at the beach. We spend most of our weekends there."

"All of you?"

"Except Ingrid." Clay's nose wrinkled. "She'd rather stay with her horses."

"I gather the two of you don't get along too well."

"My sister is a very headstrong person. She's also too ambitious for her own good."

"Ambitious to do what?"

"Let's just say she has an inflated opinion of her abilities, and a way of setting goals that are beyond them. What would you like for lunch?"

"Haven't looked at the menu," Ben said. He picked up the printed card.

"Changes every day, but I'd recommend the roast beef."

"That sounds fine."

"I'll order for us," Cunningham said. "And I'll also get us another drink. Can't fly on one wing, you know." He wrote their food order on a chit and handed it to a waiter, telling the man to bring them another round, as well.

"Tell me more about the estate," Ben said when the waiter had gone.

"It's always been kind of a home base for us," Cunningham said. "Much more than my father's house here in the city. Of course, we often got together there, too, as we did on the night he died. But usually we went out to the Island."

"You live on Park, don't you?"

"Yes, just above Sixtieth Street. I like living in town—during the week, anyway."

"And I believe you and your sister both have children."

"Two each. All the kids are from previous marriages, and all of them are in boarding school. We don't see much of them except on holidays, thank God. That's where the British always had the right idea. Keep the little beasts tucked away in school during their early years, teach them some manners. Then when they're grown up, they can become useful members of society.'' He smiled. ''Same idea as the prison system, isn't it?''

''You might say so,'' Ben said. The more he saw of the Cunninghams, the more he realized how different they considered themselves from the great unwashed masses.

He and Clay had another drink and then their food arrived. It was perfectly prepared, thick slices of juicy meat accompanied by Yorkshire pudding.

As they ate, Ben encouraged the broker to continue talking about the Cunningham lifestyle, pretending to be dazzled by what he was hearing. Cunningham grew increasingly voluble, going on about the family's possessions, their travels, and their interest in sports.

''What about winters?'' Ben asked. ''You have a house in Palm Beach, don't you? I heard some of the family talking about it the morning I came to your father's house.''

''Oh yes. It's up in the north end, near the Kennedy place. Do you know Palm Beach?''

''I've been there,'' Ben said. At the time, he'd gone to pick up a suspect who'd waived extradition. The guy was being held by the local police department for return to New York, where he was wanted in connection with a jewel robbery.

''We always spend the season there,'' Cunningham went on. ''Go down for Christmas and stay at least a month, sometimes longer. And then we're all there at Easter. Even Ingrid likes Palm Beach, which is understandable. It's a beautiful place, don't you think?''

''Yeah, it is.''

Cunningham continued to study his guest. ''Coming back to what we were talking about earlier, about your doing something different. You think you might consider it if the right opportunity came along?''

''Sure, I might.''

''Interesting that you feel that way. Hope you don't mind, Lieutenant, but I've been making some inquiries about you.''

Ben recalled what Brennan had mentioned to him, about certain people asking questions.

''And then when you called today, I made a few more. Frankly, I liked what I heard.''

''And what was that?''

''I'm told you're an outstanding officer with a superb record.''

"I've had some good luck."

"Come on, Lieutenant. As my father used to say, good luck is what you make; bad luck is what you cope with."

"That could be."

"Of course it is. What I'm getting at is that if you were to consider leaving the police department, we'd like to have you join us."

Ben made an effort to seem surprised.

"Let me explain," Cunningham said. "You see, with my father gone, there'll be a good many changes made in our various organizations—which is only to be expected."

"Sure, I can understand that."

"And as I'm sure you can also understand, we have quite a need for security. Some of it on a personal basis, some of it for the purpose of protecting the family's possessions and our other interests. At the moment, our security forces are headed by a man named Evan Montrock."

"I've met him," Ben said. "When I went to the foundation."

"Yes, of course. Evan's been with us for years. The senator hired him. Good man, but he can't go on forever."

"You thinking about retiring him?"

"Not immediately. What I have in mind is bringing in a number two, who'll take over when the time comes."

"I see."

"I think you'd be an ideal choice for the position."

"Me?"

"Why not? You're the right age, and you certainly have the credentials. From what I've seen, you'd be perfect."

Ben put the last bite of roast beef into his mouth and chewed it thoughtfully. The meat was tender and succulent.

"Well," Cunningham asked, "what do you think?"

"I don't know," Ben said. He put his knife and fork down. "Tell you the truth, I'm kind of knocked over. Last thing I expected. What compensation did you have in mind?"

The broker pursed his lips. "Oh, let's say a hundred-fifty thousand a year, to start. Plus bonuses. Also a car and a personal expense allowance. And a number of other side benefits, such as insurance, paid vacations, and so on."

"Really? Sounds terrific."

"We believe in taking very good care of our executives."

"I guess you do. That's a hell of a lot more than I'm making now."

"There's a big difference," Cunningham said, "between the private and public sectors. And just between us, Lieutenant, it'd be a shame if you were to waste your peak years on the police force. You could be part of something much more important to your future."

"Uh-huh."

"You know, there is another saying in our family. A maxim, actually, that we've always lived by. Money begets power; power begets money. A fundamental truth, don't you think? Something you could learn from, as well."

"Probably could."

"Of course. It also tells you why joining us would be a great opportunity for you."

"Would I be reporting to Montrock?"

"Yes, until he retired."

"I see. Naturally, I'd like some time to think it over."

"Of course. I'd expect you to."

"Meantime, thanks very much for the offer."

"Not a bit, Lieutenant. I have a feeling this could be an auspicious beginning for both of us. Now how about some coffee?"

"That sounds good, too."

Ben was intrigued. He'd had people try to pay him off before, but never on this scale. A hundred-fifty grand a year, plus a bunch of sweeteners? For playing bodyguard to people who were so rich they thought they could buy anything?

What was it he'd stumbled across?

36

By the time Tolliver got back from his lunch at the Metropolitan Club, it was midafternoon. As soon as he reached his office, he called Cunningham Ventures. A secretary informed him that Mrs. Kramer was not in. Ben told the woman to get in touch with her and have her call him right away. He left his number and hung up. Ten minutes later, the phone rang and Ingrid Kramer was on the line.

"It's important that I see you," he said.

"What about?"

"My investigation into your father's death."

"I'm sorry, but that won't be possible. As far as I'm concerned, that's all behind us now."

"I think it would be in your best interest, Mrs. Kramer. I just had lunch with your brother."

"You talked to Clay?"

"Yes. One of the things we discussed was you, and your relationship to the rest of the family."

He heard the unmistakable sound of air being drawn in through clenched teeth. Then she said, "I'm at my place in Connecticut. Do you want to come up here?"

"Yes."

"When?"

"Right away."

She gave him directions and hung up.

He drove up the East Side, then across the Willis Avenue Bridge, past Yankee Stadium to the Hutch, then onto the Merritt Parkway. The wind was still brisk, but the sun was out. It was a near-perfect late fall day, with only a few wisps of cirrus in the hard blue sky. He turned off at Darien and went north through New Canaan to the farm.

The place was surrounded by white fencing that stretched along the road for a quarter mile. There were pine trees inside the fence, and peering through them he caught glimpses of green meadows with horses grazing.

The sign beside the gate said FARVIEW FARM. A uniformed guard met him there, squinting at the visitor as the Taurus drew to a stop. The guy had the look of an ex-cop, putting Ben in mind of Evan Montrock. He showed the guard his ID and waited as the man spoke into a field radio and then told him to go up the drive to the main house. An electric motor opened the gate and Tolliver drove on through.

The horses were in plain sight now, a dozen or more sleek animals that paid no attention to him as he followed the winding blacktop. There were stands of trees here and there, largely evergreens but also groves of what probably were maples and oaks; it was hard to tell with most of the leaves gone. At a far-off point on the grounds, a tractor was pulling a cart.

The house stood on a rise, partly hidden from the road by more trees and with a long sweep of lawn. A rambling white Colonial, it was three stories high, with wings at either end. A row of dormers was set into the steep slate roof and massive stone chimneys sprouted from the ridges.

The elevation explained the name; from here, you could see miles of rolling hills stretching into the hazy distance. Ben slowed to a crawl as he approached, taking in the view.

Several cars were standing in the circular drive near the entrance of the house. He parked the Taurus behind a green Aston Martin and got out, walking to the front steps.

A maid met him at the door, an older woman wearing a black uniform. She led him into a wide center hallway furnished with antique Windsor chairs and settees, and with portraits of horses hung on the walls. A sweeping staircase curved upward to a balcony on the second floor. Ben followed her the length of the hall and through a door at the opposite end.

The room they entered was large, with a stone floor and a towering fireplace, hand-hewn beams overhead. The walls were painted white, and there were sofas and chairs upholstered in flowered chintz. Bright-colored vases held sprays of orange and yellow crysanthemums.

Ingrid Cunningham Kramer stepped forward to greet him. Her sandy hair was swept back casually and she was wearing a sweater and jodhpurs, her feet shod in gleaming boots. "Hello, Lieutenant. I gather you had no trouble finding the place."

"No trouble at all," Ben said. "It's a nice day not to be in New York."

"That's the way I feel every day. But I have a business to attend to, so I'm usually there during the week." She waved a hand. "Sit down, won't you? Like a drink, or coffee?"

"Coffee'd be fine," he said.

She turned to the maid. "Take care of our guest, will you, Alice, please? Nothing for me."

Alice departed, and Ingrid said to Ben, "You'll have to forgive me—I've been working with the horses." She waved her hand again and Tolliver followed the indicated direction. There was a bank of windows at the rear of the room and through them he could see barns some distance from the house.

"Frankly, I was surprised when you called," she went on. "I thought the investigation was finally over with."

''There are a number of points that need to be cleared up,'' Ben said.

''That may be. I'm also interested in hearing what my dear brother had to say. But first, I want to wash up and change.''

''Sure, go right ahead.''

''I'll only be a few minutes. Make yourself comfortable. Anything you need, just tell Alice. Oh, and don't mind Brutus. He'll keep you company.''

''Who's Brutus?''

''You'll see.'' She left the room.

A moment later, a yellow Labrador bounded in from the hall, tail wagging furiously, putting his paws on Ben's midsection and licking his hands.

Tolliver loved dogs. And despised people who kept them in the city, where they shit on the sidewalks despite the poop laws and couldn't get the exercise they needed. He scratched Brutus's ears and stroked his back and the animal rubbed against his legs. When Ben sat down in a chair, the dog curled up at his feet.

Alice was back, carrying a butler's tray with a coffeepot and a plate of cookies on it. She put the tray down on a table handy to the chair Tolliver was sitting in and asked if anything else was required. Nothing was, and again she bowed out.

Ben looked around. There were more horse pictures in here, most of them oil paintings, but many photographs as well, apparently taken at polo matches. The top surface of a bookcase at one end of the room was crowded with silver trophies. Nearby, a framed bulletin board was festooned with ribbons, predominantly blue, but also a few red and yellow ones.

He poured himself a cup of coffee and gave Brutus one of the cookies. As he sipped the hot black liquid, he glanced out the windows again. Some sort of activity was going on in one of the fields, but from where he sat, he couldn't make out what it was. Putting his cup down, he stepped to the rear door and looked out. Brutus leapt up and joined him there.

Directly behind the house was a wide bluestone terrace flanked by gardens. A walk led out past a tennis court to where the red-painted barns were. Ben could see a man riding a horse in a field enclosed by a white fence. Curious, he stepped out the door, the dog trotting along beside him, and went down the walk.

As he approached the field, he saw that two men were leaning on the fence, watching the man on the horse. This one was obviously an expert rider. Ben recognized him at once as Ingrid's husband.

Kurt Kramer was dressed much the same as his wife had been, in riding britches and boots. But despite the chill air, he had only a T-shirt on top. In the bright sunlight, his blond hair appeared almost white. He was swinging a polo mallet in his right hand, whacking a ball with it, and then racing after the ball and hitting it again. His mount was a black stallion, its flanks shiny with sweat.

The horse seemed small compared with the thoroughbreds Ben had seen on his occasional visits to Belmont Park and Aqueduct. But the animal's ability to change direction with sudden bursts of speed was amazing. He appeared to need little guidance from Kramer, following the ball and putting his rider in position to hit it as if he enjoyed the game.

Kramer looked over and noticed Ben standing near the two men at the fence. He brought the horse to the gate and the men opened it. Dismounting, he gave the mallet and the reins to one of them, and the pair led the horse toward the barns.

Kramer smiled. "Ah, Lieutenant. My wife told me you were coming to see us. You're still chasing rumors, eh?"

"You might say that. Nice horse you were riding there."

"Spartan? He's wonderful. I'm getting him ready for a match in Palm Beach. He's one of the best."

"How many do you have?"

"Altogether, about thirty here on the farm. But the string I compete with is usually six to eight ponies. In a match, you have to keep changing to fresh mounts, you see. There are four players on a team, so a team travels with quite a number of ponies. We'll have teams coming from South America and Europe, as well as from here in the States, of course. Should be fun."

"How does everybody get their horses to Florida?"

"We fly them, in airplanes specially equipped for the purpose."

Ben wondered what it would cost to transport the horses and equipment, let alone what the animals and the gear were worth. No wonder polo was the sport of kings, princes, and multimillionaires.

They walked back toward the house, Brutus cavorting beside them.

"Tell me something," Kramer said. "You must be an experienced policeman, true? To have become a detective lieutenant?"

"Sure. So?"

"So why is it you have trouble seeing this situation clearly? I don't mean to insult you, but you are totally wasting your time."

"What makes you say that?"

"Think about it. This is an open-and-shut case. Yet you go on meddling with a very powerful family, poking around with this investigation of yours. There is no possible way for you to get anywhere with it. The Cunninghams simply have too many connections, too much influence. You're only going to infuriate people who are in a position to make trouble for you personally."

"I have a job to do," Ben said, feeling like an asshole for saying it.

Kramer smiled. "That is my point, Lieutenant. If you're not careful, you might not have any job at all."

Slickly put, Ben thought. Made to sound like a word of friendly advice, when in fact it was a warning. Steel fist in a velvet glove. It was easy to see how this guy had been a con artist in Europe. Now he'd apparently found even easier pickings.

When they reached the house, they went back into the same room Ben had been in earlier, Brutus following.

"I see you were drinking coffee," Kramer said. "Like some fresh?"

"No thanks," Ben said. "I've had plenty."

"I'm going to have a Bloody Mary. Would you join me?"

Ben declined that as well, and Kramer pulled a cord beside the door, summoning the maid. When Alice appeared, Kramer asked her to bring the drink.

"Remember what I told you," Kramer then said to Ben. "It could be valuable. A word to the wise, right?"

"Yeah, sure."

"Sorry to keep you waiting," Ingrid said.

The men turned when she entered the room. Her hair had been carefully brushed and she had on a blouse of pale silk and a short, tight-fitting skirt.

"All right, Lieutenant," she said. "Let's get down to business. You want to ask me some questions and then you're going to tell me what my brother had to say. Is that correct?"

"Yes. That's correct."

Kramer leaned against the wall and folded his arms, a hint of a smile on his face.

37

Ingrid and Ben sat on sofas, facing each other across a coffee table. Kramer continued to stand, drinking the Bloody Mary as he listened to the discussion.

"All right, Lieutenant," Ingrid said. "What's on your mind?"

"You knew the writer who was interviewing your father when he died, didn't you? Jessica Silk?"

"Yes, I knew her."

"How close would you say the relationship was between them?"

Ingrid exhaled. "Let's cut out the crap, okay? That's a waste of time for both of us. What you want to know is what everybody wanted to know, after it happened. So why don't you come right out and ask me? The question is, was my father screwing Jessica Silk and is that what brought on the heart attack. Right?"

"I'd like to know what you can tell me about it, yes."

"The answer is, I don't know. My opinion? Probably he was. In fact, I'd say the odds were about a hundred to one in favor."

"Did the others think so, too?"

"Ask them."

"But if he was, that would make Ardis Merritt's version a lie, wouldn't it?"

"Look. We're all very conscious of public opinion, because that's something that's been drummed into us all our lives. Whatever went on up there in his office before he died, our attitude was, what difference did it make? At least that was how I felt about it."

"You don't seem to have any reservations about admitting that to me now."

"Why should I? The damage is over and done with. The newspapers and the TV circulated all those dirty stories, told all the rumors, invented angles nobody ever would have thought of. Not just about Jessica, either. There were plenty of sly hints about his playing around with other women, as well. And so what? It's past. He's dead, Jessica's dead, and that's the end of it.'' She glanced at her husband. ''Kurt? Tell Alice to make me a Bloody, will you?''

She turned back to Tolliver. ''You know what puzzles me?''

''What's that?''

''What makes you stick with it. You're like a leech. Is that because you don't have anything else to do, or are you just fascinated to be part of history?''

''Neither. I've been assigned to get all the facts in the case, and I don't believe I have them.''

Kramer grunted. ''That's not what he's after.''

Alice came into the room and Kramer gave her his empty glass, telling her to bring two more.

''And what are you going to do,'' Ingrid asked Ben, ''if you ever get these facts you claim you're looking for? Which I doubt very much will ever happen, but what if you do?''

''Then I deliver my report to District Attorney Oppenheimer,'' Ben replied. ''Now tell me what you know about these other friends your father had.''

''Other friends? Other affairs or mistresses, you mean? I don't know anything about that.''

Not much you don't, he thought.

Kramer spoke up. ''This so-called investigation of yours into the death of Senator Cunningham. That's not your real purpose, is it? What you really want to know about is the family's business interests. Isn't that so?''

Tolliver wondered what Kramer's reaction would be if he knew Ben had been told to stay the hell away from the subject, to keep his nose to himself. Kramer would probably laugh himself sick.

''I told you why I'm here,'' Tolliver said.

Kramer shrugged. ''Have it your way, Lieutenant. You may think you're going to run across some startling revelation, but as I told you earlier, you're not going to find anything. The district attorney's office and the federal investigators have been bothering the family for years, and they still have nothing to show for it. It's all simply a witch-hunt.''

Ingrid was eyeing Tolliver. ''You said you had a talk with Clay and he had some things to say about me. What were they?''

''He thinks you're too ambitious for your own good.''

She threw her head back and laughed. ''*I'm* too ambitious? That's a riot. And also typical of my dear brother.''

''He doesn't think too much of your abilities, either. I got the impression he'd like to push you out of the family's business.''

''Let him try. If there's any pushing to be done—''

Kurt's tone was harsh. ''Be careful—he's trying to trap you.''

She waved him off, saying to Tolliver, ''Clay is a very selfish man. I knew something like this would happen, now that my father's dead. You want to hear about relationships? What I could tell you would—''

She stopped as Alice returned to the room with a tray of Bloody Marys. The maid served one to Ingrid, the other to her husband, and left.

''What was it you could tell me?'' Ben asked.

''Never mind,'' Ingrid said. ''I don't intend to talk about Clay any further. Not about him, or about what he thinks of me and my abilities. Except for one thing.''

''What's that?''

''There's only one score that counts. And that's the final one.''

Ben was about to ask more questions, but she made it clear the interview was over. He got to his feet and thanked them for their time. Kramer escorted him to the front entrance.

The blond man opened the door. ''Have a nice trip back to New York, Lieutenant. And think about what I told you. You could save yourself a great deal of trouble.''

38

Peggy Demarest sat close to her sister, taking Jan's hand in her own and squeezing it gently. She spoke in low tones, making an effort to sound relaxed and unhurried. If Jan could understand what was being said to her, the last thing she'd want to hear, Peggy sensed, was anything that sounded like pressure.

''Hi, Jan. I just wanted you to know I'm here for you. I didn't come to ask questions or to make you think I expect a response. If you don't feel like acknowledging, no problem. Don't think I'll be disappointed if you don't. I'm only here because it's nice to be with you, and I thought you'd like some company.

''I have plenty of time today, too. That's because it's Wednesday and we closed at noon. In the summer, we close the whole day so Dr. Friedman can play golf, but that stops at the end of October. It wouldn't matter today, anyway; it's raining.

"That nice young guy I told you about? The one who studied dentistry at Tufts and maybe was going to join us? Well, he did. Monday was his first day. He's really cute, and I think he likes me. Not married, and he's already hinted around that he'd like me to help him get acquainted with the area. Be great if it turned into something, wouldn't it? Especially now that things aren't going too well with Don and me. He's kind of PO'd because I wouldn't agree to moving in together. Or I should say, agree to him moving in with me. I got the feeling it was more a question of him getting a good deal than really caring about me. Anyhow, we'll see where it goes with the new recruit.

"Dr. Chenoweth has told me about working with you, and I can imagine that's been hard for you. He said they were giving you all those tests. Just between us, I don't blame you if you don't want to go along when they're poking at you. You mustn't feel you have to, either.

"Do you remember when we were kids and the principal, Mr. Floyd, sent a note home saying you were acting up in class and that if you didn't improve you could get suspended? Mom got all upset, and when Dad came home, she showed him the note and he yelled at you. And you know what you said? You said Mr. Floyd could kiss your ass. You remember that? I never saw anybody so surprised as the old man when you came out with that. At first, he got red in the face and I thought he was going to brain you, but then he started laughing, and pretty soon we all were, until I thought we'd fall on the floor. Those were great days, weren't they? When Dad still had his job and wasn't drinking? At least not so much as he did later.

"So that's what you should say to the doctor. Just say, 'Dr. Chenoweth, kiss my ass.' "

There was the tiniest tug at her hand, but Peggy was aware of it. Yet when she looked at her sister's face, she saw no change in expression. The pale features were immobile, her eyes dull and vacant. Even the jagged scar on her cheek seemed not as bright as it usually did, as if all of her was even more subdued than usual, further away.

Peggy continued speaking in the same warm, intimate tone. "You thought that was funny, didn't you? That's why you squeezed back; I felt it. So I know you hear what I'm saying and you understand. And that's plenty for me. Eventually, you'll come out of this—whatever it is—and talk to me. But as far as I'm concerned, you ought to take your own sweet time. Whenever you feel like it, then that'll be soon enough.

"I probably shouldn't tell you this, but I have my own doubts sometimes about all these theories of the doctor's. A lot of them sound like bullshit, frankly. I mean, like your reaction when somebody mentions the Cunninghams."

There was no mistaking it this time. There was another tug at Peggy's hand, and Jan didn't relax the pressure; she kept on squeezing.

"Oh God," Peggy said, "I didn't mean to upset you, honest I didn't. I just wanted to reassure you. Let you know I'm always on your side."

A thought suddenly occurred to her. "Or are you telling me you agree with me? Are you, Jan? That you think a lot of it's bullshit, too?"

Jan's eyes moved. Ever so slightly, they turned toward Peggy. They weren't dull and lifeless now, but focused.

Peggy felt a deep thrill.

She's looking at me. She sees me.

"Jan, that's right, isn't it? When I told you the senator was dead and you cried, it was because the news made you sad, wasn't it? Because the Cunninghams have been so good to you, so helpful. I don't really know what's troubling you, unless maybe it's remembering what happened when you were hurt. Whatever it is, try not to think about it. Just shut it out of your mind. You're safe now and this place will take very good care of you. There's nothing to worry about and you can stay as long as you like to get well again. Okay?"

Jan's lips trembled and parted slightly. A dry, scratchy sound issued from her mouth.

Peggy was suddenly so excited, she could hardly breathe. She brought her face closer, until she was only inches from her sister. "Jan, what are you trying to say? I know you're trying to tell me something. If you want to say it, please try again."

What was the expression now in the deep brown eyes? Peggy wasn't sure, but instinct told her what to say next. "You can tell me,

Jan; it's okay. Whatever it is you want to tell me, go ahead and say it if you can. I promise to help you. I promise.''

The dry sound came out again and the grip on her hand tightened, her sister's nails digging into Peggy's flesh.

Peggy brought her ear close to Jan's mouth.

Jan's lips moved. ''Afraid.''

''Afraid? You're afraid? Of what, Jan? Tell me.''

''Afraid . . . he'll hurt me.''

Peggy's head snapped around. She stared at her sister. ''Who, Jan? Who'll hurt you? Who is it you're afraid of?''

It was like watching a small flame flicker and then die. Jan's eyes lost focus, lost all sign of recognition. The dullness returned and she stared blankly. The pressure on Peggy's hand eased and then relaxed altogether.

To her surprise, Peggy suddenly realized her body was damp with sweat. She still didn't know what Jan's fears were, or even whether they were imaginary, as she suspected. The important thing was that Jan had spoken to her, actually talked for the first time since she'd been here at the hospital.

She could hardly wait to tell Dr. Chenoweth.

39

It was early evening and the crowd at Max's Deli had thinned out. Tolliver and Mulloy both ordered coffee and hot pastrami on rye, taking their food to a small corner table. Ben couldn't help but think of the difference between this meal and what he'd had for lunch. Or even better, the dinner he'd had the night before at Christ Cella. The company then had been more to his liking, too; he wished he could see Shelley again.

Mulloy lifted the top slice of rye from his sandwich and slathered mustard onto the meat. ''How'd you make out with the family—and the woman at the foundation, what's her name?''

''Ardis Merritt. She slammed the door in my face. But the others opened up a little. Not a lot, but enough to let me know they hate each other.''

''Lovely. You get anything worthwhile?''

"Hard to tell. I spoke to the widow after I saw Merritt. She seemed bitter—and not only because of all the rumors about the way her husband died."

"She's bitter? Jesus, I should have it so bad. Now he's dead and she's got all that money."

"Not yet she hasn't. I got the impression the rest of them are trying to screw her out of it."

"Must be something they're born with."

"I did get one surprise, though."

"What was that?"

"Clay Cunningham took me to lunch. And then he offered me a job."

Mulloy had his sandwich halfway to his mouth. "No shit?"

"Said I could be the number-two man in their security operation. When the top guy died of old age, I'd get to be number one."

"Holy Christ. He talk money?"

"Hundred-fifty grand a year, plus a bonus and a car, some other extras."

Mulloy grinned. "So long, Ben. It's been nice knowing you. I hope you'll remember us poor folks."

"Bullshit."

"Hey, listen. You don't want it, could you give him my resume? Tell him I'd even come down a little. You know, forget the Ferrari. A Porsche would be okay."

Ben bit into his sandwich. He spoke around a mouthful. "Hard to figure, isn't it? What the hell would make him want me out that bad? Be different if I knew for sure what had killed his old man."

Mulloy chewed pastrami, his face growing serious. "Yeah, that's weird."

"All I've really done is spin wheels. I'm suspicious, but so what? He must know it's like the thing you're on. No hard evidence."

"Uh-huh."

"How about you? Did you find any kind of a pattern in those trades?"

"I think I might have, but I need to do more work on it. I can't be sure yet. Some of the same names keep popping up."

"What about the institutionals?"

"Oh, yeah. They were in almost all the deals. But there's no way we're gonna pin anything on them. With a lot of those accounts,

Cunningham's got discretionary agreements. You try charging conspiracy, their lawyers would laugh at you.''

''I suppose. What's Shackley got you doing?''

''Same old crap, tabbing a bunch of last year's figures. Just make-work, if you ask me.''

''Looks that way, doesn't it?''

Mulloy chewed on for a moment. ''You know, I can't understand why Shackley didn't ask the questions you did. Why he never tried to find out where the money went.''

''Neither can I. Unless . . .''

''I know what you're about to say. Wouldn't be the first time, right? You saw that yourself.''

''I sure did. And there's a hell of a lot of dough involved.''

''With Shackley it might not be money. Or money alone. I told you he's got political ambitions. That could be the biggest payoff of all.''

''Yeah, it could at that.'' Tolliver was hungrier than he'd realized. The pastrami didn't measure up to one of Cella's steaks, but it was hot and greasy and delicious, the juices of the meat mingling with the pungent flavor of the rye bread.

''Something like that'd also be a lot harder to trace,'' Mulloy said.

''I still might be able to get a line on it.''

''How?''

Ben smiled. ''Friends in high places. If I make out, I'll let you know.''

''Great. What about the other one—the sister?''

''I went up to Connecticut, to her farm. There's deep animosity between her and her brother, but I think you can put that down to jealousy. And also behind-the-scenes battles over who gets what from the old man's estate.''

''She clam up, too, about how the senator died?''

''Partly. But she did say she thought the old boy and Silk were getting it on.''

''Hey—an honest woman? Amazing. What else she tell you?''

''Not much. Except more slamming doors—from her husband first and then from her. I'm starting to get nosebleeds.''

Mulloy chuckled and swallowed the last of his sandwich.

Ben drained his cup. ''You finished? I want to get back.''

"Yeah, I'm set."

Tolliver reached for the check, but Mulloy beat him to it. "Allow me, Lieutenant."

When they returned to the investigators' offices, Ben got out his notes and messed around with them for a time, trying to work out a plausible scenario and not succeeding, mostly because he was finding it hard to concentrate.

He knew what the trouble was. Picking up the phone, he called her number at WPIC TV.

She answered on the first ring. "Shelley Drake."

Just hearing her voice gave him a lift. It was crisp and businesslike, but he could detect a warmth, as well. And he could picture her face, framed by the honey blond hair.

"Hi," he said. "It's me."

The tone grew warmer. "Hi, I've been thinking about you."

"Good. I thought I'd bring something to your attention."

"What is it?"

"A partnership requires cooperation. How about we get together and cooperate?"

"That sounds marvelous. I have to do an update at eleven, but after that?"

"I can't wait."

"You'll have to. Come to my place tonight, okay?"

"Sure."

She gave him the address and he hung up, feeling jubilant.

40

Hi, Shel," Jeremy Sloane said. "How's it going?"

Shelley looked up from her word processor as the editor drew over a chair and sat down beside her desk. She was putting together a piece on a shooting in Brownsville and didn't have much time to get it ready for the upcoming newscast. A young mother had been out pushing her baby in a stroller when neighborhood crack dealers started a gun battle. A stray bullet had struck her in the head and killed her. It was a good story; one of the dealers was the baby's father.

"Okay," Shelley said. "But I'm in a hurry."

The producer affected Armani suits and longish hair, a current vogue. He peered at her. ''This won't take long. Just wanted to know how you were doing with the senator and his girlfriend.''

Sloane could be a nuisance sometimes. She sat back and folded her arms. ''Doing fine.''

''Fine? What's fine? What have you got?''

''No further developments at the moment. But I hope to have something soon.''

He drummed his fingers on her desk. ''Isn't this cop giving you anything? What's his name—Tolliver?''

''He's agreed to trade information with me, yes. But that's very sensitive. I told you, I can't use anything unless he gives me the word.''

''Yeah, I know. But let's be realistic, Shel. We could be missing an opportunity here. You got started on this before anybody else did, and I encouraged you.''

''You mean you grudgingly let me work on it after I convinced you it could be terrific. That what you mean, Jerry?''

''Whatever. The problem now is, the story's already old news and we never got anything special out of it. We were just part of the pack, right?''

''So what are you saying?''

''What I'm saying is, I don't want it just to be forgotten about. I want to keep the thing alive.''

''What do you suggest?''

''I suggest you do a piece on it. Spice it up with something that sounds like a new angle. You know, there's a rumor that the writer was pregnant by the senator, whatever.''

''That's already been done. ABC did it, in a man-in-the-street.''

''Something else, then. Maybe on what she was writing.''

''I don't know what she was writing. Not for sure, anyway.''

''What happened to her material, by the way?''

''I don't know that, either.''

''The cop know?''

''The police weren't able to locate either a manuscript or her notes.''

''Hey, that's an angle right there. You know—what were the secret contents of the article that insiders say would have shocked the nation, and where is the manuscript now?''

"Um. Maybe."

"Look, Shel. I want you to do something on the case, okay? I almost don't care what it is, just so long as it sounds hot and mysterious. The cop must have told you things, didn't he?"

"A few things, yes."

"Such as?"

"I'd have to go through my notes."

"Go through them, then. Find something you can use and show it to me."

"But I'd still need to clear anything with him first. We have an agreement."

His voice took on a edge. "You also have a job, right? Anyhow, it's not up to some fucking detective to decide what we can and cannot use. Freedom of the press, Shel, and the airways. First Amendment. The people have a right to know, and we have a duty to tell them. So put something together, okay? And then get it to me. I want to be on the air with it by tomorrow, or the next day at the latest. Before the story dies of old age."

He got up from the chair and walked back across the newsroom toward his office, shaking his head.

Shelley watched him go. Someday, she promised herself, I am going to slug him right in the teeth.

She went back to writing the piece on the young mother, lying dead with a bullet in her head, her baby crying in the stroller. There wasn't much to work with; all Shelley had on videotape was a shot of bloodstains on the sidewalk.

She was also tired; trying to make a lot out of a little was a grind. But at least she'd be seeing Ben later on. And that was something to look forward to.

41

The apartment was on East Seventy-ninth Street, on the fifteenth floor of a yellow brick high rise between Second and Third avenues. Ben got there just after midnight. When she let him in, she was wearing a terry-cloth robe and her hair was wrapped in a towel. She rebolted the door before slipping her arms around his neck and giving him a warm, wet kiss. It was the best thing that had happened to him all day.

"Just got out of the shower," she said. "There's a bottle of bourbon in the kitchen. You can make us a drink while I put something on."

"Don't go to any trouble," Ben said, and kissed her again. This one lasted longer than the first and was much deeper. When she came up for air, she whispered, "Maybe I should take something off, instead."

"Good idea." They went into her bedroom and spent the next hour in bed in a state of bliss, feverish at first and then slowly winding down to pleasant exhaustion.

Later she snuggled up to him, tucking her body in against his. He lay on his back, gently stroking her flank with his fingertips. Her skin felt smooth and velvety and slightly damp to his touch.

"Ben?"

"Mm?"

"What are you thinking?"

"Tender thoughts."

"About me?"

"About a ham sandwich. I'm starved."

She dug her elbow into his ribs. "You're just like all other men."

"How do you know—been doing research?"

Her tone changed, taking on a coolness. "Maybe."

"Hey, I was only teasing. Honest."

"Better be."

"I think you're wonderful, Shelley."

"You glad I'm your partner?"

"Of course."

Her hand drifted over his belly. "I think you're pretty great, too."

"Good. Then we're friends again, right?"

"We always were. At least since you got to know me."

"I'm happy I did."

Her hand drifted lower and gripped him. "So am I."

To his delight, he felt himself respond once more. He turned to her and they made love again, slowly and easily this time.

"This is heavenly," she whispered. "I wish we could stay like this all night."

Ben wished he could, too, at the same time wondering at the differences between men and women. That was at least one area where female superiority wasn't even open to debate. Her description of what they were doing was accurate, but when this one ended, he was sure he'd have absolutely nothing left.

He was right; he didn't.

It would have been easy to sink into sleep at that point, but the thought of food was keeping him awake. He got out of bed and put on his pants and his shirt and Shelley slipped back into her robe. They went into the kitchen and she made coffee and toast and scrambled a plate of eggs for him. Then she sat opposite him at the breakfast table, watching him eat.

The eggs were delicious, done just the way he liked them, sprinkled liberally with fresh-ground pepper. He hadn't been hungry, he decided, but ravenous.

"That's another thing," Shelley said.

He spoke around a mouthful. "What is?"

"Men are always hungry afterward."

Ben looked at her questioningly.

She smiled. "I must have read that someplace."

"Uh-huh."

"How's it going?"

"The case? Sometimes I'm not sure. It seems as though a lot of people would like me just to forget all about it."

"Including the district attorney?"

"No, not him. He's the one guy who's been willing to have me keep going, although he's not convinced I'm making much progress. But at least he's given me a little more time."

"How much time?"

"He said a few days, but that's all. Wasn't for him, I would have packed it in long ago."

"I doubt that. Have you talked to the members of the family again?"

"All except Clay's wife, Laura Bentley."

"I interviewed her once. Know what she told me afterward? That she'd love to go back to her career as an actress. She was very serious about it, pumping me about how she could get started in TV. Said her agent wasn't so hot on the idea but that she was. And then she said the big problem would be her husband. He wouldn't want her to."

"And that was the end of it?"

"Apparently. Imagine, like living in the Dark Ages. I'd love to see him try that with me, if he was my husband. Know what I'd tell him?"

"What would you tell him, Shel?"

"That I respectfully disagreed."

"Yeah, I'll bet that's how you'd put it."

"What about the others—what did you learn from them?"

"Nothing much. They're not too pleased to have me still digging."

"I can imagine. The more I learn about them, the more I realize their public image is a sham. Not just now, either. When I started on the story, I read a lot of old newspaper accounts on microfiche. They've always had plenty of enemies."

"Interesting. Ties in with information the prosecutors have been gathering about the brokerage."

"How did that get started, and when?"

"It was back in the twenties," Ben said. "The Colonel would form a group of his friends and they'd pick a public company and begin buying shares. Then they'd trade the shares back and forth, driving the price up. At the same time, the Colonel would pay financial reporters to write stories about how great the company was and what a terrific future it had. The public would read that stuff and see how the stock was going and *boom,* the rush was on. When the price got to be astronomical, the Colonel and his pals would sell out, leaving the rubes holding the bag."

"Nice. No wonder he wanted to start a brokerage."

"Of course. Then he could run his schemes on a much broader scale. He'd not only be secretly pooling stocks, he'd also be brokering shares to other investors and collecting commissions."

"And that's where the senator got his training?"

"Right. The Colonel brought him into the brokerage, and eventually he headed it. Then when his children were old enough, he had them come into the family businesses, too."

"What made him go into politics?"

"From what I can see," Ben said, "they were always in it. Behind the scenes, anyway. I would guess the only difference with the senator was that he decided to run for office. Nobody can say for sure how many millions it cost him to get that seat."

Shelley filled his cup with fresh coffee. ''But that was typical, too, wasn't it? Whenever he wanted something, he just bought it. Have you turned up any more on his relationship with Jessica Silk?''

''No, nothing.''

''That's something else I've been wondering about.''

''What about it?''

''The article she was supposed to be writing. What do you suppose happened to that material?''

''I have no idea.''

''She was right about one thing.''

''What's that?''

''It'd be worth a fortune right about now.''

''I imagine it would.''

Shelley drank some of her coffee. Then she said, ''Ben? I have something to ask you.''

''Yeah, what is it?''

''My editor's been pressing me to do a piece on the story of the senator and Jessica—about their relationship, and their deaths.''

''So?''

''So I need to freshen it up, put in some new things.''

He sipped his coffee. ''You can put in anything you want, just so long as it isn't anything to do with me or what I've been telling you.''

''Hey, that's not fair.''

''Fair doesn't have anything to do with it. This isn't field hockey.''

''Who said it was? What I meant was that some of what you've learned came from me. So I should have the right to go on the air with part of it.''

''Remember what we agreed on back in the beginning. You use nothing unless I give you a green light.''

''Yeah, but damn it, you can't just muzzle me. Instead of giving me an edge, that puts me at a disadvantage.''

''Nobody's trying to muzzle you. I just have to be careful about what gets out.''

She was quiet for a moment. ''A rehash of old stuff would be okay, wouldn't it?''

''Sure it would. Listen, Shel. I'm not trying to make this tough for you. It's just that there are things I don't want to become public.

If they got to the wrong people, they could screw things up big. You already know more about this investigation than you should."

"All right, Lieutenant. Sir."

"Come on, don't be mad."

"I'm not. Just hurt. Why don't you take me back to bed and comfort me?"

"I'll be happy to go to bed, but I don't know if I can do much about the comfort part."

She got up from her chair and came over to where he sat, pressing her body against his face. "You could at least give it a try, couldn't you?"

He put his hands on her hips and drew her tight, becoming aware of a faint but tantalizingly pungent bouquet. "Yeah," he said. "I could do that."

Getting to his feet, he picked her up in his arms and carried her back into the bedroom.

42

I want him stopped," she said.

Orcus gripped the telephone. "Don't worry about it."

Her voice rose. "Don't worry about it? What am I supposed to do—just sit here, pretend he's not a problem? Do you realize how much trouble the son of a bitch has already caused? He keeps it up, he could tip the whole thing over. And you're telling me not to worry?"

"I'll take care of it."

"You'd better. He has to be out of the picture. Permanently."

"I know that. It'll be done."

"When?"

"As soon as I get it worked out."

"And how soon will that be? Tomorrow? Next week?"

He hated being goaded, especially by a female. "You think it's simple, don't you? As if he's some dummy you can just walk in on. Nothing to it, right? You snap your fingers, it's all over. Let me tell you, that's not the way it is. It has to be done in a way that he'll never know what hit him. And that takes planning."

"So plan it. I don't want this fucked up by some jerk-off cop."

"It won't be. I said I'll take care of it."

"You'd better. Or else somebody else will."

"Don't make me laugh."

"And don't make me angry. I don't care to hear any insolent remarks from you. All I want to know is that you did it, that this Tolliver no longer exists. Is that clear?"

"Yeah, it's clear. Just be patient, all right?"

But she'd already hung up. He put the phone down and ground his teeth until they ached.

43

In the morning they made love again. It was, Ben thought, a beautiful way to start the day. Made him feel relaxed and happy, glad to be alive. Put his problems in perspective, too; cut them down to size. He resolved to do it more often.

Afterward they showered together, with plenty of laughing and mutual soaping, and then they got dressed and had a breakfast of orange juice, croissants, and coffee. While they ate, they watched the news on a small TV that sat on the kitchen counter.

There was the usual stream of depressing reports, including a tape of Shelley delivering her piece on the mother who'd been shot by the crack dealer. But there was nothing on the deaths of the senator and Jessica Silk, which was fine with Ben.

Before leaving Shelley's apartment, he called Dr. Alan Stein, a psychiatrist who was a consultant to the NYPD. He told Stein what he was working on and asked whether he could have a few minutes of the doctor's time. "Come ahead," Stein said. His first patient wasn't due until eleven.

Ben dropped Shelley off at WPIC TV and from there he took Second Avenue down to East Tenth Street. The psychiatrist lived and practiced in one of the old row houses near Tompkins Square that had been built a century ago as middle-income homes. The houses now went for a fortune, if you could find one for sale.

Tolliver parked the Ford on the street and walked up the front steps. He rang the bell and a moment later heard the sound of bolts being thrown and locks undone. The door swung open and Alan Stein greeted him.

Whenever Ben saw this man, he was struck by how little the doctor resembled other psychiatrists he'd run across, usually in court cases where they'd been expert witnesses. Whereas most of them tended to be effete, Stein looked more like a steelworker. His massive chest and shoulders were encased in a red-and-black-checked wool shirt, his legs in khakis. His head was massive, too, with wiry gray hair coming down over his ears and a full beard covering his jaw. Only his eyes seemed scholarly, blinking behind thick glasses.

"How've you been, Lieutenant?"

"Okay, Doc. Glad you could see me."

"So am I. You're on an interesting case. I've been following the developments."

Stein locked the door and shoved the bolts back into place, then led Tolliver to the rear of the house, where his study was.

The room was large and cluttered: a desk stacked high with books and papers, a worn leather couch, two upholstered chairs. Packed bookcases covered one wall and a table held a PC and more books. There was a bar in the corner, but it was too early for a drink; instead, Stein poured mugs of coffee from an electric pot behind his desk. Both men sat in the comfortable chairs.

"The newspapers imply the senator died during a tryst with the writer," Stein said, "and that the rumors are what drove the lady to suicide. So tell me—did she or didn't she?"

Ben sipped coffee. "What's your guess?"

"An emphatic no. I never met her, but some things seemed obvious. For one, she was not only functioning at the time but was highly effective. A tough young woman, succeeding in a tough business. Someone like her wouldn't cave in because she was in the center of a controversy. Or because the spotlight was on her, no matter how egregious the publicity. In fact, she'd be more likely to do the exact opposite. She'd look for a way to turn it to her advantage."

Ben smiled. "That's how I see it, too, Doc. It's part of why I'm here. I don't think she went off that terrace of her own accord."

"Suspects?"

"Not yet."

"And the senator?"

"Also suspicious. But I'm getting a lot of pressure to revise that opinion. Not only from the family, but also from the powers that be. Seems that everybody'd like to see the whole thing marked closed."

"Everybody except the media."

Ben thought of Shelley and what she'd told him about her editor urging her to keep the story alive.

"Which is only to be expected," Stein continued. "They're not called vultures for nothing. What about all these innuendos concerning the old man's sex life? Anything to them?"

"At first, I didn't think so. You hear crap like that about everybody who's in the public eye. People can't get enough of it. But then I also picked up rumors about his abusing women. And after that, I went to the autopsy on the Silk woman. There were marks on her body."

"What kind of marks?"

"Bites and bruises, and burns. The burns were the worst. They were from a lighted cigar, the ME thought. Some of them were old and scabbed over, but some were very recent—raw and open. The senator smoked cigars."

"Ah. Fascinating."

"Was to me, too. Assuming he did the burning, I wondered what you could tell me about that. Might give me some better insights into what he was like, what their relationship actually was."

"Where on her body were the burns?"

"Upper thighs, and her buttocks."

Stein put his head back, thinking about it. "So if he did inflict them, it would have been during sex, in a classic act of sadism. Which is a form of rape."

That was another way this guy was different from other shrinks Tolliver had known. Most of them couldn't give you a straight answer if their lives depended on it. But Stein never failed to be objective in his appraisal of a personality, his sizing up of a situation involving human conduct. Ben knew why: The doctor had worked for eight years at Fairlawn, the hospital in Virginia for the criminally insane. Stein had no illusions about people who habitually committed violent crimes, nor did he apologize for them, as did so many of his colleagues.

"Let me make a few things clear," the doctor said. "First of all, the popular view nowadays is that sexual assault has little or nothing to do with sex. Analysts claim that a man who rapes does so essentially to exert power over his victims. It's a matter of control, they say. Or else the rapist is using sex as a weapon, because he hates women. He was abused by them as a child, so he's taking revenge on his mother, or whoever it might be. You've heard those theories often enough, haven't you?''

''Every cop has,'' Ben said.

''Sure. Prosecutors and defense lawyers both play variations on the theme. And both find it very easy to produce psychiatrists who'll back them up. The theories are also popular among other so-called experts. Sociologists, for instance—because the ideas fit so nicely with their own attitudes about the relationships between men and women in contemporary life. All examples, the social workers'll tell you, of how males try to subjugate females: dominate them, tyrannize them, through sexual aggression.''

''But in many cases it's true, isn't it?''

''Of course it is. But it's only part of the story. Fundamentally, sex crimes are the result of human instinct run amok. And as you know, nearly all such crimes are committed by men. Very rarely by women. But what's not known—or at least not accepted even in the face of incontrovertible evidence—is that many of the offenders commit their crimes because they truly *enjoy* them.''

''Okay, go on.''

''It's most apparent among sexual abusers of children. They derive intense pleasure from behavior a normal person would consider horrifying. And yet they often make a huge game of their sickness. Which is a form of denial, of course. It's really okay, they're saying—just a lot of harmless fun. So they form clubs, pass pictures around, swap victims, act for all the world like some sort of ghoulish hobbyists, which in a way is what they are. Except that what they collect are not coins or stamps.''

''A lot of that's come to light recently.''

''Right. But the sexual sadist can be even worse. Much worse. Because his aggressions more often lead to murder. Which is why this is an area in which gays and straights meet on common ground. Both groups are appalled by sadism.''

''For good reason.''

''Yes. In terms of the end results of their acts, a Jeffrey Dahmer was no different from a Raymond Shawcross. Both took their sadistic sex acts to the extreme. The gender of the victims was irrelevant.''

"Because the killers' heads were screwed up the same way."

"Precisely. All cases of serial murder are basically sexual in nature. And in *most* of them, the killer derives intense sexual pleasure from killing his victim. He may have sex with the victim before, during, or after the victim is dead, but to him, the killing and the sex are all part of the same act. That's especially true in cases where torture is involved and the process is strung out over a period of time—where it takes hours, even days, for the victim to die. And there is nothing the killer can do, or even imagine, that approaches the excitement he experiences from committing his crimes."

"Okay, but let's get back to the senator. You're not putting him in that category, are you?"

"It's only a matter of degree, Lieutenant. In the extreme, sadism manifests itself as murder. In lesser instances, the cruelty inflicted is not as severe, but the spirit is the same. At what point on the scale would we place Senator Cunningham? We may never know for sure, because the man is dead. Then again, perhaps your investigation will produce a definitive answer."

"I hope it does."

"So do I. But whether it does or not, I'll say this unequivocally. If he was the one responsible for burning that young woman's body, then all my experience tells me the man was incapable of obtaining sexual satisfaction without inflicting pain. And I'd be equally certain he enjoyed himself hugely while he was inflicting it. Now, to what extent did he indulge himself in that pleasure? Not only with this journalist but with other women? That, I can't say."

"But the odds are pretty good she wasn't the only one, right?"

"Absolutely. What's more, the senator was one of those rare people who had the wherewithal to do any damn thing he wanted to do. He had the money and the power to live on a scale most of us can't comprehend, able to buy anything or anyone he wanted. Laws and the rules of society were for the rest of us, not for him. The problem is, that has a corrupting effect not only on the people such a man controls, but on the man himself. To a personality of that type, women would be regarded simply as possessions, something he could use and then discard. He'd throw them away, get new ones. They were disposable."

"I see."

"How about some more coffee, Lieutenant?"

"No thanks, Doc. I have to move along, and you've got patients coming. But you've given me a couple of good ideas."

"Good. That's what I'm here for. Call me anytime."

44

As soon as he reached his office, Tolliver telephoned police headquarters in Washington, D.C., and said he wanted to speak to Captain Arnold Jurasky.

As he waited, Ben thought about the last time he'd seen the captain. Jurasky had been a lieutenant then. He and Tolliver had met when they attended the course for police officers that was given once a year at the FBI Academy in Quantico, Virginia. Each city in the United States was invited to send one officer, so to be selected was a considerable honor. Attendance also formed a lifelong bond among the cops who went; they became members of an elite group.

The captain picked up. "Jurasky."

"Hey, Arnie. Ben Tolliver."

"Ben! How the hell are you?"

"Terrific. How you doing?"

"Not bad. You in Washington?"

"No such luck. I'm in New York, on an investigation for the DA."

"Yeah? I figured you'd make PC by now."

"I turned it down," Ben said. "Didn't want to lose the common touch."

Jurasky laughed. "That's my man. What can I do for you?"

Ben told him about the assignment.

"Ah, the senator. That got a lot of play here, as you'd expect. The *Post* and TV did their usual job of blowing up every rumor they could find, especially after the woman took her dive. How's it going?"

"Hard to say. Still a cuppi." That was copspeak, an acronym for circumstances unknown pending police investigation.

"But suspicious, right?"

"Yeah, very."

"I thought so. He had a reputation, you know."

"Anything specific while he was in the Senate?"

"Sure. We had several incidents. Each time, the women said they'd been knocked around by him, but then they retracted, refused to sign a complaint. Said they were mistaken, that it must've been somebody else. One of them wound up in the Georgetown Medical Center. But she wouldn't press charges, and that was the end of it."

"Anything more on him?"

"No, just gossip. That's what this town operates on."

"There's something else I wanted to ask about."

"Shoot."

"The Cunninghams have their own security force, headed by a guy who used to work for your department. The senator hired him. Name is Evan Montrock. I'm curious about his record."

"Is that M-o-n-t-r-o-c-k?"

"Correct."

"No problem, thanks to the wonders of our marvelous mainframe—when it works. You want to hang on, or should I call you back?"

"I'll hold," Ben said. Thinking, Thank God for contacts. If he had to go through interdepartmental channels, it would take days to get the information he wanted.

Looking out through the glass walls of the office, he observed the usual beehive, investigators juggling reams of paper, talking on the telephone, leafing through file drawers. "When men become robots, they descend into madness." Who wrote that—Kafka? Sounded like him.

Jurasky came back on. "Okay, here we go. Evan Montrock joined the force on five June, nineteen seventy-eight. Metro Police Training six months, graduated third in his class. One year patrol officer, then . . . uh-oh. Twice reprimanded for violations, code of conduct. Disciplined, put on probationary status. Month later brought up on charges. Accused of beating a suspect, resulting in suspect's death. Insufficient evidence for indictment, but discharged from the force after investigation by Internal Affairs. Must've been before civilians started using video cameras."

"Yeah. Then what?"

"That's all we have on him in departmental records. You want me to see if he's got a rap sheet?"

"I'd appreciate it."

Ben hung on again, continuing to watch the activity on the floor outside his office. What would come after the madness? Maybe the investigators would lose it, the way postal employees had been doing. Freak out and start shooting up the work site.

The captain returned. "Ben? Nothing. Not even the arrest for battery, because it wound up like I told you."

"Anything else on him?"

"Nope, that was it. No forwarding address, whereabouts unknown."

"Okay, Arnie, thanks. Come to New York soon, I'll buy you a drink."

"How about a show girl instead?"

"What flavor?"

"I'll leave that to you."

Ben hung up. So Montrock had lied about his background. So what else was new? Had anyone in the case provided straight information? And what more might the security chief have lied about? Had he related everything he knew about Jennifer Silk's visit to the senator?

Montrock came off as smug and highly self-satisfied about his soft job and his perks. Ben wondered whether he knew his boss was readying him for the scrap heap—if in fact that was what was going on.

After making notes on what Jurasky had told him, Tolliver unlocked a drawer and got out the thick stack of folders on the Cunningham investigation. He was studying the reports when a knock sounded at the door of the cubicle. He looked up, to see Jack Mulloy come in with a worried look on his face.

"What's with you?" Ben asked.

Mulloy shut the door. "We got trouble. Brannigan heard you had the files on the Cunningham case and went batshit. Told me to get them back."

"What's his problem?"

"Shackley's been on his ass. I saw the two of them huddling together in Brannigan's office, and then after that the captain had me in there and read me out. He said you're getting a lot of people pissed off, sticking your face into things that don't have anything to do with you. He said you could've had your report finished and in to the DA a week ago."

"Why doesn't Brannigan tell me himself?"

"That's not his style. He just said I was to get the stuff back and keep it locked up. Said if you want to be a hero, do it on your own. I tried to tell you how things work around here, remember? How it's all politics?''

''Yeah, so you did.'' Ben went about stuffing the papers back into their respective jackets.

''Look out for Shackley, Ben. The guy's a buzz saw.''

''Uh-huh.''

Mulloy picked up the stack and rose to his feet, holding the material in his arms. He glanced over his shoulder and then turned back, lowering his voice. ''You want to know anything that's in here, you got it, okay?''

''Now who's violating Mulloy's rule?''

''Yeah, maybe I'm crazy, too. See you later.'' He left the office.

Tolliver sat back in his chair. If Shackley was trying to make trouble for him, better to face it head-on. Confronting Brannigan would be a waste of time. The captain would simply duck the issue and then later come down on Mulloy with both boots. Tolliver had seen enough of the type in his years on the force. The problem was, nowadays there seemed to be more of them. In his own department, as well as here.

Getting to his feet, he told himself to keep in mind what he wanted to accomplish, not let his emotions run away with him. Then he headed for Fletcher Shackley's office.

45

Striding through the corridors, Tolliver thought it was amazing, the number of ADAs in this rabbit warren. Hundreds of attorneys, battling thousands more on the private side. Someday, when humanity was in its final convulsions, when civilization was gone and the earth was blackened and scorched, there would be nobody left but the lawyers—fighting over whatever remained.

A clerk pointed out Shackley's office and Ben went to it. The layout was luxurious—by a cop's standards. It featured an outer reception area with a secretary at a desk and an inner space occupied by two trial-preparation assistants, one male, one female. Beyond that was the prosecutor's private abode.

Ben told the young woman at the outer desk who he was and she spoke into a telephone. He waited, fully expecting to be brushed off. But a moment later, the door to the office opened and the senior ADA himself came out to greet him, inviting Ben to come inside.

The interior was even more impressive than the outer trappings: leather chairs, bookcases, a rug on the floor, and a large desk that most likely was Shackley's personal property. And not only one window but three—with sweeping views of the civic center and city hall.

Shackley spoke in his customary nasal tones. "Well, Lieutenant. Captain Brannigan tells me you have your work just about wrapped up."

That was news to Tolliver. "Not quite. There are still questions I don't have answers to."

"Is that so? What questions are they?"

"I don't know for sure what killed Senator Cunningham. The death certificate says it was a coronary, but I'm not convinced. And I don't know the exact circumstances of Jessica's Silk's death, either."

A small smile tilted one corner of Shackley's mouth. "In other words, you haven't been able to disprove the facts, regardless of how obvious they might be."

"They weren't obvious to me. The district attorney asked for a complete report, and that's what I'm going to give him."

"And if this turned into an even bigger news story, that would be all right with you, wouldn't it? Might even make you a kind of celebrity."

It was difficult for Ben to sit there, having his chain pulled. "I'm only trying to finish an assignment. I think there's a connection between the deaths and the situation your group is investigating."

"What would one have to do with the other?"

"That's one of the things I want to find out. I need the files."

Shackley folded his arms. "Lieutenant, let me explain a few things. You may not be aware of it, but I have a total of six assistant district attorneys working on this investigation, and twice that many TPAs. Plus the work being done by the detectives, Mulloy and Chief Brannigan. The captain's a very experienced man, you know. Been involved with cases of this kind for many years."

"I'm sure he has."

"Anyway, the problems we've encountered have been considerable. The Cunninghams are represented by a battery of lawyers, some of the best firms in the city. We don't have their resources, couldn't possibly match their numbers. The SEC has also been investigating, and they've virtually given up on bringing charges.''

''Yes, I know that.''

''You see, it's one thing to suspect illegal activity, and quite another to pin it down with indisputable evidence. That's what we've been working to put together.''

''For a couple of years now.''

''Takes time. Not like chasing a mugger.''

''I never thought it was. But I want access to those files.''

The prosecutor thrust out his jaw. ''That won't be possible, Lieutenant. The reports are too sensitive to have them shuffled around. As a matter of fact, Mulloy never should have shown you any of them without express permission from me.''

''I asked to see them.''

''All the more reason he should have cleared it with me first. But I'll tell you what. If there is anything you need to know, feel free to ask me. That way, we won't be compromising our work. That's fair enough, isn't it? Agreed?''

''I'll give it some thought.'' He wondered how it would feel to give this jackass a punch in the nose. Great, probably.

Shackley sat back. ''Glad we've reached an understanding.''

Tolliver walked out, steaming. He went back down the corridor and got into the elevator.

If Shackley wanted to play rough, Ben had a few moves of his own.

46

Her nameplate was on the wall next to the door: FERN ROSE, ASSISTANT DISTRICT ATTORNEY. At that point, any similarity between her office and Shackley's ended.

There was a TPA outside, but no secretary. No window in the office, either. The tiny room seemed even more cramped than Ben's cubicle, every available inch piled high with case files and books and stacks of paper. A computer and a modem were on a stand beside the beat-up metal desk and there was a printer on a nearby bookcase. A filing cabinet stood alongside that, which left hardly enough room for anyone to squeeze inside.

She was on the phone when Ben arrived, standing while she yelled into the mouthpiece. "I don't give a goddamn, Arturo. You said you'd testify, and I took your word. So don't hand me that shit about you can't remember. You pull that with me, I'll go right to your parole officer. You understand? The hearing's tomorrow morning at eleven. I want you in my office an hour before that. *Diez horas,* Arturo. Be here!"

She slammed the phone down. Fern Rose was small, maybe an inch over five feet in heels. She had an elfin face and a spray of taffy-colored hair, and she wore a dark gray sharkskin suit she probably thought made her look determined.

She noticed her visitor. "Hello, Ben. You want some coffee?"

He grinned. "Sure."

"Black, right? Nancy, bring us two coffees, will you? Both black, no sugar."

Tolliver moved some books and sat on one of the two straight-backed chairs bolted to the floor in front of her desk, but she remained standing. Her fighting stance, he thought.

She eyed him. "What's up?"

That was Fern. No nonsense about how've you been or isn't this a beautiful fall day. "I'm on a special assignment for the DA," he said. "Looking into the death of Senator Cunningham."

"I heard. So?"

"I need a favor."

"Name it."

"Before I do, anything I tell you has to stay strictly confidential."

"Understood."

"I've been running into some roadblocks. There's an investigation into Cunningham Securities that's been going on at the same time."

"Yeah, Fletcher Shackley's heading it up."

"Right. The problem is, I think there could be a connection between that case and mine. But Shackley wants me nowhere near it."

"Have you told that to Oppenheimer?"

"No. I don't want to get him into it if I can help it. He'd most likely back Shackley up."

"Yeah, he would."

The TPA came into the office with two plastic cups of black coffee. She put them down on the desk.

"Thanks, Nancy," Fern said. "Better shut the door on your way out."

As soon as they were alone, the ADA looked at Tolliver. "You're not really gonna ask me to do this, are you?"

"Do what?"

"Go around Shackley's end."

He picked up one of the cups. "You know what, Fern? You have a blunt way of putting things."

"But that's it, right?"

"You said you'd do me a favor."

"I didn't say that included cutting my throat."

"All I want is some information."

"Look, Ben. I'm no longer in the Rackets Bureau. So I doubt I could be much help to you with whatever it is you're after. What I do now is prosecute dirtbags. That character I was talking to when you came in? He's the night clerk in a hot-sheet hotel on West Fortieth Street. A hooker took a john there; the john strangled her. Cops've got a suspect, but now the clerk can't remember what the john looked like, he says. I live in a different world from Mr. Shackley."

"Not so different."

"The hell it isn't. I handle about two hundred cases at any given time, most of 'em down-and-dirty. Fletcher Shackley is one of the DA's stars. He gets the good stuff, the cream. With lots of eager people to assist."

"I see." Ben sipped his coffee. "You remember about three years ago, you wanted something on a gentleman named John Bugelli? Johnny Bugs? He owned a club called the Paper Moon, on Seventh Avenue."

She groaned.

"As I recall, you wanted to know about Mr. Bugelli's friendship with people in the Lucchese family and whether he sold them an interest in the club. After which it went bust and then burned down."

She groaned again. "Jesus, don't you ever forget anything?"

"No."

"Okay, so you got me proof of the connection."

"And that's how you made the case, right?"

''The senior prosecutor made the case. I only worked on it.''

''But that was the key, wasn't it? I got what you were after, from Mr. Bugelli's former wife. You said if there was anything I ever needed, just ask.''

Fern exhaled a stream of air. Then she sat down at her desk and stared at him resignedly. ''What do you want?''

''Not much, really. Just the bank records on Cunningham Mining.''

''What am I, a magician?''

''No, I would say you're more of an irresistible young woman.''

''How would you like a kick in the nuts, Tolliver?''

''Hey, I saw you smile. Go ahead, let it all out.''

She rolled her eyes.

''I don't need everything,'' Ben said. ''All I want to know about is payouts from the account.''

''That's all? Should be a breeze, huh? I'll tell the bank to please send the books over to me—by messenger.''

''Come on, Fern. You've got ways.''

''Sure. The ways are through the issuance of a subpoena duces tecum—an order to produce records. Which has to be requested by the prosecutor in charge of the case and then signed by a judge. If I ever tried that, it wouldn't be only Shackley I'd have to answer to. The DA himself would personally pull my skin off in strips. Be reasonable, will you?''

''That's what I'm trying to be.''

''Uh-huh. What are these payouts you're looking for?''

''I think there are large sums of money that have gone missing. Millions of dollars that Cunningham Securities made in illegal trading schemes and then turned over to the holding company, Cunningham Mining. I want to find out where that money went. I know some of it would have been invested in legitimate businesses, but I can't believe the rest is just sitting in an account at Fidelity Trust.''

''Hey, Ben. You know what you're messing with? You could really get your ass in a crack. And mine, too.''

''But like I said, Fern, you have ways. What about your contacts at the IRS? They share information with the DA's office on RICO cases. True?''

''Sure, of course.''

''Okay, and federal law requires a bank to report any sum going in or out of an account if the amount is over ten thousand dollars, correct?''

''Correct. They have to file CTRs, cash transaction requirements, form forty-seven-eighty-nine. The IRS is a bitch on making every bank in the country stick to that rule, mostly to stop the laundering of drug money.''

''So?''

''So the problem is, the payouts CTRs cover are cash only. And the cash transactions for a company like Cunningham Mining might be in the thousands, or even the tens of thousands, although I doubt it. But they certainly wouldn't be in the millions.''

''Ah, good point. What about checks drawn on the account—wouldn't the IRS monitor those, as well?''

''Nope. A check wouldn't even make 'em blink, no matter how much it was for.''

''Then how about asking an officer in the bank to let you borrow Cunningham's canceled checks? You must have dealt with somebody there when you were in Rackets. You had to be talking to most of the banks in New York at one time or another.''

She shook her head. ''Same problem. I'd need a subpoena.''

Ben thought about it. ''Suppose you didn't request the checks to be sent to you physically.'' He pointed to her computer. ''Just asked to have the images scanned onto your screen. That'd be legal, wouldn't it?''

''Yeah, as long as I didn't print them. We did stuff like that all the time when we were tracking a boiler-room operation or a telemarketing fraud.''

''Then let's go, okay?''

She hesitated, tapping red lacquered nails on the surface of her desk. Finally, she said, ''All right, I'll see what I can do.''

''Terrific.''

''But then we're even, right?''

''Better than that. I'll be in your debt.''

''I don't want you in my debt. I want you out of my hair.''

''It's a deal.''

She spun through her Rolodex, then squinted at a card. ''Fidelity Trust? Yeah, I do know somebody there. Henry Travis, the VP in charge of operations.'' She picked up the phone and punched the buttons for the number.

''Ask for checks drawn in this calendar year,'' Ben said.

When she got the bank officer on the line, she said, ''Hank? This is Fern Rose, at the district attorney's office. How've you been? . . . Fine, thanks. . . . Yeah, it's been a while. Listen, Hank. I need some information on checks drawn on the account of Cunningham Mining. . . . Yes, that's right. Canceled checks drawn since the first of the year. You've got 'em on film, right?''

She listened, then said, ''I'd like to have them transmitted over here to my office so I can look through them on my computer.''

She picked up a pencil. ''Sure, that's fine. Give me the access numbers and the password.''

After scribbling the information on a scratch pad, she said, ''Thanks very much. I'll call right away. Nice talking to you, Hank. Appreciate your help.''

She hung up, then swung her chair around and turned on the computer. Tolliver watched as she called a number on the modem and keyed in a code. The red LED lighted up as the machine accessed the program at Fidelity Trust, and seconds later the host ID flashed onto the computer screen.

A panel blinked, requesting the password. Fern glanced at her pad and keyed in BABE RUTH.

Must be a Yankee fan, Ben thought.

The computer asked what she wanted to see and she keyed the numbers Travis had given her identifying the Cunningham Mining account. Moments after that, the first of the checks appeared, the face showing on the left, the reverse side with the endorsement on the right.

Tolliver took a sheaf of notes and a ballpoint from the inside pocket of his blazer and leaned forward, peering over her shoulder.

Fern turned to him. ''Okay?''

''Yeah, great. Just scroll through them . . . slowly.''

She touched the key and the images crawled upward and off the screen, to be replaced by new ones coming up from below.

As Ben studied the checks, he saw that most of them had been drawn to cover operating expenses, as he'd expected. They represented payments for utilities, rent, insurance, travel and entertainment, office supplies, furniture, catering, and dozens of other materials and services, most of them for sizable but not truly large amounts. Each had been signed by somebody named Watterson, apparently a financial officer of the company.

Payroll, Tolliver knew, would be in a separate account, paid out and recorded automatically. So would tax collections and records and amounts accrued for payments to the IRS. The main purpose of this account was to handle the day-to-day running of the business.

Some of the checks had been made out to vendors Ben couldn't immediately identify. But none of those were for more than a few hundred thousand dollars, so he didn't worry about them.

There were also some big ones, written to Cunningham Ventures, the real estate company. The amounts ranged from four to nine million, and there were six of them. No surprise; he'd been expecting to see something like that. As far as anyone knew, the transfers were for a legitimate purpose.

The real problem was the sheer volume of the checks. There were hundreds of them, and although each was scanned for only a few seconds, the process was tedious.

After thirty minutes or so, Fern grew fidgety. During that period her phone had rung a couple of times, but she hadn't picked up; Tolliver assumed the TPA was fielding her calls. He knew he was fouling up her schedule, but it couldn't be helped.

An hour passed and the checks kept rolling. By that time, Ben was getting itchy himself. He began to wonder whether he might be wrong. Maybe the holding company hadn't done anything underhanded, after all. Or maybe they had, but through some other means. Maybe some of the vendors were phony, or the payees weren't what they appeared to be.

And maybe this whole idea was a waste of everybody's time, including his own.

On top of that, the images were starting to blur: $77,541.93 to Arcom Office Systems; $114,546.30 to something called Memotex; $89,459.87 to Blake Galleries; $136,046.00 to Bridgewater Seminars. On and on they crawled, in a seemingly interminable stream. He glanced at his watch and rubbed a fist over his eyes.

When he looked back at the screen, there it was.

The rectangle was identical to all the others, except for the payee—and the amount. The check was for $50,000,000.00.

"Stop."

He leaned closer, gaping at the image. The check was made out to Banco Cafetero and had been signed by Clayton Cunningham IV. The endorsement was a stamp with scribbled initials. Ben counted the zeros just to be sure. There were so many, it seemed like a mistake.

Fern was also staring at the check, openmouthed. Her voice was soft. ''Holy shit.''

He glanced at her. ''What is it? What's the Banco Cafetero?''

''A bank in Panama. It's the biggest one down there. And it's owned by Manuel Noriega.''

47

Fern Rose looked at Tolliver. ''Did you have any idea?''

''No. I'm as surprised as you are.''

''You think drugs are involved?''

''I don't know. Doesn't seem likely. But why would a company like Cunningham Mining be sending fifty million bucks to a bank in Panama? Regardless of who owns it?''

''I can't tell you that. But I can tell you why a lot of people do business with the banks down there. The secrecy makes the ones in the Cayman Islands look like public libraries.''

''Which is why the drug cartels use them, right?''

''Exactly. Colombians, Mexicans, Peruvians, they all do. And not just the drug cartels. Money goes to banks in Panama from all over the world. The banks don't care where it comes from or whether it's clean or dirty. They'll take any amount from anybody, no questions asked. And nothing is disclosed, *ever.*''

''Customers must love 'em.''

''Sure. Because there's no way for tax officials or law officers or anybody else to get zilch on the money—least of all where it winds up. Doesn't matter who's requesting the information, either—nobody cracks those records.''

''I take it you've tried?''

''Yeah, from time to time. But forget it. They don't even acknowledge an inquiry. Doesn't help any that they hate Americans. You ever been there?''

''A long time ago. When I was in the Marine Corps.''

''You weren't too popular then either, were you?''

''Not very.''

"I assure you, now it's worse. Because of what our government did when we went after Noriega."

"Is it really true he owns that bank—a convicted criminal who's locked up in a federal prison in Florida?"

"Amazing, huh? But when you think about it, why not? No matter what he's done, the bank is still his property. And how about the United States kidnapping him, the head of a foreign state? Then bringing him here and trying him for breaking the laws of this country? You want to discuss the legality of that?"

"I'd just as soon not."

"What are you gonna do with this?"

"I don't know that, either—yet. But thanks, Fern. You've been terrific."

She folded her hands in front of her. "You know something, Ben?"

"What's that?"

"I'm glad I was able to do something for you. I really am. But I wish I didn't know this. It's not the kind of information I want to carry around. For all my bitching, I like my job. I wouldn't want to mess it up."

"You have my word. As far as I'm concerned, we never spoke."

"Okay. Good luck."

48

Dr. Chenoweth was clearly excited. His manner was much more upbeat than it had been the last time Peggy had seen him. Then he'd been in a rare dark mood, obviously troubled by Jan's lack of progress. Today, however, he was once again his usual positive self.

"I feel certain that what we're seeing," he said, "is the beginning of real improvement."

Peggy was sitting opposite the psychiatrist's desk, eyeing him anxiously. She bit her lower lip, wanting so much to believe. "Are you sure, Doctor? Really sure?"

"As sure as I can be. She's responding to just about everything I say to her. Eye movement, changes in pulse and surface temperature, every measure shows that. But the really great thing is that now she's actually spoken to me. Maybe it was only a word or two, but it was speech, nevertheless.''

''Yes, but what did she say? That she was afraid, right? The same thing she said to me. At first, I was just as happy about it as you are, but now I don't know. I mean, sure it's wonderful that she seems to be coming around. And yet all she wants to express is this awful fear. Aren't you worried about that? You were before she started to talk.''

Chenoweth wasn't to be discouraged. ''Peggy, what you have to realize is that Jan has to meet us at least partway if we're going to be successful in treating her. For her to be responding like this is remarkable. Patients who withdraw into a state of catatonia like hers sometimes stay that way for years. And sometimes, I'm sorry to say, they never come out of it at all. Jan, on the other hand, is showing definite indications that she's on the way to recovery.''

''Yes, but what about—''

''This fear of hers? What I'm trying to explain is that the first step to successful treatment is to gain responsiveness in the subject. We've got that now, and much sooner than I would have thought possible. Even though she's troubled by these deep-seated negative feelings, she's allowing us to communicate with her. Without that, we could never make progress. But she's reaching out to us, and that's extremely gratifying.''

''I see. Or at least I think I do.''

''Look, I know it may be hard for a layman to grasp. But this is one branch of medicine in which help from the patient is an essential part of the recovery process. Without her cooperation, we could never succeed. By responding, Jan is telling us she wants to get better. She's telling us she's willing to assist in our efforts to return her to emotional health.''

''What about the way she seems to react when you say anything to her about the Cunninghams? What do you make of that?''

''At this stage, I don't have an answer. But I do know we'll find out, eventually—that's part of the treatment. Whatever emotional trauma has been repressed, it's my job to get the problem out in the open. Not only so that we can see it but so that Jan can, as well. She has to recognize what's troubling her before we can help her to deal with it. Once she understands the basis for this deep anxiety, she'll be able to cope with it and overcome her fears. Now do you see?''

''I—yes. I do. Forgive me for acting this way. But I was almost afraid to hope for a while there. To tell you the truth, I was at the point where I thought a lot of what you were saying was just so much . . . nonsense, to put it politely."

He smiled. "That's also normal, Peggy. People get impatient and frustrated when they want their loved ones to overcome a serious illness. And I don't blame them. It's the most natural thing in the world. I often feel frustrated myself."

"You do?"

"Of course I do. We're human, too, you know."

Peggy felt as if she'd been relieved of an enormous burden. She returned Chenoweth's smile. "All right, Doctor. You've made me feel much better, and much more optimistic."

"Good. That's the way I want you to feel. We can't celebrate just yet, but I have a feeling we will before long. And the Cunninghams must be delighted as well, knowing that she's improving."

"Have you spoken to them about her?"

"Not directly. The person I'm in touch with is the administrator of the foundation, Ardis Merritt. Miss Merritt handles everything, including payment of the bills. She was thrilled to have the good news about Jan and I'm sure she's passed it on."

"I see."

"As you know, when your sister was first brought here, the outlook was very bleak. The family was made to understand there was virtually no hope she'd ever come out of the state she was in. So you can imagine how pleased they must be to hear about this turnaround. Almost as happy as you are, I'm sure."

"What's next, for Jan?"

"What's next is more of the same. More careful, patient treatment, until we understand fully what caused her this terrible emotional damage."

49

The NYPD's 115th Precinct covers Jackson Heights, Queens. It takes in La Guardia Airport to the north and runs south to Grand Central Boulevard. The area is densely populated, and filled with small shops and bars and restaurants. There are people on the sidewalks and traffic in the streets at all hours, and the air resonates with Latin music pounding from boom boxes.

Among the residents are countless thousands of illegal immigrants, many of them engaged in prostitution, loan-sharking, and the sale of drugs. The district is the city's largest center for the laundering of illicit cash. Cops call it Little Colombia.

Tolliver drove there in the evening, taking the Queensboro Bridge and then the BQE, turning off onto Northern Boulevard. He parked in the lot next to the precinct house and went into the building.

Except for the uniforms of the police officers, it would be hard to tell what country he was in. At the desk, cops were contending with a variety of suspects, most of them Hispanic, but with a sprinkling of Asians, as well. There were also several black prisoners, some of them speaking in Nigerian accents. A young woman was struggling with two of the officers, screaming at them as they held her by the wrists. "*Bastardos! Hijos de putas!* Lemme go, you motherfuckers!"

She was pretty, Ben thought. Olive-skinned and with long black hair, wearing a white rabbit-skin jacket and a red skirt that barely covered her cheeks. The cops were trying to calm her down, calling her Conchita and telling her to be reasonable. She tried to bite one of them, and he said if she didn't cool it, he'd punch her teeth in.

The desk sergeant had white hair and a stack of ribbons. He was busy logging a black teenager, paying little attention to the surrounding commotion. Apparently the kid had been picked up for dealing crack on the street. Tolliver flashed the tin and said Lieutenant Morales was expecting him. The sergeant pointed to the stairs and Ben walked up them, turning the corner and going into the squad room.

The scene made him nostalgic for his old crew, in Manhattan's Sixth. Detectives in plainclothes were working the phones, typing reports, talking, and drinking coffee. Two of them were questioning a fat man who was sitting at a table, speaking to him in Spanish.

One of the questioners spotted Tolliver and grinned. He was slim and wiry, wearing a sharply cut worsted suit. A pencil-line mustache decorated his upper lip. He stepped forward to shake hands.

"So what brings you all the way over here?" Carlos Morales said. "You bored with the DA's office, looking for a little action?"

"The opposite," Ben said. "I heard this is a quiet neighborhood."

Morales laughed. "Come on in." He led Tolliver to a frosted

glass door on the far side of the room and the two men went inside.

The layout in here was familiar, too: a gray metal desk, a few chairs, a filing cabinet. There was a single window, also of frosted glass, and on one wall was a bulletin board with departmental notices and memos tacked to it.

Morales took his seat behind the desk and waved his visitor to a chair. ''You want coffee, or a drink?''

''No thanks,'' Ben said. ''How's your wife?''

''Split.''

''Sorry to hear it.''

''All for the best, as they say.''

''Kids okay?''

''Oh yeah. Good as can be expected. Living with their grandmother in Brooklyn. Meantime, Rosa's running around with some asshole insurance salesman.''

Tolliver made no response, not wanting to get into it.

The slim man smiled. ''Things don't always turn out the way you want, do they? Little different from the shit they used to hand us in the Academy. You ever think about that?''

''Sometimes,'' Ben said.

''How you doing with the senator?''

''Still a few details to wrap up.''

''You really know how to pick the high-profile cases. Couldn't get much higher than that one.''

''Uh-huh.''

''The old man was a phony prick, in my book. Made a lot of noise when he was in the Senate, about the terrible drug problem. Said he wanted a broad educational program that'd teach kids to stay off it. Called for the death penalty for dealers.''

''Yeah, I remember.''

''But it was all bullshit. Just a flag he could wrap himself in, tell the people what a great statesman he was. Then he turned around and voted against the appropriations bill that would've provided the money. So what does that make him?''

''A politician.''

''Exactly.''

''There's something you might be able to help me with.''

''Sure, if I can. What is it?''

''The senator's son is Clayton the Fourth. He runs one of the family businesses, a stock brokerage. It seems the company has been making illegal profits, and they've been sending some of the money to Panama.''

Morales's eyebrows lifted. ''Panama? Why there?''

''That's what I'm trying to find out.''

''You don't think he's in the trade, do you? Maybe owns a piece of something?''

''Who knows?''

''I'll be damned. Hey, wait a minute, will you?'' Morales got to his feet. ''There's a drug detective here right now who oughta hear this. Be right back.'' He left the office.

Ben looked up at the bulletin board. Along with the other pieces of paper were several wanted posters, some of them fly-specked and curling from age. The subjects glared back at him, belligerently.

Morales returned a few minutes later. With him was the young Hispanic woman Tolliver had seen fighting with the cops at the desk.

They stepped into the office and Morales closed the door. ''Lieutenant Tolliver,'' he said, ''say hello to Detective Connie Lopez.''

Ben stood up and smiled as he shook her hand. She was even prettier up close, despite a gaudy smear of crimson lipstick on her wide mouth. ''You sure fooled me,'' he said.

She returned the smile and sat in another of the visitor's chairs. ''That's what I'm supposed to do. Carlos tells me you're looking to trace some money that went to Panama.''

''Correct.''

''How much are we talking about?''

''Fifty million.''

There was a moment's silence in the room. Then Morales whistled.

''That's a number,'' Lopez said.

''It went by check,'' Ben said, ''only a short time ago. I'm pretty sure there were others before that. The money was deposited in an account at the Banco Cafetero.''

''Noriega's bank,'' Lopez said.

Tolliver looked at her. ''How come everybody knows that but me?''

''If you worked in drugs, you'd know.''

''I'm told it's very hard to get information from banks down there.''

''Almost impossible,'' she said. ''That's why they're so popular with the trade. And besides, what you're after is a lot different from what we usually run into.''

''Because of the amount?''

''That, and sending it by check. The business here is strictly cash. And the people that run it, they know all about CTRs and how banks here have tightened up. So what they do is break it in little pieces. They got these smurfs running around with just under ten thousand each. The smurfs take the money to banks here and have it wire-transferred out of the country. Some to the Caymans, some to the Bahamas, Colombia, all over—including Panama. As long as the amount is under ten, no CTR.''

''Not just banks, either,'' Morales added.

''That's true,'' Lopez said. ''There's over two hundred travel agencies within a few blocks of here. A lot of 'em will take any amount, send it wherever you say. Most of it goes to South America. But you don't see any million-dollar wires.''

Tolliver leaned forward in his chair. ''How can I get the information I want?''

For a full minute, no one spoke.

''What about contacts down there?'' Ben said at last. ''We got a good connection?''

Morales expelled air from between pursed lips. ''You kidding? After what we did in that country in eighty-nine, they hate our fucking guts.''

Connie Lopez held up a hand. ''No, wait a minute. How about Fuentes?''

The slim detective cocked his head. ''Now there is a possibility.''

''Who's Fuentes?'' Tolliver asked.

''A police captain,'' Morales said. ''In Panama City.''

''If anybody could do it,'' Lopez said, ''he could.''

''Very true. I'll try to reach him, see if we can set something up.''

''Excellent,'' Connie said. ''I have a strong feeling he'd go along.''

''Yeah, I think so, too,'' Morales said. ''And it'd be nice to see a Cunningham get what's coming to him.'' He turned to Ben. ''I'll let you know what the captain says, right after I talk to him.''

''Okay, good. But why would this guy be willing to cooperate?''

''Because he's got a brother here,'' Lopez said, ''sitting in a cell at Rikers, awaiting trial.''

50

Orcus slowly tooled the black sedan through the neighborhood, checking out the dimly lighted narrow streets surrounding the building. The South Street Seaport and the Fulton Market were close by, and people were going in and out of the restaurants and bars along the river. His best bet, he decided, would be to park a block away, facing the most direct route out of here; when it came time to go, he'd want to go fast. He'd leave the car in a spot where he could turn into Pearl Street and then head north.

Even though it was only a weeknight evening, it took him twenty minutes to find a suitable parking place. He got one when a bunch of half-drunk revelers climbed into their car and pulled away just ahead of him. Orcus slipped the sedan into the space and got out.

He had on the usual innocuous outfit he wore on a job like this, with the hat pulled down on his head and the dark glasses and the scarf obscuring his face. His topcoat was unbuttoned, however, so that he could hide the shotgun inside the coat and get it out in a hurry when he needed to use it. Walking back to the building, he stopped on the sidewalk across the street and observed it carefully.

The structure was old, built of brick. Probably had been a warehouse at one time. Now it had a business of some kind on the ground floor and the one above, apparently an importing firm. The upper floors had been converted to apartments, and he could see that the ones looking east would have views of the Seaport and the river and beyond. That made him think of the visit he'd paid Jessica Silk.

He walked completely around the block, glancing over the building and the one next to it. On the side where the entrance to the company's offices was, there was a plate glass window with FAR EAST ENTERPRISES painted on it, and next to that was a large freight portal with a folding steel grate secured by padlocks.

Around the corner was a smaller entryway, apparently for use by the building's apartment tenants. That had an inner as well as an outer door, both of glass, but with bars over the outer one.

Farther along the wall, he saw a ramp leading down to a garage door. It was a good arrangement, he thought. The people who lived here could drive down into the garage and go on up to their apartments without having to stop outside the building. And of course they could leave the same way. It was a lot safer than parking on the street, for the tenants as well as their cars. The garage door was the type that rolled up in sections, clad in corrugated steel.

The streets here were all one-way, a labyrinth of constricted thoroughfares. He saw that to enter the garage, someone would have to drive eastbound and turn left before going down the ramp. Which suggested that the best place for him to wait would be a short distance away, where he could watch the ramp and not be seen. Cars were parked close together, parallel to the sidewalk. He stepped between two of them and sat on the rear bumper of a Honda.

It was chilly out here with the wind kicking up, and his seat was uncomfortable as hell. But he didn't let any of that bother him; rough conditions were merely something that had to be taken in stride.

For that matter, he wasn't even sure he'd get a chance tonight. He had no way of knowing when his quarry might be getting home, or whether the guy would come home at all. But that was part of doing business. If there wasn't an opportunity this time, he'd try for another one as soon as possible. There was too much at stake for him not to accomplish what he had to do.

Slipping the shotgun out from under his coat, he held the weapon in both hands and inspected it. The gun was a 12-gauge Remington pump that had been sawed off fore and aft—the barrel to a length of 16 inches, the stock shortened as well. He'd loaded it with double-0.

This time there was no reason to screw around with a cover setup, making it look like something other than murder; a cop would have plenty of people who'd be glad to see him dead. And if you were going to use a gun, there was nothing better than the one gleaming dully in Orcus's hands. With a bullet, it was possible to come up short, to wound instead of killing. But with a shotgun firing a heavy charge at close range, you turned the target into ground chuck.

He put the weapon back under his coat, holding the grip in his right hand, forefinger outside the trigger guard. The metal was cold to his touch.

A couple came along the sidewalk. The man had his arm around the girl, letting his hand slide down to squeeze her ass, and she was giggling as she pretended to slap the hand away. They walked within five feet of the motionless Orcus and never saw him sitting there.

A thought occurred to him. Getting up from his perch, he stretched, keeping the shotgun out of sight beneath his coat. Then he stepped back to where he could get another look at the garage door. It felt good to get off that goddamn bumper.

He studied the door for a moment, then turned and walked to where he'd left his car. Opening the door on the passenger side, he went into the glove compartment, taking out a screwdriver and putting it into a pocket of his topcoat. Moving at an unhurried pace, he returned to his hiding place.

From time to time, headlights blazed as a car drove past, but none went down the ramp to the garage. Orcus was cramped and stiff. Nevertheless, he sat where he was, staying low, holding the shotgun in his right hand.

He hoped the detective would show up tonight. If he didn't, Orcus would come back tomorrow night. One thing he couldn't do was to put it off any longer. Listening to the bitch criticize and complain had become insufferable. Better to get it done, get it over with, and get on with business.

He tightened his grip, slipping his finger inside the guard and lightly brushing the trigger. In his mind's eye, he pictured what he was planning to do. He could see the blast, see the impact of the buckshot when it hit the target's chest and blew it to bloody rags.

Tolliver was an arrogant bastard. It would be a pleasure to kill him.

51

On his way back from Queens, Tolliver pulled off the drive and stopped at Sparks Steakhouse on Forty-sixth Street, where John Gotti's troops had blown away Big Paul Castellano some winters before. There was a TV in the bar and he wanted to catch Shelley on the ten o'clock news. Maybe he could talk her into having a late supper with him after she finished doing the update at eleven.

Certainly that would be preferable to going home and rooting around in the freezer for something to heat up. And besides, a repeat of the night before would be lovely. He'd call her as soon as she went off the air, see how she felt about it.Sparks was busy, for a weeknight. The tables in the hokey, fake antiques–furnished dining room were mostly occupied and a number of people were in the bar. He ordered a beer and asked the bartender to tune in WPIC TV.

A moment later, the news came on, starting with a rundown of what was going on in the world. The anchor was a self-important commentator named Bert Craft, whose main talent was his ability to read a TelePrompTer. The format called for cutting back and forth between Craft and taped news clips the station bought from the networks.

The anchor was an idiot, in Ben's opinion. Everything he said was delivered in the same pompous tones, whether he was reading a piece on Paris fashions or one about mass starvation in Africa. Even his appearance was fatuous, sort of like a talking pumpkin.

There was nothing funny about the news, however: more trouble in the Middle East; the deficit was worse; Congress was legislating tax increases. All of it was interspersed with seemingly endless commercials, a half dozen of them ganged together at a time. If it hadn't been for his wanting to see Shelley, Tolliver would have given up.

When at last she came on, she looked great, as always; wearing one of her power suits, but with a soft white blouse. Her blond hair was lighted just right, and the lights also intensified the color of her eyes, adding sparkle to the deep blue. Seeing her made him wish he could take her into his arms.

Until she opened her mouth.

"There are dramatic new developments," she said, "in the case that has gripped not only the citizens of New York but the entire nation. This is an exclusive report on the investigation into the mysterious deaths of former Senator Clayton Cunningham and Jessica Silk, the writer who was interviewing him at the time he died."

He stared at the tube. Dramatic new developments? What the hell was she talking about?

Shelley continued: "This reporter has learned that the investigation, under the direction of Detective Lieutenant Ben Tolliver, has recently focused on the alleged suicide of Miss Silk."

They cut to a taped shot of Tolliver and Jack Mulloy emerging from Silk's apartment house.

Ben winced. He watched his image brush off the gaggle of reporters who were yelling questions at him as he walked toward his car, Mulloy trailing behind.

Shelley, voice-over: "Jessica Silk's body was found in the rear of this luxury apartment building where she'd been living, and where she supposedly jumped from her twenty-second-floor terrace. According to a confidential source, the police now realize certain unexplained aspects of her death call into question the decision to close the case. Was it in fact a suicide? Did she actually jump? Or was she murdered? Although Lieutenant Tolliver has refused to divulge details of police suspicions, this part of the double mystery has by no means been resolved."

Cut to Shelley on camera: "Among the unanswered questions surrounding Miss Silk's death are several that hold special interest for investigators. For instance, no trace has been found of the article on Senator Cunningham Miss Silk was writing when he died. What happened to this material? Why have the police been unable to locate it? What secrets might it reveal about the true relationship between the senator and Miss Silk? What is the complete story behind their bizarre deaths?"

Ben shook his head, wishing there was some way he could shut her up.

Shelley went on: "The police task force isn't saying what they've learned, but we have it on good authority that Lieutenant Tolliver is also looking into various business enterprises owned by the Cunningham family. Principal among these is Cunningham Securities, headed by Clayton Cunningham the Fourth. Although this company has been under investigation by the Manhattan district attorney's office for some time, little progress has been made. Is it possible there is a connecting thread running through all this? The police seem to think so. For further developments, stay tuned to this station. I'm Shelley Drake, reporting to you live from WPIC TV's studios, in New York."

"Jesus Christ," Ben said aloud. Had she lost her mind? There'd been a clear understanding between them that she wasn't to use anything he gave her without clearing it with him. And now this?

Wait a minute. Last night when they were sitting together in her kitchen, she'd said she was going to do a piece on the case. Her producer was pressuring her, she said. But what she'd use would only be old stuff, nothing new.

Nothing new? She'd stitched together a lot of wild rumors, making them sound like startling revelations.

For several minutes, he stood at the bar, boiling. Then he stepped into the hallway where the public phone was. He dropped a coin into the slot and punched the numbers for her direct line in the newsroom at the studio.

When she answered, he had to grit his teeth to keep from shouting. "I just saw your spot."

"Hi. What did you think? Did I—"

His voice rose, in spite of his resolve to stay calm. "What did I think? That you're ready for the loony bin. Do you realize you put everything I've been working on in jeopardy? Don't you know—"

"Hey! Just a minute, Lieutenant. Stop yelling at me, will you? I didn't say anything that wasn't already known. All I did was to put a little spin on it."

"A little spin? Saying I wasn't satisfied with the way the Silk suicide had been closed? You call that a little spin?"

"But that's the truth, isn't it? You told me yourself you weren't. And nobody else is, either. I mean, the whole world thinks that's suspicious, the way she killed herself right after the senator died. You think you're the only one?"

"Shelley, don't you see you made it look like I was your confidential source? That I was leaking to the media because I wanted to piss on the way the Seventeenth Precinct detectives handled the investigation into Silk's death? Showing that clip made it look like I went up there and decided the cops were doing a lousy job."

"But you *were* there. I didn't manufacture that tape. And I didn't put it that way, either, that you were being critical."

"That part about the manuscript never being found. Where did you get that?"

There was a pause and then she said, "Well, maybe that's something I shouldn't have used. But couldn't I have come up with that on my own? After all, nobody else thought of it, right?" Her tone grew angry. "You think I had to have a cop point that out?"

"It isn't a matter of whether you could have thought of it or not. The problem is that you made it sound like all that shit was coming from me."

''What I said was not shit, as you put it. I told you I was going to do a piece, and that it'd just be a rehash that I'd make sound like new developments.''

''You still don't get it, do you? What about dragging the DA's investigation into it? How do you think the prosecutors are going to take that? What you said made it seem like I'm criticizing them, too. Oppenheimer himself'll have a fit when he hears about this. Christ, maybe he already did. If he had the bad luck to be watching that stupid show, that is.''

''Now I'm stupid—after all the help I've given you? That's the thanks I get?''

''No, but—''

''But, hell. You know what I'm beginning to see here? That just because I didn't review my material with you before I went on the air, your nose is bent. Maybe my editor is right, after all. Who are you to set yourself up as some kind of a tinhorn censor?''

''Listen to me, Shelley. From now on—''

But she wasn't listening. There was a bang as she slammed the phone down, and then all he heard was the hum of the dial tone. Ben exhaled and hung up. He went back to the bar and drained his beer.

The bartender was smiling at him. ''Another?''

He was about to say no and stomp out of here, and then he thought, What the hell. ''Yeah,'' he said. ''And I'll have a hamburger. Rare. With onions.''

52

Orcus was cramped and stiff, and also chilled to the bone. He'd been out here for hours, had seen dozens of cars come by, including two that had gone down the ramp and into the garage. But there'd been no sign of the detective.

He stood up and pulled the coat closer around him, stamping his feet to get the circulation going. Apparently he'd get nothing tonight; it was time to give it up, have himself a couple of drinks and some hot food. He'd return here tomorrow—and the night after, if necessary.

Headlights flashed again, and instinctively he ducked down. The lights slowed, then swung away from his hiding place. Poking his head up a little, he saw that the car was descending the concrete ramp.

It was a blue Taurus, and the cop was at the wheel.

Orcus was instantly on full alert. He jacked a shell into the breech of the Remington and watched as the car came to a stop. The driver touched a transmitter and the garage door rattled noisily upward. When it reached the top of its travel, the car moved through the yawning opening and went on into the garage.

Orcus jumped up and sprinted the few steps to the ramp. He ran down it just as the door was beginning its return trip, automatically closing. Pulling the screwdriver from his pocket, he jammed the blade into the vertical track mounted in the door frame. The door hit the screwdriver and, meeting resistance, opened again. Crouching low, holding the gun out front, Orcus ducked into the garage.

Just ahead of him, the blue car was pulling into a space. It came to a stop and the cop turned off the headlights and the ignition. The stupid shit had never noticed the door reopening behind him. Now he was getting out of the car.

Orcus dropped to one knee, leveling the shotgun.

53

Tolliver had his hamburger and one more beer and then left Sparks.

He was still furious over Shelley's newscast and the outrageous things she'd come out with. In fact, all his reasons for loathing the media were still bubbling just under the surface, feeding his anger. He understood how reporters were driven by ferocious competition, understood how they sometimes felt they had a holy mission to bring forth the right point of view on any subject—so long as it was *their* point of view.

He also understood the greed of the owners and managers of the media, how they would put out any story they thought would sell a few more copies or boost the ratings by one extra point, while they swathed themselves in sanctimony.

But the hell with them. Because they also had a knack for fouling up an investigation worse than defense lawyers. Whatever he might feel for Shelley, it was tempered by that.

He got into his car and headed downtown. For a minute he thought about stopping off at the Shamrock, see some of his friends, get blasted. Forget this whole fucking mess, for a few hours, anyway.

And then he decided the hell with that, too; he'd do better to go home.

The run to his apartment took only a few minutes. The streets down here were all but deserted at this time of night, except in the immediate neighborhood of the Seaport. That area was brightly lighted, and he could see throngs of people moving about. Where he lived, it was dark, except for the glow of the streetlamps.

He made the left turn into his street and drove slowly down the ramp leading to the garage, pausing while he reached under the dashboard to touch the button of the garage door opener. The mechanism groaned, and the steel panels clattered and banged as the door made its way upward. Ben drove on through the opening and nosed the Taurus into the slot reserved for him, against the wall to the left of the door.

There were rows of cars parked in here and illumination was dim, provided by a naked bulb hanging from the ceiling some distance away. He shut off the lights and ignition and took his keys with him, opening the door and hitting the lock button.

As tired as he was, he'd been a cop for too many years to lose awareness of what was happening in his surroundings. Getting out of the car, he saw two things that snapped him to attention.

One was that the garage door had gone only halfway down before striking some obstruction that caused the mechanism to reverse itself. The door was now traveling upward.

The other thing was a dark shape just inside the garage. Light from the street glinted on metal in the center of the shape.

Tolliver was partly out of the Taurus, his left foot on the concrete floor of the garage. Instinctively, he jumped back into the car, rolling himself into a ball behind the door and ducking his head.

The move saved his life.

An explosion occurred a few feet away from where he crouched and a powerful blast hit the door panel, slamming the door against the top of his skull. Stunned, he shook his head, trying to clear the effects of the blow.

There was a second explosion, and this time the charge tore

through the window of the car. Shotgun, he realized. The sounds were like cannon fire in the concrete expanse of the garage. His hair was covered with bits of shattered glass and the stink of gunpowder bit his nostrils.

He had a shotgun of his own under the dashboard. He snatched it from its scabbard, thinking his best chance would be to move across the seat, get out the passenger door, and return fire from behind the car.

He slithered over and grabbed the door handle, noticing that the second charge had taken out the window on this side, as well. So much for the NYPD's bulletproof glass.

His ears were ringing, which was why he didn't pick up the sound of the footsteps right away. When he did, he opened the door and jumped out of the car, shucking a shell into the chamber of the shotgun. His assailant had run up the ramp, and the steps he was hearing now were coming from somewhere out on the street.

Ben sprinted up the ramp himself, but when he got to the sidewalk, he saw nothing but shadows cast by the streetlamps, reflecting from the silent cars parked along the streets.

He looked in both directions, noting that lights were being turned on in a few of the nearby buildings. No one came out the doors, however, to see what the shooting was about. People knew they might wind up dead themselves.

In the distance, he heard the sound of an engine starting. Not sure where it was coming from, his hearing still screwed up by the blasts, he stepped off the sidewalk between a pair of parked cars.

A block away, toward Pearl Street, he saw a black sedan pull away from the curb. The car wasn't showing lights, and it was too far away for him to see its license plate. All he got was a brief impression as the sedan roared around the corner and disappeared.

Tolliver stood in the street, looking in the direction the car had gone. He clicked on the safety of the shotgun, then brushed splinters of glass from his hair and walked back to the ramp, going down the incline to the garage door.

The thing that had jammed the mechanism was a screwdriver with a plastic handle. He pulled it out of the track and, stepping into the garage, touched the button that activated the door. It descended with a clatter.

He looked at the screwdriver. The tool was a cheap one, made in the Orient. He examined it curiously, then stuffed it into his pocket and walked over to the Taurus.

The charge that hit the door had torn a hole the width of a pie plate in the center of the panel. No ordinary shotgun shell had that kind of punch; the gunman must have fired a Magnum loaded with steel shot. If it hadn't been for the sheet of armor in the door, Tolliver's head would look something like the hamburger he'd had for dinner. Maybe not even that good.

Still carrying the shotgun, he went over to the elevator and pressed the button. From somewhere above him, he heard the muffled hum of the elevator as it came down the shaft. The ringing in his ears was disorienting. And he'd developed a pounding headache.

Both of which were preferable to the alternative.

On the positive side, he no longer had any doubts about what he was dealing with. Even though the guy had failed this time, he'd try again. He was a professional; there was no doubt about that, either.

Good, Ben thought. He was looking forward to meeting the son of a bitch. This thing had become personal.

54

"Congratulations," Sloane said. "That was a terrific piece."

Shelley looked up from the word processor. "Glad you liked it."

He half-sat on a corner of her desk. "I already got a lot of calls on it this morning. And you saw how the papers picked it up, crediting us for the story. The other stations are out of their minds trying to figure out your connection to the source."

"The source is miffed, too, Jerry."

The producer seemed surprised. "About what?"

"The lieutenant thinks I made it sound like I was getting information from him on an exclusive basis."

He waved a hand deprecatingly. "Ah, that's just city hall puffing itself up, as usual. Don't pay any attention to that shit. If we listened to jerks like him, we'd never run anything. And by the way, I wasn't the only one around here who was pleased. Art loved it."

Art was Arthur Mayer, WPIC TV's vice president and general manager. Shelley couldn't resist asking. "What did he say?"

"That we're onto a good thing. He wants you to do another one. Keep it going as long as possible."

"Based on what? I cooked the last one up out of nothing, and now I have even less than that."

Sloane folded his arms. "Shel, I'm gonna be completely frank with you, okay? This could be a lot more important to you than you think."

"Why is that?"

"There's a problem with Bert Craft. Everybody knows our famous anchor has seen better days. As you may have noticed, he's into the sauce. Some mornings he smells like he fell in a vat."

She tensed, anticipating what he might be leading up to.

"Anyhow, I've pointed out to Art that we have to make a move on it sooner or later. What I'm thinking is that we could start with you sharing the anchor job with Bert."

"He'd have a cow."

"Yeah, I know. But so what? It'd be sort of a transition period while we eased him out. You can see the kind of opportunity that'd represent for you."

She could see it, all right. First sharing the anchor responsibility with Craft, then having a chance to take over the desk herself? It would be a big step toward reaching her goals.

Sloane was watching her. "I'm sure Art'll buy it. He usually does what I tell him to in a situation like this."

The hell he does, Shelley thought. Now you're the one who's inflating your importance.

"Art's gonna want to congratulate you himself," the producer continued. "Just don't let on we've talked about this other thing, okay? Instead, tell him how you're working on a new angle that'll be even more sensational."

"But—"

"Shel, let me worry about handling it, all right?"

". . . Yes, I guess so."

"Good. In the meantime, don't worry about the routine stuff. I want you to concentrate on stories about the senator. And speaking of angles, didn't you mention you knew his daughter-in-law? What's her name—Laura Bentley, right? The actress?"

"I've spoken with her, yes."

"That's one to go after. An exclusive interview with her could be fabulous. See what you can do about it, okay?"

"I'll think about it."

"You know, sometime soon we ought to discuss all this where we can be more relaxed. At dinner, say."

He gave her another quick grin, actually more of a lascivious twitch of his mouth, and getting up from his seat walked across the newsroom to his office.

55

In the morning, Ben drove the Taurus over to Queens and dropped it off at the NYPD vehicle-repair center. The cop who looked it over was a friend of his, the guy who'd done most of the alterations when Tolliver first got the car. His name was Charley McManus and he was an expert mechanic who'd learned his trade in the U.S. Army.

McManus whistled. "What happened—you make a side trip to Beirut? Or maybe Brownsville?"

Ben smiled. "Same thing, right?"

"More or less. The brothers probably figured you were moving in on their turf." He studied the door. "That looks like a hit from a rocket launcher."

"You're close. How soon can you fix the car?"

McManus waved a hand at the garage behind him, at the blue-and-whites parked in rows inside the chain-link fence. "Be a couple days, at least. I'm all backed up here, and we're shorthanded. Do the best I can, though."

Out on the street, a flatbed truck nosed up to the entrance and the driver blew his horn. Two of McManus's men opened the gates in the chain-link fence and the truck pulled into the yard. Chained to the bed was a pile of mashed metal with flashes of blue and white paint visible on some of the surfaces.

Tolliver and McManus watched as the two men and the driver went about removing the junk from the truck. The mechanics drove a crane mounted on a caterpillar into position and dug the hook into the tangled mass, then slowly lifted it off the flatbed, the crane's engine growling.

"That a patrol car?" Ben asked.

"It was," McManus said. "Driver was killed; his partner's in Mount Sinai. Only they say he won't make it either."

The crane operator slacked off and the tangled metal fell to the ground with a crash. It lay among other junked NYPD vehicles, all of them obviously beyond hope of repair.

Tolliver looked at the wreck, not sure which end was which. "What happened?"

"They were chasing a stolen car in Harlem. Ran a red light and got hit by a garbage truck."

"Some mess."

"Yeah. Now the mayor's on the PC's ass about no more high-speed chases. Says it endangers the civilian population."

Ben took the subway back into Manhattan. The car he rode in was relatively clean, a new one built in Japan by Kawasaki of metals that shed spray paint. Must drive the graffiti artists crazy, he thought. Takes away their opportunity for free expression.

As he sat on a bench in the swaying car, he went over what had happened and what he'd do next. For one thing, he resolved to keep his mouth shut about nearly getting killed in his garage last night. Department regs called for him to file a report on the incident, but the hell with it. Maybe he was becoming paranoid, but if he was, it was for good reasons. The number of people he felt he could trust with information on what he was doing was dwindling rapidly.

He came up out of the subway at City Hall and walked to the Criminal Justice Building. When he got to his office, Jack Mulloy jumped up and followed him inside.

"Hey, Ben. Got some good stuff for you."

"Great, I could use something good for a change. What is it?"

The detective was carrying a manila file jacket. He opened it and pulled out several sheets of paper, laying them on Ben's desk. "Remember you asked me to go through Cunningham's deals, see if there was any kind of a pattern with the clients?"

"Yeah. So?"

"So the first time I looked at them, I couldn't find anything. Aside from the institutionals, I mean. Somebody might be in one or two, but that was all. And there wasn't any consistency. But then I got to thinking. Suppose they made a real effort to conceal what they were doing. Suppose they were buying through some kind of a screen. You see what I'm getting at?"

"Sure, of course."

"Then I remembered hearing one of Shackley's ADAs say he'd seen something like that, but it didn't lead anywhere. So I went back through the records, and look at this." He pointed to one of the sheets. "On this list are some of the people who were in the Biotech deal. Here's a guy, Howard Kincaid. He was in for a big block, two hundred fifty thousand shares. Only time his name appears in any of it."

Tolliver glanced down the list. "Go on."

Mulloy pointed to another sheet. "Over here, we got the Freemont-Grove acquisition. One of the biggest investors in that was a man named Michael Frost. Six hundred thousand shares. Made a bundle, as you can see."

"Where's all this going?" Ben asked.

Mulloy's face was flushed with excitement. "There are four deals here. None of these people I'm showing you was in more than one of them." He paused. "But the four guys all know each other."

"So what? Even if they swap stock tips, there's nothing illegal about that."

"There is if they were on the boards of these companies."

Tolliver looked at him. "You sure?"

"Positive. Kincaid was on the board of Freemont-Grove, but he wasn't in the deal. He had some shares, but only a few thousand that he bought years ago. But guess who *was* in it?"

Ben glanced again at the list of names. "I'll be damned."

"Right. Michael Frost."

"Who was on the board of Biotech."

"You got it. Pretty slick, huh? Works out for every one of them." He pointed again. "This guy, Roger Thurmond, was in big on Microware-Allison. And this one—"

"You say an ADA first came across this?"

"I don't know how much he learned, except there was an investment group, all heavy hitters. But, like I said, he didn't do anything with it. I just ran down the names and started checking them out."

"That's good work, Jack."

"I'm not finished, though. I got a feeling this is the tip of the iceberg, you know?"

"Could be. Keep digging."

"Don't worry."

"The ADA aware of what you've been doing?"

"No. And he won't be . . . until I get all of it."

"That's good, too. Keep me posted."

"You bet." Mulloy put the papers back into the jacket and left the office, striding back to his desk. Even his limp had a spring in it.

Ben got out his notes and jotted down what he'd just been told, including the names of the investors and the companies whose boards they served on. After that, he wrote down several theories as to what might be a master scheme that would tie all this together. Then he began testing each of the theories.

He'd been working on it only a short time when the first of the phone calls came in. It was from a reporter at the *Post* who'd seen Shelley Drake's so-called newsbreak the night before. The reporter tried to pressure him into giving out more information, but Tolliver cut him off, saying curtly that he had no comment.

After that, he received several more calls, and as the morning wore on, they became a flood. Not all of them were from the media, either. Some were from civilians who'd also seen the program, apparently nutballs who got their rocks off by talking to a detective about a notorious case.

One was a lady psychic who said she'd been contacted on the suicide of the journalist. She claimed she'd been informed as to what really happened and was willing to share it with him.

Who was it she'd heard from? he wanted to know. Jessica Silk, the psychic said, so it had to be the truth. Ben said he'd be in touch and hung up.

There were also calls he didn't get, although he was half-expecting them. He thought one would be from Captain Brennan, and another from Shackley, or even the DA himself, demanding to know what was behind the newscast. But he didn't hear from any of them. Maybe they'd simply put the report down to typical stirring of the pot by the media and ignored it. He certainly hoped so.

Shortly before noon, another call came in, and this was the one he'd been waiting for. The caller was Lt. Carlos Morales.

"I spoke to Fuentes," Morales said, "the captain in Panama. He says if we'll spring his brother, he can get what you want."

"Can you do it?"

"Yeah, I think so. After that, I talked to the ADA who's got the case. The brother's at Rikers on a drug rap, but the prosecutor's willing to knock it down. He says it wouldn't be any big deal—they don't have a strong case anyhow. Which Fuentes doesn't know, of course."

"That's great," Ben said.

"Yeah. But there's a hitch."

"What hitch?"

"The captain won't say anything more over the phone. If you want what he can give you, he said you'll have to go to Panama."

56

Jan's hand was thin, clawlike. It grasped Peggy's wrist in a fierce grip, nails digging into the flesh.

Peggy was astonished. This had to be one of the few times Jan had moved of her own accord since she'd been admitted to the facility.

The expression in her eyes was also different. There was an intensity that said she not only was focusing on Peggy's face but that she was also rapidly forming conscious thoughts.

For a moment, Peggy was afraid to breathe for fear of breaking Jan's concentration or upsetting her. The last thing she wanted was to cause her sister to retreat into that secret chamber somewhere deep in her mind. That was what Jan had done previously; she'd been like a small animal that emerges from its den and then, recoiling at the sight of a predator, scrambles back into its hiding place.

As gently as possible, Peggy said, "Jan, take it easy, will you? It's only me. And there's nobody here but the two of us. You can relax, honest."

The green eyes narrowed.

"Really, Jan," Peggy went on. "I'm just here to visit. You can talk to me if you want. But if you don't, that'll be fine, too. I can be quiet, or I can babble on the way I do, give you all the latest dumb gossip on what's going on in our office. Or maybe you'd rather have the two of us just sit here."

Jan's tongue darted over her lips, moistening them. She spoke then, in a tone so low as to be barely audible. "Not safe."

Peggy felt a jolt. She leaned forward. ''What's not safe?''

''Here. Where we are.''

Peggy exhaled. This had to be another surfacing of the blind, unreasoning fear that had haunted Jan for so long. ''That's simply not true. You're in Brentwood. Are you aware of that?''

There was no reply.

''Brentwood is a—'' She'd been about to say mental hospital. Instead, she said, ''Nice place. Where you can be warm and comfortable while you get well. Everyone here is your friend. They all want to help you.''

''He might . . . find me.''

''Who might find you?''

''If he does, he'll hurt me.''

''Jan, what are you—''

''He tried to kill me. He only stopped 'cause he thought I was dead.''

That brought another jolt, but one that made a much greater impact, because it fit what the police had told Peggy about Jan's brush with death.

She tried again. ''Who was it, Jan? Who tried to kill you?''

The younger woman shook her head slightly. The movement was quick and jerky, like that of a bird. ''Can't tell you. He'd find out and come after me.''

''Nobody can come after you. There are people here all the time. The attendants and the nurses—there's even a guard. And Dr. Chenoweth himself is here.''

Jan's mouth quivered. ''I'm afraid.''

Peggy felt a wave of compassion sweep over her. She put her arm around the thin shoulders. ''There's no reason to be afraid. You're completely safe, I swear to you.''

Instead of reassuring her, the words seemed to inspire greater anxiety. Jan's entire body was trembling now, breasts rising and falling as the pace of her breathing increased. The jagged red scar on her face had become more vivid, twitching with each heartbeat. ''Don't let him hurt me. Please don't let him.''

''Jan, you've got to believe me. No one's going to hurt you. No one.''

The grip on Peggy's wrist tightened and then suddenly relaxed. The thin hand fell away. Jan slumped back in her chair and her head lolled. The intense expression faded from her eyes, as if a cloud had passed over them, obscuring the light.

"Jan? Can you hear me, Jan?"

There was no response.

Peggy felt wrung out. She sat there for several minutes, not moving. Jan seemed so helpless, so vulnerable.

Finally, she reached over and drew the robe close around her sister's frail body. She stood and, pulling a tissue from the pocket of her coat, wiped her eyes, then blew her nose.

"Good-bye, Jan. I'll be back tomorrow." She bit her lip, refusing to let herself cry again. Then she patted Jan's shoulder and left the room.

57

In the afternoon, Tolliver took a taxi to La Guardia. At the American counter, he bought a ticket for Flight 948 to Miami and produced his ID, then filled out the form allowing him to carry a firearm aboard the aircraft. He used his credit card to pay for the ticket. Regulations called for him to get clearance for such a trip, a formality that mainly had to do with cost control. But that would also entail explaining his plans, which was the last thing he wanted to do.

In Miami, he connected with AA 999 to Panama City, and that leg seemed to take forever. The aircraft was jammed, many of the passengers carrying kids who screamed incessantly. Harassed flight attendants served a meal that appeared to be inedible, so he passed it up, settling for coffee. There was also a movie, which looked worse than the meal.

Despite the cacaphony, he managed to do some thinking about the case. Getting out his notes, he studied the list of investors Jack Mulloy had come up with. If Mulloy had it right, the scheme these guys were involved in had been immensely profitable, and illegal as hell. The problem was to determine how it tied in to the other activities of Cunningham Securities.

Ben also thought about Shelley. He regretted having blown up at her; she was the best thing that had happened to him in a long while. He'd try to call her and mend some fences, tonight if possible.

At least the flight was on time, touching down at 8:27 P.M. Getting through passport control was another pain in the ass, with long lines of people at the mercy of pompous officials who moved very slowly. Fortunately, he didn't have to wait for his luggage, having brought only carryon, a nylon bag containing a few essentials.

When he left the terminal, it was like walking into a furnace. The air was moist and heavy, the temperature well into the nineties. It had been years since he'd first come here, courtesy of the U.S. Marine Corps, but the heat and the odor of dank vegetation instantly brought back memories.

He walked to a line of waiting taxis, the drivers all standing beside their vehicles and yelling and waving at him, and climbed into the first one he came to. The cabbie slammed the passenger door and hopped in behind the wheel.

"*La ciudad, por favor,*" Ben said. "*Llevame para el hotel esta bien, pero no muy caro.*"

The driver said he would recommend La Paloma, which was in the new section. Ben told him to go there.

Tocumen Airport was seventeen miles from the city, which gave the driver plenty of time to talk. He claimed he had cousins in New York and for that reason was more friendly toward Americans. He said most of his countrymen hated them.

But who could blame them? he wanted to know. The *yanquís* had always treated Panamanians with contempt. When they moved on Noriega, they shot people in the streets and bombed the city and all the region around it. Then they captured the general and destroyed the government and afterward they forced Panama to set up what they called a democracy, but in fact all that did was put another band of thieves in power. The difference was that under the new ones there was more unemployment, more crime, and runaway inflation. Things had been better under Noriega, he said.

And by the way, would the señor like to have a girl—only sixteen years old and beautiful? Or maybe some very fine cocaine? Or both?

No thanks, Ben said. He had enough problems.

When they reached the city, they went through the old section, Casco Viejo, many of its buildings vine-covered ruins. Among them was the arch of Santo Domingo, which Tolliver remembered was famous because it had proved to engineers that Panama was not earthquake-prone and therefore was a suitable site for the canal.

From there, they crossed King's Bridge into the new part, where the architecture was a mixture of colonial and modern. A lot of it had been built since he'd last been here, but he recognized the National Theatre and the ancient cathedral with its mother-of-pearl tower. And the Presidential Palace and the French Plaza. The shop windows were filled with duty-free bargains from Europe and the Orient, as well as from the United States.

He also spotted a few members of the U.S. military, who were probably stationed at the two remaining U.S. air force bases. After the big shoot-out in 1989, Panama no longer had an army; instead, they now had thousands of police officers. The cops wore tan uniforms that were similar to those of the old Guardia Civil, and they were everywhere.

La Paloma looked out on the center of the bay. The hotel was a glitzy pile of pink stucco with bougainvillea climbing on it and a fountain out front. Palm trees and red-blossomed hibiscus bushes bordered the circular drive. The doorman saluted as Tolliver climbed out of the taxi.

Ben paid the fare in U.S. dollars and went into the lobby. The area was thronged with what appeared to be businessmen, many of them accompanied by women. From what he could see, there were few *Norteamericanos* besides himself, and even fewer Europeans.

Lack of a reservation was not an obstacle. He registered and was assigned a single on the third floor that was indistinguishable from ones he'd occupied in Stateside motels, except for a huge basket of tropical flowers that sat atop the dresser.

Once he'd tipped the bellboy and was alone, he stripped off his clothing and took a long shower in the lukewarm water that came out of the cold tap, then toweled down and sat on the bed. He telephoned the number he'd been given by Morales. The man who answered said he would be picked up at the hotel at midnight.

Next he tried reaching Shelley. It took twenty minutes to get through to New York, and when he reached the WPIC TV newsroom, he was told she wasn't in. That was strange, he thought; normally she would have been working tonight.

He then called her home number, which took another twenty minutes, and this time got the answering machine. At least that enabled him to hear her voice, if only on a recording. He left a message, saying he was out of town and would try again.

It had been hours since he'd eaten anything. He got dressed, putting on his blazer but not bothering with the tie, and went down to the dining room. When he was shown to a table, he drank a Carta Blanca and studied the menu, then looked around the room.

None of the men in here seemed younger than forty and none of the women older than thirty. In fact, the spread among most of them was much wider than that. That was another custom in Latin countries; you took your girlfriend to dinner, your wife to church.

He ordered *patacones y carimanola con puerco*—fried green plantains and yucca with pork—an old favorite you flat out could not get in New York—and it was wonderful. Later, he had coffee that was so rich it would dissolve a spoon, and by the time he finished it was midnight. He went out to the front entrance of the hotel.

Two cops were waiting for him. They put him in the rear seat of a patrol car that had a gold star on the side and black letters that said PANAMA CIUDAD POLICÍA. As they drove through the darkened streets, Ben tried to get them into a conversation, but they responded with little more than grunts.

Their destination was the Palace of Justice. Built of stone and profusely decorated, the structure was obviously a holdover from colonial times. The cops escorted him up the wide stone steps to the entrance, which had elaborately carved doors under a marble arch. Two officers armed with submachine guns stood at attention as the group went past them into the building.

Inside, more police with automatic weapons were posted at various places in the halls, although at this hour the place seemed relatively quiet. Apparently, the courtrooms did little business at night, which was in sharp contrast to the tumultuous activity that went on around the clock at 100 Centre Street in New York.

From the main floor, Tolliver was led one flight down to police headquarters. He saw that the offices here were swarming with cops, both in uniform and plainclothes, but he wasn't taken into the area. Instead, the pair who had brought him continued along a dimly lighted, low-ceilinged hallway with holding pens on either side.

The pens were packed with prisoners, wailing and reaching out to them through the steel bars. The men were filthy, hollow-eyed, and bearded, clothed in stinking rags. A pervasive stench of human waste, a mixture of feces, urine, and vomit, hung over them like a shroud. Compared with this place, Rikers Island was a picnic ground.

At the end of the hallway, they came to a door guarded by another submachine gun–toting officer. He unlocked the door and Tolliver was led down a second flight of stone steps. They walked along a corridor narrower than the one above, lined with metal doors.

Ben realized these were the dungeons that had been used by the Guardia Civil as well as the police. It was said that many of the prisoners confined here were never brought to trial at all, but were simply left to rot.

Midway along the corridor, an officer stood outside one of the doors. He opened it and the cops led Tolliver inside.

This was an interrogation room. It was perhaps ten by fifteen feet, the walls and floor built of granite blocks. At one end of the room, a number of uniformed men were clustered. Brilliant lights shone down from overhead and the air was thick with tobacco smoke.

One of the men looked around at Tolliver. He was squat and wide, with gold braid on his cap and more of it on the epaulets of his tunic. Under the cap, his brown features seemed more Indian than Hispanic. Smallpox scars pitted his cheeks and his eyes were hooded like a lizard's.

''Welcome to Panama,'' he said. ''I am Captain Manuel Fuentes de Cardona. In a little while, we will go and talk.'' He returned his attention to where the others were standing.

Tolliver stepped closer and saw that the subject of the interrogation was a male prisoner sitting on a wooden chair. The man was naked and dripping sweat. His wrists and ankles were handcuffed to the chair, and on the floor beside him was a transformer with a length of wire attached to it.

As Ben watched, one of the cops picked up the wire and held the bare end to the prisoner's genitals. A blue spark flashed as the copper strand touched the head of the man's penis. He howled in agony, writhing in the chair. The cop held the wire there for several seconds and then the prisoner fell unconscious, his head lolling. Another officer threw a glass of water into his face.

Fuentes turned to Tolliver. ''Here we are more efficient than you are. When we need to know something, we are very direct in our questioning. A better system, no?''

Ben glanced at the naked wreck in the chair. The man was coughing, his eyes closed, each convulsive burst from his lungs spraying the air with a fine mist. Tolliver had no illusions as to why he'd been brought down here to witness this.

He looked at Fuentes. "What if the suspect dies?"

The captain shrugged. "That is an advantage of using electricity. No one can tell for sure what killed him."

The cop with the wire leaned toward the prisoner. "Speak up, you miserable shit, or I will shock your dick off."

A deep groan issued from the prisoner's mouth and then the cop repeated the process, with the same results.

"Come," Fuentes said. "We'll go to my office. Sooner or later, this scum will tell us what we want to know."

Tolliver followed him out the door, the two cops who'd escorted him walking close behind. They four of them went back down the corridor and then up the stairs, past the holding pens, to where the police facilities were.

The captain's office was large and handsomely furnished in dark wood. A collection of antique swords decorated the wall behind his desk and a Panamanian flag was hanging on the wall opposite. Fuentes gestured toward a chair across from his desk and then took his own seat. Ben sat in the chair, but the two cops remained standing behind him.

"So," the captain said. "This must be very important to you."

"It could be, or it could be nothing."

"The police in New York do not send a detective here if it is nothing."

"Then let's hope it turns out to be worthwhile. If it doesn't, the deal is off."

"How do I know if it is on? I have only the word of your Lieutenant Morales."

"And my word," Ben said.

The captain studied him with his lizard eyes. "You have to realize, information of this kind is worth a lot."

"As much as your brother?"

"In Panama, it is different from your country." His tone was derisive. "Here, our laws are based on the Napoleonic Code. We protect our citizens in all matters, including privacy. That is why this could be very dangerous—for both of us."

Tolliver thought of the man the police were interrogating, wondering what protection he'd been given. "Then call it, Captain. You want to make this happen, or are we wasting each other's time?"

"I told Morales I could get what you wanted."

"And did you?"

"Yes, I have it."

"Okay. When I'm satisfied it's genuine, I'll give New York the word. Charges against your brother will either be reduced to a misdemeanor or thrown out altogether. Fair enough?"

"The charges are ridiculous. Totally false. All part of a vendetta against the Panamanian people."

"Your move, Captain."

The hooded eyes were fixed on Ben's face, not blinking. "When Banco Cafetero received the money, it was deposited into the account of Aguila Associados."

"What is that? Sounds like a company."

"It is. The man who heads it is Tomas Aguila."

"Who is he, and what are they?"

"He is a businessman, an investor. Very rich, very powerful. His business is mainly import/export."

"I see." In this part of the world, as in a number of others, import/export was a catchall that could cover trading in a wide range of goods—anything from legitimate commodities to drugs, arms, or people. Noriega had been in that business, dealing in all three.

"And he's located here, in Panama City?"

"Yes. His offices are in the Torre Plata, which is on Paitilla Point."

"What else can you tell me?"

"Nothing," Fuentes said. "I have delivered what I promised. After this, you must deliver at your end. And therefore, I make you another promise."

The captain got up from chair and came around the desk. Stepping close to Tolliver, he drew a 9-mm Beretta from the black leather holster on his belt and jacked a round into the breech.

He held the pistol close to Ben's face. "If you renege on the offer for my brother, or if in any way you have deceived me, I will make sure that you are dead. No matter where you are or how long it takes, I will make sure."

Ben remained silent. He could see the lands and grooves in the barrel of the pistol, could see the captain's finger tighten on the trigger.

He was about one-thousandth of an inch away from getting his brains blown out.

"Well?" Fuentes said. "Do you understand?"

Tolliver locked his gaze on the lizard eyes. "You shoot, and your brother's in jail forever."

There was a moment of silence and then Fuentes's mouth twisted in a lopsided smile.

He returned the pistol to its holster and stepped back. "Very well, Lieutenant. Good night. Enjoy our city while you are here."

58

"As I told you the last time we talked," Laura Bentley said, "I'm very excited about reviving my career."

"I know you are," Shelley said. "That's why I thought we could do each other a favor. You give me an exclusive interview, and I'll slant it as big news. Famous movie actress launches exciting new career in TV. That way, you'll get maximum PR value from the interview. It could be almost like a personal promo for you."

They were sitting in the grillroom at the Four Seasons. Shelley had called to say she had some ideas about how Laura could get started in television, and Laura had gone for it, suggesting they meet there for a drink.

"I like that," Laura said. "I like that a lot. I'll give you the interview and also tell you things about people in the movie business—things you'll find fascinating. Some of them are kind of freaky even. But of course you'll have to be careful how you handle the material."

"Of course."

"And it's understood there can be no questions about the death of the senator or that writer who committed suicide."

"There won't be," Shelley said.

"I have to be sure of that. Didn't you do a report on it not long ago? I remember seeing it."

"Yes, but that was just one of many things I've worked on. Anyway, the story's all over by now. It's ancient history."

"Maybe so, but the family's touchy about it—especially my husband."

''I promise I'll avoid the subject entirely.''

''Good. And there's one other point.''

''Yes?''

''I don't want Clay to know what I'm planning. I wouldn't want to do the interview until I was sure I had everything lined up. He seems to think being married to him is career enough in itself, but you know how men are.''

''Yes, I do know.''

''Multiply it by ten and you have some idea of what it's like being a woman in the Cunningham family.''

''I can imagine.''

''But that's another story, too. What's important is that I think TV would be the perfect medium for a new start. Much better than going back into movies or doing something on Broadway.''

''I think you're right.''

''My agent doesn't. He tells me I'm being silly, but I don't trust his motives, either. The thing about me is, I'm a realist. I know my days of doing romantic leads are over.''

Shelley could understand that. Bentley's face was still beautiful by any standard, except the one that counted most: It was no longer youthful. The high cheekbones were still sharply defined, the nose short and straight above the full-lipped mouth directors had loved back in her heyday. But now there were tiny sags and a network of lines around her eyes. Her hair was subtly different, too; its chestnut color didn't look as natural as it once had. Men wouldn't notice those things, but women would—just as Shelley did now.

The net of it, she decided, was that Laura was getting on and wasn't sufficiently talented to take on character roles.

''What I really want to do,'' the actress said, ''is host a talk show.''

Oh God, Shelley thought. You, too?

''When I look at some of the crap that's on today, I can't believe it.''

''Neither can I,'' Shelley said. ''You have a format in mind?''

''Yes, but that's one of the things I'd like your advice on. As a trained actress, I could handle it any number of ways. In fact, doing a show of that kind would be a snap—especially because I could attract so many great people to come on as guests.''

''I'll bet you could.''

"Friends of mine in the entertainment world, and also painters, authors, sculptors, people like that. I thought we could talk about trends in the arts. And I'd tape the show in a lot of fabulous places, not just here, but in Europe."

"Sounds wonderful." And guaranteed to put an audience to sleep, she thought, if it ever got on the air—which it wouldn't.

"Just between you and me," Bentley said, "I'm looking for an apartment to buy . . . in Paris. That would be my base over there."

"That's exciting, too." And revealing. Apparently, Laura was getting her ducks in a row. For what—an impending divorce? A settlement from Clay Cunningham could be quite a jackpot. "How soon are you hoping to have all this happen?"

"As soon as possible. You must know some packagers, don't you? My agent tells me everything is syndicated nowadays."

"Yes, that's true." And he tried to talk you out of it, but you wouldn't listen. Like a lot of other people, you hear what you want to hear.

"Let's have another drink," Laura said.

"Sounds fine."

While Bentley sought to catch a waiter's eye, Shelley glanced about the famous French rosewood–paneled restaurant with its black leather upholstery and the rippling copper-chain drapes. Elegantly dressed patrons were eating dinner at the tables while others jostled for places on all four sides of the bar. She liked this room better than the more formal one with the pool that was on the opposite side of the building.

The waiter brought them fresh drinks: vermouth cassis for Laura, Chardonnay for Shelley.

Laura raised her glass. "Here's to a new beginning."

"Yes, here's to it."

They sipped their drinks and then Laura said, "Maybe there'd be a spot in the package for you, too. Would you consider that?"

Shelley smiled. "Sure I would," she said, thinking, I'd consider it a bald attempt to buy me. But we're talking fair exchange here, right?

"Tell you what," the actress said. "I'd like to discuss this at some length, get your ideas as to what producers I should be dealing with, where to shoot the pilot, stuff like that. Why don't you come out to Long Island for the weekend?"

''At the family estate?''

''Sure, why not? As far as Clay is concerned, you'd just be one of the guests. He wouldn't pay any attention to us, anyway—all he does out there is talk business with his sister and brother-in-law and sometimes their lawyers. We'd have a chance to explore ideas for the show in much greater detail. And we could also go over the kind of material you want for the interview. What do you say?''

''All right, fine. That's this weekend?''

''Yes. We'll fly out. I'll send a car for you, to take you to the heliport. I think it could be productive for both of us.''

''I think so, too,'' Shelley said. ''Very productive.''

59

In the morning, Tolliver ate a breakfast of sliced papaya and drank a pot of the thick, rich coffee. Then he checked out of the hotel. At this point, he had the name Aguila and a hazy description of an import/export business, but not much more than that. At least it was something; he'd known when he came down here that he was betting on a long shot.

Paitilla Point, the address the police captain had given him, was an area of tall buildings in the business district. Part of the new section of the city, it was a jut of land extending into the Bay of Panama. Riding toward it in a taxi, Ben found the locality jammed with people and vehicles, all moving sluggishly in the brilliant sunshine. The heat was much more oppressive than in the night—the temperature had to be close to a hundred now.

Approaching the building, he saw that Torre Plata was indeed a tower, rising twenty stories above the crowded streets. Where the silver part of its name had come from was a mystery, however. Probably out of some developer's feverish head. It looked little different from any of the thousands of other metal-and-glass boxes that had sprung up in cities all over the world.

A black Cadillac limousine was parked out front. As Ben's taxi drew up, the big car pulled away, and then the cab took its place. Tolliver paid the driver and went into the lobby, carrying his bag.

The directory said Aguila Associados occupied the penthouse

suite. He took the elevator up there, and when the doors opened, he stepped out into a reception room that was sleekly furnished with white sofas and chairs and white carpeting, the walls clad in teakwood. A garden terrace surrounded the space and blue-tinted curved windows gave a panoramic view of the coastline and the Pacific Ocean.

The receptionist was dark and very pretty, wearing a flowered silk dress. She greeted him with a smile. Using his best Spanish, he told her he was there to see Señor Aguila. Sorry, she said, but Señor Aguila was not available.

Tolliver took his case from his back pocket and flipped it open, giving her a quick look at the gold shield and then putting it away again. Police business, he told her. It was imperative that he talk with her boss at once.

It made an impression. She was wide-eyed but still apologetic, saying Señor Aguila was on his way out of town—in fact, he'd just left for the airport.

Ben recalled the black limousine that had left the building as he was arriving. He asked whether that was Señor Aguila's car and was told it was. Where was Aguila headed? he asked next.

She hesitated and then said she didn't know, which clearly was a lie.

Nevertheless, he wasn't going to stand there and debate it with her; there wasn't time. Which airport? he demanded.

She claimed not to know that, either, probably another lie.

Instinct told him it would be the international. The other one was small and handled only domestic flights. He turned and hit the button for the elevator.

When he got to the lobby, he ran out into the street, waving for a taxi. It took several minutes to flag one down; when he finally succeeded, he waved the shield again, telling the driver to make the run to Tocumen as fast as he could.

That turned out to be very fast. The cabbie was obviously overjoyed to have a cop on board—he could forget about laws. He whipped in and out of traffic, blowing his horn and passing slower vehicles, infuriating some drivers and scaring the shit out of others, his brown face split in a wide grin. Twice he came within inches of slamming head-on into other cars on the narrow road.

If he only knew, Ben thought.

They made the airport in what must have been record time. The cab skidded to a stop in front of the terminal and Tolliver jumped out. There was a jam-up of vehicles near the entrance, but the limo wasn't among them.

Looking around, he caught sight of the long black car disappearing through a gate in the high chain-link fence, a hundred yards farther down the line. He got back into the cab and told the driver to go there.

When they reached the gate, Ben was again frustrated. There was no guard; the gate was the electronic type that opened when a passcard was inserted into the lock, and now it was closed. As the taxi pulled up to it, he saw the Cadillac drive past a hangar and onto the apron, where a white Falcon jet was parked.

The car stopped beside the aircraft. A uniformed chauffeur and a bulky guy in a light-colored suit got out and opened the rear doors. Two people emerged: a man in a lime green jacket and a woman with dark hair and long legs, carrying a small bag. The Falcon's pilot and copilot stepped forward to greet them, looking snappy in short-sleeved white shirts and caps, and then the couple boarded the jet.

Tolliver sat where he was, watching. The chauffeur opened the trunk of the limo and he and the other man took suitcases out of it, setting them on the cement apron. There were five pieces, all large and apparently heavy. The men then loaded the suitcases into the Falcon's aft luggage compartment, assisted by the crew. When the guy in the suit was finished with the bags, he too entered the passenger cabin. Ben figured him for a bodyguard.

Minutes later, the jet moved slowly out onto a taxiway, navigation lights on and engines whistling, and rolled toward the active runway. The chauffeur watched also, standing beside the car.

Tolliver slammed his fist into the palm of his other hand. ''Goddamn it,'' he said aloud. To come this close—

He turned to the cabbie and told him to drive to the control tower, pointing to it. The taxi sprayed gravel as they pulled away.

This time there was a guard—evidently a police officer, judging from the tan uniform. The guy was standing in the small patch of shade beside the door of the tower, asleep on his feet. There were dark crescents under the armpits of the uniform blouse and a heavy automatic rifle was slung over his shoulder.

As Tolliver got out of the taxi, he broke out his shield once more and barked at the dozing guard. The man's eyes opened, and when he saw the gold, he looked as if he might pass out. He snapped to attention and saluted. Tolliver stepped past him through the door, returning the case to his pocket.

The elevator whisked him up to the large room atop the shaft, where three controllers were working at desks next to the tall windows. A radar technician was sitting nearby, monitoring a screen on which a number of blips were visible. Through the windows, Ben could see a Varig 737 landing and another commercial airliner taxiing out. The white Falcon was number one for takeoff.

As the Falcon was given clearance, Tolliver listened to the exchange on the loudspeaker between the controller and the pilot. He noted that the aircraft carried an *N* number, which meant it was under U.S. registry, not Panamanian.

The slim jet wheeled onto the runway, then surged forward as the engines went to full power. It streaked down the concrete ribbon and leapt into the air, climbing out at an impossibly steep attitude, as graceful as an arrow. Departure control ordered the pilot to fly a heading of 005 degrees, and then the aircraft was gone.

Ben waited until there was a momentary lull in the air traffic. Then he stepped over to one of the controllers, giving the guy one of his patented half-second glimpses of the gold shield. "That white business jet that just took off," he said. "November one-three-six-two Charlie. Where's it going?"

The controller picked up a telephone and pressed a button. He spoke briefly—to Flight Service, Ben assumed—listened, and hung up.

"He filed for PBI," the controller said.

"Where's that?"

"In the States . . . in Florida. PBI is Palm Beach International."

60

Jan's voice was a whisper. "It didn't seem like much . . . in the beginning. We'd . . . have sex, and he'd be rough. He'd slap me, bite me."

Peggy looked over her shoulder. People were walking by in the hallway—hospital personnel, other patients. She got up and closed the door, then returned to her sister.

''Who did those things to you?''

Jan shook her head. She had that taut expression on her face again, the jagged scar twitching, her eyes sunken deep in their sockets and shining with an odd light. ''Don't ask me that. I can't tell you. I can't tell anybody. He'd kill me.''

Peggy had learned not to push it. The thing to do was to be grateful Jan was talking and to let her find her own pace. ''All right—go on.''

''He said it wasn't anything, that he was only pretending. But after a while, he started beating me. With his fists. And then later with a whip.''

''How could you let him do that?''

The words began tumbling from Jan's mouth, so rapidly that it was hard to understand her. ''It just gradually got worse and worse. He started really hurting me. I didn't know what to do. By then, I'd gotten in so deep. I had my own apartment and he was paying for it and buying me clothes, anything I wanted. Jewelry, anything. Even bought me a car.''

''I remember that,'' Peggy said. ''I didn't know where it was all coming from, and you wouldn't tell me.''

''I was . . . ashamed.''

''But why didn't you—''

''What? Break it off, or go to the police? I thought about doing that, but I didn't want to give up all the things I had. And to tell you the truth, I was scared. Then it got to a point where it didn't matter so much.''

''Even though he was hurting you?''

''Yes. We were doing a lot of coke together. And this one time, he knocked me around until I was a bloody mess. I screamed and carried on, tried to hit him back. I was pretty hysterical, and it took a long time for me to calm down. He promised he'd take it easy, wouldn't hurt me again. Then after that, he started bringing other stuff.''

''Other stuff?''

''Little glass tubes you break and inhale. He said it was amyl nitrite, and that it was harmless—just made the sex better. Pills, too. Red capsules he said were uppers. With the coke and all the rest of it, I'd get so high that I didn't care what what was happening. It didn't hurt anymore then—even when he burned me.''

''Burned you how?''

"With a cigar."

Despite her resolve simply to listen, Peggy was horrified. "Jan, have you told Dr. Chenoweth any of this?"

"No! Oh God, no. I wouldn't tell anybody except you."

"But—"

"It's too dangerous. I'm taking a terrible chance by talking about it at all."

"You're not taking a chance. You're absolutely safe. And you have to trust the people who are trying to help you—if you're going to get well again."

"*No!* I'm not safe. You have to get me out of here. If he finds out—"

An idea came into Peggy's mind. "Tell me something. Were you still working for the Cunninghams when all this began?"

Jan looked away, not answering.

Behind them, a knock sounded. The door opened and Jay Chenoweth stepped into the room. He smiled. "Hello there. How's everyone doing today?"

"Fine, Doctor," Peggy said. "We're doing fine, aren't we, Jan?"

She turned back to her sister. The intense expression on the thin features had disappeared. Jan's eyes were dull and vacant, staring straight ahead, at nothing.

61

Tolliver caught American's 998 out of Panama City with less than five minutes to spare. The trip to Miami seemed even longer than the one going down, probably because he was suffering from a severe attack of impatience. He had the circle now; he was sure of it. New York to Panama to Palm Beach, with Cunninghams on both ends. But the big question was as elusive as ever: What the hell were they up to?

In Miami, he went through immigration and customs and then connected with American Eagle's 4:30 P.M. flight up the coast to Palm Beach International, arriving there at 5:10 P.M.

At this airport, customs was housed in a separate facility. He took a shuttle bus over to the one-story building that was the U.S. Port of Entry.

The man he spoke to was rumpled and congenial, an older agent named Chuck Groening. Looking at Ben's ID, Groening smiled. "Worked in New York a couple years myself, Lieutenant. You got no idea how happy I was to get out of there."

"Maybe I can imagine it," Tolliver said.

"Yeah, I guess maybe you could. Don't get me wrong—down here it's not all roses. There's plenty of street crime, other problems. But nothing like what you guys have to cope with. And you can keep the winters. What can I do for you?"

"I'm interested in a private airplane that was due in earlier today from Panama. A Falcon, one-three-six-two Charlie."

"Sure, got here a few hours ago. Handled it myself. What do you want to know?"

"Everything you can tell me. I'm trying to trace some people in a case I'm on."

"Yeah, all right. Come on in the office."

Ben followed him across the central area, where two other agents were inspecting bags.

This was a small operation. Despite the International part of its name, most of the flights that came into this airport were domestic. The others were from Canada and the Bahamas, infrequently scheduled.

As a result, the pace at customs was leisurely. Only about a dozen arrivals were waiting to go through at the moment, people wearing bright-colored casual clothing and looking relaxed and happy. Nothing like Miami, with its swarm of tired, sweaty passengers jamming the inspection counters at all hours of the day and night, after voyages from every part of the world.

"Here it is," Groening said. Standing at his desk, he pointed to the listing in a logbook. "Three people. Mr. and Mrs. Tomas Aguila, and Pablo Chavez. Plus the pilot and copilot."

"What were they carrying?"

"Just personal belongings. Mostly clothing, and some binders with business papers. A camera and a laptop computer. The lady had a jewelry case and a bunch of cosmetics."

"How many bags?"

"Three. And the pilots each had a small valise and a Jepp case."

"What's a Jepp case?"

''They're used to carry Jeppeson aerial navigation charts. And also plates showing instrument approaches for different airports.''

''And that was all the luggage on the airplane?''

The agent peered at Tolliver. ''Tell you what, Lieutenant. Why don't you let me in on what it is you're looking for. That way, I could probably be more help to you.''

''I have reason to think they might be hauling something they shouldn't have been. Contraband of some kind, but I'm not sure what.''

Groening frowned. ''If they were, it couldn't have amounted to much.''

''Why not?''

''For one thing, we gave the airplane a good going over, and it was clean. If there'd been drugs on board, even small amounts, Lucy would have picked it up.''

''Who's Lucy?''

In answer, Groening turned and made a smacking noise with his lips. A German shepherd jumped up from where it had been lying on the floor and trotted over to the agent, wagging its tail. The dog had been so quiet, Ben hadn't noticed it.

Groening scratched the animal's chin. ''That's a good girl. You didn't smell anything, did you, baby? Have to be pretty slick to get past you. Now go on back over there and take your nap.'' The dog returned to its place, settling down onto a small rug.

The agent turned to Tolliver. ''Let's face it, Lieutenant. If somebody's a smuggler, the last thing they're gonna do is come waltzing in here with a nice business jet, saying, Here we are; please inspect us. I don't care what it is they're running, drugs or anything else.''

''If not drugs, what else could it be?''

''Only other thing that's important is jewels. There's some of that, but not much. Emeralds, for instance, from Colombia. Drugs, though, are where it's at. As you know, most of it comes into the big cities like Miami or New York, with mules carrying it. There's thousands of those people, running back and forth all the time. I'd say the DEA intercepts maybe ten percent of the dope, if that much.''

''Still, plenty comes in on private airplanes too though, right?''

''Oh yeah. Mostly from the Bahamas, but they don't land here. They're small airplanes that put down on country strips. With so many square miles of ocean, there's no way the Coast Guard or the DEA can patrol it all.''

''Getting back to the Falcon.''

''Uh-huh. I hate to disappoint you, but that flight was totally legitimate.''

''And you're sure of that?''

Again Groening pointed to the log. ''See here? They followed exact procedures for a private jet coming in from a foreign country. Faxed us a a complete rundown a week ago, stating the aircraft type and registration and their ETA. Also gave the names, addresses, nationalities, and dates of birth of everybody on board. If any of 'em had a record or there was any other reason to deny entry, computer would've spit it out for us. But there's nothing on any of 'em. So now tell me—they look like smugglers to you? Or any kind of criminals?''

''No, I guess not.''

''Sorry, Lieutenant.''

Tolliver wasn't ready to give up. ''This says the Aguilas and Chavez are Panamanian and the pilots are U.S. citizens.''

''Correct.''

''And the aircraft is registered in the United States.''

''That's right.''

''Can you tell me who owns it?''

''Not offhand, but I can find out.'' He opened a drawer in his desk and took out a directory. ''The FAA office in Oklahoma City can give us that.''

Ben waited while Groening made the call. The agent spoke to someone and then waited for a few minutes. He made notes on a pad, said thanks, and hung up.

''Belongs to the Amvest Corporation. Four-twenty Park Avenue, in New York.''

Amvest. Why was the name familiar? An instant later, Ben had it. Amvest was one of the companies owned by Cunningham Mining.

62

Daylight was gone now and there was a light breeze. The temperature was about seventy-five, Tolliver guessed, much more comfortable than last night's steam bath in Panama City. He got back on the shuttle and returned to the main terminal, where he rented a small Chevy sedan at the Hertz counter. As he took the keys and the contract, he asked the girl where private planes were parked. On the south side of the airport, she said, and told him how to get there.

At least a hundred airplanes were on tie-down, most of them small and with single engines. There were also several crop dusters and a half dozen ancient DC-3s that were being operated by some airline he'd never heard of, as well as rows of private jets, parked in front of a complex of hangars run by Butler Aviation and Bizjet. Spotlights illuminated the area, which was accessible by a number of open gates.

Locating the Falcon was easy. It was standing between a Lear and a Citation, its distinctive profile unmistakable, and he picked out the *N* number as he approached. He parked the Chevy in front of an administrative office attached to the hangars and went inside.

A young woman behind the counter asked if she could help him. He identified himself and inquired how he could get in touch with the pilots of one-three-six-two Charlie. She looked in her book and said she had no local contact; charges for fuel and services were being billed to a company in New York.

He thanked her and went back outside. Lights were on in one of the cavernous hangars and he could see a mechanic standing on a platform, working on one of the engines of a large corporate jet, a Gulfstream. He walked over to the platform and called up to the man.

The guy pulled his head out of the intake and looked down. He had short-cropped gray hair and a lined face. "Yeah—what is it?"

Tolliver held up his shield. "Police officer. Like to ask you a few questions."

The mechanic drew a rag from the back pocket of his coveralls and wiped his hands on it. Then he came down the metal steps, continuing to rub grease off his fingers.

"What's your name?" Ben asked.

There was a look of wariness in his eyes. "Joe Bellamy."

"I'm Lieutenant Ben Tolliver, Joe. You happen to know anybody who was on that Falcon out there—the one next to the Lear?"

Bellamy spoke with a corn-pone drawl. "Naw, I got no idea whose airplane that is. Folks who come in here, they like their privacy."

"Then maybe you can just give me some general information, okay?"

"I was about ready to knock off. But yeah, all right."

"Come on outside."

They walked out to where the Falcon was parked. When viewed from a distance, the aircraft hadn't looked as large as it actually was, probably because its lines were so graceful. Up close, it loomed above them, the white surfaces reflecting the glare of the spotlights.

"You familiar with this type?" Ben asked.

"Sure. I done a lot of work on 'em."

"Then tell me something. Suppose you wanted to hide something in a plane like this. Nothing too big, but say a couple of suitcases. Would that be possible?"

Bellamy looked at him sideways. "I don't know if I—"

Tolliver held up a hand. "Let's just say it's hypothetical, okay? Could you do it?"

"It'd be easy."

"Why is that?"

"On account of this airplane has got a hellhole."

"A what?"

"Back there in the tail, just forward of the stabilizer, there's an empty space. It's called a hellhole, but don't ask me why. Lot of airplanes're built like that. You have to unscrew the cover off a bulkhead to get at it, but it's there."

"And you could put suitcases in that space?"

"Sure. Matter of fact, there're a couple places like that in a Falcon. Another one's just aft of the luggage compartment. How much weight we talking about?"

"I don't know—but not more than a few hundred pounds."

"Pilot'd have to trim the airplane a little, but it wouldn't be any problem." The mechanic squinted. "You think they might've been hauling dope?"

"Maybe."

"Be a pretty dumb way to do it."

"Why's that?"

"Too expensive. If a doper ran an airplane like this one, he'd have all the seats pulled out so he could get a real payload on board. He'd want to haul a couple thousand pounds, not a few dinky suitcases."

"Uh-huh. Tell me something. How tight is customs at this airport?"

Bellamy got out the strip of waste cloth again and resumed rubbing his fingers with it. "I wouldn't want to make trouble for nobody."

"Hey, look," Ben said. "I won't quote you. Anything you say stays between us, okay?"

"What you're asking me is, would customs pull that bulkhead, really get into the airplane. That right?"

"Yes."

"Answer's no. Not unless they had a damn good reason to. Like if they knew ahead of time there was something they oughta be looking for. Otherwise, forget it. They ain't gonna do any more work than they have to."

"All right, Joe. Thanks for your help."

"That it?"

"That's it. Have a nice evening."

Bellamy turned and walked back into the hangar.

Ben took one last look at the airplane. Whatever it might have brought in from Panama, there was no way for him to check it out now. Not after customs had inspected it and pronounced it clean. And besides, what did he have other than hunches?

There was a public phone on the outside wall of the administration office. He went to it and called the Palm Beach Police Department. It was getting late, but he still might reach the man he wanted. When he got an answer, he asked for Sgt. Peter Dennison.

He was in luck; the sergeant was in.

63

Ben drove from the airport to Okeechobee Boulevard and then over the bridge to the narrow island that was Palm Beach. The moon was up, its rays silhouetting the palm trees and shining on the waters of Lake Worth, where rows of yachts were tied up at the docks.

The police station was like no other Ben had ever seen. It was two stories high and built of orange stucco, with a red barrel-tiled roof and an arched loggia, surrounded by beds of elephant-ear ferns and neatly clipped ficus hedges. Just four blocks from Worth Avenue, it looked more like a golf club than a police headquarters.

When Tolliver walked in, he was the only person in the lobby. Opposite the entrance was a glass partition, with a lone female officer behind it, sitting at a desk and reading a newspaper. He took the elevator to the second floor, where the detectives' offices were.

There was a circular balcony up there with potted plants around the railing, and you could look down from it and see the lobby. He couldn't help comparing this station house with the Sixth Precinct's in the West Village, with its stink of disinfectant and the daily complement of whores, muggers, boosters, and burglars fighting with cops while they screamed their innocence.

Peter Dennison clapped Tolliver on the back. "Man, you're lookin' good. That easy life in New York must agree with you."

"Wouldn't trade it for anything," Ben said.

Dennison headed the PBPD detective squad. He'd gone to Tulane on a football scholarship and had graduated with a degree in criminology. Long past his playing days, he'd become jowly and his hair was thinning. He'd also developed a paunch that pushed out the front of his trendy linen jacket.

"How about we get something to eat?" the sergeant suggested. "You can bring me up to speed on what you're doing."

Ben said that sounded fine. Dennison led the way, driving a patrol car, with Tolliver following in the rented Chevy.

The place they went to was a bar and restaurant that had been built back in the twenties by a gambler named Ed Bradley, who'd also run a wide-open gambling casino across the street. The casino was gone now, and so was Bradley. But the bar was booming, filled with a raucous crowd dressed in plaid shorts and loud shirts and pants, enthusiastic boozers of all ages.

Both cops drank bourbon, standing in the crush at the bar.

"So what's this case you're on?" Dennison asked.

"Investigation of Senator Cunningham's death."

"Ah, the senator—I should've known. That's why you're in Palm Beach?"

"In a roundabout way, yes."

"What is it you're looking for?"

"I'm not sure," Ben said. "Does the name Tomas Aguila mean anything to you?"

Dennison pursed his lips, thinking about it. "No, never heard of him. Who is he?"

"Somebody I wanted to talk to. How about Pablo Chavez?"

"Not him, either. They Cuban?"

"Panamanian. I think they might have a business connection with the Cunninghams."

"Are they here in Palm Beach?"

"I don't know that, either."

"If you want, I'll run a check. Let you know if I turn up anything."

"How about the family—are any of them here now?"

"No, too early. They usually come down just before Christmas, when the real season starts. Hey, the senator dying made some big splash, didn't it? How's the investigation going?"

"All right. More or less routine."

"Not according to what I've been seeing. He had this woman with him, right? And then maybe she killed herself and maybe she didn't. Anyhow, there's never anything routine with that outfit. We've had our own problems with them."

"Like what?"

"Let's order some chow and I'll tell you about it."

Despite the crowd, they were given a table immediately; Dennison was obviously well known here. He recommended snapper, telling Ben it was fresh and hard to screw up. They had another drink while they waited for their food.

"First year I was on the force," the sergeant said, "there was this nineteen-year-old kid who'd been beaten. She was a hostess in a restaurant on Royal Poinciana. Some people found her on the beach at night with a broken arm and her face pushed in. Ambulance took her to St. Mary's, and when she could talk, she told us she'd been to a party at the Cunningham house. Said the old man got her off in the guest cottage and worked her over. At first, she was gonna press charges, but then she changed her mind. Said she'd been mistaken. After that, she dropped out of sight."

The story had a familiar ring. "Where is she now?"

"I have no idea. Her folks live in Lantana. Whether they ever hear from her, I couldn't say. There've been other things, too, with the Cunninghams. But one way or another, they all got hushed up."

"How far is the house?" Ben asked.

"Couple miles. It's up near the Kennedy place, on North Ocean."

"And you say there's nobody there?"

"Just some of the permanent staff. Gardeners, the housekeeper, one or two maids. They always bring more with them when they come down from New York."

Dinner arrived, and it was as Dennison had promised; the fish was fresh and simply cooked, served with lemon and baked zucchini. Ben attacked his food ravenously, as usual.

While they ate, he pressed the sergeant for more information about the Cunninghams. Dennison told him the Colonel had built the place just after World War I, when so many of the big estates were constructed. Like a lot of other families, they were always leaders in the social world, but with plenty of skeletons in their closets. You wouldn't believe it, he said, what their kind of money and power could do. Tolliver said he had a fairly good idea.

"After a while, I got smart," Dennison said. "It's one thing to handle the nickel-and-dime cases, burglaries, car theft, shit like that. But when you get something where one of the important families is involved, that's another story."

Ben sensed what he was going to hear next.

"These people have got just too many resources," Dennison went on. "There's more money per square foot here than in any other town in America—maybe in the world. There're the du Ponts, and the Fords, the Newhouses, even the Sultan of Brunei. So what chance do you think you've got if one of 'em trips over the law? Lot of times, it won't even make the papers."

Tolliver listened politely. Dennison wasn't the first cop he'd run across who was awestruck by wealth.

''And if something does go public,'' the sergeant said, ''look at the kind of firepower they can call up. You take the rape case. Two prosecutors up against a whole battery of hotshot lawyers from Miami. We knew goddamn well he was guilty. But there wasn't any way he was gonna be convicted, either. I heard the legal fees ran over two million.''

''So what are you saying?'' Ben asked him.

Dennison spoke around a mouthful of fish. ''Just that it took me a while to catch on. Our job here is to keep the streets safe, run a nice clean town. But what I learned is, you don't go looking to be a hero, take on something bigger than you are. That's not healthy. I guess you know all about that, huh?''

''Yeah,'' Ben said. ''I know all about it.''

Dennison looked at his watch. ''Getting late, and I promised the wife I wouldn't be too long. She gets pissed sometimes about my hours. Hope you don't mind if I take off.''

''No, I understand. Thanks for dinner.''

''My pleasure. Next time we'll do it in New York, okay? If I ever have the bad luck to get up that way.''

The sergeant signed the check, winking at Tolliver. When they walked out the entrance, he said, ''Forgot to ask—you got a place to stay?''

''I'll go to one of the hotels near the airport,'' Ben said. ''There's no flight out until morning.''

''You need anything else while you're here, just let me know.''

''Yeah,'' Ben said. ''I'll do that.''

Dennison waved, got into the patrol car, and pulled away. Tolliver watched him go. The sergeant had been friendly and polite, but the message he'd given Ben was about as subtle as a punch in the mouth. Behave yourself, and don't mess with any of our prominent citizens, because it won't get you anything but trouble.

The Chevy was parked nearby. As Ben went over to it, a young couple walked past on the sidewalk. He asked them for directions. Then he climbed into the car and drove up to County Road, following it until it joined North Ocean Boulevard. From there, he drove along the beach.

The moon was high now, and there were roof lights on some of the mansions, casting beams out over the sea and picking up the phosphorescent glow of the breakers. He had no trouble finding the Cunningham house, a huge Mediterranean villa that sat on a bluff, with a high wall surrounding the property. He pulled over and parked some yards up the road, then walked back.

Through the latticed gates there were only a few lights showing, and there were no cars in the circular driveway. Just as Dennison had said, it was too early for the Cunninghams to be here; there would be no one in the house but members of the permanent staff. The place was silent except for the distant roar of waves breaking on the beach.

Ben shook his head in anger and frustration. The prospect of winding up with nothing was more than he could wrap his head around. There was something going on here; there was a link—he *knew* it.

And what proof did he have? Zero. Zip. He felt like kicking the goddamn gates down.

So now what? Admit failure and go back to New York? That was depressing, but what choice did he have?

He turned away, and as he did, he saw a glimmer of light appear at one end of the house.

A garage door was opening. He watched as a car backed out onto the tiled driveway, a black Rolls-Royce Corniche convertible. The garage door closed and the car swung around to the main entrance.

The front door of the house opened and a man stepped out. He was silhouetted in the doorway and Ben couldn't make out his features. But then as he opened the passenger door of the Rolls, the light shone on his blond hair. He ducked into the car and slammed the door. The Rolls pulled away, heading down the drive, toward where Tolliver was standing.

Ben turned and sprinted back to the Chevy, reaching it and jumping in just as the gates opened and the black convertible emerged. The car came out onto North Ocean Boulevard and turned in the direction Ben had come, toward the town center.

Tolliver waited until the red taillights were almost out of sight. Then he started his engine and flicked on the lights, easing the small car onto the road and following the Rolls at a considerable distance.

Maybe he'd have some luck, after all. The man who'd gotten into the convertible wasn't a Cunningham, but he was married to one.

64

The Rolls maintained a moderate pace, running down County Road past the Breakers Hotel and turning left at the church, Bethesda by the Sea, and then right again onto South Ocean Boulevard.

There were beachfront mansions along here as well, each more pretentious than the one before. Many of them looked like hotels rather than private houses, immense pseudo-Mediterranean villas with fluted columns and balconies. All had lush plantings of bougainvillea and alamanda and oleander under tall royal palms.

Tolliver kept the black convertible in sight as it left the island via the Southern Bridge, then he moved closer. They were on the mainland now—in West Palm Beach, where there were a lot of stoplights and more traffic and the Rolls could slip away from him if he wasn't careful.

They crossed I-95 and continued west, and he realized they were approaching the side of the airport where he'd been earlier. Suddenly, the other car swerved off onto Congress Avenue, a strip lined with honky-tonk bars and topless joints.

One of the places was called the Pussycat Lounge. The Rolls pulled into the parking lot behind the rambling one-story building and Tolliver drove on by. He went down the road a quarter of a mile, then turned around and came back.

When he entered the parking lot, he saw the Rolls at the far end, looking oddly out of place alongside the other cars and the pickup trucks: a princess among the frogs.

The convertible's headlights were off and he could make out that the driver was alone, sitting at the wheel. Ben parked the Chevy some distance away, got out, and went around to the front entrance. Huge red neon letters over the door said GIRLS! GIRLS! GIRLS!

He stepped inside. There was a single large room, with a bar that ran down one side of it, and the place was busy. Slow rock, heavy on drums and bass guitars, was slamming out of wall-mounted speakers and a pair of topless dancers were gyrating on the bar. The girls had on only G-strings and heels and were waving their butts in the customers' faces as they made their turns.

Most of the drinkers were rednecks, sporting beards and baseball caps, but there were some guys in business suits as well, looking frazzled and maybe half-drunk after a hard day at the office. Kurt Kramer was nowhere in sight.

A bartender in a T-shirt that showed off his weight lifter's body moved over in front of Tolliver and placed his hands on the mahogany surface. Ben said he'd have bourbon on the rocks.

One of the dancers was kind of cute, he thought, a redhead with a turned-up nose and nipples that pointed in the same direction. The other girl looked as if she was ready to go back to the minors. Or maybe this was the minors, and the redhead was being primed for stardom. It seemed unlikely.

He was on his second swallow when he caught sight of a face he'd seen just once before. Recognizing the guy was easy; he was wearing the same lime green jacket he'd had on at the Tocumen Airport in Panama.

Tomas Aguila walked straight past where Tolliver was sitting at the bar, and this time Ben got a good look at him: slicked-back black hair and dark skin, a square jaw and a thin, aquiline nose. As he watched, Aguila walked across the room and sat at a table in the corner.

One other man was at that table: Kurt Kramer. Tolliver hadn't spotted him earlier in the semidarkness. A waitress went to the table and moved off again; the two men huddled together. A match flared briefly as Aguila lighted a cigarette, and Ben could see both faces clearly.

He sipped his bourbon, pretending to watch the bumping and grinding on the bar but keeping his eyes on the table in the corner. The waitress returned and set drinks down in front of the men, then left them. They continued to talk, Aguila gesturing with his hands.

I would give a lot, Tolliver thought, to hear what those two are saying to each other.

Abruptly, both men stood up. Kramer pulled money out of his pocket and tossed it down on the table. Then they came toward the bar.

Ben turned his face away and the men walked past him. Kramer was saying something, but with the pounding of the rock music, Tolliver couldn't make out what it was.

He waited for a few seconds, then watched them go out the door. Dropping a bill on the bar, he slid off the stool and followed.

Out in the parking lot, Kramer and Aguila were continuing their conversation, Aguila still waving his hands. There were lights on the rear of the building and Ben could see the pair walking toward the Rolls. He hung back in the shadows.

A pickup truck rolled into the lot, its lights illuminating him briefly. He retreated around a corner, flattening himself against the wall. The vehicle stopped and two men got out. They didn't notice Tolliver as they went by him on their way into the Pussycat.

When he stepped out of his hiding place, the Rolls was gone. He cursed under his breath, his gaze sweeping the parking lot as he tried to catch sight of the green jacket. But Aguila had disappeared, as well. Ben reached into his pocket for the keys to the Chevy and strode toward the place where he'd parked.

There was a crunch of gravel behind him.

Instinctively, he threw himself to one side. A knife blade ripped down the shoulder of his blazer. He felt a sharp pain, then hit the ground rolling. He lashed out with his foot as a dark shape leapt onto him.

The kick must have caught his attacker in the belly. Ben heard the air go out of the guy and then the heavy body crashed down onto him. Steel glinted as a knife blade flashed toward Tolliver's face. He grabbed the man's wrist with his left hand and held on, halting the point of the knife an inch from his eye.

Garlic breath washed over him like fetid gas. Ben strained, his teeth clenched, and drove his other fist into the knife wielder's jaw. The punch shook the guy, but it didn't dislodge him. Ben could feel him pulling himself forward, trying to bring his weight into play so he could drive the blade through Tolliver's eye and into his brain.

Ben twisted the wrist and at the same time brought his knee up between the assailant's legs, ramming it into his groin. The man screamed and let go of the knife. With a mighty heave, Tolliver threw him off. Then he rolled to his right, drawing himself up onto his knees and reaching behind him for the Mauser.

He was a fraction of a second too late.

At the instant his hand closed around the pistol grip, he caught a kick on the point of his jaw. It lifted him up and over backward. He landed flat on his back.

After that, everything was in slow motion. He tried to move and couldn't. There was the sound of footsteps and voices, and then for what seemed like an hour, he was moving through a black tunnel whose walls were a spiraling yellow light. He could hear the voices, but it was as if they were coming from a great distance.

When he opened his eyes, he realized he'd been out of it, but he didn't know for how long. Strange faces were looming over him.

One of the faces said, "Hey, buddy—you all right?"

Another face said, "Yeah, he's okay. Let's get 'im up."

He felt hands grab him under the armpits and then he was lifted to his feet.

Three men were standing in a half circle around him, big guys wearing jeans and short-sleeved shirts. One of them had a beard.

The beard grinned. "Man, he really kicked the shit out of you."

Ben's jaw felt numb, and when he spoke his voice seemed to belong to somebody else. "Where is he?"

"Aw hell, he's gone. Soon as he saw us, he took off. Jumped in a car and hauled ass."

"You can catch the mother some other night," another one said. "Come on inside and have a drink."

"Thanks," Tolliver said, "but I'll see you later."

He trotted to the rental car, leaving the trio shaking their heads.

65

Pulling out of the parking lot, Ben was disgusted with himself for having been so careless. It wasn't as if he didn't know Aguila had a bodyguard—he even knew the guy's name, for Christ's sake. Yet he'd let himself get taken like some bubble-brained rookie.

Driving back to Southern Boulevard, he headed for the hangars where the Falcon was parked. This time when he arrived, there was a uniformed guard near the gate, but the man merely waved lackadaisically as Ben drove in.

He pulled to a stop in front of the administration building and jumped out.

The Falcon was gone.

Ben stared at the vacant space, feeling all the more like a prize asshole. He heard the roar of jet engines and, looking up, got another view of the airplane as it took off. The Falcon climbed at the familiar steep angle, rising sharply from the eastbound runway and vanishing into the night.

Turning away, he looked at the parked aircraft standing in rows, wishing he'd gotten here a few minutes sooner. The empty space was like a confirmation that he'd blown it.

Something else was different, he realized. Not only was the Falcon no longer there but the space next to it was vacant, as well. What was the airplane that had been there?

It was a Lear, he remembered.

He stepped to the one-story office building and went inside. The same young woman was on the desk. When she caught sight of him, her mouth fell open.

Which wasn't surprising; he looked as if he'd been run over by a truck. His blazer was ripped open and the front of his shirt had blood all over it from the kick in the jaw Pablo Chavez had given him. His face was swollen and his shoulder was stiff where the knife had nicked his flesh.

Ben got out his case and waved his shield at her. "I was here earlier," he said. "The Falcon that was here just took off, right?"

She nodded, staring at him.

"What happened to the Lear that was next to it—when did that leave?"

"Just before the Falcon."

"Whose airplane is that?"

She looked at her register. "I don't know. It just says—"

He grabbed the book and turned it around. "Where is it?"

She pointed. "The *N* number is five-six-four-nine Tango."

Next to the number was the billing address: Amvest Corporation, 420 Park Avenue, New York, NY 10022.

Bingo—there it was again.

Ben glanced up at the young woman and grinned. "You know something? You're the best-looking girl I ever saw in my life."

She continued to gape at him as he went out the door.

When he got back into the Chevy, he sat there for a moment, thinking.

It wasn't drugs; he knew that. And it wasn't jewels or gold—that made even less sense.

But he had no doubt whatever that after the money had been

laundered through the Banco Cafetero, Aguila had smuggled something of great value back into the States and transferred it to Kramer.

So what was it that would fit into a couple of large suitcases and be worth 50 million bucks?

Fifty million bucks, of course. The suitcases hidden in the Falcon had almost surely been packed with cash. But was that physically possible? How much space would that amount take up, and how much would it weigh?

Some years ago, Tolliver had worked on the hijacking of an armored bank truck. Most of the money had been recovered, and there was so much of it in loose bills that instead of counting, the feds had weighed the bills. A million in twenties, he remembered, came in at 115 pounds.

Doing some calculations in his head, he figured there were fifty thousand twenties in a million dollars. And fifty thousand pieces of paper currency would have the same weight, regardless of their denomination.

Assuming the Banco Cafetero had cashed Cunningham's check in thousand-dollar bills, Ben reasoned that fifty thousand such bills would come to $50 million. He went over it again slowly, to be sure he hadn't screwed up the zeros.

Okay, he was right.

He went on thinking: Take out both the bank's commission and Aguila's cut—a couple of pounds or whatever—and what you had left could be split into two bundles of roughly 24,000 thousand-dollar bills each. The bundles would fit into two large suitcases, no problem.

Ben started the engine and backed away from the building, then pointed the car toward the gate, banging a fist on the steering wheel in exultation.

66

Orcus drove his car onto the grounds of the Brentwood Treatment Center and followed the winding drive to the parking lot. He pulled into an open space not far from the main entrance and turned off the ignition. It was twilight and lights were on in the building; through the tall windows, he could see much of the activity going on inside.

Hunched down in his seat, he was confident no one would notice him sitting there, especially in the gathering darkness.

It was important that he plan this well. He was still smarting over the way he'd missed taking out that goddamned detective, bumbling the job like some amateur. He wouldn't miss next time; you could bet everything you owned on that.

And he wouldn't miss this one, either, which was why he was scouting it now, checking out every detail, making sure he knew exactly what he had to do and what he could expect, when the time came.

A half hour later, it was pitch-dark. A number of staff members came out, got into their cars, and drove away. Over the next few hours, Orcus sat where he was, observing the ivy-covered stone structure.

For a mental hospital, Brentwood was surprisingly casual about security, he thought. There was no wall around the grounds, no gate with a guard stopping visitors to ask for identification—just this rambling old building on the eastern end of Long Island, surrounded by pine trees and exposed to the cold winds that were blowing in off the Atlantic. He'd seen summer houses out here that were better protected.

But then, Brentwood wasn't a state facility, a place where hard cases were treated. An asylum like Wingdale, for example, where there were corrections officers armed with rifles and where spotlights were trained on the high steel fences throughout the night, making the area as bright as day. Where confined inside the forbidding red stone buildings were homicidal psychopaths who had to be watched around the clock to prevent them from killing hospital personnel or other inmates. Or themselves.

No, Brentwood seemed more like a country club or a rest home. The nurses were wearing pale blue outfits, but without caps, and many of them had on gaily colored sweaters over the uniforms. The attendants were even more informally garbed, in sport shirts and slacks.

The patients were easy to pick out, as well. They were all adults, ranging in age from young to the last stages of doddering senility. No one bothered to draw the shades or pull the drapes over the windows, so Orcus could see people sitting in their rooms or walking through the halls. Most of them also wore leisure clothing, although a few had on pajamas and bathrobes.

On each of the upper two floors was a space that appeared to be some sort of lounge, with card tables and TV. He couldn't see into the one on the top floor very well, but he assumed it was more or less the same as the one below, where inmates were playing games or watching the tube. Occasionally, one of them would wander past a window.

By now, it had to be long past visiting hours. In a place like this, visitors probably weren't permitted in the evening. This meant that after the office workers left, there would be fewer staff members wandering around. And if Brentwood was like other institutions, it would be at its quietest after the evening meal.

Satisfied that he'd seen all there was to see from his vantage point, and confident that he had a clear impression of the hospital's nighttime routine, Orcus started his engine and pulled out of the parking lot. When he reached the narrow blacktop road, he turned toward the small village he'd passed on his way here.

It was amazing, he thought, that there were still stretches of Long Island that were sparsely populated. Yet when you got out past Port Jefferson, you saw many good-sized open areas. Couldn't last, though. Someday they'd be converted to developments that looked like all the others—rows of chicken coops.

The village was little more than a crossroads with a few shops and a scattering of houses. Orcus reached it in less than ten minutes. There was a gas station on the corner of what was apparently the main street. The station was closed, but he saw what he was looking for: a public phone booth standing off to one side.

He parked near the booth and got out of his car. There were streetlights along here and occasional traffic whizzing past. He tugged the brim of his hat down over his eyes and flipped up his coat collar as he stepped over to the booth.

As usual, she answered on the first ring. He could picture her camping beside the telephone, anxiously waiting for him to check in. Women were like that; even when they thought they were tough, they acted like nervous Nellies when it came down to it.

"It's me," he said.

"Have you been to the hospital yet?"

"I just came from there."

"I hope nobody saw you."

"They didn't, I guarantee. I didn't go inside, just sat in the car and watched."

"Do you know which room she's in?"

"No, but I won't have any trouble finding her. The whole thing should be easy."

"If that's so, why didn't you do it while you were there?"

"Because I wanted to plan it carefully, that's why."

"So plan it, and then get it done. Fast. She's running her mouth off, don't you realize that? Can't you see what would happen if it got out?"

"Don't try to push any of this off on me. It should've been taken care of a long time ago. I told you that."

She bristled. "Nobody ever thought she'd live, let alone come out of it."

"Still was a dumb mistake."

"You're telling me about dumb mistakes? You? After you fucked up the other one?"

"I'll take care of him, too. Don't worry about it."

"One of us has to."

He hung up. More and more, she pissed him off. Maybe that was another thing he'd handle when this was over.

She'd be just one more bitch to get rid of.

67

Tolliver spent the night in the airport Hilton and in the morning took American's first flight out of West Palm Beach. He was still a little stiff, but a few hours of sleep had helped.

The cut on his jaw and the one on the back of his shoulder he'd cleaned and patched up with alcohol and tape he bought in a drugstore. What was left of his blazer and the bloodstained shirt, he'd thrown away. The shirt he had on now was the one he'd worn to Panama, and it was getting ripe.

Breakfast on the airplane wasn't bad; at least there was plenty of hot coffee. And despite the soreness from his encounter with the guy who'd tried to knife him, he was feeling pretty damned good. He had answers now; he'd closed the loop. And he was almost certain he knew how the Cunninghams were running the scheme.

The problem was, did he have enough to take to the DA?

That was where it got sticky. No matter what he'd learned, he was still facing the same dilemma that had plagued him from the beginning of the case: He had no hard evidence.

And yet, look at what he did have.

He knew that Cunningham Securities had made staggering sums through illegal trades and he was certain they were laundering the money by sending it to Tomas Aguila's account in the Banco Cafetero. Aguila would then bring the cash into the United States, using ports of entry like Palm Beach International because slipping the money past such operations was a breeze.

Ben had to admire the ingenuity of it. No playing hide-and-seek with border patrols, no dodging U.S. government aircraft or the Coast Guard. Instead, they even *announced* they were coming—in a fancy corporate jet, following all proper procedures and being greeted with courtesy and respect upon their arrival. Once in the States, the money was then transferred to Kurt Kramer, who also had long experience in illicit financial dealings. Amvest Corporation was the repository, and it was owned by the Cunninghams.

As far as the deaths of former Senator Clayton Cunningham and Jessica Silk were concerned, Ben not only knew both had died under suspicious circumstances but he would bet his soul they'd been murdered.

And yet there was so much he *didn't* know, let alone what he could or could not prove. The ultimate question was still how all this fit together, and why.

Take the laundering operation. There was nothing new about turning dirty money into clean. What was different here was that instead of going into phony front companies or even lawful ones, with the money eventually winding up in Swiss bank accounts or legitimate investments, he felt sure it was coming back into the United States in cash. If that was true, what the hell would anybody want with all those bills? It would be like starting the process all over again.

And if the senator and Silk had been murdered, who had killed them and what was the motive, or motives? And how were those issues related to the money schemes?

He wrestled with it all the way to New York, but when the airliner made its final approach, he still hadn't come up with anything definitive. All he had was a bunch of theories, and none of them quite worked.

At La Guardia, the air was a good thirty degrees cooler than what he'd been experiencing the last couple of days. He got his raincoat out of his bag and put in on, then stopped at a pay phone.

He called 115th Precinct headquarters first and told Lieutenant Morales the plan had worked, that he had the information he'd been hoping to get. He also told Morales to be sure the ADA kept his end of the bargain involving Fuentes's brother. For a number of good reasons.

Next he called Shelley at WPIC TV, was relieved when she answered. "I've been out of town," he said.

"I know. I got your message."

So much for civility, he thought.

He tried again. "Shel, look. I'm sorry I blew up at you, okay? I think we both made mistakes. You went too far in what you said on the air and I overreacted. Maybe we both learned something."

She softened. "I'm sorry too, Ben. I've missed you."

"Me, too. How about we get together tonight?"

"Can't. I think I just might be getting close to something."

"What's that?"

"Laura Bentley has invited me to the Cunningham's estate on Long Island for the weekend."

"She *what*?"

"Now don't go into orbit again, okay? What happened was, I talked to her about doing an interview on her career. She's planning to revive it, only in TV this time. She wants me to help her with her plans. That's what brought on the invitation."

"Shelley—"

"Relax, I know what I'm doing. No matter what happens, I'll get a damn good story out of it. Might even get some things that could help you."

He knew better than to argue with her or to launch another tirade. He exhaled. "Listen, be careful, will you?"

"You know me." She hung up.

Ben put the phone down, wishing she'd stayed the hell away from Bentley. This thing had enough complications as it was. He walked out of the terminal and took a cab to the NYPD repair shop, which wasn't far from the airport.

The Taurus was parked outside the garage. Charley McManus led him over to it. "Good as new," McManus said. "We filled up the holes in the door with Bondo before we painted it. Came out okay, huh?"

Ben crouched beside the door on the driver's side. There was a slight ripple in the metal and the blue color wasn't an exact match, but you'd never notice the imperfections if you weren't looking for them. "Not bad, considering."

McManus pointed. "Put in a couple new windows, too."

Ben straightened up. "So I see. Hope you didn't use the same glass as last time. Stuff went out like Saran Wrap."

"Hey, don't kid yourself—there's no such thing as bulletproof glass. Bullet-*resistant* is the best we got. And besides, whoever was shooting at you was using heavy artillery. Wasn't for the armor in the door, we'd be filling you with Bondo, too."

"Might be an improvement." Tolliver tossed his bag into the backseat of the Taurus, then climbed in behind the wheel. "Appreciate the good work, Charley."

"Stay out of Brownsville," McManus said. He looked at the piece of tape on Ben's jaw. "And take care of yourself."

"I'll do that." Tolliver started his engine and the men opened the gates for him. He drove past the lineup of wrecked patrol cars and out of the yard.

At this time of day, the Queens Midtown Tunnel would be his best bet. He was right: traffic was light. He made the Criminal Justice Building in just under twenty minutes.

When he walked in, Jack Mulloy jumped to his feet with a big grin. He followed Tolliver into his office.

"Man, am I glad to see you," Mulloy said. "Where you been?"

"Took a few days off," Ben said.

"And cut your chin shaving, right?"

"Right. What's going on?"

Mulloy pointed to a pile of messages on Tolliver's desk. "Lot of calls, people looking for you. Brannigan's been asking me, and then yesterday Shackley was over here nosing around."

Ben hung up his raincoat and sat at his desk, leafing through the messages. Captain Brennan had left word to call him, nothing urgent. None of the others seemed important; some of them were from reporters, and many others appeared to be of the nutball variety, from people claiming to have vital information.

"Hey," Mulloy said, "you ready for the good news?"

"Sure—what is it?"

"That group I came across, the guys who were feeding each

other information they got from boards they sat on? I got four more of them.''

''You sure?''

''Sure as I can be. And get this—one of them has a son who's gonna marry the daughter of another one. It was in the *Times*. You believe it?''

''Yeah, I do.''

''The trouble is, I'm not crazy about laying it out for Shackley. I wouldn't want to see this get shoved into the same shit can where all the rest of it goes. I was hoping you'd have some ideas.''

''Let me think about it,'' Ben said. ''Just keep it under wraps until I tell you.''

''Okay, will do.'' Mulloy left the office.

Tolliver thought about this latest development. What Mulloy had uncovered was another pattern of illegal dealing, without question. Unfortunately, it also raised a further set of questions Ben didn't know the answers to.

Resignedly, he resumed looking through his messages, tossing most of them into the wastebasket. One of them was from a woman on Long Island who said she wanted to talk to him about her sister, who was hospitalized. He crumpled the slip of paper and dumped it with the others.

At the moment, what he wanted most was to go to his apartment for a shower and some clean clothes.

68

When Jack Mulloy returned to his desk, he noticed Captain Brannigan standing in the doorway of his office, watching him. Brannigan had his arms folded, leaning against the door frame and wearing a shit-eating smile. The captain glanced over at Tolliver's office and back at Mulloy, then turned away and went back to his own office.

The prick.

Mulloy had no illusions about the chances he was taking, hooking up with Tolliver. It was like walking a high wire across the East River. One false step and it'd be all over.

Maybe when it came right down to it, what he'd been doing was too risky, after all. It was one thing to latch onto a great opportunity when he saw one, but it was another to piss away everything he had.

And yet, would he really want to deal with this any differently? You never got anywhere unless you were willing to lay your ass on the line for what you believed in. And that belief started with yourself.

He looked at his desk: the records, his notes, all his work he kept carefully locked away in the drawers. What would happen if Brannigan got into the stuff and started questioning him—or if he told Shackley about it and the two of them worked on him? He'd be in deep shit.

He tensed, thinking about it, and then forced himself to relax. There was nothing he couldn't handle. He'd just be extra-careful, that was all. Maybe it'd be smart to move the material, too, store it someplace else.

In the end, it was just a question of keeping his wits about him—the same as always. Jack Mulloy hadn't made it this far without being one smart, tough operator.

He picked up his mug from his desk and went across the area to the coffee urn.

69

The helicopter was larger than any of the ones Shelley had flown in. It looked like a giant dragonfly, ready to buzz off from the southeastern tip of Manhattan. The aircraft was painted pearlescent white, gleaming under coats of wax, the main rotor blades turning lazily as it sat on the pad at the Port Authority Heliport. The pilot, a young guy in a crisp blue uniform, had stowed the baggage and was waiting for his passengers to board the aircraft.

There were two others besides Shelley: Laura Bentley and Claire, the senator's widow. Laura introduced her to Claire and then the pilot helped them up the step and into the door. All three women were dressed casually in slacks and sweaters.

When they were ensconsed in the passenger compartment, Shelley was even more impressed. The seats were upholstered in glove-soft beige suede, luxuriously deep and comfortable. There were also magazine racks and a folding desk and a combination bar-refrigerator, plus a TV and a stereo. The floor was covered in thick carpeting.

In all, the helicopter was nothing like the thrashing machines she'd broadcast traffic reports from back in her early days in the business. Those were raucous and uncomfortable, while this was more like a flying limousine.

"The others went on ahead," Laura said to her, "in one of the other helicopters. They always do that, so they can talk business. They leave this one for the ladies."

"The camp followers, you mean," Claire said.

Shelley was in the left-hand seat aft, with Laura sitting beside her and Claire facing them. As the helicopter lifted off, they had a marvelous view of the city. Late-afternoon sunlight was reflecting from a million panels of glass in the windows of the skyscrapers.

Claire opened the liquor cabinet in the bar. "Anybody want a drink? Besides me?"

Shelley shook her head. "Not for me, thanks."

"Maybe later," Laura said. "After we're airborne."

"Suit yourselves." Claire got out a glass and filled it with ice and gin, then sat back and took a long swallow.

They leveled off, sailing over the Brooklyn and Manhattan bridges, and a little farther up went over the Williamsburg, the river like a wide gray-green ribbon below them. The pilot kept the craft low, which Shelley knew from her own chopper experience was so that controllers wouldn't confuse them with the traffic on their radar screens, jets arriving and departing from the local airports, Kennedy, La Guardia, and Newark.

They crossed the Queensboro and at Hell Gate swung east, going over the Triborough this time, with Wards Island on their left. Then they ducked lower, following the air corridor that would take them past La Guardia. It seemed to Shelley that they didn't clear the Bronx Whitestone and the Throg's Neck bridges by more than a few feet.

Once clear of the TCA, the pilot lifted the helicopter to a slightly higher altitude, then the ship settled down for the trip out to the eastern reaches of Long Island.

Laura turned to Claire. "I'll have that drink now. A Scotch, if the offer's still good."

Claire was already working on her second. "Sure. How about you, Shelley?"

"No thanks, I'm fine. Just enjoying the ride."

"You'll enjoy the whole weekend more if you stay slightly

tanked. The alcohol tends to offset having to be around this bunch.''

''Don't mind Claire,'' Laura said. ''She tends to judge us all a little harshly.''

''But accurately,'' Claire said. She poured Scotch into a squat glass and handed it to Laura. ''And who are you kidding, Laura? You feel the same way.''

Laura smiled indulgently, as if putting up with a fractious child. ''Maybe I just handle it better than you do.''

''That's not true, either. You're like this rug. You lie there and let Clay walk all over you.''

''That's Eaton's Neck down there,'' Laura said, obviously anxious to change the subject. ''Those tall smokestacks are a great landmark. And the ones farther ahead are Port Jefferson.''

Shelley looked down at the stacks, and at that point the helicopter changed course slightly, angling inland.

Claire was squinting at her. ''You're a TV reporter, aren't you?''

''Yes, but not this trip.''

''Shelley's helping me with some plans I have for a television appearance,'' Laura said.

Claire kept after it. ''After my husband died, didn't you do a story on him and that woman?''

''I just read what they handed me,'' Shelley said. ''I'm sorry if it offended you. And anyway, that's all over now. The story's in the past; it's time to move on.'' Thinking, Listen to you, you liar.

''Even so,'' Claire said, ''you'd better stay out of Clay's sight. He's furious about all the publicity, and for once I don't blame him.''

''Right now I'm just concentrating on interviewing Laura for television.''

Claire turned to Laura. ''You don't have any illusions about reviving your career, do you—after all this time? The audience wouldn't know who you were.''

Laura smiled sweetly. ''They don't forget, not when you're as big as I was.''

''*Was* is right,'' Claire said, draining her glass.

The gin wasn't doing the older woman much good, Shelley thought—she had a tongue like a razor blade. Thank God this wouldn't be a long trip.

Coming out here was taking a considerable chance, she knew. And half-bombed or not, Claire was right about one thing: The rest of the Cunninghams wouldn't be thrilled to have her show up at the estate—especially after the reports she'd made on the air. Maybe she shouldn't have been so quick to jump into this. Or maybe she should have let Ben know more about what she was planning.

Which was a ridiculous thought. She was still angry with him for the way he'd reacted after seeing the last piece she'd done. And yet, now that her emotions had quieted down and she could look at the situation more objectively, maybe what he'd said when he called her was true: They'd both been wrong.

In any event, she wished they hadn't quarreled and that she didn't feel she'd been forced to swallow her pride. It would be lovely to feel his arms around her again.

And it would be good to have him with her now. She'd thought she was being so clever, worming her way into this. Now she wasn't so sure.

The steady beat of the rotor blades underwent a subtle change and the attitude of the ship changed slightly. Their forward momentum slowed and they began to descend.

Shelley pressed her nose against the glass. Another helicopter was parked down there. As they slowly settled toward the landing pad, she caught sight of the house. As hard as she'd tried to imagine it, the great rambling mass of stone was more imposing than anything she could have conjured up in her mind. It was huge, dark, and foreboding.

What the hell was she getting herself into?

70

The woman's voice on the telephone was hesitant. "Are you the Lieutenant Tolliver who's in charge of the Cunningham investigation?"

"Yes, I am," Ben said.

"I saw you on the news . . . after Senator Cunningham died. I called you earlier today."

"I've been out of the office." He wondered whether she was yet another nutcase.

"The reason I called is that my sister used to work for the Cunningham family."

"Is that so?"

"Yes. But now she's hospitalized. The place she's in is a private treatment center on Long Island. It's called Brentwood, and it's in Farmington, not far from where I live."

He remembered then—he'd thrown the slip away earlier. And the name Brentwood was also familiar. "What's wrong with her, Miss—what did you say your name was?"

"Demarest. Peggy Demarest. My sister is Jan. The trouble is, she has very severe emotional problems. They're the result of something that happened almost a year ago. She was beaten and nearly died."

Ben felt a crawling sensation at the back of his neck. "Who was responsible for the beating?"

"I don't know. She's afraid to talk about it. But I've gotten bits and pieces from her. She's terrified whoever did it will come back and . . . kill her."

"Go on."

"This may sound crazy to you, but I think that what happened to her might have something to do with the Cunninghams. Or at least that they know about it."

"Where are you now?"

"At home. In my apartment in Farmington. I work in a dentist's office and—"

"Give me your address, please."

"Seventeen Maple Avenue. The Morningside Apartments. I'm in Two A."

"It's important that I see you. Stay where you are and don't talk to anyone until I get there. I'll drive out, be there as soon as I can. Okay?"

"Yes, of course. But does this sound like—"

"We'll discuss it when I see you," Ben said. He hung up and, grabbing his raincoat off the hook, ran out the door.

71

Driving from Manhattan to the eastern end of Long Island on a Friday night was Chinese torture, the death of a thousand cuts. You crept and you crawled in the heavy traffic, bumper-to-bumper, on a road that had been obsolete for years. The road was laughingly called the Expressway, and after a few hours, you longed to be put out of your misery.

The one saving grace, Tolliver thought, was that this was late fall. In the summertime, it would have been worse.

Nevertheless, by the time he turned off and followed the route that led to Farmington, he felt as if he'd been traveling forever. When he arrived, he had no trouble finding the address he'd been given; this was a small village, and Maple Avenue intersected with the main street.

The apartment was in a Victorian house that had been converted into four units. He pressed the buzzer for 2A. When he identified himself, the door latch clicked open. He walked up the stairs to the second floor.

Peggy Demarest was waiting for him in her doorway. She was a good-looking young woman, but obviously upset. She was wearing an olive green sweater and a brown skirt, colors that set off the deep auburn of her hair. He showed her his ID and she asked him to come inside.

Ben stepped into the apartment and she shut and locked the door behind him. "I hope you don't think this is nonsense, Lieutenant. I just didn't know where else to turn."

"Have you talked to the local police?"

"Not since right after Jan was hurt."

"Then you haven't told them what you said to me on the phone."

"No. I don't trust them, and neither does Jan. They're the last people I'd tell this to."

"Then suppose you tell me, but from the beginning."

"Yes, of course." She indicated a sofa. "Please sit down. Can I get you something to drink? Coffee or a Coke or something?"

He declined the beverage offer and sat, taking in his surroundings. The apartment was small and simply furnished, apparently a couple of rooms and a bath. The young woman sat on a chair opposite him, nervously twisting a handkerchief in her fingers.

"You said your sister used to work for the Cunninghams," he said.

"Yes. At their estate, which is just a few miles from here."

"Doing what?"

"Something in the office. It's a big place, and they have people managing it. I don't know what her job was exactly."

"How old is she?"

"Twenty-one. Two years younger than me."

"Go on."

"She seemed happy enough while she was there, but then she left. Why she quit, I don't know—I couldn't get her to talk about it. And then after that, she was never the same. She changed so much, it was as if she'd turned into a totally different person."

"Different how?"

"She moved into a fancy new apartment, got herself a new car and a bunch of clothes and jewelry. At the time, I had no idea where the money was coming from. When I asked her, she said it was none of my business, and then after awhile she wouldn't talk to me at all. Then one morning . . ." Her voice trailed off.

"Yes?"

She wiped her nose with the handkerchief and took a deep breath. "Some kids found her in a ditch beside the road. She'd been stabbed and beaten. Her face had been slashed and there were stab wounds all over her body. They thought she was dead."

"But she was still alive."

"Just barely. An ambulance took her to the county hospital and the doctors gave her quarts of blood. Then they operated on her for something like seven hours. She was in the hospital for weeks. It was a miracle she lived. But it left her in a state that wasn't much better than if she'd died. At least that's what I thought at the time. She couldn't talk, couldn't walk. She wasn't a vegetable, but close to it. The doctors called it catatonia. They said it's rare, but not unheard of when someone has the kind of severe trauma she did."

Ben had seen cases of it, as well. "And she went from there to Brentwood?"

"Yes. At least they offered some hope of treating her. And that's when the Cunninghams got involved. They told the people at Brentwood they were fond of Jan, even though she worked for them only a short time. They said their foundation would take care of all Jan's medical expenses, no limit to the amount for as long as she was sick."

Ben remembered the name then. Brentwood was one of the places in the folder he'd been given, listing the recipients of charitable contributions from the Cunningham Foundation. "Were you surprised they were willing to do that?"

"I suppose I was. But I was so thankful and so relieved, I wasn't about to question it. My mother and I were all the family Jan had, and we didn't have any money. The bills were staggering."

"I'm sure they were."

"The psychiatrist who was treating her said at first she might never come out of it. In fact, I got the impression that deep down he didn't expect her to."

"When she was attacked, was she robbed?"

"I don't know. That is, she was wearing an expensive watch and a gold bracelet, and some rings. None of those things were taken, but her purse was missing."

"Did the police come up with any suspects?"

"No, not a one. I don't think they tried very hard. They said it looked to them like she was a hooker and she'd run into the wrong man, or somebody who had a grudge against her."

"Did you think that was possible?"

"Yes, I suppose so. I did think it was pretty strange, the way she had all that money all of a sudden. Especially because she didn't have another job, as far as I knew. But that's no excuse for the way they acted. As if she'd gotten what she deserved."

"What happened to her possessions?"

"I sold them to help pay her bills. But the money didn't go very far. If the Cunninghams hadn't stepped in, I don't know what I would have done."

"So she was being treated at Brentwood. Then what?"

"For months, she was in this awful condition. And then Senator Cunningham died and I told her about it. I didn't expect her to respond, but she began to cry."

"And that was the first time you'd seen a reaction from her?"

"Yes. And then after that, she gradually started to come out of it.

She began speaking to me. But what she said was that she was afraid someone would hurt her. She was terrified.''

''Did she say who that someone was?''

''No. But later she told me the truth about what she'd been doing. Told me someone had been keeping her, doing drugs with her and beating her when they had sex.''

''You said on the phone you thought the Cunninghams were somehow involved or that they knew what had happened.''

''Yes. I know that sounds terribly ungrateful, after all they've done for her. But listening to her, I just became more and more suspicious. I didn't dare go to the police. Around here, the Cunninghams are like God. It's amazing the kind of influence that family has.''

''Isn't it, though.''

''That was why I called you. I'm so worried about Jan. She says I have to get her out of there, that she's in terrible danger.''

''I think,'' Ben said, ''we'd better have a talk with her. Right now.''

72

At ten minutes before five in the afternoon, Orcus parked the sedan in the visitors' lot at Brentwood. Twilight was deepening; the days were short at this time of year. He was wearing his working clothes: topcoat and scarf, the felt hat pulled down over his eyes. No dark glasses, however; that would be a detail someone might remember. He got out of the car and surveyed the building, then walked up the steps to the front entrance and went inside.

The receptionist looked up and smiled. Instead of approaching her, Orcus merely waved casually as he stepped over to one side of the room and sat on a couch, telling her he was waiting for someone who was visiting.

Next to the couch was a table stacked with magazines and newspapers. He picked up a copy of that morning's *Times* and pretended to immerse himself in it. The receptionist went back to her own reading, a paperback novel.

Two other people were in the outer area, white-haired women who were sitting together on the opposite side of the room, chattering away. One of them was knitting what appeared to be a sweater. They paid no attention to him.

He waited until his watch read three minutes before five. Then he got up and went to the desk, asking if there was a men's room on the floor. The receptionist pointed to the hallway behind her. Orcus mumbled thanks and made his way down the hall to a door bearing the letter *M*.

There was no one else in the room, which contained three urinals, three stalls, two sinks. He'd have a long wait ahead of him; he could take his time. He entered a stall and locked the door.

First, he removed his scarf and his topcoat and hat and hung them on the hook on the back of the door. He had on a navy blue bathrobe he'd been wearing under the coat. He opened the front of the robe and reached into the waistband of his pants, getting out the folded nylon gym bag he was carrying there. Next, he unzipped the bag and stuffed his outer garments into it, then zipped the bag shut. After that, he sat down on the toilet to wait.

The shift change, he knew, would take place at five o'clock. At that time, a different receptionist would come on, one who wouldn't be aware of his presence. Nor would she become aware, he reasoned, because he hadn't signed in.

Orcus had observed that there were fewer attendants on at night than during the day. He assumed this was because the facility had no violent patients. They were all harmless, the majority of them just dotty old folks.

By eight o'clock, the kitchen staff would have left, after tidying up following supper, which was served at six. Then the center would settle down to the evening routine, with patients watching TV and playing cards or checkers in the lounges, some of them shuffling through the halls. By ten, most would be in bed, with their lights out. The attendants would themselves be drowsy and some of them would be nodding off, as well. He also knew from his surveillance that no cleaning people worked here at night. Those chores were all done in the daytime.

As usual, waiting was the most difficult part of the operation. Over the next few hours, he stood up from time to time, stretching stiff muscles in his arms and legs and back, then resumed his place. Unfortunately, the toilet seat was the horseshoe type, with no lid, and sitting on it for long periods caused his thighs to become crampy.

The discomfort reminded him of the night he'd perched on the bumper of the car near the South Street Seaport, waiting to do another job and then blowing it. Recalling that made him bitter, but it was a mistake he wouldn't repeat. Tolliver was still right up there on his list. The thought of the detective produced a sharp twinge of anger.

While he sat on the toilet, Orcus counted six visits to the men's room by persons he couldn't see but could only hear, men who used the urinals and drifted out again. The sounds told him that four of them washed their hands after urinating; two did not. Other sounds indicated that a seventh visitor occupied a neighboring stall and defecated mightily. That one also washed his hands afterward, humming to himself as he did.

At shortly after ten, Orcus exited the stall. There were cramps in both his legs and his feet tingled. He paused to massage the muscles in his thighs and his calves for a minute or two, then bounced up and down on the balls of his feet to restore circulation.

He was reasonably sure no one would be using the stall he'd occupied until the next morning, but just to be safe he didn't leave the gym bag there, instead placing it in the cylindrical waste container, under a pile of crumpled paper towels. He'd pick it up before leaving the hospital.

When he stepped back into the hallway, it was deserted, as he had expected. The lights had been turned down to half their earlier level. The only sounds he heard now were the rumble of a furnace and a low babble of voices coming from one of the floors above, probably from a TV set still on somewhere.

Along this corridor, the rooms seemed to be either administration offices or those for public use, none of them housing patients. Elevator doors were located at the end of the hallway, and just beyond them were swinging doors he thought might lead to a stairway.

They did. Walking slowly and carefully, he went through the doors and climbed the stairs, on the theory he would be less likely to encounter someone there. Anyone moving around would be more inclined to use the elevator.

On the second-floor landing was another set of swinging doors. He pushed them open and stepped through.

And jumped a foot.

A man was standing directly in front of him, grinning.

Orcus tensed, reflexively reaching for the Browning in his right-hand pants pocket. He had the pistol halfway out before he saw the man clearly.

He was old. Incredibly old, his deeply lined face twisted by the grin. Only a few wisps of white hair remained on his skull. He too was wearing a bathrobe, over pajamas, and there were slippers on his feet. The dim light in the hallway was reflecting weakly from his false teeth.

"Hello, Father," the old man said. "Are you going to take me home now?"

Orcus exhaled, and pushed the Browning back into his pocket. He was about to brush past when an idea occurred to him. Taking the old man's arm, Orcus said, "Not just yet, but soon. Okay?"

The ancient head bobbed once and the grin stayed in place. "All right, Father."

Moving slowly and sticking close, Orcus guided the man down the corridor, speaking to him in a low voice. He'd taken a half dozen steps when he saw something that made him glad he'd hit on the plan. Coming toward them were two of the hospital staff, a man and a woman.

Orcus ducked his head, holding on to the old codger's arm and continuing to talk to him in a tone just above a whisper, about how nice the fall weather was and how it probably would snow soon and how that was a good thing because then they could all go sledding.

Out of the corner of his eye, he saw that the staffers were a nurse and an attendant. They were deep in a conversation of their own. As they drew closer, he picked up a few words—something to do with overtime pay. The nurse was gesticulating with her hands, saying it was unfair. They paid no attention to Orcus and his new friend, striding past and going on down the hallway.

Orcus relaxed and kept walking. He also continued to talk to the old man, at the same time checking the small name signs beside the doors of each of the rooms. There was another floor above this one; he hoped he wouldn't have to go up there. If he did, he'd have farther to go when it came time to get out of here—which would make the trip just that much riskier.

They'd gone the length of the corridor and turned the corner before he saw what he was looking for.

JAN DEMAREST, the sign next to a door said.

He turned back to the old man. "Where's your room, sonny?"

"What?"

"I said where's your room? Where do you live?"

"Where do I live? Oyster Bay. Can we go home now, Father?"

"In the morning. Where's your room?"

"What?"

"Come on, we'll go down to the lounge there. Okay? You can watch TV."

He guided the man a few steps farther, to where an open archway led into a sitting room equipped with a television set and a card table. A handful of men and women were sitting in front of the TV, all wearing bathrobes. Not far from them, an attendant was sprawled out in an armchair, reading a magazine.

Orcus gave his friend a little shove, whispering, "You go on in and sit there, enjoy the show."

To his relief, the geezer did as he was told, moving into the lounge with small jerky steps and taking a chair alongside the others.

Orcus turned and walked quickly back to the room with Demarest's name on it. When he got there, he looked up and down the corridor, making sure it was deserted. From the pocket of his robe, he took out a pair of rubber gloves and drew them on. Then he opened the door and stepped into the room, closing the door behind him.

73

Ben drove, with Peggy Demarest giving him directions. She said Brentwood wasn't far, but he was finding it hard to make good time on the backcountry roads. At an intersection, a pickup truck with a large black dog in the bed pulled out in front of them and hogged the center of the narrow blacktop.

Tolliver blew his horn, but that only inspired the driver of the truck to slow down more. Ben hit the horn again, and this time the guy stuck his arm out the window and gave him the finger.

"Some people around here are like that," Peggy said. "They think that's standing up for their rights."

"Some people are like that everywhere. This the only way to get to the hospital?"

"It's the shortest way."

He put his thumb on the horn again and then thought, The hell with it. The important thing was to get there.

''You said your sister never mentioned a name, never gave you any idea of who the man was who was keeping her?''

''No. I tried to get it out of her, but she became very upset when I did. She said he'd find out and then he'd kill her.''

''What about the psychiatrist—how much of this did he know?''

''Not nearly as much as I've told you. Jan didn't trust him any more than she did anyone else.''

''Who is he? What's his name?''

''Jay Chenoweth.''

''And he's on staff?''

''Yes. Chief of psychiatry, in fact.''

''What are your impressions of him?''

''A nice guy, very bright. Quite young, too, for somebody with that much responsibility.''

''Why did your sister distrust him?''

''I don't know. She said I was the only person she'd be willing to confide anything in. But she wouldn't even tell me very much. She was just so afraid. Kept saying that this someone would find out and then he'd come and kill her.''

''And she never told you any more about her experiences with the Cunninghams?''

''Nothing more than I've told you.''

''How secure is the hospital? Are there guards?''

''I guess so, but I've never seen one. It's more like a rest home. There's nobody violent there. Mostly old people who're senile.''

Tolliver looked at the pickup truck, rolling along at an easy pace, smack in the center of the road. The dog's eyes reflected eerily from the headlights of the Taurus.

Damn it, Ben thought, that's enough. He flicked his headlights to high beam and pulled over to the left as far as he could go.

As expected, the truck moved over to block him. When it did, Ben flipped his steering wheel and put the accelerator on the floor. The Ford shot by on the right, missing the pickup by a coat of paint.

Behind him, the truck driver blew his horn and put his lights up. But in seconds, the other vehicle was left far behind.

''It's just around this next bend,'' Peggy said, ''where you see the stone pillars.''

74

She was in bed. The room was in semidarkness, illuminated only by a tiny night-light, but Orcus could make out her features. In the faint glow, her auburn hair appeared almost black. She was wearing pajamas, lying on her back, breathing slowly and deeply.

He looked about the room. There was a single window with the drapes drawn over it and two vinyl-covered chairs, the woman's robe lying on the back of one of them. Her slippers were on the floor beside the bed.

In the wall opposite was a built-in chest of drawers; on its surface was a hairbrush and a small framed photograph, a snapshot of several people. Next to the chest was an open closet space with a few articles of clothing hanging in it.

There was a door near the head of the bed. He opened it silently, finding it led into a bathroom, as he'd thought. The only indication the room was in use was a toothbrush in the holder over the sink.

He turned back to the woman. Her lips were parted slightly and he could see the jagged scar that ran down the side of her face. Her breasts rose and fell in a steady rhythm, telling him she was in a deep sleep.

He stepped to the chair where her robe was and picked up the garment. It was made of wool and had a belt. He slipped the belt out of the loops and dropped the robe back onto the chair.

The belt was thick and strong; he tested it by wrapping the ends around his fists and tugging on it. When he was satisfied, he moved once more to the figure lying in the bed.

As he bent over her, he could still hear muffled noise coming from the TV in the lounge. It was the sound of canned laughter.

75

Tolliver drove between the stone pillars and along the winding drive. Only a few lights were showing in the sprawling old building, apparently coming from the hallways. Nearly all the outside rooms were dark.

He pulled to a stop before the steps leading up to the front entrance and he and Peggy got out of the Taurus. A number of cars were parked in the lot, vehicles that he assumed belonged to staff members. It was cold out here and he could hear the wind moaning in the pines. He ran up the steps, Peggy following as he went inside.

A uniformed guard was sitting at the desk, his feet up, his cap pulled down. When Ben approached, the guard jumped to his feet, blinking and adjusting his cap. ''Visiting hours are over,'' he said.

Tolliver waved his shield. ''Police officer. I need to speak with one of your patients. Her name is Jan Demarest. This is her sister.''

''Listen,'' the guard said, ''I'm not supposed to let anybody in here at night. I have orders to notify Dr. Chenoweth if—''

''Notify him, then,'' Ben said. He turned to Peggy. ''You know where her room is?''

''Yes, it's on the floor above. Come on, I'll show you.''

They rode in the elevator. He wished they'd used the stairs. The car took forever to creak and groan its way up there. When the doors opened, Peggy led the way down the corridor.

Light from ceiling lamps reflected from the mottled gray vinyl floor tiles and from the pale green walls, but nothing else was visible in the hallways. No nurses or attendants were around; the place seemed deserted. Tolliver could hear snoring coming from behind some of the doors they passed.

Peggy turned a corner, into another empty corridor. Halfway along it, she stopped and held up her hand. They were standing outside a room that had Jan Demarest's name next to the door.

''Better let me go in first,'' she said softly. ''I don't want to startle her. Give me a couple of minutes, okay?''

''Yeah, sure,'' Ben replied. ''Go ahead. I'll be right here.''

He waited as Peggy gently opened the door and slipped into the room. The hallway was quiet, but he could hear the murmur of a TV coming from somewhere far off and, above that, a rumbling that probably was the sound of the furnace.

Peggy came back out, looking confused. "She's not there."

"What?"

"Her robe and slippers are inside, but she's not in her bed."

"Let me have a look," Ben said. He stepped past her into the room.

There was only a dim glow in here, coming from a small night-light. He flipped on the overhead. The bed had been slept in, but except for the robe and slippers, he saw no sign of the room's occupant.

There was a door next to the bed, most likely leading into a bathroom. He turned the knob, but the door was hard to open. He pushed and it swung in. He saw no one in here, either—until he poked his head inside and looked around.

A young woman was hanging from a hook on the back of the door.

He turned on the light, knowing at once that she was dead.

She was wearing flimsy pajamas and bore an eerie resemblance to Peggy, with auburn hair and startlingly green eyes. A jagged scar ran down the side of her face. The belt from her robe was tied around her neck, the other end knotted to the hook on the door. The green eyes were bulging from their sockets and fixed in a grotesque stare, the whites a network of broken blood vessels. Her tongue was protruding from between her lips and a cyanotic shadow had formed around the base of her jaw.

Peggy moved close behind him, trying to see what he was looking at. "What is it? Is she in there?"

Ben backed out and closed the door. Turning to Peggy, he placed both hands on her shoulders. "Don't go in. I have something very bad to tell you."

76

The room was full of people. Nurses were in there, as well as several of the young male attendants, and whenever Tolliver shooed them out, they managed to slip back in again. A number of patients were milling about in the corridor outside the room.

Peggy Demarest had been near collapse when he told her what he'd found, and two of the nurses had taken her to another room and given her a tranquilizer.

A Farmington cop was present; Ben had called the police as soon as possible after he discovered Jan Demarest's body. The officer spent a lot of time in the bathroom, looking at the corpse.

Dr. Chenoweth was also on hand; he'd hurried over from his home when someone telephoned him with the news. Apparently, he'd been in bed. Now he was wearing khaki pants and a ski jacket pulled over his pajama top. As Peggy had said, he was surprisingly young for his job; Ben thought he probably grew the beard to look older.

To Tolliver's consternation, the doctor insisted on taking the body down before a medical examiner could be summoned to the scene. Ben argued, but Chenoweth was icily stubborn, and the local cop supported the psychiatrist.

''No need to wait for the ME,'' the officer said. ''Could be a couple hours before he gets here, and anyhow, it's pretty clear what happened.''

''How can you be so sure?'' Tolliver asked. ''Don't you at least want him to see her exactly as she was when she died?''

The cop's name was Jaworski. He was beefy and redfaced, not hiding what he thought of having a New York City detective commenting on his procedures. ''Listen, Lieutenant. A suicide is a suicide. You got crazy people here, and crazy people do crazy things. And besides, it wasn't like we didn't know anything about her. She wasn't exactly what you'd call stable, even before she came to this place.''

''Very unfortunate,'' Chenoweth said, ''to have something like this happen, especially when she'd been making such good progress.''

Tolliver kept his mouth in check, with an effort. In the end, Chenoweth had the attendants clear everyone from the area except one of the nurses and several other male medical staffers. Then they cut the belt from around Jan Demarest's neck and placed her body on a gurney.

The corpse was covered with a sheet and wheeled away. It would go to the basement morgue, Chenoweth said, where the examiner could see it when he arrived. In the meantime, Officer Jaworski could wait in the reception area.

In the hallway, Chenoweth asked Tolliver what he was doing at Brentwood. When Ben told him he was conducting an investigation into Senator Cunningham's death, the psychiatrist seemed dumbfounded.

"As you know, Miss Demarest used to work for the family," Tolliver said. "I had a discussion with her sister and wanted to speak with Jan."

"At this time of night? That's incredible. In fact, I think you had no right to come here at all without contacting me first."

Several staffers overheard the exchange. They stopped to listen, gaping at Chenoweth and the detective.

"I think we'd better discuss this in my office," Chenoweth said. Ben followed him down the stairs to the main floor.

The office was no more impressive than the doctor. Only the framed diplomas, inscribed in Latin with the names of several heavyweight educational institutions, suggested Chenoweth might be a heavyweight himself.

"I'll tell you right now," the psychiatrist said, "I intend to report this to the proper authorities in New York."

"Fine," Ben said. "Go right ahead. But there are some things I find strange. For instance, why wasn't she being watched? And how can you run this place with almost no security? You had one guard on duty when we got here, and the guy was asleep."

Chenoweth bristled. "How we conduct our affairs is our business, Lieutenant. This is a private facility, and we get along very well without outside interference. What's more, we've never had a problem with security. For you to come bursting in here this way is outrageous. And so is the attitude you're now displaying. Miss Demarest's suicide was terrible, but those things happen. What's more, there was no indication whatever that she might be suicidal. None."

"I understand the Cunninghams were paying all her expenses."

"That's something else that's none of your business."

"But it's true, isn't it?"

The doctor folded his arms. "The Cunninghams are very generous people."

"The estate's not far from here, is it?"

"No. It's only a few miles farther along the road. And now if you're finished prying, I'd appreciate it if you'd leave. Don't concern yourself about Peggy. I think it would be best if she spent the night here with us."

"I'm on my way, Doc." Tolliver stood up. "One other thing. Are you the head of this place?"

"I'm head of psychiatry, but I'm not the director."

"Who is?"

"The one we had resigned some months ago. A new director is scheduled to arrive in a few days."

"What's his name?"

"It's not a he, Lieutenant. Her name is Ardis Merritt. I've already called her to let her know what happened."

77

Shelley joined Laura Bentley for dinner in a glass-enclosed sun room. They'd be more comfortable here, Laura said, and more private. The room was in a wing of the mansion, overlooking a terrace and a garden that were illuminated by spotlights. It was decorated in bright stripings and filled with plants, huge ferns that made Shelley feel as if she was sitting in a jungle. Laura called it the Florida Room.

The meal was excellent: mushroom caps stuffed with crabmeat, followed by Dover sole and braised endive and accompanied by a superb white Burgundy. It was served by a maid and a butler.

Both women had changed for dinner but were again dressed casually, this time in sweaters and skirts. As they ate, Laura pumped Shelley on how to go about getting her TV career started. Most of what Shelley told her was accurate, but a lot of it she made up as she went along.

The biggest hurdle, she explained, would be to get a packager to back the project. That would involve shooting a pilot and guaranteeing that at least thirteen installments would be produced. The show would then have to be auctioned among syndicators, who would try to sell it to potential buyers—the stations that would carry it. All of that was factual; understated, if anything.

The parts she stretched concerned Laura's ability to attract and hold an audience with a program that sounded like a half hour's worth of dull crap. The chances of that happening were right up there with the return of Elvis, but Shelley was careful not to say so.

They talked for a long time, skipping dessert and drinking coffee and after that snifters of cognac. Shelley only sipped her brandy, but Laura drank several. After about the third, most of the actress's pretensions disappeared. "Let me ask you something," Laura said. "Be frank, and don't be afraid of hurting my feelings. I want to know the truth."

"Sure, what is it?"

"What's your honest opinion of this idea? Do you think it would be as interesting as I do?"

It was the kind of opening Shelley had been hoping for. "Maybe. But I think it could stand some spicing up."

"How would I do that?"

"For one thing, the audience would be much more interested in your guests' private lives than in their opinions about art or politics or anything else."

"Yeah, I guess that's true."

"Take your own life," Shelley said. "A beautiful, glamorous woman who made it big in the movies and then married into a rich and powerful family. Great stuff, isn't it? *That's* what would fascinate the audience—the juicy, intimate details."

Laura smiled. The brandy had loosened her up considerably. "The details just might be a little too juicy and intimate."

"Why is that?"

"I guess because nothing's perfect, ever." She swallowed more cognac. "Especially my marriage. I thought my troubles were over when I married Clay. Instead, they were just beginning."

"What happened?"

"A lot of things. When I met him, he was married to his first wife. He came to California for a big blowout put on by a company called Beverly Hills Investors. Junk bond traders. The chairman was a guy I used to go out with, and he took me to this thing. It was at the Ambassador, in L.A. There were a lot of other actresses there, too, mostly to impress people like Clayton. Anyway, I danced with him, and he flipped. Decided I was going to be his next acquisition."

"And so you were."

"Right. That's exactly what I was."

Laura drained her glass and the butler stepped to the table. He poured more cognac for her and then looked over at Shelley, who shook her head. The butler bowed and moved away.

"You were saying?" Shelley said.

"Clay heard I was in town for the opening and called me. I was staying at the Plaza. He gave me quite a rush. Dinners, flowers, presents. I was dazzled, of course. Not long after that, he divorced his wife and we got married."

"And your dreams came true."

"For a time, yes. I loved the role, too. The great lady, moving in glittering social circles. With an apartment in Manhattan, weekends here on Long Island, winters in Palm Beach. To say nothing of trips to Paris and London in between. It was heavenly."

"What went wrong?"

"I forgot the past. So of course, it repeated itself. And now Clay has other little friends he doesn't think I know about. Listen, this is all off the record, isn't it? I mean, we're just talking now, right?"

"Sure," Shelley said. "We're just talking."

"The mistresses are one of his main interests, but not the most important. That one is business. Even when we're out here, that's all he and the others talk about. Most of the time, they hole themselves up in the cottage."

"The cottage?"

"It's down at the beach. It's a house, actually, but they call it the beach cottage. That's where they hatch a lot of their schemes."

"What kind of schemes?"

"You know, the financial operations and the real estate. And the—" She caught herself. "The other things."

"Will they go out there tonight?"

"I don't know. They were having dinner in the dining room. They might go down there afterward. They often do that at night."

"What are they working on at the moment, do you know?"

"Yeah, I have a pretty good idea." She sat back in her chair, suddenly looking befuddled. Then she leaned forward again. "Listen, I shouldn't be talking about this stuff, least of all to you."

"Don't worry about it," Shelley said. She wished she'd brought along a pocket tape recorder.

"And remember," Laura said, "anything I said stays between us, right?"

Her speech was getting sloppy. She's drunk, Shelley thought. All that wine and brandy has gotten her bombed. "Sure, absolutely."

"That's good. You know, I'm so glad we're doing this. You have no idea what it's like, seeing some of my old pictures, knowing what I gave up."

Yeah, Shelley thought. What a sacrifice.

"Did you see *Eternal Love*?"

"No, I missed it."

"One of my best performances. The reviews were lousy, but it was one of the top grossers that year."

"Must have been great," Shelley said. "Maybe I can pick up a video. Listen, Laura, it's been a long day and I'm really bushed. I'd like to turn in, okay?"

"Yes, of course. Sure you won't have another brandy? I'm gonna have a nightcap."

"I've had plenty, thanks. But you go right ahead. I'll just go on up to my room."

"Okay, sleep well. We'll do some more tomorrow on the show."

"Fine. Good night." Shelley got up from the table and left the room.

The guest quarters were on the floor above. She walked along the corridor and went up the wide staircase, and when she reached the landing, she heard the sound of voices. She looked back as a group of people emerged from a room on the main floor.

Shelley got only a glimpse of them, but she spotted Clay Cunningham and his sister, Ingrid. Behind them were Ingrid's husband, Kurt Kramer, and some others she couldn't see well enough to recognize. The group went out through French doors at the rear of the house.

She turned and looked out the window on the landing.

The people crossed the terrace and stepped out onto a flagstone walk. In the distance, Shelley could make out lights in another building, realizing that must be the beach house.

Turning back, she ran up the stairs and down the hallway to her room, going inside and closing the door.

She took off her skirt and put on a pair of black slacks and a black zippered jacket. Then she exchanged her shoes for a pair of black Reeboks. Lastly, she pulled on a black knitted watch cap, tucking her blond hair under it and rolling the cap down over her ears.

From her travel bag, she took out a small flashlight and put it into a pocket of her jacket. Glancing into a full-length mirror hanging on the wall opposite the bed, she saw that the only part of her appearance that wasn't dark was her face, but that couldn't be helped.

Moving quietly, she opened the door and slipped out of the room.

78

Tolliver got into his car and started the engine. Never in his years as a cop had he come up against anything like this. Three deaths, all of them suspicious as hell, and yet with no evidence they were anything but what they seemed on the surface. One heart attack, two suicides.

Which added up to a ton of bullshit.

Why had two attempts been made to kill Jan Demarest, the second one successful? He felt sure she'd been murdered and that the Cunninghams were involved in some way. But how?

And what about Ardis Merritt becoming head of the institution where Demarest had died? How did that figure?

For that matter, how could the family run their affairs with such utter contempt for the rules the rest of the world lived by?

And how could one guy stand up to them? Ben felt like an infantryman who'd been given the point and contacted the enemy, only to discover there was nobody backing him up.

He sat there for a few minutes, his anger building. He'd been told the estate was only a few miles farther down the road. Going there would mean putting his ass on the block once more, but by now he didn't give a damn.

And besides, Shelley was there. She could be in danger.

He drove down the winding driveway, turning onto the road and accelerating rapidly.

His headlights illuminated a desolate landscape, remote and inhospitable. He passed no buildings of any kind as he drove along the narrow road. The night was cold and dark, with only a sliver of moon showing and with a stiff wind coming in off the sea.

Identifying the estate was easy. There was a high brick wall surrounding the grounds, with wrought-iron gates at the entrance. He didn't see a guard as he went past, but he was sure members of Evan Montrock's security force would be around—and probably Montrock himself.

He parked some yards down the road from the gate, pulling the Taurus into a grove of pines that had been stunted by the salt-laced wind. Getting out, he looked over at the wall and judged it to be about ten feet high. He took off his raincoat and tossed it into the backseat, then went around to the rear of the car and opened the trunk.

He took out a grappling hook and, rummaging around, came up with a length of nylon rope, which he bent onto the hook.

Lastly, he got out his old standby, the Smith. Carrying an extra weapon just might give him an edge. He checked the cylinder and strapped the holster containing the pistol to the inside of his left ankle.

Then he crossed the road and approached the wall.

The hook caught on the first try. He tested it, tugging at the line, and when he was satisfied it would hold, he clambered up the brick surface. Once on top, he lay flat on his belly and squinted into the darkness.

Across a long span of lawn and trees was the mansion. He'd expected it to be impressive, but even so he wasn't prepared for what he saw. The place was huge, a turn-of-the-century Gothic monstrosity, built of granite. Enough lights were showing for him to make out the imposing center section, the wings and cupolas, the steep roofs and pointed arches, the tall chimneys. Before the entrance was a large paved area where cars were parked.

There were also a number of outbuildings. Stables, he supposed, and garages, plus storage sheds for groundskeeping equipment. In the far distance was another house, close to the beach, and perhaps a hundred yards from that was an illuminated landing pad with two helicopters on it.

And set back farther than any of the others was still another structure. There were no lights in that one, but he could see its pale shape in the faint moonlight. Probably the mausoleum, he thought, where the senator and the Colonel and various other members of the clan were entombed.

He looked at the mansion once more and wondered how he could hope to get inside it. Not only would there be guards, but every inch of the place would be covered by television cameras. And yet he couldn't figure out a way in by staying where he was.

When he had a good fix on the layout of the estate, he tossed the line over the wall and reset the grappling hook, then eased himself down to the ground. Crouching low, he trotted across the long expanse toward the mansion, his gaze constantly sweeping the area.

A man stepped out the front door and into the recessed entryway.

Tolliver dropped facedown onto the frost-tipped grass. He could see that the guy was wearing a uniform and carrying a submachine gun.

The guard stayed in the entrance, apparently to keep out of the wind. A moment later, a match flared. He leaned against the wall, smoking his cigarette.

Getting to his feet, Tolliver again crouched low and ran toward the end of the mansion nearest him. When he reached it, he crept toward the rear of the building, hoping the man out front would be the only one on patrol. He turned the corner.

And ran head-on into another guard.

For a fraction of a second, both men gaped at each other. Then the guard grabbed for the submachine gun that was slung over his shoulder.

Tolliver was quicker. In one rapid motion, he reached behind him and snatched the Mauser from its holster, then shoved the muzzle into the guard's left nostril.

"Don't move," Ben said. "And don't make a sound."

The man's mouth was hanging open, his eyes fixed on the pistol that was halfway up his nose.

Ben held it there. "With two fingers," he said, "take the strap off your shoulder and drop the gun on the ground."

The guard did as instructed, never taking his eyes off the pistol. The submachine gun fell to the grass.

"Now your clothes."

"What?"

"Your clothes. Take off your fucking clothes. And hurry." He twisted the Mauser's barrel. "But be careful. This might go off."

The guard stripped, leaving his uniform and cap in a heap beside his weapon. When he was down to his skivvies, socks, and shoes, Ben stepped around behind him, pressing the pistol against the back of the guy's neck.

Tolliver pointed to the wall. "We're going there. Move."

He steered the guard to the wall at an angle that kept them out of sight from the front of the mansion. When they reached it, Ben pushed the man along in front of him until they came to the place where the rope was dangling from the grappling hook.

He took off his belt and used it to bind the guard's hands behind him. Then he put the pistol away and lashed the nylon rope to the belt, hauling on it until the man's toes were barely touching the grass.

The guard gasped. "Christ, you're gonna break my arms."

"Don't talk so much," Ben said. He knelt and pulled off one of the man's shoes, then his sock. Straightening up, he got out a handkerchief and stuffed it into the guard's mouth, binding it in place by tying the sock around his jaw and knotting it behind his neck.

Lastly, Ben took off his blazer and draped it over the guy's head.

Turning, he sprinted back the way he'd come, until he reached the place where the uniform and the submachine gun lay. He took off his pants and put on the uniform, buttoning the jacket up to his throat and tilting the cap low over his forehead. His pocketknife, keys, and the case containing his shield, he put into a back pocket.

Picking up the guard's gun, he saw that it was an Uzi with a thirty-two-round magazine. He slung it over his shoulder and walked around the corner to the rear of the mansion.

Back here was a large lighted terrace and walks leading from it to formal gardens and the house on the beach. He crossed the terrace and gently tried the knob of one of the doors. It was unlocked.

He opened the door and cautiously pushed aside a heavy drapery.

This was a sitting room of some kind, and there was no one in it. He stepped into the room and closed the door behind him, then put the drapery back in place. For the next several seconds, he stood completely still, listening. No sound reached his ears; the great house seemed eerily quiet. He was aware of a TV camera mounted high in one corner.

Again moving with caution, he stepped out into the hallway. It was wide, with a vaulted ceiling and gold-framed portraits hanging from the walls. Most of the subjects were old-time politicians. Warren Harding was there, and Alfred E. Smith, Herbert Hoover, Jimmy

Walker, and others. Apparently, the Colonel had his kept his feet on both sides of the political fence.

Ben checked room after room, finding no one in any of them. He turned a corner and went down another hallway, opening more doors, with the same results.

At the end of the corridor, he peered into still another room, realizing that this one was a library.

Like everything else in the place, the room was constructed on a mammoth scale. Bookcases extended from the floor to the high ceiling, the upper shelves accessible via a balcony running around three of the walls. In the center of the fourth wall, at the far end of the room, was a stone fireplace big enough to roast an ox.

But it was the niches that were cut into the bookcases at ground level that caught his attention. There were more than a dozen of them, and in each one stood a statue of a Roman god. The figures were life-size, much larger than those he'd seen in Clay Cunningham's office on Wall Street. They were made of bronze, blackened from age. Some of the effigies were male, some female.

He studied one that occupied a nearby niche. It was of a woman, holding a lance in one hand and a shield in the other, mounted on an ebony base. The inscription on the base said she was Juno Lucetia, the goddess of light.

Curious, he walked around the room, looking at the statues. Some of the names on the pedestals were familiar to him. Mars, for example, and Jupiter. But many of the others he'd never heard of. Such as Consus, the sower, and another female, called Pales, who, the legend said, was the protectress of flocks. That they'd survived down through the centuries, and in remarkably good condition, was amazing.

Again he thought of how different the Cunninghams' lives were from those of ordinary people. Just one of these things would most likely be worth more money than he'd earned in his lifetime. Yet here was a whole collection of them, representing only a scrap of the family's wealth.

He stepped to another niche and stared at a sculpture that was different from any of the others.

This god was male, with a deep, powerful chest and broad shoulders, crouched slightly in a wide stance. His left hand wore a cestus, the studded glove of a gladiator, and his right clutched a double-edged dagger. His muscles were tensed, as if he were poised to attack.

The face was different as well, neither heroic nor benign. Instead, the lips were drawn back to expose clenched teeth. Above a hooked nose, deep-set eyes glowered back at Tolliver with a hatred that made the bronze form seem startlingly alive.

The features reminded Ben of the faces he'd seen on career criminals, on psychopaths, killers who enjoyed their work.

He looked at the inscription on the ebony base. It read:

ORCUS
God of the underworld, god of death
Bearer of the damned to the inferno

It was like a punch in the gut.

Here he'd been trying to track down a name and had failed because he'd misspelled it. It wasn't Orkis at all, but Orcus.

And yet that was the way Silk had spelled it, too, when she wrote it on the pad in her kitchen. The phonetic spelling could mean she'd never seen the name, only heard it.

But no matter how anybody spelled it, Tolliver felt sure he'd found a direct link between her so-called suicide and the Cunninghams. The trouble was, he didn't know any more than that. What did the name on a two-thousand-year-old statue have to do with Silk's death?

He took one more look at the savage bronze features and then left the room to continue his prowl of the mansion.

79

The wind coming off the ocean had a sharp, salt-tanged bite. In the distance, Shelley could hear surf pounding on the beach. She avoided the walks, moving stealthily over the frost-encrusted lawns toward the sea.

Lights were showing in the beach cottage. As she advanced toward it, she saw that the architecture was similar to that of the mansion—Gothic, old, and ugly. It was two stories high, built of stone, with a hip roof and gables. A wide wooden veranda faced the sea.

Crouching low, she crept closer, trying to get a glimpse of what was going on inside. Peering into the windows on the ground floor, she could see figures moving about, but she wasn't near enough to make out who they were. She inched forward.

And heard footsteps.

She stopped suddenly, her heart hammering in in her rib cage. Turning slowly, she saw that the sound was coming from the walk. A guard was stepping along, moving away from the cottage.

She watched him for a moment and then decided he was on routine patrol. She could make him out clearly in the glow of the lights from the cottage. He was a tall man in a gray uniform, carrying a walkie-talkie in one hand, an automatic weapon in the other. She waited until he was a considerable distance away, barely visible on the walk, and her pulse had returned to near normal. Then she resumed her approach.

Steps led up onto the veranda. She went up them slowly, wincing as the wood creaked, hoping the sound would be muffled by the roaring surf. Looking out toward the beach, she could make out the white crests of breakers crashing onto the sand.

She held her breath and, keeping her body lower than the windowsills, darted across the veranda and knelt beside the wall of the cottage. From inside, she could hear voices raised in an argument, but she couldn't tell who was speaking. One voice might be that of Clay Cunningham, but she wasn't sure.

The dispute grew louder. She raised her head, praying no one inside would be looking at the window at that moment.

No one was. Only one lamp was lighted, but she could see Clay shaking his fist and shouting at someone. "Goddamn it, we should've known what was going on. Should've realized it a long time ago."

There were others present, but they were on the far side of the room and she couldn't identify the shadowy figures. One of them said, "Let's not argue about what we should have done. That doesn't get us anywhere."

Shelley strained to hear. The voice was soft and low-pitched and it was hard to tell whether it was male or female.

Another voice spoke up, this one unquestionably male: "The important thing is, it's done. And the way I see it, the main issues are under control. Compared with them, these other problems are nothing."

Clay turned in the direction the voice was coming from. ''That's the kind of thinking that caused the problems in the first place.''

''Go easy, will you?'' the voice said. ''It'll all work out just the way we planned.''

''It damn well better,'' Clay said. ''And for God's sake, get rid of that thing in the mausoleum!''

Shelley tensed. *What thing?*

''I told you,'' the voice said, ''it'll be taken care of. For now, that's the best place for it.''

One of the figures was coming toward the lamp. As he stepped into the pool of light, Shelley recognized Kurt Kramer. ''Anybody want a drink?'' he asked.

''I do,'' Clay said. He turned back and seemed to glance toward the window. Shelley ducked, her pulse again racing.

From inside the room, she heard someone else say, ''That's better. Let's all settle down a little, okay? Have a drink and relax.''

''Pour me a Scotch,'' Kramer said. ''I want to step outside for a minute, get some fresh air.''

Shelley felt a surge of panic. If she moved, they might hear or see her. If she didn't, Kramer would spot her the minute he came out the door. Moving as quickly as she dared, she scuttled back across the veranda and rolled off the edge, dropping into a bank of shrubs at the foundation of the cottage.

She heard the door open, heard footsteps on the wooden floor of the veranda, coming toward her hiding place. They seemed to stop directly above where she was lying. Peering up, she found herself staring at Kurt Kramer.

He was looking out toward the ocean—wearing a heavy sweater, hands jammed into his pants pockets. If he so much as glanced down, he couldn't miss seeing her.

Please, she thought. Make him keep on looking at the damn beach. Don't let him look down.

He stood there for what seemed like forever, although it couldn't have been more than a few minutes. She didn't dare move a muscle or so much as blink. Kramer scratched his jaw and folded his arms, continuing to look toward the ocean. Then at last, he turned and went back inside.

Shelley let out her breath. She could hear voices once more, but from where she was now, she couldn't make out a word of what was being said. She pulled herself up onto her knees, needles from the shrubs scratching her face. Then she got to her feet and, again bending low, ran as fast as she could away from the cottage.

Get rid of that thing in the mausoleum? What did that mean? And did she have the guts to find out?

When she was far enough away, she straightened up and raced across the grass, again staying clear of the walks.

The mausoleum was on the far side of the estate. She'd spotted it on her way out here. As she ran toward it, she could see the outlines of the structure, the white marble showing faintly in the reflected light from the helicopter pad.

80

The clatter of pots and pans told Tolliver he was near the kitchen. He rounded a corner, and saw that it was off to his left. People were moving around inside, apparently cleaning up.

There was a stairway on his right. He was about to go up it when he heard the heavy thump of footsteps on the treads. Ducking back against the wall, he watched as another guard came down the stairs.

Like all the others he'd seen, this guy was tall and burly. His uniform jacket was unbuttoned and he wasn't wearing a cap. Nor was he carrying a weapon. The guard went across the hall and into the kitchen, where he began talking to one of the maids.

Apparently, the stairs led up to the guards' quarters. If they did, Montrock's room would be up there, as well. Tolliver was sure the security chief was one man who knew the secrets of this ancient pile of stone, and the people who owned it.

And whatever Montrock knew, it was time to force him to reveal it. Stepping quickly to the stairs, Ben went up them as quietly as he could.

On the floor above was a hallway with doors on either side and one at the end, facing him. If he was right about what was up here, the door at the end would be to Montrock's room.

There was one other problem. A TV camera was mounted high on the wall, its fish-eye staring down into the hallway.

Ben knew there were dozens of rooms in the mansion. Which meant that, just as in the senator's house in Manhattan and in the foundation building, the monitors wouldn't show the interiors of all of them at once but would skip around at random. Or would show whatever somebody scanning told them to show. The odds, therefore, were in his favor.

He walked steadily down the corridor and when he came to the place where the camera was, he took off his cap. Reaching up, he dropped it over the camera. The move had taken no more than two seconds. If the monitor was to show one dead camera, no one would get upset about it, he reasoned, at least not for a while.

Stepping to the door, he listened for several seconds. No sound came from inside. He tried the door and found it locked. The lock was the snap type; he got out his pocketknife and slipped the blade into the crack, forcing back the tongue and opening the door. He stepped inside, feeling for the light switch and flipping it on.

There was no one in the room.

He glanced about, taking in the furnishings. The room was large, with a bed and a dresser and a sitting area with a sofa and several comfortable chairs, an upright gun cabinet, a writing desk, and a TV plus a closet and a bathroom.

Tolliver had guessed right; on the desk was a bill from Exxon, addressed to Evan Montrock. He took the gun off his shoulder and laid it on a chair.

Going to the closet, he checked the contents. There was nothing in it but clothing and several pairs of shoes. He was about to back out when he glanced up at the shelf. There were two hats up there—one felt, the other a fur-trimmed cap.

And a slim black attaché case.

He pushed the hats aside and pulled down the case. It was made of fine-grain leather and was secured with a combination lock. Next to the handle were initials stamped in gold: JS.

He carried the case over to the desk and laid it on the surface. He pried open the lock with his knife and swung back the lid. The case contained a single brown manila envelope. Opening it, he took out a thick packet of photographs.

They were color prints, of good quality and in sharp focus. Most were four by six inches, but some were eight-by-tens. Each featured a man and a young woman in a sex act, some conventional, some bizarre. In many of them, the man was inflicting punishment on his partner, striking her with his fist or lashing her with a whip.

But the pictures weren't what Ben had thought they'd be. For one thing, the women were all different. They were young and very good-looking.

And none of them was Jessica Silk.

Even more curious, the man was not former Senator Clayton Cunningham.

It was his son, Clay.

Ben went through the stack quickly, then again more slowly. He returned the photographs to the envelope and put the envelope back into the case.

Looking around the room, he wondered what else of interest might be here. If there was something more, the likeliest place to find it would be the desk. He tried the drawers, finding them also locked. The locks had inset bars; he'd need something heavier than his pocketknife to force them.

Among the pens and the box of paper clips and other junk on the desk was a letter opener with a long steel blade. He jammed the blade into the file drawer and exerted pressure. The lock broke with a loud snap. He opened the drawer.

Inside was a stack of videocassettes. On each was a strip of masking tape with initials and dates written on it. He went through them until he found one that was identified as CC-JS 11/3.

November third was the day Senator Clayton Cunningham died.

There was a VCR attached to the television set on the far side of the room. Ben went over to it, shoved the cassette into the machine, and turned on the TV. Then he sat down in one of the upholstered chairs to watch.

Seconds later, the image of Senator Cunningham loomed onto the screen. He was standing beside the table in his office and Jessica Silk was seated at the table.

As Ben stared at the tube, he saw the senator draw Jessica to her feet and embrace her, holding her in a long, deep kiss. Then the old man led her over to the leather sofa and began to undress her.

81

When she drew close, Shelley could make out details of the mausoleum's construction. It was built in the style of a Greek temple. Carved into the tympanum under the tiled roof were figures of warriors on foot and in chariots, and on three sides of the building Doric columns stood like tall sentinels.

Approaching the steps, she saw a pair of heavy bronze doors, just inside the columns. The doors were almost sure to be locked, but she wouldn't know until she tried them.

She stood there for a few moments, willing herself to have the courage to go up the steps. Whatever she did, remaining here was out of the question; she was too visible. After one last glance over her shoulder, she walked quickly up the wide treads and past the columns to the doors.

The handle on each was a thick vertical cylinder, also of bronze. She reached out and gave the handles a tug. To her surprise, the doors opened easily.

The interior was shrouded in darkness. She stepped inside and the doors swung shut behind her, enclosing her in pitch-black silence. The air in here was cold and damp, infused with a musty odor that crawled into her nostrils and stayed there. Grateful that she'd brought along the tiny flashlight, she dug it out of the pocket of her windbreaker and thumbed the switch.

As the small cone of light swept over the area, she saw that she was standing in what appeared to be a single large room. Set into three of the marble walls were smaller bronze doors, stacked one above the other, and she realized these were the actual tombs. Each of the doors bore engraved inscriptions identifying the tomb's occupant.

In the center of the wall opposite where she stood was a door larger than the others. She went over to it and read the legend that had been carved into the metal. What she was looking at was the final resting place of the founding father of the clan, Colonel Clayton Cunningham.

Below that door were a number of others, set into the wall in a horizontal line. In the flashlight's beam, she saw that they were the tombs of two of the Colonel's wives and of his son and daughter-in-law, who had died young in the skiing accident Shelley had read about, an avalanche in Austria. The son had been the father of Senator Clayton Cunningham III.

But where was the senator?

She played the light over the walls. Some of the doors were inscribed with the names of other Cunninghams, many of whom were unknown to her, and some doors bore no inscription. The spaces behind these, she reasoned, were empty at the moment, waiting for family members who were yet to die.

She found the senator's tomb on the wall to her left. He was also in what was obviously a place of honor, behind a door set on the same level as that of the Colonel. Impulsively, she reached out and touched the clammy bronze surface. The door was locked.

For the next few minutes, she walked slowly around the dank, gloomy room, trying the other doors and finding all of these securely locked, as well.

She studied the inscriptions. Judging from the dates, the life spans of some of the Cunninghams who were entombed here approximated that of the Colonel, while others ranged over more recent years. Many of these people had lived long lives, but some had died in infancy.

Not all had the name Cunningham. Who were they? Cousins, perhaps, or in-laws? It struck her as odd that so little was known of them, compared with the Colonel's direct offspring, who had always enjoyed a certain celebrity—or notoriety. The engraved inscriptions gave no clue, stating only names and the dates of birth and death. Shivering in the damp cold, she felt a growing sense of disappointment.

That thing in the mausoleum.

What was it—and where?

An idea struck her. Perhaps what she hoped to find—whatever it was—had been stored in one of the empties. Stepping to an unmarked door, she tried to open it. No luck; this one was also locked. She tried another and was again frustrated.

Damn it. She'd better get out of here. See if she couldn't figure out some other way to approach this place and its secrets before one of the guards found her.

She flicked the flashlight beam over the room once more and

turned to leave. As she did, she caught sight of an upright doorway she hadn't noticed, at the end of the far wall. It was painted white, the same shade as the marble wall, which was why she'd overlooked it.

Stepping across the room to the door, she tried the knob. It was unlocked. With growing excitement, she opened the door and stepped through, into a space that was smaller than the one she'd come from. She swept the area with her flashlight.

Inside this room was a row of coffins.

Each was made of highly polished wood, so dark as to seem almost black. Handles on the sides appeared to be of hammered silver. Some of the caskets were larger than others.

For a few seconds, she simply stood gawking at what she'd discovered. Then she went to the nearest one and bent over it. Holding the flashlight with one hand, she reached down with trembling fingers and touched the gleaming wood. Taking a deep breath, she grasped the lid and opened it.

The coffin was empty.

The lining, she saw, was as elegant as the exterior. It was of tufted white satin, with a lacy pillow at the head end. But there was nothing else inside, and she felt deflated.

Stepping to the next, she repeated the process, gripping the heavy lid and raising it—and was disappointed once more. She tried the next, then the one beside that, and the sense of excitement she'd felt a moment ago turned to one of frustration. There was nothing in any of them.

But she wouldn't give up until she'd looked inside each one. She went to the next and swung the lid upward.

And was stunned.

Looking down at what lay on the white satin, she felt faint and sick at the same time, her knees turning to rubber and bile welling up in her throat. She opened her mouth to scream.

At that moment, a thick arm clamped around her neck and she was lifted off her feet. The cry died in her mouth and bright lights exploded like rockets going off in her head. She tried to bite the arm, tried to kick at whoever was behind her, but her efforts had no effect. No matter how hard she struggled, she couldn't break free, nor could she breathe.

Seconds after that, she couldn't think. There was a roaring in her ears, as if she was standing in the path of a freight train. The lights in her head began spinning faster and faster and then she fell into a deep black void.

82

It was like watching an X-rated movie, which had never been Tolliver's idea of a good time. But this was worse, because the old man kept biting Jessica's neck and touching her thighs with a lighted cigar. Seeing it made you want to puke, he thought. You could almost feel the sting, smell the stench of burning flesh.

They went at it for some time, writhing on the leather sofa, the old man groaning and slobbering, sometimes whispering into Jessica's ear, sometimes squealing with pleasure. She was responding the same way, but Ben couldn't help wondering whether that wasn't a put-on.

Gradually, the coupling grew more and more animated, until at last Cunningham jerked spasmodically, Jessica gripping the back of his neck and gasping. He shuddered and let out one last wail. Then both of them collapsed, sprawled in a tangle of flaccid, sweaty limbs, breathing hard. The cigar lay in an ashtray on the floor.

After that came a long period in which the pair remained relatively still. Ben kept his eyes fixed on the screen, however, sensing this wasn't the end of the action.

It wasn't.

Jessica got to her feet and went over to the table. There was a sheen on her naked skin and a number of red spots were visible on her legs and buttocks.

Again Ben recalled the scene in the autopsy room and the condition of her body when he'd seen it there. Some of the wounds had looked raw then, when he'd observed them close up.

Now the tape showed her opening an attaché case, the same one Ben had found the photos in. She took something out of the case and returned to the sofa, hiding the object behind her back.

The senator raised himself on one elbow, watching her. "What have you got there?"

Jessica gave him a kittenish smile. "Close your eyes and do as I tell you."

"Is that the new toy?" he persisted.

"Don't be so nosy. Just close your eyes. You'll love it."

He did as instructed and she got back onto the sofa, sliding under him and spreading her legs so that he was lying between them. It took a little coaxing, but finally she succeeded in helping him reenter her.

At this point, Ben could see what she was holding in her free hand. It was a slim, shiny cylinder, perhaps six inches long. As the senator again began a slow, rhythmic thrusting, she inserted the device into his anus.

Cunningham tensed, but Jessica cooed reassurance, and he resumed his lovemaking. Another few seconds went by and then she pressed her thumb down on the end of the cylinder.

Instantly, the old man grew rigid. He arched his back and a strangled cry issued from his mouth. Ben could see his eyes protrude, spittle forming on his lips. He twisted and bucked, his hands fluttering, feet kicking. For several seconds, he flopped about, still in position between her legs. He cried out once more, but now the sound was a muffled grunt. Finally, he stopped moving and his body became totally limp.

Jessica shoved him off her and got to her feet. She stood beside the sofa, looking at him lying facedown. Then she pulled the shiny cylinder out of his rear end and put it on a table.

Tolliver stopped the tape, thinking of what he'd seen in the dungeon under the Palace of Justice in Panama City.

He rewound the tape to the beginning of the sequence with the love toy and started it again.

Once more, he watched as Jessica inserted the cylinder and the pair went through the action on the sofa. After removing the toy from the senator's body and placing it on the table, Jessica stepped over to his desk.

She opened the drawers and quickly went through them. There seemed to be nothing of interest to her, until she pulled an envelope from one of them. She opened it and, after leafing through the contents, went to her case and put the envelope inside.

After that, she hurriedly put her clothes back on. She picked up the telephone, speaking into it so softly, Tolliver couldn't hear what she was saying.

Ardis Merritt came into the office. She knelt beside the senator's body and felt for a pulse. After a moment, she looked back at Silk and shook her head.

Straightening up, Merritt said, ''Where is it?''

''There, on the table.''

Merritt picked up the shiny cylinder. She wrapped it in a handkerchief and tucked it into a pocket in her skirt.

So intently was Ben watching that he never heard the door open behind him. The first hint he had that he was no longer alone came in the form of a cold, hard object pressing against the back of his head.

A voice said, ''Hold still or you're dead.''

He froze and the voice said, ''Now get up and put your hands on top of your head. Go over to the wall and stand against it with your feet spread apart.''

When his nose was flattened against the wall, the object was withdrawn from the back of his skull and he was frisked. Hands relieved him of the Mauser, the case containing his shield and ID, his keys and his knife.

''Turn around,'' the voice said.

The guard was like the others in Montrock's security force, tall and husky. He was holding a submachine gun and pointing it at Tolliver, his finger curled around the trigger.

''Get in front of me,'' the guard said. ''And walk slow. You try anything stupid and I'll blow your backbone out your belly.''

83

The pain in Shelley's head was a fierce pounding in synch with her pulse, as if a demon were inside her skull, smashing against the bone with a sledgehammer. Each time her heart pumped, it felt as if the top of her head would come off. After a while, she wished it would, to end her suffering.

The pain was also affecting her stomach. It made her weak and queasy, made her want to vomit. But the contractions of her belly muscles produced only a scalding sensation in the back of her throat, leaving a sour taste in her mouth.

She tried to think of what had happened to her, as much to get her mind off the agony as anything else. She remembered going into the mausoleum, seeing the tombs of Cunningham family members. Remembered finding the smaller room where the coffins were stored, the dark, gleaming boxes squatting there like a row of vultures, waiting.

And most of all, she remembered looking into each of the caskets, one after another. Opening the lids and peering inside. Finding all of them empty.

Except the last.

When she'd directed the flashlight beam down into that one, she'd wanted to scream. Now, seeing the ghastly contents once more in her mind's eye, she again opened her mouth. But all that came out was a thin whimper.

She tried to recall what had happened after that. Remembered being hoisted off her feet, a heavy, muscular arm pressing against her throat, cutting off her air. Remembered kicking and biting and struggling until the lack of oxygen had set off a burst of fireworks and a horrendous roaring in her ears.

And after that, nothing.

But where was she now? Her eyes were open, but she couldn't see. Because she was in total darkness, she realized. Lying on her back in a place that was cold and dank.

She tried to sit up, but instead banged her head on a hard surface. She lay back and groped with her fingers. What that revealed was that she was confined in a narrow space, not much more than a couple of feet wide, whose ceiling was scant inches above her face.

Realization struck her, and this time she did scream, a long, piercing screech that left her trembling in horror and made the hammering in her head more violent.

Panicking, she beat on the surfaces with her fists, but they were as unyielding as stone. She kicked and clawed and thrashed her legs and her elbows against the walls of her tiny prison but achieved nothing but bruises and more pain. After a time, she grew limp, sobbing in the darkness.

Think, she told herself. *Think.*

And don't give up. Nothing's hopeless, ever.

Or is it?

No, no, no. Don't give in; don't feel sorry for yourself. And above all, don't flail around like some kid having a tantrum—that'll only use up the oxygen faster.

But what if it does?

Wouldn't that be better than prolonging this? You're thirsty, aren't you? And cold. Your legs and your arms hurt. And this god-damned pounding in your head is more than you can take.

But there has to be a way out of this; there has to be.

You were stupid, weren't you? Thought you could bring this off all by yourself. Thought you could play detective, become a big hero. You'd show that damned Tolliver, wouldn't you?

And what would you give now to have his help? To have him get you out of this hideous trap?

If only he knew now where you were. He wouldn't leave you like this, would he? Hell no he wouldn't. He'd rip this place wide open to free you.

But he doesn't know, does he?

And so here you are, alone in your little black dungeon, cold and in pain. Waiting to die.

84

You stupid bastard,'' Clay Cunningham said.

Ben looked up from where he was sitting on a straight-backed chair in the living room of the beach cottage. He still had on the uniform he'd swiped, and his hands were tied behind his back. A guard was standing beside Cunningham, the muzzle of his submachine gun trained on Tolliver's gut.

Kurt Kramer was there as well, wearing his cynical smile. And his wife, Ingrid, Clay's sister. Also Evan Montrock, with light from the room's single lamp gleaming on his bald head. The group formed a half circle around Ben, glowering as if he were something smelly that had washed up from the ocean. In the shadows on the far side were still others, apparently more of Montrock's guards.

Cunningham shook his head. ''Did you really think you could get away with this? Creeping in here like some two-bit burglar? You and your girlfriend must both be idiots.''

''But don't worry,'' Kramer said, ''she won't make any more trouble, either.''

Ben said, ''Where is she?''

Montrock answered. ''In the mausoleum, asshole. Dead. Same as you're gonna be in another minute.''

Dread washed over Tolliver like a cold wave. And then he felt a surge of anger. ''You're only making it worse for yourselves. I know more than enough about your scam to blow it away, and you along with it. All of you.''

''You don't know shit,'' Montrock said. ''You haven't got—''

Clay held up his hand, silencing the security chief. He turned back to Tolliver. ''What do you know?''

''Everything.''

Kramer spoke up. ''He's just stalling, trying to stay alive. Come on—let's get rid of him.''

''No,'' Clay said. ''I want to hear this. Go ahead, Lieutenant. Tell us what you know, or what you think you do.''

Ben looked at them gaping at him like witnesses to an execution. If he was to have any chance, he had to keep this going. ''You've been making huge profits from illegal trading. Hundreds of millions of dollars. Part of the money goes to the holding company, Cunningham Mining, which then invests some of it in your various deals, including real estate through Cunningham Ventures. The rest you've been laundering through Tomas Aguila's account in the Banco Cafetero in Panama. Aguila brings the money back into the States in cash, turns it over to the Kraut here. Then it's used for payoffs. You bribe everybody from city commissioners and judges to congressmen. Anybody who has political influence, you buy them. Including prosecutors in federal agencies and in the DA's office, which is why you've never been indicted. And no one can trace a nickel of it, because it's all in cash.''

They stared at him in icy silence.

''I'm right, aren't I?''

''Partly,'' Cunningham said. ''But that wasn't a bad guess. Maybe you're not as dumb as I thought.''

''Maybe not, but I should have gotten it a long time ago. You even laid it out for me. 'Money begets power; power begets money.' The Cunningham family maxim. What it really means is how you people use corruption. How you got rich, and how you stay rich.''

''That's true enough,'' Clay said. ''But you won't live to tell it to anyone else.''

''I also know what happened to the senator,'' Ben said. ''And how you were conned.''

''Conned?''

"Sure. You thought you were being clever, concocting a cover story around Ardis Merritt. Thought you were using her. But in fact, she was using you."

"What are you talking about?"

"Jessica Silk killed him with what he thought was a love toy. She shoved an electric prod up his ass and shocked his prostate. He thought he'd be getting a big thrill, that he'd get off like never before. He got off all right. For good. But of course that's not what Jessica told you, was it?"

Clay frowned. "Where did you get this?"

"I'll tell you about that later. But come on, admit it. You were had, weren't you?"

"That's ridiculous."

"Is it? Jessica and Ardis were working together, but it was Ardis's idea. Her term at the foundation was coming to an end and she was worried. So she laid out a plan that would make them both a pile of money, and Jessica went for it. Their scheme was to kill the old man but make it look as if he'd died from a heart attack while he was screwing Jessica. They figured you'd pay a bundle to have them keep their mouths shut, avoid a scandal. And they were right."

"Jesus," Ingrid said. "Those bitches."

"Shut up," Clay said to her. "He's just grabbing at straws."

"Am I? Let me tell you some more. Jessica was supposed to call in Ardis as soon as the senator was dead. But before she did, Jessica did something else."

"Which was?"

"She went through his desk. It was too good an opportunity to pass up, even with him lying dead a few feet away. What she found was a collection of photographs. Pictures of you, Clay, engaging in your favorite sport. Or maybe I should say the family sport."

"Don't listen to this shit," Montrock said.

Clay waved a hand. "Let him finish."

Ben went on: "She knew what she had could be sold for a fortune, one way or another. So she tucked the photos away in her case, and after that she brought in Ardis. Then they went into their hysterical act, calling security and the police, and the family. You and Ingrid came over, and it went just the way they'd planned it. Jessica said the old man was fucking her and he keeled over. You bought it, of course. Promised them a payoff for putting out a cover story. They were to claim they were both there while the senator was being interviewed and that he'd suddenly dropped dead.''

Clay's face reddened. ''Jesus Christ.''

''The payoff was in cash, of course. How much was it? Couple million each? More? And on top of that, you agreed to give Ardis a cushy new job, right? Head of the Brentwood Treatment Center. Then when your tame doctor arrived, he did what all your other employees do. He saluted and did as he was told. Signed the death certificate, stating the cause as a coronary thrombosis. He might even have believed it, because heart failure as the result of an electric shock is one of the hardest causes of death to determine, even with a postmortem. But you weren't worried about an autopsy, either, thanks to Dr. Phelps.''

''Not bad,'' Clay said. ''But nothing anybody can prove.''

''I told you,'' Ben replied, ''I can prove every bit of it. Including where the photographs came from. They were taken with the fancy video equipment the senator had installed everywhere. But you didn't realize the system was being used to spy on you, did you? The old man knew all about what you were doing, because he watched. He had you on tape, and in the stills, courtesy of your security chief. Now who's an asshole?''

''That's a bunch of fucking lies,'' Montrock said.

''What else?'' Clay asked.

''Jessica tried to blackmail you with the photos. So you sent Orcus to kill her. That's right—Orcus. Your code name for your assassin, taken from Roman mythology. Orcus the killer, the agent of death. Who at the moment is standing right beside you. Only most of the time, he calls himself Evan Montrock.''

The security man sneered. ''Wrong again, dickhead.''

''You made it look like a suicide,'' Ben said to him. ''First you raped her and then you threw her off her terrace. Matter of fact, there've been a number of accidental deaths among people who've crossed the Cunninghams.''

Ben strained against the ropes and they gave a little. ''Like that poor kid who supposedly hanged herself,'' he said, ''the patient at Brentwood, Jan Demarest. She was your playmate, wasn't she, Clay? And when you gave her that last beating, you thought she was dead. But somehow she survived. So you had the foundation pay the bills, figuring she'd never give you any trouble, not in the state she was in. And you'd know what was going on with her."

Ingrid looked at her brother. "I warned you, didn't I? Told you we should have eliminated her sooner. I even ordered it done. And it took that son of a bitch forever to get around to it."

Clay's voice grated: "Will you shut the fuck up?"

"Another suicide," Ben said. "That was Orcus's work as well, wasn't it? And why did it happen? Because to your surprise, Jan was beginning to show signs of recovery. That meant she just might recall what had been done to her—and who had done it."

Clay Cunningham was eyeing him. "You know something, Lieutenant? I was serious when I told you we had a place for you. You would've had a better life than anything you could have hoped for as a cop. But now you're not going to have any life at all. You'll be gone, and your girlfriend with you. And there won't be a scrap of evidence you were ever here."

Montrock grinned, the light shining on his naked skull. "Look out the window."

Ben turned his head. A station wagon was parked near the house, and behind it was his blue Taurus.

"We knew you'd hidden your car someplace, when we took your keys," Montrock said. "Wasn't hard to find. Now it goes to the same place you're going. In the Atlantic."

"They'll trace me," Tolliver said. "I was at Brentwood earlier. A lot of people saw me."

This time, Clay laughed out loud. "There'll be a flurry of activity, Lieutenant—for a day or so. But those people you're talking about will tend to be confused. Might even develop amnesia."

Kramer was impatient. "Come on, let's get it done."

"Just one more minute," Clay said. He turned to Ben. "You almost had it right. I'll give you credit for that much. Except that you screwed up your operatives here and there."

Ben looked at him. "My what?"

"You got the people wrong, Lieutenant."

"What does that mean?"

Clay beckoned to the shadowy figures on the far side of the room. One of them approached and the others made way for him. He was a big man, thick-bodied and heavy, wearing a topcoat and a felt hat, dark glasses obscuring most of his features.

''Say hello to Orcus, Lieutenant,'' Clay said.

The big man took off the hat and glasses and bent closer to Ben, grinning.

Tolliver found himself looking into the face of Detective Jack Mulloy.

85

Ben was speechless. He stared at the rogue cop, his senses reeling.

Mulloy smirked. ''You know what your real problem is, Tolliver? You haven't caught up with the rest of the world. Just about everybody's got something going nowadays, except for a few cement-heads like you. Should've got smart, saved yourself a lot of trouble.''

''Come on,'' Kramer said. ''Get him out of here.''

Ben ignored him, turning to Clay Cunningham. ''This was how you beat the DA's investigation, wasn't it?''

Cunningham smiled. ''Of course. I told you how you had a few things mixed up. Detective Mulloy has been very useful to us. He's a much more practical man than you are, Lieutenant.''

''Sure. You never had to worry about the prosecutors, because this slug was tipping you to everything that was going on. Whatever Shackley tried, you were always one jump ahead. Then when I was assigned, Mulloy must have thought I was a gift from heaven. That gave him a direct line on what I was doing, as well. Made him just that much more valuable to you.''

''Quite true.''

''Then if you and Ingrid wanted to shut somebody up for good, you had him do it for you. Your last resort was Orcus—Jack Mulloy.''

Cunningham shrugged. ''Mulloy's right about one thing, Lieutenant. Everybody's for sale—that's the way things work. You're the one who's out of step. So when once in a while we run across a fool like you, we take care of it. The way we're going to take care of you now.''

''This one's mine,'' Montrock said.

Cunningham nodded. ''Go ahead. Do it.''

The security chief reached into his jacket pocket and took out a switchblade. ''With pleasure.''

Tolliver saw the blade snap out of the handle, six inches of gleaming steel. Montrock held up the knife, a sadistic smile twisting the corners of his mouth. He leaned closer, waving the blade. ''Watch, asshole, while I cut your throat. You get to see yourself bleed to death.''

Ben looked at him. ''Anxious to get it done, aren't you? Before I tell your bosses what you've been up to.''

Montrock gripped the knife and aimed for Tolliver's jugular. ''Die, you fucker.''

''Hold it,'' Clay said. And then to Ben, he said, ''What are you saying?''

''How do you think I saw those photographs—the ones of you playing your weird sex games with all your little chippies? And how did I know about Jessica and Ardis? I'll tell you how. I saw a videotape of your old man dying, showing me exactly what they did to him. And I saw the photos in the same place—in Montrock's room.''

''It's all crap,'' Montrock snarled. ''He's just—''

''Shut your mouth,'' Clay said to him.

''Then after Mulloy killed Jessica,'' Ben went on, ''he brought the case from her apartment and turned it over to Montrock, didn't he? And I'll bet you told Montrock to destroy it, right? The case and the photos. But he didn't do that. Instead, he kept building his stash, figuring he could blackmail you himself later on.''

Clay looked at the security man. ''What about it?''

''Hell, I can explain everything,'' Montrock said.

''Explain this, then,'' Ben said. ''Why is the case in your room now, with the photos in it? And what about all those videotapes that you had locked up in your desk? You not only have the one that shows Jessica shooting sparks up the senator's ass; you have a whole collection in there. What's on those, Montrock? Maybe they're porn flicks? Featuring Clay Cunningham?''

Montrock lunged with the knife, but Cunningham and Mulloy blocked his way. Montrock's security guards moved forward, seeming uncertain whether to protect their chief.

''You want to hear more?'' Ben said to Clay. ''Then let me ask you this. What happened to the manuscript Jessica was writing, and where is it now? You know what I think? I think your buddy Mulloy here kept it. So he could do a little blackmailing of his own.''

Mulloy's mouth fell open. "He's full of shit. I never saw a manuscript."

Ben pressed it. "The hell you didn't. You took it out of her apartment, after you killed her. Probably took her computer disks too, didn't you? Figured all her material'd be plenty valuable when the time came."

Sweat popped out on Mulloy's face. He backed away, turning toward the door.

"Stop him!" Clay snapped.

This time, the guards reacted fast. Both men jumped on him, holding his arms, struggling to restrain him.

Mulloy let out a roar of rage. He grappled with his attackers, slugging one, kneeing the other in the crotch. One of them slammed him in the head with the barrel of an Uzi, but the blow only staggered him.

Montrock got into it as well, obviously eager to have the heat directed away from him. He grabbed Mulloy's wrist with one hand, swung the knife with the other. The detective howled as the blade sliced into his flesh, opening a gaping wound from hairline to jaw.

Blood pouring from his face, Mulloy pulled a police revolver from his pocket and shot Montrock in the belly. The security chief doubled over, and Mulloy shot him again, putting this one in the top of his bald head.

Kramer drew a gun of his own as Ingrid threw herself to the floor and covered her head with her arms. Cunningham pointed at Mulloy, yelling to the guards to kill him.

Now, Ben thought. Dragging the chair behind him, he kicked over the table with the lamp on it. The lamp shattered with a crash and the room was blacked out.

Summoning all his strength, he strained against the bonds holding his wrists. One of the submachine guns ripped off a burst, which was answered by pistol shots. The roar of gunfire was deafening, muzzle blasts flashing in the room like strobe lights.

Tolliver tore his hands free and scrambled for the door. Behind him, he could hear one of the guards screaming for somebody to turn on the fucking lights. More shots were fired.

Ben got as far as the veranda, when a bullet ticked his hip. He hit the floor and rolled over, clawing the Smith from its ankle holster.

A man appeared in the doorway, holding a pistol in both hands.

The man stepped forward. In the semidarkness, Ben saw it was Clay Cunningham.

Standing over him, Cunningham said, ''You son of a bitch. You think I'd let you out of this alive? You're less than dirt, Tolliver. Nothing but a cheap, ignorant cop.'' There was an oily click as the weapon was cocked.

Ben shot him in the chest. The slug knocked Cunningham backward, slamming him into the wall behind him, a dark stain spreading on his shirtfront, his mouth hanging open in astonishment. He made one more attempt to raise the pistol, and Ben shot him again. He slid down the wall, the expression frozen on his face.

Tolliver got to his feet and went down the steps, running to the rear of the house, where the Taurus was parked. He jumped into the driver's seat and reached for the ignition key.

It wasn't there.

''Oh shit,'' he said. ''Oh sweet shit.''

86

Shelley was growing drowsy. She no longer felt as cold as she had earlier, and the pain in her head had subsided. It was still there, an incessant pounding that matched the rhythm of her heartbeats, but now it didn't seem to matter.

In fact, nothing did. The bruises on her elbows and knees, she could hardly feel at all. And the terrible claustrophobia, the horrifying comprehension that she'd been buried alive, had gradually seeped away, leaving in its place a sense of hopeless resignation. It was as if she was becoming detached from physical sensations, her mind gradually moving outside her body. Was this what it was like to die?

If it was, it wasn't nearly so harrowing as she would have imagined. Instead, she was experiencing only a feeling of sadness as she realized what it meant to be trapped here, what it meant to confront the end of her life. She'd never again enjoy the sunshine on a summer's day, never smell the fresh air after a spring rain.

And that was a lot of poetic crap, wasn't it?

And yet . . . the awful part was that it was *real.* She'd never again have any of those experiences.

Even more sorrowful, her dreams were not to come true; there would be no triumphant success somewhere down the road in her career, no marriage to a man she loved, no kids, no home in the country. She'd never have the things she'd almost taken for granted would someday be hers. Not now, not ever.

But goddamn it—she couldn't let this happen. She *couldn't*! Again she kicked and flailed, beating her fists and her feet against the walls of the tiny prison, screaming until her throat was raw.

And then she fell back, sobbing.

She thought of Ben, and that made it all even worse. She wished she could tell him she loved him.

But that wasn't to be, either.

It was becoming increasingly hard to breathe. She gulped air but couldn't get enough oxygen to supply what her lungs were demanding. Pinpoints of light appeared in front of her eyes and the burning sensation in her throat made her desperately want a drink of water.

Better not to think of that. Better to will her mind once more to leave her body, to leave the pain behind—to deaden the mental anguish, as well as the physical.

She forced herself to relax totally, and began to slip away.

87

Tolliver groped for the keys. They weren't on the sun visor, nor in the glove compartment. The guards must have taken them. As he searched frantically, he heard more shots in the beach cottage.

He found the keys on the floor. He fumbled for the ignition key and shoved it into the lock. When the engine caught, he put it in gear and skidded the car in a half circle, the rear end fishtailing as he drove across the grass.

Montrock had said Shelley was in the mausoleum. Ben didn't turn on his lights, but he could see the building's dim white shape some distance ahead of him. Squinting into the darkness, he pointed the nose of the car toward it.

When he reached the building, he slammed on his brakes, stopping before the entrance. He left the engine running, got out, and ran in through the heavy bronze doors.

Inside, there was an eerie silence, and no lights. He called Shelley's name and stood still, listening. No reply. He shouted again, yet the only sound he heard was the echo of his voice bouncing off the marble walls.

He turned and went back out to the car, opening the trunk and rummaging for a flashlight. When he found one, he ran back into the mausoleum, turning on the light and directing its beam around the area. What it revealed was a large, musty room, its high white walls relieved by the bronze doors of tombs.

Some of the doors were inscribed, he saw, while some others were not. He stepped to one at the far end, which seemed to be in a special position, inset at a higher level than the ones near it. Playing the beam over the inscription, he saw it was the tomb of Colonel Clayton Cunningham.

Once more, Ben shouted Shelley's name. As before, he got no answer.

He swung the flashlight around, casting the beam over the other tombs. The doors to these appeared to be locked, as well. But as the light swept the walls, he noticed another door, in a corner not far from where he was standing. This one was upright and painted white. Stepping over to it, he tried the door and found it opened into a storeroom in which lay a row of caskets.

Apprehension gripped him. Montrock had said Shelley was dead. Was that true, after all—and was this where he'd find her body?

Fearful of what he might see, he raised the lid of the coffin nearest the door. It was empty. He repeated the process with the one next to it: also empty, as was the next one and the next.

But when he opened the one after that, he looked down at a dead body.

Claire Cunningham was lying on the white satin. Her eyes were open, and in the glare of the flashlight Ben could see at a glance that she'd been strangled. There were flecks of blood in the corneas, and petechial hemorrhages on the skin of the upper and lower eyelids. Bruises and scratches were visible on her neck, and there was lividity in the flesh under her jaw.

He touched her face, and found it still warm. She probably hadn't been dead more than an hour or two. He dropped the lid of the casket and stepped back.

There was one more coffin in the room. He went to it and grabbed the edge of the polished wooden lid. Raising it, he directed the beam of his flashlight down into the interior.

There was nothing inside.

He didn't know whether to cheer or to curse in frustration. Slamming the casket shut, he ran out the door, going back into the main room of the mausoleum.

Where was Shelley?

As he stood there, he heard a faint tapping sound from behind him. Turning, he listened, wondering whether he'd imagined the noise.

The tapping continued and then stopped.

Ben shouted, ''Shel—where are you? Was that you? Can you hear me?''

There was a moment of silence, then the tapping sounded again.

And stopped.

''Shel! Where are you?''

The noise had to have come from one of the tombs—which would mean she was behind one of the doors in this room. But which one?

He ran from one to another, rapping on each slab of bronze with his flashlight before going to the next. When he'd covered several of them, he began to wonder whether his mind had been playing tricks on him.

Tap-tap-tap.

There, by God! He'd heard it that time; he was sure of it. ''Shel, keep it up, will you? I'll find you if you help me. Keep it up!''

Moving as quickly as possible, he covered tomb after tomb, listening before the bronze panels that were inscribed, as well as those that were blank. At a door on one of the side walls, he found the source.

The tapping was more faint now; he could barely hear it. But, like all the others, the door was locked. He clawed at it for a few seconds, then again turned and hurried out to the Taurus. His tools were in the trunk. He opened it and got out a pry bar and a hammer, then slammed the trunk shut. Carrying the tools, he ran back inside.

Placing the flashlight on the floor, he jammed the sharp edge of the pry bar into the crack between the door and the jamb. He gave the bar a mighty whack with the hammer, the metallic clang reverberating from the marble walls.

The door swung open.

Shelley was lying on her back, her head toward him. He dropped the tools and grabbed her, sliding her out of the narrow enclosure. Then he held her in his arms, pressing her body against his.

She was alive; he could feel her breathing. But they had to get out of here fast. The guards would be searching the grounds. If Montrock's squad spotted them, they'd be dead.

He picked her up and carried her out to the Taurus, depositing her in the passenger seat. Running around to the driver's side, he jumped in and jammed his foot down on the throttle. The car kicked up a spray of gravel as he swung it onto the driveway that led to the main house.

By the time they reached it, Shelley was showing signs of coming around; the fresh air was reviving her. She put out her hand and gripped his arm, and he felt a flood of relief.

Ben wheeled the car around the mansion and onto the long stretch running toward the main gates. With no headlights, it was hard to see.

As they approached the gates, a security guard moved in front of them, holding up one hand in a signal to stop and raising a submachine gun with the other.

''Get down,'' Ben shouted to Shelley. He kicked the accelerator to the floor and headed straight for the guard.

At the last possible second, the guy dived out of the way. An instant after that, the Taurus slammed into the heavy gates.

There was a violent shock as the car hit the iron grillwork, but the gates burst open, raking the sides of the Taurus and sending up a shower of sparks as it roared through. Behind them, Ben heard the sound of shots, but whether any of them had hit the car, he didn't know. Seconds later, they rounded a curve. The estate was no longer in sight.

88

Jack Mulloy staggered to his feet. He was dizzy and there was a burning pain in his side, as if he'd been stabbed with a red-hot knife. He put a hand on the wall to steady himself until his head cleared.

In the darkness, he could hear groans. It's a wonder anybody is still alive in here, he thought. The guards had gone berserk after he shot Montrock—firing wildly, spraying bullets in all directions.

He'd shot back, and he was pretty sure Kramer had, too. Who'd been hit and how badly, he didn't know. Nor did he give a shit.

Ingrid was lying on the floor. He couldn't tell what shape she was in, either. After all the crap he'd taken from that bitch, with her high-handed orders and her snotty attitude toward him, he hoped she was out of it for good. In the end, when the crunch was on, she'd flopped on her face and whimpered.

He touched his side, feeling a sticky wetness. He'd been shot through himself; that was where the pain was coming from. The cut on his face was throbbing as well, but not as much as when the knife had first sliced his flesh open.

Nevertheless, he could move, and that was what counted. There had to be a way to salvage at least some of his plan, even though it had been blown apart.

He didn't know what had happened to his pistol. But as he moved toward the door, his foot touched an object. He knelt, and found it was a submachine gun—one of the Uzis the guards had been carrying. Taking the weapon with him, he went out onto the veranda.

There was enough light there for him to make out Clay Cunningham sprawled dead with his back against the wall, his eyes open, his shirtfront covered in blood. Mulloy looked at the body with contempt, then stepped over it.

Much of what had gone wrong was Cunningham's fault, he thought. The fool had gone crazy when the senator's widow demanded more money from the estate, and then when she threatened to expose him, he had choked her. How in hell had he thought they could cover that one up?

Cunningham had also dragged his feet after the guards caught Tolliver, giving the bastard an opportunity to run his mouth, instead of ordering him killed at once. And that was when everything exploded.

At the thought of Tolliver, Mulloy was again enraged. He should've taken him out long ago—blown his fucking head off. Then things would have gone the way they were intended to go.

Walking was hard, yet Mulloy managed. The bullet had hit him on the same side his bad leg was on, but the leg was something else he hadn't let bother him. Gambling for the big score? That's what he'd done all the way, and he wasn't about to quit now.

The station wagon was behind the cottage. When he reached it, he got in and started the engine, then wheeled the vehicle down the drive toward the mansion.

There was a telephone in the car. He picked it up and punched the buttons.

This thing wasn't over yet—somebody else had a stake in it, besides himself.

89

A short way down the road, Tolliver turned off onto the shoulder and stopped. He drew Shelley close once more and held her in his arms. Her breath was coming in sharp gasps and he could feel her trembling under the black windbreaker.

''Just take it easy,'' he said. ''I'm right here with you.''

She nodded, shuddering.

''You okay?''

''Yes.'' She began crying and laughing at the same time, and he knew she was on the edge of hysteria. He tightened his hold on her and she buried her face against his chest.

After a moment he said, ''Try to put up with this a little longer. I have to keep going, get us out of here. The village is only a few miles farther. When we reach it, we can get help. All right?''

''Yes.''

She tucked her legs up under her and he kept one arm around her as he pulled the Taurus back onto the road.

''What happened back there?'' she asked.

He recounted all of it, starting with what he'd learned about how the senator had died, what had happened afterward to Jessica Silk, and on through the series of events at the estate. He left nothing out, including the Cunninghams' financial maneuverings and the murders of Jan Demarest and the senator's widow.

''That poor girl,'' Shelley said. ''And the old lady—I'll bet that wasn't planned.''

''No. When I went to see her, she told me Clay and Ingrid were trying to screw her out of her share of the senator's estate. She must have forced the issue, and they killed her.''

''How awful. That family was completely amoral. They dirtied everything they touched and destroyed anybody who got in their way.''

''Exactly. You know, I always had the idea that in politics you could trust people who were as rich as they were. I figured that with all their money, they were incorruptible. What didn't occur to me was that they'd use the money to corrupt other people. They bribed some, bought others. And the ones they couldn't touch, or who wouldn't bend, they got rid of. Goes to show you how naïve I was.''

''Believing in honesty isn't naïve.''

''Maybe not. But if I've learned anything on the job, it's this. Trust nobody. Give people a fair chance, but only one.''

''Is that the Gospel according to Tolliver?''

''It'll have to do.''

''The detective, the one who was Orcus. What was his name?''

''Jack Mulloy. He was another one who fooled me. But in the end, it turned out he sold his soul, too.''

Ben drove the Taurus at a snail's pace, wheeling along the narrow blacktop through the forest of pines. He couldn't help thinking how good a cup of coffee would taste—hot, rich, and black, with a good shot of rum in it.

From behind the slow-moving Taurus, the glare of headlights appeared. The distance between the vehicles closed rapidly, until the lights were only a few yards back.

Shelley sat up, turning in her seat and looking out through the rear window. ''What is it? Is somebody following us?''

Before Ben could answer, a burst of machine-gun fire rang out, the slugs bouncing off the rear deck. He slammed the accelerator to the floor and the car leapt ahead.

''Oh God,'' Shelley yelled. ''It's a big station wagon, but I can't see the driver because of the lights.''

Ben whipped the Taurus around a curve, fighting to hold the rear end on the road as he revved the engine. ''There's a shotgun there under the dash,'' he shouted. ''Give it to me.''

''No, you drive—I'll handle it.'' She snatched up the gun and pointed it rearward, working the pump slide.

More bullets hit the rear of the car, whining through the air as they ricocheted off the armor plating of the trunk.

Shelley leaned out her window and rapidly fired three shots. Then she pulled her head back in and yelled, ''The gun's empty!''

''There are more shells in the glove compartment!''

She got the door open and fumbled for the box.

Ben cursed, whipping the Taurus along the winding road as fast as he could drive it. The station wagon was almost touching their rear bumper. He knew that as soon as they were on a straight stretch of road, the bastard would have a clear shot at the passenger compartment.

Tires screeching, he roared around another curve, reaching out with one hand to hold on to Shelley, who was still trying to load the shotgun. The village was just ahead, he knew. If he could make it that far—

Suddenly, another car appeared directly in front of them, parked across the road and blocking it completely.

The car was a gray sedan. Standing before it was a woman wearing a heavy coat, a scarf wrapped around her head. She was holding a pistol in both hands and aiming it at the Taurus.

Ben slammed on his brakes and wrenched the wheel, sending the car into a sickening skid. They missed the other car by inches, sliding off the road and smashing into a pine tree, snapping it off at the base as if it were a matchstick. The Taurus flipped over, landing on its roof.

The station wagon had been only a few feet behind them and there was no way for it to stop. It crashed into the sedan and rode up onto it, and both vehicles' gas tanks exploded.

Ben was stunned. He was lying upside down in the Ford, Shelley slumped against him. His left shoulder felt as if it was paralyzed and the salt-sweet taste of blood filled his mouth. He wiped his face with the back of his hand and looked out at the blazing wreckage of the other cars.

The station wagon had become a crematorium. Inside, Tolliver could see Jack Mulloy writhe and twist as the flames ate at him, his skin blackening, his hair on fire. Then the man who had been Orcus grew still, his incinerated body stiffening into the boxer's stance of a burned corpse.

Ben became aware of a new danger as the smell of raw gasoline stung his nostrils. He crawled through the hole where the windshield had been and with his good hand reached back to drag out Shelley, who was still clutching the shotgun.

Supporting each other, they hobbled to a place some distance from the burning cars and flopped down onto the forest floor, resting their backs against a tree.

Shelley looked back at where flames and oily smoke were billowing up from the wrecked vehicles. ''Jesus,'' she whispered. ''That's hideous.''

Ben followed her gaze. ''Saved the world a lot of trouble.''

A voice said, ''Not quite.''

He turned his head. The woman who'd been standing in the road was less than a dozen paces away. The pistol was in her hand and she was pointing it at him.

She reached up and pulled away the scarf. Ben found himself staring at Ardis Merritt.

Shelley shook her head. ''You! You were as rotten as the rest of them.''

Merritt swung the pistol toward her. ''Shut up, bitch.''

''You had your own plans, didn't you?'' Ben said to her. ''You and Mulloy. You must have figured out what he was up to and demanded a cut. What else were you planning, more extortion? Doesn't matter now. It's too late for both of you.''

''The hell it is.'' Merritt thumbed back the hammer of the revolver. ''I'll still make it, but you won't.''

The Winchester was lying on the ground somewhere. Had Shelley managed to reload it? Ben wasn't sure. And if she had, was there a shell in the chamber now? He didn't know that, either.

He'd get only one chance. His good hand, his right, felt for the shotgun.

And couldn't find it.

Merritt must have sensed what he was doing. Holding the big pistol in both hands, she aimed it at his face.

Shelley raised the shotgun and fired. The charge tore into Merritt's body with the force of a sledgehammer.

At that instant, the pistol discharged as well, driving a copper-jacketed slug into the tree a quarter of an inch from Tolliver's head. Merritt landed on her back, a lifeless, bloody heap.

For what seemed like a long time, there was no sound in the forest, only the echoes of the shots and the crackle of flames that were consuming the wrecked cars.

Shelley looked at the body of Ardis Merritt, the smoking pistol still clutched in her fist. She turned away. ''I think I'm going to be sick.''

In the distance, Ben could hear the wail of approaching sirens.

Ben put his arm around her once more. ''It's all right,'' he said. ''This time, it's really over.''

She shuddered. ''Merritt was corrupted, too, by being around them. Just like all the others. I thought the senator was a totally evil man. But his offspring were worse.''

''They weren't worse,'' Ben said. ''They were only the same. They were his flesh and blood.''

90

The media went into a feeding frenzy. The *Times,* the *Daily News,* the *Post,* and *Newsday* all ran stories on the Cunningham case for days on end, as did the *Washington Post,* the *Chicago Tribune,* the *Boston Globe,* and many of the nation's other metropolitan newspapers. *Time, Newsweek,* and *U.S. News and World Report* gave the subject heavy coverage, as did *Der Spiegel* and *Paris-Match.* Reporters from all over the United States and Europe converged on New York to squat on the developments and pick meat from the bones.

The TV spotlight was even brighter. Not only did CNN and the network news shows focus heavily on the story, but the talkers, including Donahue, Geraldo, and Oprah, outdid themselves in presenting weirdly contrived angles they claimed as both exclusive and authentic. *A Current Affair* and *Unsolved Mysteries* ran specials on the case.

Nevertheless, none of them got the whole truth, or even much more than a semblance of it. And as Ben Tolliver realized early on, it was unlikely anyone ever would. The case was cleared by the DA and the New York Police Department, although in a form he found hard to recognize.

Most of the culpability for the killings fell on Clay Cunningham. But even there the family's power and money combined to produce an adroitly concocted explanation. Clay was unbalanced, the story went, by grief over his father's death. He blamed his stepmother for creating marital discord that caused the old man to suffer a fatal heart attack, and in a fit of blind rage, Clay had choked her. A psychiatrist who testified at the coroner's inquest asserted that Mr. Cunningham was unquestionably deranged at the time, and therefore not responsible for his actions.

The NYPD announced that Lieutenant Ben Tolliver killed Cunningham in self defense, after the detective tried unsuccessfully to restrain the mentally unbalanced man when he went berserk and began shooting at everyone around him.

Separately it was revealed that Clay Cunningham also had established a corrupt relationship with Jack Mulloy, an obscure investigator in the DA's office. Unbeknown to Cunningham, Mulloy had in turn conspired with Ardis Merritt—who was described to the media as a former administrator of the Cunningham Foundation—in an extortion scheme.

Evan Montrock, who for many years had been the family's loyal head of security, was said to have been shot by Mulloy when Montrock discovered the investigator's duplicity. Mulloy then died in a fiery auto crash while attempting to escape.

The cops further determined that Shelley Drake, a reporter for New York television station WPIC TV, shot Ardis Merritt when Merritt threatened her life and that of Lieutenant Tolliver by firing a pistol at them. Ms. Drake was not charged.

Although Tolliver reported suspicions to the district attorney as well as to his superiors in the NYPD, no evidence was produced to refute the official findings in the death of former Senator Clayton Cunningham, nor those in the suicide of the journalist Jessica Silk. Videotapes the lieutenant claimed were taken when the senator died were never found.

No link was established between any of these events and the death of Jan Demarest, a patient in the Brentwood Treatment Center in Farmington, New York. Although Lieutenant Tolliver argued that there had been a connection, support for the hypothesis was not forthcoming. Dr. Jay Chenoweth, head of psychiatry at the center, said that Ms. Demarest had shown suicidal tendencies in the past, and although she had been watched closely, the patient had managed to elude staff members and take her own life. An autopsy confirmed that Ms. Demarest had died of asphyxia caused by hanging. The Farmington Police Department declared her death a suicide, and marked the case closed. Dr. Chenoweth was later named director of the Brentwood facility.

The death of Clayton Cunningham IV also resulted in the Manhattan District Attorney's office dropping its investigation into the activities of Cunningham Securities. In a brief statement, DA Henry Oppenheimer averred there was insufficient evidence to seek an indictment from a grand jury. Insofar as rumors of a money-laundering scheme were concerned, he said there was no proof of such activity, and no law prohibited the transfer of funds from a U.S. bank to one in a foreign country.

Fletcher Shackley, the senior prosecutor who had headed the investigation, resigned from the DA's office in order to pursue a career in politics. Shackley immediately began organizing a campaign to win nomination in the upcoming race for the congressional seat representing Manhattan's 17th District.

Ingrid Cunningham Kramer and her husband went into a period of deep mourning. It was pointed out that they had put their own lives at risk by bravely trying to stop the outbreak of violence at the family's Long Island estate. Both were considered fortunate to have escaped without injury. When they resumed normal activities, the couple flew with their team to the polo matches in São Paulo, Brazil. Upon their return, it was announced that the board of directors of Cunningham Mining Corporation had elected Mrs. Kramer chairman and chief executive officer. Her husband, well-known international financier Kurt Kramer, continued as president of Amvest Corporation, an investment banking firm in New York.

At a press conference, Mrs. Kramer declared her intention to uphold the Cunningham tradition by devoting increased time, money, and effort to the family's many charitable and political causes. For example, she vowed to give her whole-hearted support to Fletcher Shackley's bid to win election to the United States Congress. Mrs. Kramer also hinted that she might at some point seek elective office herself, although no specific plans were revealed at that time.

The case had a major impact on the career of Shelley Drake. Overnight she went from news-reader on a local station to star in her own right. She was a guest on a number of talk shows, and was featured in articles appearing in *People, New York* magazine, and *Vanity Fair*. Several producers approached her with TV miniseries and movie offers.

Ben Tolliver was also deemed lucky to have survived the events at the estate. It took three hours of surgery and over a hundred stitches to repair the bullet wound in his hip. If the slug had hit him a little to the right, he might have wound up with a shattered pelvis. Or dead.

He spent two weeks in St. Vincent's and then several more on leave confined to his apartment, going crazy from the inactivity. When the therapist put him on a moderate exercise program he overdid it, which landed him back in the hospital. Now he was again ready to be discharged, and this time when he promised the doctor he'd take it easy, he meant it.

"You'd better," the surgeon said. "I don't like to see my work screwed up by somebody who thinks he's still a kid."

"Can't help it, Doc," Ben said. "I'm young at heart."

"That's fine, but go slow, give your body time to heal. That bullet did more damage than you think. Tore a channel through your transverse abdominus and oblique muscles, and chipped the bone. I had a hell of a time repairing the damage. You rip those tissues loose again, you could suffer a permanent impairment."

"Yeah, okay. But how soon can I work out?"

"Not for several weeks, anyway. And when you do start, stick with the regimen. The idea is to get the muscles limber, not to over-exert them. You're to do nothing strenuous until you're much further along toward full recovery."

"How about pushups—with a partner?"

The doctor smiled. "Let her do the work. For the time being, anyway."

"Yeah, I guess I could stand that."

"I'm sure you could. You're getting out of here tomorrow, and I don't want to see you again until it's time for a checkup on your progress. Clear?"

"As a bell. And Doc? Thanks. I appreciate the embroidery."

"Good luck, Lieutenant." He left the room.

Ben lay back and switched on the tiny TV set that hung over his bed. After a moment he turned the set off; if he never looked at another soap opera it would be too soon. And every half-hour or so CNN began to repeat itself.

He'd also done all the reading he cared to for one day: magazines and newspapers—even that morning's *Wall Street Journal*. Conversation with the occupants of the other three beds in the room wasn't practical; they were a comatose, a broken jaw wired shut, and an Asian who spoke no English.

Ben looked at the pile of newspapers on the bedside table. At least the storm of publicity on the Cunningham case finally seemed to have blown away; for a long time the media had pestered him for interviews, but he flatly refused to talk to them. Now at last they were on to other disasters, other scandals. There was never a shortage of horrendous developments; New York had a new serial killer, another crazed judge, a teenager who'd blown away his parents. Tomorrow there would be something else.

The door opened, and Captain Michael Brennan walked into the room.

Tolliver had seen the zone commander several times since the Cunningham case had come to a violent head, but today Brennan was making no attempt to appear cheerful. Under the misshapen nose, his mouth was set in a grim line.

''Hey, Cap,'' Ben said. ''Good to see you. But why the gloom?''

Brennan drew up a chair and sat down beside the bed. ''Got some bad news. I know you're getting out of here tomorrow, and I wanted to tell you myself before you heard it through channels.''

''What is it?''

''You been passed over for promotion.''

Ben didn't reply. After the case was cleared, he'd often thought about his chances for making captain, and had concluded they weren't good. Hearing now that he'd be stuck in grade wasn't really much of a surprise.

''I'm sorry,'' Brennan said. ''I know you been kind of counting on stepping up, but that's what happened.''

''Uh-huh.''

''The trouble is, the PC thinks you're too controversial. So do Houlihan and Galupo. The media blasted the department over the Cunningham case, and if there is one thing the brass don't like, it's taking heat. They got enough problems with the mayor as it is.''

Ben looked at him. ''So why didn't they just can me?''

''Don't kid yourself, they would have. Except it would've given the reporters more rocks to throw at them.''

''How about you, Cap—what about your own promotion?''

''It came through.''

''Inspector Brennan. Congratulations.''

''Thanks. But as far as your situation's concerned, it's not all bad. The DA wants you for a special investigator.''

Tolliver groaned.

''Hey, keep your shirt on. You'd have a lot more room to move around in that job than you'd ever get as a zone commander.''

''I don't have a shirt on—I'm wearing this fucking nighty. And I don't want to be one of Oppenheimer's boys.''

''Listen to me, will you? You'd be working on some of the most important cases to hit the city. And with him behind you, there'd be nothing to keep you from going all the way.''

''Yeah, but—''

''But relax, Lieutenant. Think, for once, before you take a swing. The game today is politics, and you better learn how to play it.''

''Seems to me I've heard that before, someplace.''

''Good. Maybe it'll start to sink in.''

Ben exhaled, and stared at the ceiling. ''I doubt it.''

Brennan stood up. ''Give me a call, when you've thought it over. We can talk about it some more. Meantime, what I told you stays between us, right?''

''Yeah, it will. So long, and thanks for coming.''

When he was again alone, Tolliver continued to stare at the ceiling. It was painted pale green, and there were cracks in it. Leaving this place would be a pleasure.

He tried to keep his mind off what Brennan had told him, but it was difficult. Each time he thought of what had happened, his anger grew, until it reached the edge of bitterness. The game today was politics? Christ, wasn't *that* the truth. In some ways, it was no wonder a guy like Jack Mulloy had become disillusioned, and then had turned rotten.

So immersed had Ben become in his thoughts, he wasn't aware she'd entered the room. Until he smelled her perfume, and turned his head toward her just as her lips brushed his.

She really was a spectacularly good-looking woman, he thought as she stood smiling down at him with that lushly curved mouth, the honey-blond hair softly framing her face.

Her voice was gentle. ''Hi. I know you'll be going home tomorrow, but I couldn't wait to see you.''

''You've been busy.''

''Yes, I know. It's been wild. I feel guilty about not having spent more time with you.''

''That's good. But you can redeem yourself.''

''I'm way ahead of you. I'm taking two whole weeks off, and I'd like to spend them with you, if I'm invited.''

He put his arms around her. ''You're invited.''

''Sure I won't be a strain on you?''

''Yeah, I'm sure. The doc was even telling me how we could do some exercises together.''

''What kind of exercises?''

He kissed her nose. ''I'll show you tomorrow.''